THE UNPOSSESSED

THE UNPOSSESSED

A Novel of the Thirties

Tess Slesinger

With an Introduction by Alice Kessler-Harris and Paul Lauter and an Afterword by Janet Sharistanian

THE FEMINIST PRESS
Old Westbury
New York

Published in 1984. Printed in the United States of America
88 87 86 85 84   6 5 4 3 2 1

Library of Congress Cataloging in Publication Data

Slesinger, Tess, 1905–1945.
  The unpossessed.

  (Novels of the thirties series)
  Originally published: New York; Simon and Schuster, 1934.
  I. Kessler-Harris, Alice. II. Lauter, Paul. III. Sharistanian, Janet. IV. Title.
PS3537.L48U56 1984   813'.52   84-20840
ISBN 0-935312-21-8

First Feminist Press edition

Cover design: Marta Ruliffson
Cover art: Self-Portrait, Florine Stettheimer, 1939. Courtesy of Columbia University Collection. We wish to thank art historians Thalia Gouma-Peterson and Linda Nochlin for their suggestions and assistance.
Text design: Lea Smith
Manufacturing: BookCrafters, Inc., Chelsea, Mich.

CONTENTS

INTRODUCTION

Alice Kessler-Harris and Paul Lauter

The first phase of the women's movement, so the historical tradition goes, ended in the twenties. Its passion spent in the successful campaign for the vote, its remnants torn apart by divisions between those who wanted equality at once and those who insisted on retaining hard-won protections, the movement was stifled finally by a depression that mocked individual ambition. But if one kind of feminism ended in the twenties, another emerged in the thirties. Largely overlooked by historians, its existence is documented by the literature of the period.

The old movement that ended in the twenties declined in the affluence of that decade. After the vote was won, activist women set out to translate their political success into the economic equality it seemed to promise: Alice Paul's Women's Party pushed for an Equal Rights Amendment; coalitions of women's groups supported the Sheppard-Towner Act to provide maternal and well-baby care; the Women's Bureau successfully defended the rights of wage-earning women to minimum wages and shorter hours. The prosperity of the twenties made room for ambition, nurturing the talents of such writers as Edna St. Vincent Millay, Katherine Ann Porter, Zora Neale Hurston, and Anzia Yezierska. For a while it seemed as though the women who flooded into arts and letters as well as into banking and insurance were merely the vanguard of a new generation of self-confident and fulfilled womanhood.

Then came the depression, and widespread unemployment put an end to illusions of economic equality for women. The crisis of the thirties revealed the extent to which women's ambitions had relied on the opportunities offered by an expanding economy. With 25 percent of the work force unemployed by 1933, the picture changed dramatically. State and local governments tried to drive women, especially married women, out of the work force. Private industry took advantage of socially sanctioned discrimination against women to undercut the wages of poorly paid men. Opportunities for promotion and advancement shriveled.

To return to the home was no answer for most women. Families doubled up. Husbands and fathers lost their jobs. The home reflected the poverty and insecurity of unemployment as women and their children coped with the psychic tensions of maintaining family life and the economic pressures of insufficient incomes. Young women postponed marriage to help their parents survive, and they avoided pregnancy for fear of its economic consequences.

But women did not abandon the search for women's rights. Rather, as the crisis exposed their vulnerable positions, they began to question the degree to which the ambitions of the twenties were circumscribed by social reality. There would be no freedom for women at work while millions were unemployed; no genuine partnership in the home while clothing and food remained luxuries; no equality of opportunity for male or female children who grew up without medical attention or education. To women of the thirties, poverty and the social conditions that fostered it seemed as much women's issues as individual advancement had seemed in the twenties. To fulfill their own thwarted ambitions, women were required to connect themselves with the larger struggle for social justice. They would rise or fall with it. In this new generation, women who might earlier have been called feminists became social activists of a broader stamp.

As the old individualism gave way to concern for eliminating unemployment, preserving home life, and collective survival, women began to turn to available political movements for answers. Some moved into New Deal agencies, hoping to find a cure for despair in government social programs. Others chose to organize workers into the newly militant trade union movement. Many turned to the socialist and communist parties of the Left. Here, in an atmosphere of revolutionary possibility, they introduced questions of equality between the sexes, of women's education, and of reproductive and sexual freedom.

Left-wing groups like the Communist Party, USA, welcomed women into their ranks. They provided increased opportunities for women to act in the political arena, but they remained ambivalent about specifically women's issues. Though leftist ideology in the 1930s recognized the "special oppression" of women and formally espoused sexual equality, in practice, the Left tended to subordinate problems of gender to the overwhelming tasks of organizing the working class and fighting fascism. Both ideology and practice opposed feminism, fundamentally on the ground that it drew working-class women away from their male working-class allies and into the orbit of bourgeois women. Women constituted a formidable proportion of most left-wing groups, and Unemployment Councils, neighborhood groups, and even the emerging CIO relied heavily on them for leadership and support. By the end of the decade perhaps 40 percent of the membership of the Communist Party, USA, was female.[1] If the Communist Party did not provide a comfortable haven for women, if it subordinated women's questions and often refused to challenge sexual segregation on the job or rigid gender roles at home, its language of equality provided women with opportunities for debate, and its political programs opportunities for organizing and leadership experiences. The Left offered a forum and more serious attention to women's questions than any other group of the decade. It also provided women with a community of shared experience.

Female voices, primed by the rhetoric of equality, resonated on the printed page. A remarkable number of politically active women wrote. Their poems, stories, and songs, as well as their novels and essays, give us access to some of the issues seldom addressed in political practice, even on the Left. If the nature of women's participation in political action limited the issues about which they wrote, it also provided depth and insight into the critical social and personal conflicts that underlay activism. Their political views help clarify why most of the women writers of the thirties and in this series worked in a variety of forms: each form had both an artistic and political motivation as well as a particular audience. Fielding Burke, for example, had published many volumes of verse under her real name, Olive Tilford Dargan; Josephine Herbst was an active reporter throughout the thirties, as well as a critic; Mary Heaton Vorse, whose novel about Gastonia was a rather crude and obvious effort, wrote some of the decade's best books and articles about the developing labor movement. These writers strove not only to perfect the forms in which they wrote but to choose the forms most appropriate for the various political tasks in which they engaged.

We have chosen in this series to begin with fiction because it seems to reflect most closely the unfettered consciousness of women in the decade. The books in this series are part of a long tradition of literature about working-class life. Because they are written by women, these novels do not sit comfortably inside most accounts of that tradition, nor do they conform precisely to theories of "proletarian fiction" produced in the thirties. Yet the ways in which this women's fiction differs from that of men alert us to the particular qualities of some of the best female writers of this century, including Agnes Smedley and Meridel Le Sueur, and provide the most important reason for The Feminist Press to undertake this series.

In the 1920s, literary rebellion, in the words of Jack Conroy, "was directed principally against the fetters of form and language taboos."[2] By the thirties, literary theory had provided a systematic alternative to the modernist emphasis on formal experimentation, ironic distance, and linguistic complexity. Its major breakthrough, particularly for the work of left-wing and working-class writers, was to validate the experiences of working people. In her speech to the 1935 American Writers' Congress, Meridel Le Sueur made the point this way:

> It is from the working class that the use and function of native language is slowly being built. . . . This is the slow beginning of a culture, the slow and wonderful accumulation of an experience that has hitherto been unspoken, that has been a gigantic movement of labor, the swingdown of the pick, the ax that has hitherto made no sound but is now being heard.[3]

"Proletarian Realism," Mike Gold's widely adopted phrase, would thus deal in plain, crisp language with the lives and especially the work of the proletariat, optimistically urging them on "through the maze of history toward Socialism and the classless society."[4]

Though this is in fact a rich and complex aesthetic, it presented immediate problems for women who took their own experiences seriously. Less than a quarter of all women and fewer than 15 percent of married women worked outside the home during most of the

1930s. If the workplace was to be a major focus for art, as it was for Communist Party organizing, then, as "workplace" did not include work done in the home for the support of the family, only small fractions of women's lives would find their way into art. The rest would be ignored, subordinated once again to the demands of male politics. More important, since proletarian fiction, by the definition of the times, rested upon the central distinction between the experiences of the working class and those of the bourgeoisie, it would underplay, even deny, the relevance of other distinctive group experiences. Blacks, Hispanics, women—as groups suffering their own persecution—would have no place in it. In denying the commonalities of female experience, the vision of the proletarian aesthetic undermined such crucial issues for women as the uneven division of household labor, the sexual double standard, and male chauvinism within the working class or the Party itself.

Women writers who perceived such problems were placed in a certain dilemma: theory maintained that their work should be based upon the experiences of the working class; yet the experiences of one half of the working class—males—were clearly of more significance than the experiences of the other half of the working class. Where did that leave distinctly female experiences, like childbearing, or those, like the nurturance of children, which continued to be primarily women's tasks? And where in that theoretical framework could one find a place for the strengths and ambiguities of love, of rearing children, of family life, of the problems of control over one's body, the struggle to find emotional and sexual fulfillment?

Women writers of the Left chose to flout male convention and to write about themes that fell outside the frameworks of their male peers. But so strongly masculinist was the cultural theory and practice of the Left that it remained virtually immune to the feminist implications of their themes. The cultural apparatus of the Left in the thirties was, if anything, more firmly masculinist than its political institutions. It is not that women writers were ignored. Josephine Herbst was a "guest delegate" to the Kharkov conference of the International Union of Revolutionary Writers in 1930. Tillie Olsen and Meridel Le Sueur were among the (few) invited women speakers at the American Writers' Congress in 1935. The Communist Party's book club, the Book Union, selected as its representative "proletarian novels" Fielding Burke's *A Stone Came Rolling,* Clara Weatherwax's *Marching! Marching!*, and Leane Zugsmith's *A Time to Remember*. Herbst, Le Sueur, Zugsmith, and Grace Lumpkin, among others, were active reviewers for *The New Masses* and certain other Left journals.

But women were often, in fact, tokens at major conferences. Accounts of the John Reed clubs (the Communist Party's cultural associations), of the editorial boards of magazines like *The Anvil, Blast,* or *The Partisan Review,* and of other Communist Party and Left cultural organizations hardly acknowledge the existence of women—though many did, in fact, work in such groups. The hitchhiking Wobbly style of life extolled by writers like Jack Conroy left room only for the rare Boxcar Bertha, while the hairy-chested polemics of left-wing critics like Mike Gold placed women's issues squarely in a male context. The worker-poet was inevitably male, his sexuality "evidence of healthy vigor"; his comrades, cigar-smoking talkers, in from the wheat fields or the Willys-Overland plant. In a *New Masses* editorial announcing the advent of "Proletarian Realism," Gold pictures the new writer as "a wild youth of about twenty-two, the son of working-class parents, who himself works in the lumber camps, coal mines, and steel mills, harvest fields and mountain camps of America. . . . He writes in jets of exasperated feeling. . . ."[5] Women writers were recognized on the Left, indeed occasionally puffed, just as women's issues were recognized. But the values and outlooks *institutionalized* in magazines, editorial boards, conferences, and theories of the Left were decidedly masculinist.

At the same time, there appear to have been few distinctly female cultural groups or networks of support among women writers on the Left. Meridel Le Sueur mentions in her American Writers' Congress speech a group of "a hundred and fifty women from factory and farm" who "wrote down their great proletarian experience." Myra Page, novelist and reporter, recalls the way experienced women took newcomers under their wings, but notes that women "felt that the general issue was the most important thing: depression and unemployment."[6] Support among women was directed at achieving the larger goals. Women intellectuals in books like Tess Slesinger's *The Unpossessed* and Josephine Herbst's *Rope of Gold* seem, from the perspective of the 1980s, strikingly isolated from one another. While there were female-centered cultural institutions during the 1930s—the YWCA, for example, supported a Women's Press—they were not of the Left. In fact, they were likely to be noted by the Communist Party, if at all, with suspicion. In short, there was little institutional support on the Left that might have validated any distinctly female culture, and much that discouraged it. Not perhaps by design, but effectively for all that, any female—much less feminist—tradition was submerged.

Within a few years, the entire world of left-wing culture was ploughed under by the attacks of McCarthyism. It is not always easy now, thirty years later, to perceive how successful the campaign was in silencing and burying writers on the Left. One good indicator is that copies of books by the writers with whom we are concerned are absent from libraries and used book shops. After the thirties, some of the women turned away from "political" subjects; some fell into silences; others continued to write but could find no publisher; many, like Tillie Olsen, were subjected to public attack. That happened, of course, to men as well as to women. But, in addition, women were confronted with that hostile ideology we have come to call "the feminine mystique." More profoundly, perhaps, the concern for working-class life and for understanding the relationship between gender and politics was suppressed in the fifties as anticommunism, suburbanization, and consumerism controlled the environment. As the cultural soil dried up, writers lost their audience. The run of stories, novels, poems, and songs that had established for an audience certain expectations, artistic conventions, and ideological perspectives, came to an end.

When the writing of the thirties began to be re-discovered twenty-five years ago, critics persisted in denying its feminist proclivities. In his comprehensive book, *The Radical Novel in the United States,* for example, Walter Rideout suggests that "the explicit linking of political revolution and sexual freedom rarely appears" in left-wing novels of the thirties "as it did in *Daughter of Earth.*"[7] In fact, however, sexuality, personal liberation, and radical politics are closely intertwined in Fielding Burke's *Call Home the Heart;* sexual politics are at the center of conflicts described in Tess Slesinger's *The Unpossessed;* personal and sexual relations provide the critical counterpoint to emerging political differences in Josephine Herbst's *Rope of Gold.*

Female writers who accepted the central class division of socialist realism nevertheless paid attention to women-centered issues. In Tillie Olsen's *Yonnondio,* as Deborah Rosenfelt argues, "the major transformation is based on human love, on the capacity to respond to beauty, and on the premise of a regenerative life cycle of which mother and daughter are a part." For feminist proletarian writers, these issues are not separable from the capacity to effect a successful political transformation. As Rosenfelt tells us, "Women's work in preserving and nurturing that creative capacity in the young is shown in *Yonnondio* to be an essential precondition to social change."[8] Such themes, ignored by male critics, are not peculiar to Olsen. Both in her story "Annunciation" and in her novella *The Girl,* Meridel Le Sueur focuses on the regenerative power of pregnancy and birth. The action in Leane Zugsmith's *A Time to Remember* concerns a department store strike, but the emotional conflict that constitutes the dynamic tension of the novel comes from the attempts of strikers and their families to cope with the social reality of women's subordinate positions.

The books in this series demonstrate the substantial and vigorous tradition of women-centered literature. We find in these books women of intellect and strength—like Victoria in Herbst's *Rope of Gold*—seeking work that is politically meaningful and yet consonant with their need for personal independence. We encounter in Slesinger's *The Unpossessed* many of the same conflicts between ostensibly progressive politics and real chauvinist behavior that helped generate the women's liberation movement of the late 1960s. With Ishma in Fielding Burke's *Call Home the Heart* we experience the contrary appeals of full-time, heroic but often grubby, work in a movement for social change and of the rich, green pastures of the hill country. These books present women (and men) in varieties of workplaces—including the home—participants in strikes and demonstrations, observers and reporters of what seemed a growing, international revolutionary movement. Their steady grasp of sexual politics illuminates the inner contradictions and struggles of movements for change. These writers are the sisters and comrades of Agnes Smedley, Meridel Le Sueur, and Tillie Olsen: their work asserts the richness, as well as the continuity, of the traditions of left-wing feminism in the United States.

Certainly all the female authors of the thirties did not write in ways that distinguished them from men. But some of the best works written by women addressed the distinctive experience of both working-class and female lives. Women in that decade produced a body of writing with qualities that overlap but are not identical with those of the male writers of the period. This literature—we might now call it "socialist feminist"—is only beginning to be explored by scholars with an eye to what it tells us about the complex factors that encouraged women to write both as activists and as critics. In presenting these books as part of a series, The Feminist Press hopes to underline the need to reconstruct the cultural context that helped shape them.

That process will require us to re-examine questions around which debate swirled in the thirties. What is the function of art in a revolutionary movement? Do we cast aside as merely absurd the notions of some socialist critics, who suggested that art was a "weapon" in the class struggle, that writers must under all circumstances convey a sense of "proletarian optimism," and that they must write only in language plain enough for plain people? Or are we to understand the criticism of the Left in that period as a creative effort to confront issues with which the artists themselves were struggling? Are there ways to resolve the tensions between the slow, sustained discipline which the artful rendering of experience demands and the more immediate requirements of writing hitched to the needs of a political movement? How can a writer bring alive the vision of a triumphant socialist future, which no one has seen or fully imagined, with anything like the power to evoke the struggles and devastation of capitalism in decline? Just who is one's audience? And if the audience for socialist art should, at least in part, be working-class people, what functions does art serve in their lives, and are these different from its functions in the lives of the traditional audience for writers?

The writers in this series largely avoided the more formulaic demands of thirties criticism. Their endings are not always unambiguous and hopeful as "socialist realism" theoretically required. Their heroines, like Ishma in *Call Home the Heart,* share both the virtues and the profound limitations of their class origins. They portray retreat as well as triumph; confusion and ambiguity as well as possibility. But struggle was never simple. Together these books provide another piece of the puzzle that illustrates how women have come to consciousness over the years. In publishing this series, The Feminist Press calls attention to the varieties of feminism and its expressions. The fiction of the thirties is part of our common heritage. We hope it will be useful in conceiving of our future lives.

Alice Kessler-Harris
Hofstra University

Paul Lauter
State University of New York,
College at Old Westbury

Notes

1. See Robert Shaffer, "Women and the Communist Party, USA, 1930–1940," *Socialist Review* #45 (May–June 1979): 90 for this and for additional information on women and the Communist Party.

2. Jack Conroy, "Introduction," *Writers in Revolt: The Anvil Anthology* (New York, Westport: Lawrence Hill, 1973), p. ix.

3. From "Proceedings of the American Writers' Congress," New York, 1935, reprinted by West End Press, Minneapolis, 1981.

4. Edward Seaver, "Socialist Realism," *The New Masses* 17 (23 October, 1935): 24.

5. "Go Left, Young Writers," *Mike Gold: A Literary Anthology*, ed. Michael Folsom (New York: International Publishers, 1972), p. 188.

6. Interview with Alice Kessler-Harris, December 1, 1982.

7. Walter Rideout, *The Radical Novel in the United States* (New York: Hill and Wang, 1956), p. 219.

8. Deborah Rosenfelt, "From the Thirties: Tillie Olsen and the Radical Tradition," *Feminist Studies* 7 (Fall 1981): 398.

THE UNPOSSESSED

to my contemporaries—

ONE

I.

Margaret Flinders

MR. PAPENMEYER was ashamed of his celery!

Look at it. Frozen, for one thing; coarse; brown; ill-natured. He let the stalks snap toughly from his fingers.

Eric Papenmeyer could not find it in his heart to sell her celery, with celery in the shameful state it was!

There was plenty would sell it to her without a second's thought. But not Papenmeyer.

Yes; she knew that.

Unless she would cut it up for pot-roast? For a nice stew? His eyes brightened. His voice cajoled. His hands holding the frozen stalks begged.

Mrs. Flinders shook her head, widened her eyes coyly at the grocer like a woman confiding in her doctor. "*Mister* Flinders is from New England, you know."

There was a moment during which it seemed that Mr. Papenmeyer's eyes would fill with tears. Then he nodded wisely; dropped the whole business of pot-roasts at once; grew brisk and detached, still nodding, oh of course, if Mr. Flinders is from New England then let us say no more about it, the least said about *that* sort of thing the better; and turned with admirable tact to potatoes.

"See that you pick them without too many eyes," she said coldly. (Mr. Papenmeyer's hands brooded among the potatoes.) For the man deserved a little taking down.

Standing there with all that heavy German *Verstandt* in his eyes; as if he were indeed a gynecologist (his white apron spattered with vegetable stains!); as if it were too much for him that Miles was a New Englander. "And your lettuce is frozen! But the cider! the cider looks lovely, the first I've seen this Fall. I'll take a jug of cider," she said, relenting.

"Everything's withering," Mr. Papenmeyer said, as though corroborating. "I might never step out of this store. But still I'll know. I'll see the vegetables freezing and the prices going up, and I'll know winter's coming. I'll say here's another winter with everything to do again. Will I send it, Mrs. Flinders?"

"Send it? Dear Lord no! Why it might get there in time for breakfast, Mr. Papenmeyer—and how is your little girl?" Dear Lord no! there would be Miles come home ahead and waiting, and she must not come to him empty-handed. Oh no; give me the world all wrapped in bundles; let me carry it home resting on my breast; let me bring the world home to Miles and lay it at his feet. A dash of salt, a skillful stir; and I will serve him the world for his supper.

"Good after*noon,* Mr. Papenmeyer."

"Good day to *you,* Mrs. Flinders." He had his dignity too.

Certainly the street lay quieter now, the air upon it darker, the wind big with solemn tidings. For summer with its suspension of life, its long and endless days of sun like the days without end of one's childhood, was gone again. And another Fall, another year, another round of life (Mr. Papenmeyer was right!) to do again.

Soon the chestnut vendors would warm their hands in

the whistling steam on their little wagons; the Scottsboro boys would be called for re-trial; butter would go up, eggs would go up. Would there be apple-sellers again, crying their fruit on cold corners? The wind would whinny down the chimney; and in the mornings after the alarm-clock one of them must brave the cold to shut the windows while the other cowered in bed, clinging to last night's nest like a slow-witted chick.

The Sunday papers would issue their supplementary book sections for the Flinders to strew over the bathroom floor on Monday, Tuesday, Wednesday. Mr. Worthington would reduce the summer's amount of ice for the office water-cooler. Elections again; and whether one voted for the Republicans or the Democrats, or tossed one's vote to the left in futile protest (but Miles said it was *not* futile) would the scabrous unemployed be swept from one's sight off the public parks? Then the smell of camphor in the house! its glint where it fell shining and secret in the cracks of the old floor! Soon the last leaf would be off the last tree in Sheridan Square; there would be that feeling in one's chest of ending and beginning again, expelling the last of one breath and expanding the lungs for the intake of another; sorrow for the departing year curling smaller and smaller until it was dead, excitement and wonder opening their eyes and catching their breath as the winds grow colder, the nights fall quicker, the curtains are early drawn and the fires lit. Was there progress? was there change?

At the office he let her sign his name with her own hand now, and she marvelled to see how day by day her writing as she flourished Adolph Worthington over *Business Manager* so gravely typed grew less and less her own. He wondered too at her smiling so much; with your husband gathering pay-cuts right and left, Miss Banner? Miss Banner-that-was, that is, he adds with his daily tic of humor. Ah, signing his name with her own hand! Carrying the only key to The File in her purse! Answering the telephone in the cabalistic tones of the hired, "He is in Conference, We have changed our Policy, We have closed our Autumn List." Ah, what glory is yours, Maggie—Miss Banner-that-was, Missis Flinders-that-is! As long as you can play school all day at the office with Adolph Worthington, *Business Manager;* dance home through the shades of the evening to play house all night with Mister Flinders, husband; live the year round, make a leisurely circle through the seasons and come safely back to the starting-point again, the Fall. This was progress? this *was* change? Well, last year she left the letters on his desk for Mr. Worthington to sign; last year it seemed that the Scottsboro boys must hang without much ado; last year Miles' soul was worn about the edges but displayed no gentle fraying in the seams.

One got older. One grew soberer. One would like perhaps to see a thread drawn through the years as though they were beads. (Twenty-nine! what was the deadline for babies? for clearing out and starting somewhere else?) This year on Charles street, last year on Tenth; surely these were stations along some route? One's world too, which had been a tight nut, expanded; burst; until there you were, stepping out over the broken shells, soberly trotting down a street—toward what, and why, one vaguely wondered. And was there something else?

There had been small Maggie, child of a family, fastest girl-skater on a city block, most important child in the world (had the world known it? now she had been sure, again it seemed it waited for enlightenment). Growing and growing; then squeezed back into something resembling all other children (she remembered sashes; the day they cut her bangs because her forehead so high and naked made the other children stare) and sent off to school; where to her surprise and terror—and something like relief—she was given not the best desk nor the worst desk nor the farthest nor the nearest nor the most nor the least of anything. The feeling of deprivation! But rising out of it a sense of importance, of social responsibility: the blackboard erasers must be in line, chalk must not strew the school-room floor; one was song-book monitor once a week. So the world of school opened until it took in Saturday morning concerts and Irma Haliburton's father explaining Damrosch over lunch. And whenever (then) you took stock in the Fall, up another grade, maybe a floor higher, granted more freedom this term—you found a newer and bigger world, you belonged to a larger and deeper fraternity. Now you and Miles, you live in a room on Charles street (the richness of their daring, of their living together and calling the same place home, caught her suddenly unawares), you have never been out of your country or even to the south of it; yet you make out checks from your meager income to send to the Scottsboro boys quaking in Alabama jails; you subscribe to a German paper which names writers you will never read; you visit Russian movies whose characters you comprehend no more than you do their machines.

Is this because the room on the fourth floor is too small, because Charles street is too narrow? Because one's horizon must stretch till it takes in the world?

Here she turned a corner and came upon the last street, and because it was home her heart must do something, it must go up, or it must go down; she must hurry or her feet must lag. She shifted her bundles (the world in her arms had grown heavy; the cider weighed it down) as if in indecision. For the street ran too smug, too sure, between the same rows of houses, too properly studded with corners, with lamp-posts. There is satisfaction implicit in recognizing, in coming back to the known—the pink house again, the house with one shutter hanging loose, the Italian speakeasy, the only tree. But a finer excitement would lie in change, in things concealed from view. The pink house moved down the block! why the shutter has been taken down at last, the speakeasy closed! The street ought to wind at the middle; the lamp already glowing die: catch your breath as you round the turn! anything might happen! But there was the house again squatting smug on its rump like an injured woman. The fourth floor still there, its windows like a train of cars above the third. O drop the bundles on the nearest stoop; turn round and run, run back, run the wrong way for once up that right street, run and chase the world that hides around the corner!

For she would come in. She would drop her bags on the kitchen table. There would be Miles in the leather chair, his feet lifted to the wicker one; his New England conscience ticking neatly on his desk, beside the clock. He would look up. He would check her home-coming with a smile, as in the morning he acknowledged the ringing of the clock by pressing down the jigger. Jeffrey called up, he might say—called *you* up, he would put it if his mood demanded hurt. What happened to you all day, Miles? (The moment of her standing there and waiting, jealous a little of his day which had not held her, fearful at the same time that another day had passed without leaving its mark on him, another day like a sheet of Mr. Worthington's calendar to be torn off and dropped heedlessly away.) No, what did *you* do, Margaret? you are the one things are always happening to, you make them up if they don't, you liar: what did *you* do all day? . . . And then the cider in the jug. If he didn't see it, not as cider, but as cider she had bought for him, as cider which had come out of the country from the apple trees specifically and courageously for them, for Miles and Margaret, to sit in a jug on their checkered tablecloth, why then the fine apple-y taste was nothing, the tang was bitter, the color dull.

Suppose she said What happened! why darling, things happened to me all day long. In the first place the beggar on the subway stairs noticed my straw hat was gone; and then I signed thirty-seven curt letters Adolph Worthington and I crossed the t at thirty-seven different angles; furthermore, Mister Flinders, it is emphatically *not* our policy to wrap soap in cellophane; at four-seven P. M. the carbons blew off my desk and feeling the breeze anyway on my wrists and under my skirt I knew it was Fall again. And celery isn't good any more, being brown and coarse-fibred, but tomorrow or maybe the day after I think I can promise you the chestnut vendors will be out, and the grocery man's little girl has a nasty runny cold again and darling I hope you understand I talk this way because I love you. Suppose when she said all that on one breath it didn't work, it didn't reduce him to smiling his fine reluctant smile reserved for nonsense, suppose it didn't bring back to him and so to her the softness of her, the woman-ness of her, that part which passed all day unknown and undesired, by Adolph Worthington *Business Manager*, by the beggar in the subway, by Mr. Papenmeyer whose little girl had a nasty cold again?

The street lay cramped between its rows of houses, leading inexorably to its end. Down its center ran a groove; and try as she would to escape, her feet ran down as helpless as a trolley. At one end Mr. Worthington, to whose bell she responded all day, in whose aura she lived all day; on the way home Mr. Papenmeyer (who dared commiserate, because Miles was a New Englander!), a brief stop at Mr. Papenmeyer's station; and then Miles Flinders, who made his wishes felt not by a bell in her ears but by a constant frightened consciousness in the very lining of her being.

The janitor's wife leaning out the first floor window with a shawl about her shoulders called:

"Chill in the air, ain't it, Mrs. Flinders."

"Winter is certainly coming, Mrs. Salvemini."

There was the bell marked Banner-Flinders. There stood the door which could open and close a thousand times in a day without her knowledge, although it was the door to her home. Perhaps the door had opened and quietly, secretively, released Miles, who might also have sensed the new year waiting round the corner! perhaps he had slid through like a cat never to come home again! (But he would be there, come home ahead and waiting.) The mail-box hung like a sealed packet on Christmas day, that might contain anything; that must contain the world; her nervous fingers crawled and clutched: a milliner's card came out. (But what did she want, this woman who—*surely she loved her husband?*) "Madame Bertha invites you . . ." Well what was she after then—a letter from Jeffrey, from Bruno? a letter from Miles, "goodbye, my dear, I've gone away"? No, no, it was some thread, some meaning she was looking for; some way of finding the world without reading papers from Germany . . .

She raced up the stairs in terror, in doubt.

She burst the door open—and in the pit of her being peace vanquished regret, for there was no change and no sign of a change; for he sat there with his feet on a chair and with all that she loved and all that she hated him for written plainly on his face; he had come home, like a child, for his supper. He took off his glasses and his eyes opened and closed several times patiently like a baby's growing used to her light. And she herself was taking off her hat to stay (enormously bored, enormously relieved) at the same moment that she advanced to kiss him.

His hand shot up as though to ward off something. "Old Son-of-a-Bitch cut me again today," he said; "and before I forget—Jeffrey called, to speak to you I think." His hand wavered with an air, she thought, of laying a smoke-screen between them. "A ten percent cut," he said with a certain grim complacence.

She paused, startled by the irrelevance; "Old Son-of-a-Bitch?" she faltered, trying to focus her wits: her impulse being to cry impatiently "What of it? that has nothing to do with *us*"; then fluttered, lost to the notion of their being children playing at being adults, pretending to *care* about such irrelevancies; and rushed to him dropping the bundles, perceiving how his pride lay bleeding out of all proportion, tortured by how, in coming home to him, she had in her mind deserted him, had turned and fled from him twenty times.

She would pierce his wavering smoke-screen and purge him with her comfort.

2.

Miles

BUT comfort was salt to his wounds. He had been reared to expect just punishment from an angry God; then God was mercilessly withdrawn and since then nothing adequate supplied. In punishment one found the final solace; in repentance the blessing of convalescence, return to grace. All of his life women (his aunts, his frightened mother, now Margaret) had come to him stupidly offering comfort, offering love; handing him sticks of candy when his soul demanded God; and all of his life he had staved them off, put them off, despising their credulity, their single-mindedness, their unreasoning belief that on their bosoms lay peace. For if he were once to give in, to let their softness stop his ears, still the voices that plagued him this way and that, they would be giving him not peace, but death; the living death of the man who has consented to live the woman's life and turned for oblivion to love as he might have turned to drink.

For Son-of-a-Bitch he had felt sharp admiration, when the man, by virtue of his superior position, bent to deliver perfunctorily to him the cut. He had bared his chest, had taken the *cut* without flinching, as his just due from Mr. Pidgeon pinch-hitting admirably for God; and then because he felt complacently like a dog he had wheeled his bleeding chest about and exposed for Mr.

Pidgeon's further flagellation the humble seat of his pants. "Has my work fallen off, Mr. Pidgeon?" And Son-of-a Bitch, stirred by no womanly compunction, led further perhaps by temptation than his original desire would have taken him, added to the cut a well-placed kick in the pants: "We might have cut you anyway, Flinders; but we don't feel you've been getting much punch in your work."

Gratefully stung, Miles *thanked* him; that is, he said in so many words, "Perhaps you're right." And felt as he had felt when Uncle Daniel, flogging him with a wand of birch, said "Maybe that will teach you," and he had answered "I'll ask God to help me." There had been a God then. Now God like Uncle Daniel had been a long time dead.

And sitting at supper (to which the aunts timidly bade him come) on the raw stripes of Uncle Daniel's licking, he would be filled with a righteous exaltation. It was more blessed to sit on stripes than on a bottom unlawfully padded with deceit. Uncle Dan flogged harder than the immediate sin deserved; this was because Uncle Daniel, wise, like God, knew vaguely of many other sins which had not come to light, which might have been stored up on a small boy's conscience almost since his birth. In this Uncle Daniel was a loyal representative of God. So before his eyes, as before God's, he lowered his own; in fear—for something in him loathed those floggings; in guilt—if ever all the sins were guessed then flogging was not enough; and also, obscurely, in hope, for once they were all read that one lacked the strength to own to, then would come absolution complete: an end to evil thoughts preventing sleep at night, end to the sudden threats of God sounding in guilty ears—one would be like "other children" that the aunts, not knowing, dimly fancied.

Here came Margaret, *at* him, it seemed (a wistful aunt, a helpless mother, ill-disguised) with that peculiar look of hope planned to seduce him; he described it to her fondly, at times when he could bear it, as her "balmy" look. Dropping the bags at his feet as though she brought a sick child toys from the Five and Ten and fully expecting his fever to go down at sight of them, not knowing them for trash! Poor little Maggie; it took stooping to enter the doll's house in which she lived; which she furnished so tenderly with chairs that were too little and too soft, always struggling to draw the curtains so a man could not see out; and rushing to the miniature door with her hands outstretched, her face gone "balmy" with her filmy hopefulness, begging a man to come in and be stifled. He could have borne it better if her face had sprung to life for Jeffrey.

He waved her back: "Ten percent. So now *you* will be bringing home most of the bacon"; and watched her, with compunction yet with pleasure, withdraw and stoop as though for refuge to the bags. Her face looked hurt as though his need for hurt hurt her. But since she would not stab him, he longed to reach and scratch out forever the "balmy" look from her mild, uncomprehending face.

"Leave them, leave them," he said, slumped in his chair. "We have time before we eat." The paper corner on the bulkiest lifted suddenly with a crackle, like the ear of an animal, rather hurt. He prodded it with one toe and shoved it an inch or two farther from his chair.

So lately had she held it! He could feel his toe gently

prodding her shoulder where the helpless bag had lain. Well, now was her chance: why didn't she scream out in anger and strike him back? When would she learn that a man could not live with such unrelenting kindness?

"But darling!" she protested. "I—" She stopped. She seemed to eye him humbly; perhaps ashamed of her bucolic unawareness, her gift to him of vegetables! She sighed, her protest skillfully withdrawn. She has her own way, he thought, of knifing me! her cowardly pulling *out* the sword—that wounds!

"But what did he say—Mr. Pidgeon?" she asked, as though rousing herself (concession number one!) to pretend acquaintance with his world of facts; so might his aunts have inquired kindly about a game of baseball played at school. "Old Son-of-a-Bitch?" she added painfully (concession number two!); did she think to win him with this condescending loyalty?

"*He* doesn't matter." Contemptuously Miles dropped Mr. Pidgeon along with Margaret's concessions out of his picture. "He is just a symbol. He gets *his* from the higher-ups, just as I get mine from him."

She was choked with silly laughter. "Such a fat symbol, honey! I mean, it's hard to recognize a symbol with a belly like that—and so *many* warts . . ."

He wished to God she wouldn't use nursery humor on him. She'd had a good malicious wit before she was a wife.

"You wouldn't see a social trend," he said, "unless it was crammed down your own personal throat: and *then* you'd try to think it funny. You know what I mean when I say Pidgeon is a symbol."

"Then doesn't it seem wrong to call him Son-of-a-

Bitch," she said thoughtfully. "I mean—an epithet—if he doesn't himself determine his status, if it's all—" she waved her arm; deprecated her own ignorance, but falsely, he thought—"if it's all, as you say, ec-o-nom-ic."

That perverse female logic again! Did they know what they were talking about? or did they bandy words, caught from the male-grown-ups' table? "Miss Banner! you win your M for elementary Marx," he decided to be gallant and smiled reluctantly.

"You surely aren't worried, Miles!" she rallied warmly. He hated the way she picked up his crumbs! "We can still afford cigarettes and gin and a Charles street roof over our heads—Mr. Pidgeon or no Mr. Pidgeon. *We* don't give a damn!"

He looked at her slowly, with distaste, the still-born smile sticking in his throat. (But thank God she had not said "each other—we still have each other!" Some tact, some happy accident, prevented that!) "I should hate to think that cigarettes and gin are what our life is made of."

She seemed to sit plunged in defeat, her foot making sad little designs this way and that on the floor. Then she strengthened suddenly, as though from the bottom she bounded up, reborn. "Cigarettes and gin!" she said scornfully. "When we have each other!" She seemed to flow toward him borne strongly on a tide of joy, suddenly too big and too amoeba-motherly to hold out against. She put her arms around him and drew him against her and he could feel himself like a bundle of dry sticks gathered to her side.

He leaned against her, not unwillingly, but awkwardly, joint by joint, as though he did not know how. He was ashamed before her sudden largeness. He did his best for her. But his dryness would not melt.

"The best things in life are free, my love," she whispered merrily; and ran her hand wickedly inside his shirt as she pressed him closer.

He grew less brittle. The faint suggestion of wickedness in her tone and the sudden invasion of her hand on his unsuspecting chest warmed him, even thrilled him faintly, as though the thrill were sensed through veils of prohibition.

"Pinocchio!" she whispered.

His heart ached for her. He felt indeed like the puppet-boy—he remembered pitifully how Bruno said (incredulously admiring, nevertheless, for Miles's stiffness was a miracle to him, a mystery to Bruno's rich amorphous Jewishness) that if he presented his friend Miles Flinders on the puppet-stage the audience would boo, demanding a more life-like marionette.

"Will you wait, Blue Fairy, will you help?" he said gently. He wanted to be taken out of his shell; but at this moment he wanted it, guiltily, more for her sake than his own.

"Dear little Pinocchio," she said; "of course, forever!"

She seemed to hold her breath, hoping for the miracle. It irked him; but he felt he owed it to her to lie still in her arms.

He closed his eyes. Pinocchio! It was an old story between them, a sad little joke. She had read him the whole book one night, after Bruno had called him a puppet; the story of the little wooden boy who wanted to become real, whose dear papa and whose Blue Fairy waited and waited patiently for that happy day to come. She leaned over to show him the pictures; he said she exactly resembled the Blue Fairy. He had felt pleasantly pathetic; pointing out that no one had read him Pinocchio when he was a child; that until Bruno came along he had never had a friend; that now he had a wife he wanted her to slowly give him all the childhood he had missed on that New England farm where he had feared the wrath of God. Strong in his faith in his new wife he repudiated Uncle Daniel; forgot the forgotten God of his childhood.

"I'm a hard guy to live with," he said. "But have patience with me, Maggie."

Between them, first Bruno, then Margaret, they had taught him to take pride in the childhood he had thought so barren. Margaret had made him remember what he thought had never been: the good things, the warm bits, the isolated rays. He had found for her the story of his first hay-wagon ride, his uncles drinking corn and singing with the farm-hands; he had given it to her baldly, take it for what it's worth. She had looked at the story; taken it up in her hands and breathed on it; turned it round, admiring it (from her own flat urban background); and handed it back a story he could feel. He found himself proud of his stern uncles relaxing (with Uncle Dan's permission) and getting drunk; of his own solemn self jigging up and down with the motion of the wagon; proud that before God had died, before he had found a friend and then a wife, before Tenth street and Charles street, he had known long dusty roads with rocks piled on their sides, farm-hands singing in the harvest moonlight, and little jumpy hay-ticks hopping from his grimy hands to his bare scratched knees.

So he was a man with a childhood behind him like

any other man, and why couldn't he lean back in peace against his wife's soft breast. He had earned it, he deserved it, like any other man. He leaned back now, knot by knot unravelled in his mind. His stiff joints eased, his dry bones bent. Only, he could not come all of the way. One breath caught on a snag; he sighed, lightly, inquiringly. There must be more than this?

But Margaret was wise, he countered, allowing himself momentarily to be seduced. She was not like his befuddled aunts who would have made him into someone else than who he was. She took him (if you were a gangster! she had said; if you were a one-armed paper-hanger! *I* don't care!) demanding nothing—but surrender of his restlessness. Whatever I am, she loves me, her message is that we can be "happy" together (my Uncle Daniel used to say his *pigs* were "happy.") "We have each other!" she could say. With what joy, what faith! She needed (it would seem) no other purpose, no other God; perhaps that "balmy" look was holy? perhaps he must respect it, as one sits dumb in the presence of another person's religion? For him there *was* no longer religion—curious that what was *rational* could be so incompatible with man's emotion!—and what else was there, once one's God was dead? Margaret herself was the greater sceptic, born and reared in flippant, urban agnosticism; yet Margaret, blandly, with that "balmy" look, faced life and lived it, asked no questions, sought no answers; like a calm angel, he thought; like a woman rocking a cradle, he thought; like a cow chewing her cud. *Was* Margaret wise?

She sat as still above him as though she had gone to sleep. He knew that she had not. He knew she was there, a pillar of consciousness, awake to his smallest movement, ready to open and take him in if he asked for it in the subtlest way; ready, her face gone "balmy" with her ecstasy, to swallow him whole. He knew that she reduced even her physical being to suit his, softened her breathing now so they could breathe together in a common rhythm. He knew that she was physically so minutely aware of him that he had only to put up his hand for her to find it. Her consciousness rebuked him; lowered on his head a debt it irked to meet. He wanted to breathe in his own private rhythm. The nearness of her female flesh, her female awareness, surrounding him with warmth he did not want, was stifling.

Yet peace sat on his eyelids. Gently his head rose and fell, drifting on the ecstatic tide she strained herself to regulate. Drift! Drift off together, floating out of the world to ecstasy, to sweet oblivion. Ah! if he only dared! if Pinocchio only dared give in! Give in to the blessing of forgiveness without punishment, give in to love. Let the world (which Margaret—blindly? wisely?—hated) with its hideous turmoil spin over their heads, unheeded. "We have each other!"

But that was death! cried out agonizingly the one knot still holding open parched eyes in his breast. That is surrender! cried the part of himself that to this day felt itself the cause of Uncle Daniel's death, for wishing it to be. Save me! cried the little boy who turned from love as Uncle Daniel turned from drink. Peace—such peace as he saw ahead was death.

His sense of wrong against Margaret turned slowly to a sense of injury. What sort of woman had he got that offered her man the breast when he needed the sword and the power behind him of her own resentment? And what sort of weakling was he, standing meek while he was *cut* (cut so his wife, earning more than he did, was left more of a man than himself) to come bleeding home and forget his wounds. . . .

He found his bones going dry again, his shell closing over.

A drafty doubt against her stood in the road and winked to him. Loyalty struggled and died. He sensed conspiracy in the pressure of her arm about his shoulder. Woman is man's temptation, Uncle Daniel sternly said, classing Miles' mother (whom Margaret said he must have loved to have hated so) as a Limb of Satan for her sin of being pretty. The real class struggle, twenty years later Bruno dryly said (but one never knew what Bruno really meant), is the struggle between the sexes . . . from an old Chinese adage, he added hastily to dodge responsibility.

The pressure now of Margaret's arm: too light to be love, too deliberate to be unconscious. Coaxing, rather, as his aunts once urged him out to play, like "other people's" nephews. Was it seduction? proselytism? was she carrying on the aunts' campaign? On the floor the bundle he had pushed looked on with its ear expectantly cocked like a pleasant little animal, signalling her above his head.

Conspiracy! Her touch said nothing at all to him; it spoke beguilingly to her hope of what he might become, the prototype of the boy "like other boys" his aunts had wooed. She wanted him soft. She offered him the bribe of female flesh. So the mother tempts the child; so the rich man soothes the poor; so a woman bribes her man. Perhaps she was pleased his pay had been cut? hoped it would melt him down? hoped that the cut emasculated him? "You will be bringing home most of the bacon," he had said casually; and she had made no reply. But perhaps her arms had gone round him in triumph? And "Jeffrey called you," he had said; she had ignored it as one would a child's obsession. (Yet he had said it only to torture himself; it miserably failed; was even the sharp joy of pain to be denied him?)

The real class struggle, Bruno said, is the struggle between the sexes; and rebellion begins at home.

He squirmed in her arms.

Her hold relaxed at once. He was shot like a lonely arrow out into the void again. (She gives up easily, he thought with bitterness.)

"I've been cut twice," he said, shattering the silence grimly as though he had thought of nothing else.

She quivered behind him loosening her hold. "As if it mattered!" she said; but he could detect defeat in her voice and it gave him subtle pleasure.

"Next I shall be fired."

She stood before him now, straightening her dress. She seemed less like a woman straightening her dress than a soldier pulling his uniform in place after leave. Her "balmy" look was gone. She looked oddly militant to him.

"No doubt you will," she said with her kind of cheerful malice; "as long as you reckon so consistently, as Bruno puts it, that the world owes you a beating."

"Just think," he said, roused by the challenge in her tone, "just think of the men all over the country, sneaking home to their wives tonight, their tails between their legs. 'Darling, the big shots cut me again today.' Not unlike being castrated, you know (let her have it): the word *cut* has an admirable folk-basis. And the wives, who ought to feel themselves cheated too . . ."

"I know!" She laughed, pulling her dress firmly over the shoulder. " 'How much, darling? oh, only ten per cent? well, we can get along on *that!*' "

He shouted with laughter, his tension momentarily snapped. "You do know how to put a man in his place, don't you, my gentle little wife?" This was how he valued her, brittle sword in hand.

But her face went soft again. "It's a place I don't much like to see you, dear." Her damned face looked sick again, like weeping. "Oh Miles! I wish you trusted me more. I wish you let me *help.*" Her voice broke on the *he-elp* unbearably; like a tragedy actress in the sticks.

"And just how could you help?" he asked her dryly. "Can you find me a job that's interesting? can you fix the world so it's a decent place to live in? can you even" (oh let her have it strong, let her suffer from what was eating him, let her damned female superiority cower in knowing inadequacy) "can you even share my ideas? my indignation? can you help me to express them?"

Discouraged she looked, but resourceful; as though no child could come hungry to her and find her without cookies in her apron. He could see her searching through her meager cupboard.

"There's Bruno's Magazine," she said thoughtfully; and her eyes brightened, wistful, as she offered him her findings.

"The Magazine!" he uttered, strong in his rejection; it was like offering him warmed-over cake, his last year's love. "There'll never *be* a Magazine. Try again, Missis Flinders," he said for the recollection hurt him.

"What did Jeffrey *want?*" she said calmly.

"Oh yes, of course," he said quickly. "I said if you liked, we'd pay them a visit. I suppose you'll want to hurry with supper?"

"Hurry?" Her eyebrows raised, she was gathering the bags up off the floor. "Hurry?" she said; and wearily he saw that her patience had snapped, that a quarrel between them was imminent.

"Why yes. To change your dress for Jeffrey. Let me help with the supper." He spoke with gentle malice.

She gave him the onions to peel.

3.

Professor Bruno Leonard

THE cable lay conspicuously on his desk, adding to his gloom. "*Professor Bruno Leonard* (the *professor,* he felt, was ironic) *Am threatened with marriage and slightly drunk please advise. Elizabeth.*" A modern odyssey, he thought, could be hardly better couched: phrased to conceal the meaning, to understate the feeling, to ridicule the appeal still (one didn't entirely outgrow being human) humanly necessary. He pushed it aside; the business of the Magazine—or Jeffrey's interpretation in terms of filing cabinets—must come first. It seemed today the world was out to frame him, force him to decisions when he much preferred to float. First his peaceful bachelor life disturbed by a ridiculous cablegram (and she might be already married); and then his placid dream-world ruthlessly invaded under the nervous adolescent eye of Emmett Middleton, by a Filing Cabinet arrived unheralded in the moment of his worst confusion.

The business of the Magazine came first; but his eye like his mind returned tortuously to the cable. The form as well as the wording was so pathetically fitting, so hauntingly recalling Elizabeth at her most ambiguous and lost; what could be briefer and fleeter than a cablegram? it touched him to see how she had put all she had to say in ten short words. He thought for a mad second of cabling her a wedding-present, a check the exact amount of her passage home, alone; but her marrying or not marrying had really nothing to do with him. Twice he had kept her from marrying, fifty times altered her life in some other way; mustn't there be an end to this interfering like an aged uncle in other people's lives? But a fine Frankenstein he was, he thought, and almost groaned aloud as he saw his Idea turning on him and become reality embodied in a Filing Cabinet, emerging green and indisputable like fate under the salesman's crafty hands.

"Listen, my good fellow." He addressed the back of the man who fed his wife but not, from the look of him, his own vanity, by demonstrating Filing Cabinets. "Don't unwrap that thing, I hate it. I didn't order it. I haven't anything to put in it. For thirty years man and boy," he said grimly, "I've hated Filing Cabinets. My young secretary there will tell you." He designated Emmett Middleton wavering on the window-sill, backed by the campus outside. "Filing Cabinets and progress—explain my defeatist inclinations, Emmett."

Emmett squirmed inadequately in his flimsy undergraduate shell. The salesman, resigned as he was to the legitimate vagaries of the upper classes, smiled his faint, thin, up-state smile; and continued to rip heavy paper from his livelihood.

"It's only fair to tell you," Bruno concluded firmly, "that you haven't a devil's chance of selling me that thing. It's a pink elephant in a china shop and I don't care for it."

"That's perfectly all right, professor," the salesman muttered soothingly; "my orders is to set it up. Orders is orders," he added insincerely. His loyal goiter trembled.

"Look—" Bruno relapsed into a coaxing tone. "That thing was ordered for my Magazine. . . . But I haven't *got* a Magazine; I'm not even sure that I want one."

"That's perfectly all right, professor," the salesman said. "You haven't got a Magazine, today—no. But then" he said wisely, "there's no use having an inferiority complex, is there? Is there, son?" he said nodding with wistful brightness to Emmett. "No, there isn't," he answered himself, crestfallen and obedient; and winding a little ball of cord about his finger dropped it with trembling assurance to the floor.

Bruno subsided in bewilderment. Where there's a Filing Cabinet, he reflected uneasily, can the Magazine be far behind? One ought to have time to think things out—yes, and he had had, he reasoned dryly, only about ten years of playing with the Idea. The Filing Cabinet (like the damnable persistence of the cablegram on his desk and in his mind) was profoundly disturbing by its concrete presence. One could deny its implications no more than one could deny its being Saturday. And Saturday in Paris too; it must be nearly midnight there. Too late to get married tonight, young Elizabeth! "Nothing," he said thoughtfully, "is more baffling than an assistant editor who orders Filing Cabinets. . . . After all," he ended with a despairing glance at the silent Emmett, "it's as well to remember, just by way of practice: there *is* no Magazine."

"I think maybe my mother," said Emmett shyly, "I know she's interested, I think maybe we could get Merle to give us m-m-money. . . ."

"What, you in the conspiracy too, Emmett?" Bruno

groaned. "My God, mister Demonstrator, I'm framed."

To *have* the Magazine. . . . But it was the Idea that Bruno was in love with. As he saw his Idea tampered with, taken up, exposed, Filing Cabinets ordered to put it into action, it became less clear, less dear to him. Build it up, concretize it—and one must compromise; face a public; recognize a policy and in thus limiting the horizon deal only with a portion of life instead of perceiving the whole illumined by the Idea; and finally admit that no matter how lofty the hopes, how valid the Idea, reality must consist in dealing mediocre articles to mediocre readers. The Filing Cabinet was yesterday's blushing sweetheart turned coarsely to a bride. . . . But how his images today were colored by Elizabeth's maddening cable (why he should feel that her act in marrying meant treachery to him he couldn't say; but there it was: he felt deserted).

"Listen," he said persuasively to the salesman's balanced back, "listen, I'm going to take you into my confidence. How long have you been with the Filing firm?"

"Four-star man," said the salesman thinly. "Star for every five years. My card, professor." He kept one hand on the neck of the Filing Cabinet as though he were groom to a captious horse, and peering behind a row of patent pencils in his upper pocket selected a card from what seemed a miniature Filing Cabinet within his chest; consulted it; handed it to Bruno and snapped back to his fiery charge. "In the lower right-hand corner, sir. Walter Payton Harrison. With four stars."

"I congratulate you, Mr. Harrison." Bruno saluted with the card in his fingers. "A noble name—with a name like that I could get you a job in our English department; they're overstocked at the moment on Jews with Harvard accents. Now listen, Mr. Harrison—are you listening," he said sternly.

"I'm listening, professor," Mr. Harrison said and put his narrow Anglo-Saxon shoulder to the wheel. "Just don't want to waste time, sir, yours *or* mine."

"You sound like a man with his head on his shoulders, Harrison," said Bruno admiringly. "And I don't want to waste time either, mine *or* yours. Now look Harrison: you understand the system of barter, I'm sure? You're no stranger to the fundamentals of historic materialism? You've been with your firm four-star years; you know they aren't giving me this thing from some ill-judged motive of generosity? No. Your boss, Mr. Harrison, is a crass materialist. He wants money for that God damned thing. Well, I haven't got any money. That's reasonable, isn't it, Mr. Harrison? No sugar, Harrison; no cash; no shekels." For Emmett's benefit he shaped in the air a series of empty bank accounts.

"Yes sir," Mr. Harrison said. "But I've got orders to leave her here ten days. *Then* if you don't want her. . . . But might as well look on the bright side, professor." He stooped and taking strips and pieces of things out of a box began to fit them deftly into place.

"Mr. Harrison is a bigoted realist," Bruno sighed to Emmett; and was surprised and disconcerted to see the boy's face lit with interest as he watched the Cabinet inexorably emerge. Heresy in the ranks, he thought; would he lose his disciple to Jeffrey? But as he watched, he caught Emmett slowly swinging round, his gaze lingeringly departing from the Filing Cabinet to stare with timid adoration at himself. "Do you think you could help me explain our ideology to Mr. Harrison, Emmett? The superiority of the shadow to the substance, for instance? Look, Harrison. Yesterday was the Idea. Today, because of a literal-minded assistant editor, suffering from a rush of printers' ink to the brain, is the Filing Cabinet. . . ."

The fine aristocratic stupidity of the Nordic! (He felt suddenly certain that if Elizabeth, lost in Paris, were marrying anyone tonight, she would not be marrying a Jew; so he was doubly deserted and doubly left alone.) Jeffrey said Magazine and immediately he saw himself assistant editor of a Filing Cabinet; he saw the whole thing complete, in its concrete form; complete with office desks and typewriters, lavatories, water-coolers, telephones on hinges, office girls named Miss Diamond, waste baskets, desk calendars, erasers tied to drawer knobs, fire extinguishers, supply closet, bench in the reception room, wire baskets for incoming mail, wire baskets for outgoing mail, all ticketed, docketed, billeted, and in all four corners threatening the editorial desk. Filing Cabinets groomed by up-state four-star salesmen swallowing their goiters manfully. . . . Where then was the Idea?

"The Black Sheep," said Emmett suddenly at the window. "I think I see them. Yes. They're at the Cross. They must be waiting for the girls—C-C-Cornelia and Kate—to come out of their gym class, Bruno." His voice grew a little rueful as he recognized his classmates.

The Black Sheep! To have to make their decisions now as well as his own. What right had he to set himself up to solve other lives when his own (and young Elizabeth's, for which he held himself responsible) wavered so hopelessly in a treadmill? The Black Sheep, with their turbulent indignation! incredibly long ago himself and Miles and Jeffrey had been the Black Sheep of this very campus; twelve years had passed since their bold triumvirate had burned the campus with their angry pacificism, since a wakened faculty pinned blame to Bruno for being what he was, a Jew, of German origin. He felt a quick nostalgia for their old meetings, held beyond the Cross, in a wing of the old gymnasium, now torn down. He remembered Miles, painful New England ingrown sprout, clamping an ascetic jaw against temptations of New York. But it was Jeffrey for whom he had felt the most affection, Jeffrey leaving the meetings early for his eternal dates with girls, Jeffrey with his quick and generous blindness plunging into every pool he saw; impossible for Bruno, even now, to stay angry for long with Jeffrey.

"The Black Sheep," he said, with a certain tenderness. "Maybe that will move you, Mr. Harrison. We are expecting a group of bright, dissatisfied undergraduates. They'll stare at you. They'll glare at you. They'll examine the whites of your eyes to see if you're a proletarian. They'll tap you on the knee to see if you're class-conscious. If you would care," he urged kindly, "while there is still time, to jump out of the window . . ."

"I'm nearly done now," Mr. Harrison explained courteously. "You see we learn to set them up in seven minutes. That's the simple ones. But this Mr. J. Blake ordered you a model double nine-two-five, drawers for cards three different sizes besides the regular eight-by-eleven letter containers. . . ."

"The most expensive model, I hope, Mr. Harrison?"

"Why no," Mr. Harrison admitted, "it's not; not by a long shot. There's eight-one-three for doctors and nine-o-five for lawyers, both comes higher. But this nine-two-five," he punched it gently, "it's a pip, this model is. You can't go wrong," he finished didactically, "on nine-two-five."

"Thank God for that." He spoke absently, returning in his mind to the curious phenomenon of Jeffrey, still at thirty-odd, plunging headlong into whatever offered itself. No Jew, he reflected, could see anything so straight, so clear; no Jew, if he was besieged by thoughts, could set the thoughts aside and leap, unhindered. A Jew, if he had any brains at all, had twice as much as anyone else; he saw all sides at once and so his hands were tied, his brain stood still, he couldn't leap here and he couldn't leap there. (In this matter of Elizabeth, for instance! Jeffrey would obey his impulse; but Bruno had a hundred impulses, balanced evenly, at once.) A Jew said Magazine and he was content, dancing on the point of a needle for his life thereafter to investigate the concept of Magazine, to explore the function of Magazine, to dream the fulfillment of Magazine conveying the Idea . . . which he knew, from the vantage point of his superior philosophical needle, could never be accomplished in the world. So what it came to in the end (for the Jew died before the end, perhaps even before he presented the world with one sentence clarifying the Idea) was that Jeffrey Blake who could not comprehend the Idea covered it over with Filing Cabinets, that Jeffrey who had no Idea had written seven novels concealing that fact while Bruno Leonard who could conceive behind his desk of The Novel must content himself or not content himself with the knowledge that if he never wrote a book at all it would still be a better book than any written by his colleague Jeffrey Blake. Yes, and you knew the football signals better than the half-back too, in your day (his own bright-boyhood seemed to mock); all the same it was the dumb bastard of an athlete that got his letter.

"Forgive me, gentlemen," he said, "while I indulge in a little insincere race solidarity. It can't be done except when I'm the only Jew present." From the very nature of his position in the world, he continued to himself (observing with amusement Emmett's discreet Christian embarrassment, the salesman's four-star hired-man's indifference), the Jew is born to think, as he must live, on two antipathetic levels at once; one the ordinary level and the other his own peculiar subterranean Jew-level. Every Jew a dual nature, split personality; if he coordinated the two levels he got to be a banker, or a jeweller, like the elder Leonard; if he couldn't, if he couldn't reconcile them, couldn't bring himself to sacrifice an iota of the integrity necessary in order to accomplish one concrete fact . . . then he was an idiot, he concluded witheringly. Or a genius—he wavered. A genius, a dementia praecox, a genius, a demented peacock . . . wearily he maintained his balance, teetering on the point of the eternal needle.

"Now take you, Mr. Harrison," he said. "I ask you, I beg you, to take that thing out of my sight. Your reaction is to continue ruthlessly to hammer it together. Why? Because you believe in the God damn thing—you believe in the Filing Cabinet as in an eternal verity. No room for doubts in your mind—I find you, even, a trifle narrow there—but let's not speak of that. No hedging for you, no seeing the other fellow's point of view till you can put it better than you can your own. . . . My assistant editor's the same kind of animal. Now if you were a Jew, Mr. Harrison, God forbid! you'd have a little streak of madness, you'd want to smash those things sometimes instead of putting them together. And if you were a bright enough Jew you'd stay home wondering whether it would be better to smash them or better to put them together, and after a while you'd stay in bed wondering, unable to get up because you couldn't decide . . . and then you'd get a cable from Paris and think of so many answers you wouldn't send any . . . and by the time you got to the office you'd find someone else had your job; an Anglo-Saxon named Walter Payton Harrison."

"I'm very nearly done now," said Mr. Harrison solicitously.

All right, get married, young Elizabeth, he thought; go on and get married; live in Paris too. Everybody's doing something but Bruno—who has sat on his ass for twelve years now planning a Magazine, running everybody's life except his own. The voices of the Black Sheep floated clear across the campus. The children coming to their mentor, the live seeking help of the dead—all at once he was plunged in such depression that a great weight sat on his chest, his breath came and went in a small constricted area in the bottom of his lungs, it was difficult to draw a fresh one. For all of them, all of his friends, Jeffrey, the youngsters, Emmett, even Miles to some extent, the poor gentle salesman bowing a narrow back before him, and finally Elizabeth—they lived in such a different world from his. They crashed up against the rocks while he floated safe and obscure among the shadows. Little dents would be left where their lives had smashed; his own would make no mark, floating down through a series of whirlpools, sinking through the shadows, sinking to the dense bottom in pursuit of the illusory Idea. . . .

"Listen Emmett," he said rapidly, "I can't see the Black Sheep today, I can't do it, I—I'm too busy. Run down, Emmett. Stop them. Tell them next week, any time; not today." He covered the cable with a sheet of paper to hide it from his sight. "Hurry Emmett, catch them at the door, make my apologies. Tell Firman I'm sorry. . . ."

"They'll be awfully disappointed," said Emmett generously; and glowing with self-importance he scrambled for the door.

In a minute he would see their backs, he would hear their voices, growing dimmer, as they retreated over the campus. So vulnerable, so terribly vulnerable! The weight on his chest made it difficult to breathe. He felt a sadness so wide it included everything democratically; even inanimate objects, so that the Filing Cabinet, shiny and new and confident as it was seemed a blustering projection of Jeffrey shouting for recognition, and at the same time the symbol of wan Mr. Harrison's modest four-star life; so that the cablegram actually resembled Elizabeth —Elizabeth, wandering in Paris, reaching over human abysses bravely for his hand. What did she want of him? he could give her nothing because he had nothing to give; yet he felt guilty as though he knew he owed her something. Perhaps better if he let her go her way, let them all go, let them go plunging and smashing while he . . .

"I suffer, Mr. Harrison," he heard his voice unnaturally rising from the grave, "from a touch of the Christ complex now and then. Whenever I get it I crave whiskey. Will you have a spot with me?"

"Thank you, no," said Mr. Harrison compassionately, "not on the job, professor. In my game," he said meagerly, "it's best not—in my game," he repeated vaguely.

"But what in the devil—" Bruno was frantically pulling at the cork; exorcizing by a spurt of physical energy the strange visions that beset him—"what in the devil is the object of the game? Ah there's a sticker, Mr. Harrison! When do you reckon they give us the low-down? Who in the hell is supposed to let us in?" His hand holding the bottle shook. "Well, life goes on, as the Chinese were noted for saying. Sure you won't have a drink, Harrison? Well—have a drink, professor! thanks old man, I will. . . ."

"She's ready, professor," said Mr. Harrison. "Now if you'll just listen to me a minute, sir, I'll explain the workings." He stepped back, rather dapper, and surveyed his life-work; portentous and pathetic, it topped him by a head. "She's a pip all right, professor," Mr. Harrison said; and swallowing humbly he produced his four-star smile.

4.

Flinders Blood

"It got cooler, just as I expected," called the janitor's wife. They turned and nodded in assent. "You ought to have dressed warmer, Missis Flinders," she called after them down the street; "feels like snow in the air," she urged upon them. They turned and waved; and Mrs. Salvemini in her window could be seen drawing her shawl around her shoulders to demonstrate her point. They edged away.

Evening was lowered all around them; and Miles felt that the street they paced together ran like an armistice before them. With sober step—how they had caught each other's tread!—they made it; past the tea-room closing for the day and the speakeasy opening for the night, to the corner where some hours earlier he had wavered, indecisive (Mr. Pidgeon's message in his brain), not feeling where he had to go. Habit—and a vision of Margaret who would eagerly round the turn, impatient to be home—had brought him home; something else, perhaps the indecision undefined, had brought him to the edge of quarrel; when Margaret stepped in (with her wisdom? with her cowardly longing for peace?) and pulled him back, held him safely to a truce. Some day they would face it out—or was it something, he asked himself perplexedly, that was all within himself, that he must fight out alone, without her?

"Fall—I used to go away to school then," Margaret said, holding his arm tightly as if to share it with him.

"Sometimes I think your childhood," he answered slowly, "is the realest thing about you. It gives you a root, Maggie, a funny kind of peaceful super-basis. I never had it," he said suddenly; and they walked a little faster, past the store where he bought his pipe-tobacco because the tobaconist sold communist papers on his stand. "My own was stony," he said with pride; and thought of the difficult New England soil where he had grown. "Not bleak, as I thought before you taught me better," he responded to the instant pressure of her arm, "but stony—like my Connecticut earth."

They walked quietly with the evening. "I wonder," she said thoughtfully, "whether one can ever be successfully transplanted. But of course!" she cried, rushing to tear down the doubt she herself had placed, "why the whole history of the human race—migrations and settlements, your Plymouth Rock and my own Peter Stuyvesant . . ." She finished vaguely. He found it charming, her nebulous feeling for what she could never document, never put correctly into facts. She had a touch, a feel, he thought, glancing at her calm yet eager profile, for what he could only arrive at through laborious mental process—and then it was doubtful if they came out at the same place.

For they were after such different things, he and she (he felt it keenly, through the truce she had involved him in). She wanted to be *happy* (his Uncle Daniel used to say his *pigs* were "happy"); and he wanted—oh God knows! Margaret was fine; but if there was no more simplicity in her mind than his, there *was* simplicity in her nature. There were no gloomy, unlit corners in her. When he exposed his own she brought forth her eager lamps, and, in lighting them, destroyed. What she destroyed, or what he felt she threatened to destroy, he was not sure; whether it might be good for him in the end, he did not know. But he felt a compulsion to *fight,* and she (all gentle fairness, mild intelligence) brushed away his grounds. Yet it seemed, as they walked the familiar streets (past the play-house now, the Greek's tiny flower window), so soberly arm in arm, while evening deepened about them, a good and possible thing—a peace he almost thought he could endure. But in his soul he knew it was not possible.

"The history of the human race," he spoke gently as one might to a child, "at least each new step, each new transplanting, is always a stony thing, it takes more than a generation to recover from it."

He thought of the hard summers, when each day had been packed for even a boy with units and chores, each one another hurdle, another set of stones, and of the meager harvest that resulted in the Fall. He saw his Uncle Daniel fighting his yearly losing fight, struggling with blight in the tobacco fields. He saw his lean aunts, spreading the butter more thinly week by week; his mother, fading as it were deliberately, to pay the penalty for her sinful beauty; and his father sneaking off, because there was an evil strain in him that wanted pleasure, that could not meet the look in Uncle Daniel's eyes.

"My own New England," he said, "my own ancestors, are a good example. Pioneers and zealots—they never should have landed where they did. The thing about them is, they *aren't* farmers; they aren't peasants. They're people with hard brains who *hate* the soil; they stayed, they put up with it, only because it challenged them. And of course, for economic reasons," he added hastily, as if to cancel his own sentimentality; but let it go, he knew there was more at the bottom of it than his new god, economics. "The soil's so bad it's a hand-to-hand fight for existence—a personal struggle between each farmer and his own particular plot of dirt. The profoundest individualists," he threw in, again in the tone of self-discipline, to assuage his intellectual conscience; and let it go, abandoning himself to memory. "My Uncle Daniel was almost insane with personal struggle. . . ."

"I love to hear you talk about it," said Margaret warmly. But he sensed her turning from him to the sight which momently drew her eyes: Mr. Papenmeyer's meat-and-grocery emporium; he felt the link existing between a woman and her market. "Look dear—now prices are going up again," she said absently. "You make it," she came loyally back to him, "as fascinating—both as real and unreal—as O'Neill does in his plays."

"O'Neill," Miles said, piling up on him the lack he felt in Margaret, "didn't get my people straight. He made them far too Irish, almost quaint; and too explicit. My Uncle Daniel would have sneered at 'Beyond the Horizon'; even my father would have walked out on it—staggered out, to the nearest saloon." The thing was, he thought—and did not bother saying, for he knew that Margaret, and perhaps anyone of urban birth, could never understand—that they at once despised the soil for giving them a living and respected it for making that living a hard one. They couldn't stand rich, easy earth;

they *needed* the stones in their fields—but how could he ever make that clear to Margaret who would gladly spend her life on her hands and knees plucking the stones up out of his path!

But she saw his background, and would never see it otherwise, as picturesque—O'Neill; a little Freud; a little Yeats dragged in from somewhere; and the whole made a curious travel book to her. She pieced it together and it looked very neat; he admired Margaret's ingenious puzzle-map. But the blood was left out of her picture. For to call Uncle Daniel, as Margaret blandly did, "pathological," did not materially affect his uncle's ghost. To talk of the "incest pattern" that had kept his three aunts from marriage, that had driven Aunt Fan cuckoo till she lived like a leper up over the barn. . . . He had accomplished all that, for himself, in his mind; but like rationally dismissing God—it didn't cover the ground.

"Shall we go the long way round, Maggie?" he said—and was not sure whether he thus postponed her meeting with Jeffrey, or whether, because he had got back in his mind to home and himself, he would find it unbearable to break the thread. "Or do you think, since they expect us—" He inquired of himself: no, the thought of Margaret meeting Jeffrey was perfectly endurable, meaningless now in fact, since he had worked his way back to where his present life meant nothing.

"Of course, dear—it's such a lovely evening. Norah won't mind our being late; and I wonder about Mrs. Salvemini's snow, it's possible." He smiled; he felt she avoided the use of Jeffrey's name to spare him pain; and he guided her easily toward the openness of Washington

Square, which at the moment did not exist for him except in its faint resemblance, from the distance of one block, to the square in Galloway opposite Town Hall.

He wondered for a minute if his struggle must not end where it began, on that New England farm; if he could ever go back; if it were not implacably too late—now that God, like Uncle Daniel, was so rationally buried. His Uncle Daniel, whose approval he had struggled for and never won (whose approval even now he desired and could never win) had died because of him; that thoroughly irrational fear, laid many times by Miles in cold and adult thought, remained, emotionally, a fact. He lay ill, and the people in his house crept guiltily from stair to stair with frightened faces. The little boy had cried to God in his attic Please let him die! In the morning they broke it to him gently—as though they did not *know* that he had killed him. The look on his own father's face haunted him still; obscurely he had known that his father too had helped to kill, had wished his strong and righteous brother dead; a shame existed between father and son from that morning until the father died. Did not some sort of justice point . . .

Margaret had wondered if one could ever be transplanted; it struck him now that he had never been—that his roots had stayed behind in the stony soil, and that what of him had come on down (to live with Margaret in New York, to work for Mr. Pidgeon in an office) was an aberration, a part of himself that was scarcely valid, which must flounder and die unless he traced back his course to his roots and his home again. Was it possible, he thought with a crazy hope, a longing that touched him to life as nothing these days was able to, to go back some day? (but he was no farmer!) and could that life still hold the meaning this one lacked, in spite of God and Uncle Daniel being gone?

For those early days—and all his later life he failed to make it clear—had held something (which he now supposed was God) that made living, if terribly painful, meaningful. Something was there, in black and white. One was damned or one was saved; and in between there were no finer shadings. There was always the rough soil to be struggled with; and in the Fall there was either enough food or less than enough. One faced the problems daily; there was no drugging oneself from the final issues, either of the earth or of heaven—one lived, as one's neighbors did, by some guiding rote combined of practical and spiritual.

They reached the Square. One certain memory caught him by the throat, a memory that contained, he thought, the essence of his childhood, half understood and never to be outgrown. He slowed his pace, drawing Margaret back beside him; he addressed her politely, as though she were the stranger she had suddenly become.

"Do you mind? I feel like walking slowly. . . ."

"Of course, darling! It's such a grand old night! It's so exhilarating—Fall always is to me. It makes me look ahead so eagerly. . . ." But with that seventh sense she had acquired, born of marriage, that seemed to tell her what was wanted of her, her words trailed into grateful silence.

She could look ahead, he thought, because she was finished with what was past, and grew without transplanting out of childhood; but Miles must go back and go back because he had been torn out, leaving his roots behind. . . . Walking slowly beside her, he abandoned himself utterly to that nostalgic memory.

The air, rain-sodden that memorable summer's day, added its weight to the burden of guilt already borne by a little boy of seven. Looking back he felt that even before the thing took place the air had told some hint of it. So many days dawned in his childhood with the pregnant horror of Judgment Day; but afterward he saw so clearly all their faces, heard on the air the ring of their prophetic voices . . . yes, surely the morning air had known something of what the afternoon would bring.

They were picking berries, the little boy and the Limb of Satan, his mother, condemned by Uncle Daniel and convicted in her own and her son's eyes for her sin of being pretty; Aunt Mart was with them. They set out accompanied by Uncle Daniel's dog; but King grew tired quickly and deserted; they thought perhaps he'd run back home. The little boy was ashamed of the woman's occupation of berrying forced on him because he was young, not yet a man. But unlike King, he was not free to desert. The Flinders women and the Flinders child wandered into Brown's Lane, not far from home.

Brown's Lane was named for Old Man Brown who held what was left of him from the Civil War on a porch austerely facing back. The "Italians" had already begun to invade the Lane. The "Italians" were always referred to in a special voice, as though the word implied description, not mere nation; one said "Italians" as one said "the boogey men." And a piece down the Lane from Brown lived the Picketts, frowned on by all around as trash; they fraternized, one said, with the "Italians."

Brown's Lane lay buried in a valley; farm-land sloped down to it, Old Man Brown's tobacco fields hid from the potatoes of the "Italians" by stony fences. The Flinders place was quarter of a mile above, just out of sight.

The berrying took them to the end of the Lane, right by the Picketts' barn. All at once Aunt Mart shrieked: "The chickens—look!" then covered her mouth in fright, for Uncle Daniel's dog had been suspected once before. They looked. The ground before the Picketts' barn was strewn: a dozen strangled chickens lay there.

"Let's say we never saw!" Miles's mother, limp, held weak hands before her pretty, sinful face.

The little boy felt sick at sight of the chickens, although he had witnessed killings of fowl that left him cold. But this was different; something unnatural, blasphemous, in the way these chickens sprawled.

Aunt Mart was Flinders-born, closer to her brother Dan than mother; and somehow she was on closer terms with God. "It's our duty, Hester," she said.

The little boy felt vaguely threatened. If there was a crime around, he was sure to feel himself guilty, born cursed, as he was, of a mother who was *pretty* and a father blinded by beguiling sin. So now, he crouched; he had wanted to run away with King: did that mean, before God and Uncle Dan, he shared King's sin?

A Pickett boy approached. His mouth opened wide in horror; then, his hands in his blue jeans' pockets, he surveyed the Flinders standing there in guilt. "I bet it's that there dog of yourn," he sneered, identifying them with King. "I'll go git Pa. He said, the *next* time . . ." And he was off across the Pickett field.

"Oh Martha! what shall we do!" his mother whimpered. "Poor King! I'd rather they shot *me.*" It seemed her evil prettiness had made her soft; Aunt Mart might be weak with fear, but she was born a Flinders and she was never *soft.*

The Pickett boy was like the rain. Wherever he ran, the ground was fertile, and people sprang up at his words. And soon the Lane was full. "Who did it?" "*Sure,* it *must* have been the Flinders dog." "Where is he now?" "Once a dog's got *chicken* on the brain!" "Dern right: they can't be cured." "Best to kill 'em off." "Does Dan'l Flinders *know?*"

This was the snag on which caught all their thoughts. "Does Dan'l Flinders know?" The Flinders women and the Flinders child cowered together.

John Pickett, summoned, came at last; angry, but pleased in spite of himself that such an audience was gathered there.

"Where's that damn dog?"

But the dog must not be killed in anger. This the people in the Lane seemed to know. He must be killed in cold blood, for doing wrong. Just act of a just God.

They wavered now; hummed uneasily in the valley of the Lane; hostile a little toward John Pickett. "Might be one of them dogs belonging to the 'Italians' " someone spitefully called. "We mustn't act in haste," he was supported.

"Go get Old Man Brown," John Pickett ordered his son. This was right and felt to be. It was Brown's Lane; Brown had fought the Civil War; Brown was the oldest man in Galloway. The Pickett boy sped up the Lane.

The "Italians" gathered shyly; clustered together gesticulating mildly. The Hired Men, drawn democratically, flocked to the Picketts' barn. Soon there were twenty in all in Brown's Lane: a brilliant crowd.

"What, Flinders dog?" "I saw him; noon." "Made off, did he?" "One thing sure, he wouldn't have gone *home.*" "No, that he wouldn't dare." "Flinders dog? well, he'll come skulkin back, you wait." "They never do go far, you know." "No, *chicken's* stronger in their blood than fear."

As if born from this conjecture, in the road suddenly King appeared. (A little moan of pity went to him from the "Italians.") There was no doubt about King's guilt. His tail hung low; his head was ducked. He slunk, rather than walked; and he eyed the people weakly. He would not come too close. But he would not run away. A good New England dog, he stayed for punishment.

The people in the Lane grew still. Only John Pickett, whose chickens lay dead, could hate the slinking culprit.

Miles' mother sobbed. "I can't bear it, I can't bear it! King, here Kingie-boy! I'd rather they shot *me!*" The "Italians" moaned their grief.

Miles knew the dog would die; he thought the dog knew it too. He was proud of King, not because he had killed the Picketts' chickens, but because he stayed to meet his death. No one made a move to catch him. He could have run away. Everybody knew he would not. He was a good New England dog. But Miles was puzzled by his own kind, by the people. He could feel that they did not *want* to kill old King; King was a fine dog. They could banish him, send him down to Galloway where there were no chickens loose to kill; or Uncle Dan could keep him tied. They didn't *want* to kill him. But they were going to. All of them together, because not one cried out to spare him. Why, if they didn't *want* to kill him, must they? Even his soft mother, snivelling her weak disgust, was not protesting; she was merely voicing grief for a King already dead.

The Pickett boy came running back. In his wake Old Man Brown came hurrying, as fast as his Civil War leg let him. By his side he carried his old gun, which everyone knew was the gun he had used in the War.

Old Man Brown was in a fine state of excitement. He cackled on ahead of himself, "Wait for me! Wait until I git there. I'm acomin, fast's I ken."

He was a little man. Old age had shrunk him smaller than his gun. He had no teeth. But he had fine white gums with bloody scallops where his teeth had been.

"Where's that dern dog? where is he?" he croaked, arriving in their midst, and peering with his blue, blind eyes. "I've brought my gun. Reckon I can't lift it, though. Not and hold it steady. Reckon it's for John Pickett to do the shootin anyhow."

"You figure there ain't nothin else to do but shoot?" respectfully inquired one.

"Why sure, there ain't no curin dogs once they got *chicken* on the brain." Old Man Brown snapped his head in certain affirmation.

"Reckon he's right, sure enough." "Why sure, there's nothin *else* to do." "What ken you do with dogs got *chicken* on the brain!"

The dog with chicken on the brain lurked, self-condemned, before them all. It was his last hour. He let it be.

Then Aunt Mart sprang to her full, scrawny height, the man's felt hat on her head pushed back. She had been seeking help, perhaps in prayer, or perhaps had found it in her Flinders pride. "Nobody is goin to shoot that dog!" she said, speaking in a loud clear voice. "Nobody will tech that dog unless Dan'l Flinders tells 'em to. It's Dan'l's dog, and Dan'l's got it to say what happens to him."

It seemed the last word had been spoken. "That's right, Marty." "You've spoke right there, old Miss Flinders." "Why sure it's up to Dan'l." "You don't go killin a man's dog without you ask him first." "Flinders'll know what's right." "Dan'l will do what's right."

"Who'll fetch him?" "Who's goin to tell Flinders?" No one stirred.

"Go fetch your uncle, Miles." Aunt Mart spoke proudly.

The little boy cowered against his mother's skirt. She soothed him apathetically. Uncle Dan would be in the tobacco field now. King was the only living thing he loved—he *couldn't* tell him.

Aunt Mart gave him a little push. "He'll take it better from the family, son," she whispered. "You go, now. Let him go, Hester; it'll do him good." His mother released him with a sob.

He felt important running over the hill, taking the short cut from Brown's Lane to the Flinders place. Never had he run so fast. He was for the moment *not* afraid of Uncle Daniel; he was his equal. They both were Flinders-born; they both must do God's will.

He found him in the backer patch, the leaves shoulder-high to Miles. He floundered through to Uncle Dan, weeding under the cloths stretched pole-to-pole to keep the leaves in shade. He would never forget Uncle Daniel's straightening back as Uncle Dan reared himself like God above the leaves. His blue eyes, used to taking in horizon vistas, narrowed as they focussed on the boy.

He didn't say a word; slapped down his tools and pulled his straw hat lower on his head. Then, his face not changing, he spoke: "You go on down. Tell them I am coming"; and stalked with giant's paces toward the house.

Miles knew he must not wait. He turned his eyes from Uncle Daniel's form and they streamed tears as he ran blindly down the hill, important with his message.

The people took the message silently. King took it flattening down his ears in fright. He ran to and fro, unhappy, like a condemned man spending his last minutes in his cell. Miles clung with both his arms to Aunt Mart's waist; she was stronger than his mother, she could give him help; also, like himself and Uncle Daniel, she had Flinders blood.

"He's coming." "Look!" *"Look what Dan'l Flinders' bringin!"*

Miles saw, and knew before he saw. Till then he had not been sure; now he knew it *was* the Judgment Day. The crest of the farm-hill held his first vision; Uncle Dan was God; behind him the clouds broke and the sun streamed in angry mercy; it was the Day of Judgment; and Uncle Daniel strode to it with his gun across his shoulder.

Moving in just wrath he slipped closer, his black shape descending from the sky and climbing fiercely down the side of hill. "Dan'l will do what's right." "Flinders knows what to do." The people stood proudly, waiting his coming. The "Italians," quivering, hemmed in closer.

The dog left off his guilty pacing; turned and faced his master. He made a movement forward, as though straining at the leash of memory; then stood still, his ears flat back, his tail lifting in a single wag of recognition.

Uncle Daniel never stopped until he stood on a little hillock, fifty paces from his dog. There was nothing readable in his face; but at that moment, if at no other in his life, Miles knew he loved him, more than any person living. He lifted the gun to his shoulder; it was already primed; and squinted down its length.

"Brother Daniel! Oh for God's sake!" Miles' mother fell to the ground and wept.

The little boy took his last look at King, standing a knowing target in the road. He saw King's tail move slowly up and down. Then he buried his eyes and his ears in Aunt Mart's skirt. He felt her body stiffen. Through the folds of calico and his own layers of fear he heard the shot: one single sound, booming in the valley. He thought he heard a yelp; it blended with his mother's weeping.

When he dared look up King was a brown mass on the ground, and Uncle Daniel's back, half up the hill again toward home, mounted with the muzzle of his gun pointed to the sky.

"Twere the right thing to do," said Old Man Brown in closing benediction. "Dan'l knew," murmured all around.

Nobody would touch the Picketts' chickens. At last the "Italians," wiping their moist and volatile eyes began to smile again, came forward and bargained with their friend

John Pickett. In the end they got all twelve chickens for a dollar. They rode off slow and easy, carting John Pickett's dead white chickens, their eyes looked back and shone with lazy pleasure.

The valley sighed. The air lightened. Justice had been done. The people dispersed back to their fields, the Hired Men moved fast, knowing democracy was finished for the day.

The Flinders women and the Flinders boy took the short cut home, up over the hill the way their man had gone. They placed their men's felt hats over the pails of berries to keep the sun from wilting them. Miles could see across the field his Uncle Dan, already back at work, under the cloths stretched pole-to-pole to keep the backer in shade. When they went in the kitchen to wash the berries they saw his gun hung back in its place on the kitchen door. No one ever spoke of King again . . . but Miles knew well that day that there was something bigger in men than themselves, that could drive them to do what alone they would never have dared. . . .

"Here we are," said Margaret, and he gathered from the inflection of her voice she must have spoken twice. He looked up in haste—for he knew that it was as unendurable to her as it was incomprehensible, to be forgotten, to have their world together even for a moment so ignored—and saw, to his faint surprise, that his journey down Brown's Lane had brought them ineluctably to the door of the house where Jeffrey and Norah lived.

"Of course, if you don't feel like seeing them," said Margaret somewhat acidly.

"Oh sure I do," he said protestingly; and added, filled

with compassion at the thought of how far he could wander from her, "Mrs. Salvemini was right dear, you ought to have dressed warmer, you look cold—maybe we walked too slowly?" He could feel her eyes penetrating gravely as, hiding his reluctance, he rang the bell.

5.

Norah's Jeffrey

SHE stood listless at the kitchen door, watching Jeffrey range his bottles. From the living-room beyond came the sound of Miles' and Norah's voices, carrying on their desultory off-stage drama. "Yes," Miles was saying, "oh yes, of course; living in the country is quite another thing; there you're less aware of trends because you're busy making them—grubbing away knee-deep in dirt, you can't haul off and get a mental eyeful." And Norah's hearty murmur, scarcely audible, muffled by the din of Jeffrey opening bottles; words here and there like the thrusting undercurrent of the second violin, her father's orchard, her mother's brood of hens; and Miles again, patient, didactic, uninterested, politely intoning the theme-song from a corner of his shell. Margaret Flinders shivered. Cold? *why yes, Mrs. Salvemini, chilled to the bone and heart; it was the coldest walk I ever took—winter is certainly in the air, Mrs. Salvemini.* But another coat, Mrs. Salvemini's shawl itself, would not have helped. For Miles had effectually shut her out, locked and double-barred the door which closed his shell; she had wandered many times around it, her fingers ached with battering vainly on its brittle walls. Let Norah try the empty shell-step now! She thought of Miles; and turned with relief to Jeffrey, preparing an altar on the kitchen table for the rite of mixing drinks.

"no age for repressions, my dear," Jeffrey spoke in a low and irritable voice, its deadline the kitchen door and the discretion of her ears. "Will you hand me the squeezer, please Maggie? Your repressions are unhealthy, a damned unhealthy lie."

"not a question of repressions, I've told you that before." It was such a very old play; her lines came easily. She rummaged on the shelf for Norah's lemon-squeezer.

"so utterly bourgeois, not like you." He took the squeezer angrily. "This gin," he pointed to it proudly, it might be a bonus offered with himself, "is made with hardly any juniper; but lots of glycerine to make it smooth. And it's not just that I'm arguing my own case," he brought his large and beautiful eyes to stare like a baleful preacher's into hers, "it's for your sake just as much. I wish you'd read my book—where in hell is the ice-pick? the dynamics of healthy sex," he finished absently. He forgot her; the dynamics of healthy sex slithered to the floor. His eyes and his quick nervous hands darted through the kitchen drawers.

"You really don't mix cocktails, you perform them," Margaret said; and gave herself over to the joy of watching a man in love with what he did. She thought of Miles; from the outer room the sounds came vaguer, Miles withdrawing deeper in his hard impenetrable shell—poor Norah! She thought of Miles. But Miles for all his scorn of Jeffrey's catholic amours, had brought her here himself; Miles had not lifted his eyes when on the flimsiest pretext (for she had shivered in his presence, found it impossible to raise her voice from spirits sunk so deep) she had followed Jeffrey wildly to the kitchen. Then let Miles go! forget him! forget Norah too, her friend. Forget them both (she urged herself on; she needed courage); let them go on sitting there, discussing Marx, if she knew Miles! in whatever state they might: Norah in her hearty silence, Miles laboriously making faces from the safety of his cloistered shell. She thought of Miles; and turned with warmth to Jeffrey. "Two parts gin without juniper, and about ten parts Jeffrey's soul," she said; she paused; "if you put as much ardor into your *courtship,* Jeffrey . . ." She let her eyes smile mockingly.

"And that's just where you're wrong," he said, taking her look and swallowing it with his own egocentric brand of salt, "that's just where you're wrong, my dear. I don't believe in courting, any more than marriage. *Dynamics,* I tell you—I only believe in nature. I tell you honestly how I feel—and I know damn well you feel the same. So there isn't any courting needed. It's entirely up to you. Either you go against your nature; or you follow where it leads." Yet in the very face of nature she observed he lowered his voice; as though nature were something belonging exclusively in the kitchen and by no means to sidle down the hall to the room where Miles and Norah sat. "You resent that I seem to put more ardor into making drinks? Why Margaret! you romantic lady! back to the middle-ages, darling, I'm no Galahad." His voice changed—she loved his trick of turning with a grin, feeling quick joy from some little thing: disarming, almost admitting his own absurdity. "But really—I confess it: I *do* get a kick out of mixing drinks. Why not? it's part of living. And out of so many things besides, Maggie—and that's all the courting I can give you darling, invite you to share things with me, get a kick out of something together, you and I and nobody else. . . ."

That was it, that was the whole thing, she reflected, handing him the can-opener for which he had not asked, on an impulse to contribute something to his joy—he got a kick out of practically anything: men, women, gin without juniper, jokes and espousing justice and his own shallow sparkling books; there was nothing Jeffrey could not eye with pleasure. (She heard Miles in the other room explaining to Norah how economic determinism was responsible for even private motives; "even most marriages" he said in what sounded to her a grim and disillusioned tone.) Avidity immediately followed; insatiable hunger to capture, to make a part of Jeffrey whatever caught his eye—what Miles called spreading himself thin like synthetic cheese to reach indiscriminately everywhere. (*Oh Miles, it wasn't economic determinism darling, that was responsible for us—why Miles, have you forgotten everything?*) And Miles was right about the cheese, he always was right in some meaningless mental zone that took nothing human in account; but that Jeffrey was democratic to the point of spreading indiscriminately she found she suddenly could forgive. It was a pleasant quality, and pliable, proof of his being alive and young. ("Well, I don't really know, Miles," she heard Norah's calm and laughing answer; "now take my father's rooster; you can't tell me he only thought of ways to earn his keep! And I never heard a banker crow so loud!" Then Norah too had found the shell-door bolted! but Norah could stand on the shell-step laughing; she knew she had no rights inside.) That capacity of Jeffrey's for uncritical enjoyment—Miles would condemn it forever, Miles would never understand it—but let Miles go! who sat and explained the nature of economics and forgot to consider his pulse-beats; who turned deliberately from her warmest gifts and chose to wander off alone, carrying his hard-shell integrity on his back like a hard-shell baptist beetle—let Miles go!

"I do like to enjoy things," she said; "and I like to enjoy things with you. But Norah—she's my friend, Jeffrey, after all, as well as you." This *was* taking Jeffrey seriously! she was almost frightened.

"I don't put much value on a friendship embalmed in vinegar—which is all that denial is." She thought it odd that Jeffrey, with all his talk of nature and denial, continued to resemble a poetic, fair-haired priest. "Now let me see. Oh yes—I have the bitters: it's the sugar I want next." He worked his way happily with the can-opener around the seal-tite grapefruit. "If you can find it, Maggie. And when you come to your senses, darling, about life, I mean, let me be the first to know."

The ice-cubes clinked; the liquid thrashed—and Margaret's spirits rose. Why of course! (she opened the door of Norah's cupboard); she had reckoned, on that lonely walk with Miles, altogether without Jeffrey, without the world outside of Miles that Jeffrey stood for. She had fallen (loosening her hold experimentally on Miles' unwitting arm, vainly seeking company from Mr. Papenmeyer's passing store) into a state of injured apathy she now could hardly credit; creeping beside him in the tempo of some demoded world (but not the middle-ages; her mother's world perhaps) where drinks and men beside one's husband had no place. Now Jeffrey and his cocktail rite, Jeffrey and his warming words, lifted the curtains again on the world of faster rhythms; in Jeffrey's eyes and Jeffrey's admiration she could feel Margaret recreated, Margaret standing for herself again, no longer Mrs. Salvemini's shivering Missis Flinders. She faltered, facing Jeffrey's gayer world, for what she left behind was far more dear. But one must compromise! one must evade; fatuity got one nowhere. She searched through Norah's cupboard for Norah's store of sugar; and found it in the crock marked GINGER.

She held it out with the faintest suspicion that she gave him more than sugar. He turned and meeting her eye, swiftly kissed her hand and held it quietly in his. She strained for a sound from the other room, some perceptive signal (but God knew what she wanted!) from Miles perhaps; but there was silence. She was frightened; and drawing back her hand she spoke in the high artificial voice of an actress stressing the cue.

"The reviews, Jeffrey, tell me what they did to you."

"The reviews," he said obediently; and taking the sugar returned with characteristic absorption to his task. "Idiotic as usual," his hands moved competently opening bottles; "all that economic drivel, you know—well, Miles subscribes to it, and Bruno too—about my not dealing with 'social distinctions'—when I'm concerned with *life* transcending classlines . . . will you hand me the lemons now Maggie? and anyway (thanks darling) I'm something of a mystic." He poured with an expert narrowing of the eye from a brown bottle into the cocktail shaker. "They *did* speak of me, though—two of them," he numbered modestly, and fastidiously pushed the lemon peels back off the cocktail altar, "as America's D. H. Lawrence." More ice-cubes tumbled in. "I'm terribly fed up with grenadine, aren't you? to hell with it. And of course, they missed my most symbolic meanings. . . ."

"I thought you were a communist," she murmured—and thought how Miles would add *'this week.'* (She wished that Miles' ghost would stay outside with Miles, arguing Marx to Norah.)

"Of course, I am; a Marxist intellectual, I *should* say." He stirred and tasted; added another spoon of sugar. She wondered if his Revolution existed just as cocktails did, something for Jeffrey to enjoy. "And as a matter of fact, I have it on good authority that certain members of the Left Wing, you know I'm pretty close to them . . ." He paused and thought; his fine brow wrinkled. "Oh yes! I'm ready for the bitters, Maggie."

It struck her how from her earliest days it had been dinned into her that a woman's life was completed by her husband; and now (taking the sugar, handing him the bitters, in short building with Jeffrey toward something, the ingredients the lightest symbols if she wished them so) how utterly false that might be. The bond, for instance, that she plainly felt with Jeffrey—it was surely more than friendship? strengthened and put to the test by Margaret's long denial of it, it certainly existed in itself and was extraneous to Miles. Convention, her mother's sweet and trustful code, dictated that denial. But it might be one thing for her mother and another for her mother's child, she found herself reflecting now—and Mrs. Thomas Banner had had something, the sanctity of the family she had called it, to preserve. But Miles and Margaret Flinders had no such tender thing, their rooms housed nothing but each other—and what had they, Miles and Margaret, what thread, that Jeffrey could destroy? For fidelity—there, it was out! she slipped it recklessly free of her conscience and looked it in the face; the word and its antithesis must have been playing in her mind since early evening, surely since she chose a dress to wear for Jeffrey. For fidelity—it must have some object larger than itself; it must achieve some end; and what had come of hers, tonight and many times before?

For coming faithfully home from the market had she not paused at sight of her house, before her again! smitten with the longing to turn back and lose herself somewhere in the city out of sight forever of that house, to chase madly in pursuit of some world around corners (and might Jeffrey possibly be its door?). But had she not also, drawn there surely by her loyalty, raced up the stairs in terror? had she not joyfully greeted Miles when she half-hoped to find him gone? And better so, better so, she had thought, and thought repeatedly. Let us have no change; let us have no hurry; let us have no infidelities. Let us lull the men till they leave off their restlessness and come and sit in the cynical shade of our bosoms—grown large (how ripe and fine her mother was, just before her death) to comfort them; let them be at last like our fathers, our children, with bald heads pressing them down and in, safe and sweetly defeated. So she had turned, as she had a hundred times before, from infidelity even in her mind; and what had come of it?

She was Miles' faithful wife. Yet Miles could wander (even now, she heard his voice, droning on to Norah, and it sounded strange to her) walking even by her side, so many dark turns from her. And she could not leap jealously in pursuit because the grounds were so intangible, because he took his road alone and went unaccompanied by what it would have been comparatively light to bear—some other woman. She turned from a twinge of loneliness determinedly to Jeffrey. *His* infidelities were something a woman could grasp and meet; Norah could offer him the same gifts that lured him off to win him home again. Or was Margaret Flinders telling herself this, to pave the way for disloyalty to Norah, just as she coached her soul for infidelity. . . .

"This will knock us for a goal," said Jeffrey happily.

She watched him keenly. Jeffrey Blake (she said his name with pleasure to herself, as if it became a part of her) was too often absurd—she would admit it freely again to Miles; occasionally seemed mad; certainly was obsessed with the importance of himself and his enthusiasms. But all the while there was this healthy appetite in him, a capacity for absorption and enjoyment, that she knew could match her own. Even his beauty—strange anachronism in a male, as Bruno said—seemed a symbol of his inner glow, his inner generosity: he wore it, showed it, loaned it, with such frank delight. His laugh, his joy, his childlike glow. . . . Was it infidelity if she turned to another man for what Miles could never give her?

His voice came floating muffled down the hall; his words stopped short just at the kitchen door. But she thought that even if his words came in and stood about her, they could not touch her now, so completely had she moved to Jeffrey's world. The world of gayety, of warmth! it might be as closed to Miles as his New England shell to her.

And if it *were* infidelity? if it *were* disloyalty? Mustn't she be Margaret first, before a friend and wife? And if her life, unlike her mother's, were *not* completed by her husband?

He had said it himself, in a hundred different little ways, during their loyal drinking of the cider (which had tasted like tears in her throat): "Something is wrong with our life." And she might have agreed, they might have faced it down—but that it seemed two people never bravely spoke the truth at once; she had manufactured peace. She sighed. Such peace was fraudulent, she knew it. Clearly something *was* wrong, and wrong for her part too. On her side it consisted perhaps in a failure to keep her identity apart from his; she sought a thread and a meaning, and expected them both from him. But that was impossible; it was sentimental; moreover, it had failed.

"And last but not least," said Jeffrey with joy, "the gin. Did I tell you my man said—less juniper and lots more glycerine—is what does the trick?"

He rattled the shaker high over his head. Then he poured a little in a glass; sipped, his brows raised quizzically. He handed the glass to her. "What do you think Margaret, taste it carefully?" He watched her anxiously, his forehead beaded with sweat like a baby's.

She tasted it and holding the glass in her hand as though she weighed it against the delicacy of the moment, swallowed slowly. She came to decisions and reversed them; sipped again, her eyes gravely meeting his. It was a fine moment; fidelity hung in the balance; she wanted to prolong it. "A little sweet," she said at last, "a very little too sweet, I think," she said faintly (for she liked it sweet, it was Miles who would want it dry) and handed him back the glass. Now they almost held their breaths as he with infinite precision added infinitesimal drops of bitters, the final touches to their masterpiece. They tasted again—first Jeffrey, then Margaret; then Margaret again, then Jeffrey to make sure. Their eyes met; they nodded; and she trembled so her hands went cold.

He set a full glass before each of them. She was not sure if her voice would come clear; she tried it; it was a soft and shaky tenor. "Plying me with liquor, are you." He rose and softly closed the kitchen door. They lifted their glasses with one motion and drank slowly like people mesmerized, their eyes spinning a tenuous vibrant thread. (*Drink deep of the gin without juniper, drown Miles in the gin with glycerine to make him wash down smooth.*)

He set down his glass and holding his eyes on hers as though he were magnetized, as though he feared to snap the tenuous thread stretched taut between their eyes, he advanced as warily as a tight-rope dancer and took her hands in his. "Margaret!" The moment held her like a vise.

His arms went lightly round her. But while she stood and waited, locked with him into a strange paralysis of everything but hope, he did a curious thing: with one oddly disembodied hand (wearing a painful smile upon his face) he hurriedly unfastened the buttons of his coat. The poignant moment passed, releasing her. Something in her shuddered and drew back; but that must be how these things were done; and as she had hardened herself earlier against Miles, so now she closed a door on her own too-sensitive self—and taking a hasty gulp from the glass he had taken from her (it would be accomplished now, she knew, on a considerably lower level) she slipped with a feeling almost of despair into his arms again, against his carefully erogenous shirt. The sides of his coat flapped back reproachfully.

She felt with curiosity—and marvelled at her standing there, so passive—his hands upon her shoulders, moving vague, dispirited, she thought; then leaping, quick with frenzy, through her hair. He drew her closer to that vulnerable shirt; she was surprised that beneath it his heart could beat so fast. Well, this was what she had wanted, what she had made up her mind for once to take; but she felt more distant from him in his arms than she had during the seconds they stood eyeing each other over the rim of a glass.

She had wanted to lose her head; now she found herself too steadily regaining it. She had expected some surge to draw them together, to sweep them all at once to some high, oblivious place. Infidelity—yes; she could face it; she had consented to it in her mind; half expected this might be an understood preliminary. But she had not counted on—mechanics.

His hands moved quickly, desperately, as though they would achieve some tour de force—a fire with no paper perhaps; no matches; rubbing together two dry unfitted spheres of flint; he was laying his fire with damp sticks. It struck her that he was playing some sort of game, that having forgotten her he was engaged in proving something to himself. "I am something of a lone wolf," he whispered suddenly; and she shook with repressed laughter—yet if they lived in a world where there were no jokes, it might have been the truth, she granted that;

she reflected how no man could speak words entirely foreign to his nature, how even a technique partook of truth. She caught a kind of anguish in him; she felt he reached for her not as Jeffrey Blake for Margaret, scarcely even as man for any woman, but as one rather lonely human being for another; that the fire he was passionately fanning was more for friendliness than sex; and that he did not know it, had overshot his mark, must feel this as his only way of speaking to her.

He went through the motions like an old actor relying on a patient memory. There was something strained and something gallant in his efforts, that won her pity—and left her cold with curiosity. From time to time he drew back his head and looked at her full with his fine blind eyes and murmured "Beautiful. Joy. Atoms dancing like happy pagans" and she did not know whether his words were spoken about her or even to her, and had a ridiculous conviction that he was plagiarizing either from his own or someone else's novel; and surely he looked like anything but an atom or a happy pagan himself, he resembled nothing so much at this moment as a tortured saint. It was an incredible thing that she should be leaning back on Norah's kitchen door with Norah's Jeffrey making love to her. The kitchen door itself was ludicrous; that Miles was talking Marxian determinism on its other side was the final crowning idiocy. . . . But with one ear cocked to that room beyond (she would see it through, this once at any rate) she played her end mechanically; stood and maintained her balance while he hurled himself against her; stood calm while he withdrew to murmur his curious verbal aphrodisiac.

"Margaret, are we never—" he whispered in her ear;

"are you never going to throw away your bourgeois notions, are we always condemned to sin against ourselves and our desire, oh this is evil, you must read my book and see, it's the only evil. . . ." He continued his impassioned speech; punctuated it with kisses oddly lacking in sensual intelligence. It persisted in her mind that this was *fake,* that desire had started from nothing, that she was taking part, however passively, in a drama much beneath her. "This is terrible," he whispered, "this making love in kitchens, it can't go on, this is no age for repressions. . . ." His eyes ran from one of her eyes to the other, asking his hundreds of questions—but he waited for no answer; he whipped himself up to have something to beat, just as he fought for possession of her mouth which offered no resistance.

"Your bourgeois notions," he muttered furiously; "will you never get over them?" She had not answered him directly for something like five years, since the evening when she met him first; he had scarcely expected an answer since. She thought a moment (she was a novice in these matters; the poignant moment had safely passed, leaving her able to coldly calculate) and then spoke blandly: "Yes; I think I *shall* get over them, what you call my bourgeois notions. Now what do you think of that?"

What he thought of it he wouldn't say; but she had an idea, as he drew back in surprise, that his eyes held a moment's dislike of her, as though she had spoken out of turn or in some way broken the unwritten law of his code (which suddenly she recognized, the clearer for his denying it), that he must be seducer. Then he fell to fighting her again, murmuring "Oh this is terrible, this half-love, my God how much I want you" as though she had never spoken at all.

She thought, and wondered if she had not known before, he is trying, at bottom, to seduce himself! Oddly Puritanic, that he should bother then with words; but he needed them, he needed them, for his own inside assurance. "I am highly over-sexed," he said indignantly as though he challenged a denial; and all at once succeeded in convincing himself.

He seized her as though she were the last human on earth and clung to her ready to die in her arms; then pressed himself against her bitterly (she feared the kitchen door might give) as though she were no human at all but some wall that denied him entrance; and drew back, because he had not found her at all, had found nothing worth his nervous seeking, smiling sheepishly.

She felt completely sold, discovering in a shameful flash that she had been less unfaithful to Miles than to something in herself. She helped Jeffrey locate his sadly floating hands, retrieve them from her flesh which shrank, dishonored, to let the strangers pass. He left one hand a placating hostage on her shoulder while with the other he buttoned himself resentfully into his coat against her (for she had failed him too); and when he had both of his hands back in his own possession again he rubbed them one against the other as though he somehow washed them and forgave them. Their problem was to leave each other now that they so terribly wanted to.

They stood embarrassed like a pair of tired actors wishing the curtain would fall on a play they knew was rotten. She wanted to cut and run—she longed to get back to Miles again, to escape those falsely glowing eyes of Jeffrey's which had failed to take possession of her; she longed to creep back humbly into the circle of Miles' notice. But still they lingered, looking for an exit line.

"I suppose we've been out here pretty long, I suppose we'd better be joining the others," he said with a loyal showing of reluctance. She saw with mild pain how before returning to Norah he wiped his hands again (or was it Miles he feared) as though he hoped to purge them, guiltily on the sides of his jacket.

"Oh yes, by all means—now that we've mixed the drinks," she said coldly; and discovered a similar weakness in herself, smoothing her hair (and hoping to God that Jeffrey didn't notice). He lifted the shaker and carried it before them, shining container at once of their apology and both their failures.

"Of course," he said, as if continuing absently after he had opened the door and waited impersonally for her to pass out first, "of course the critics this year are bit hard by the social consciousness bug, there's a regular blight on them;" the "blight" brought them to where the others sat (and there was Miles again! sitting faithfully where she had left him; but she knew she never *had* left him and prayed that he would know it too); "but in a deep way of course" (what was it, in Norah's mild compassionate eyes? just what *was* Norah anyway, beside a wife and friend? and Miles, *dear Miles,* at whom she could not look directly, gathering his forces perhaps before he dared look up?) "in an important way my characters did symbolize. . . . Oh say, you two, we've mixed a knock-out of a drink!"

"I made him put in bitters, Miles—I knew you liked it dry." She spoke too quickly; the blood rushed to her temples as though she had called right out before them all *I love you dear, I haven't been unfaithful.* And still she couldn't look at him, fearing to meet what might be in his eyes as she slowly crossed the room toward Norah, renouncing openly (so she felt), denouncing, Norah's husband. And still Miles didn't speak.

"But you forgot the glasses, children," cried Norah rising gayly.

"This gin," said Jeffrey bravely (Margaret couldn't bear to look at him) "is something very special, Miles. My man gave me the inside dope. It seems when they put in less juniper—"

"And glycerine to make it smooth," said Margaret cruelly; (*do you see, Miles, do you see, how he means nothing at all to me?*) "The stuff we have at home is just as good."

"Flinders chauvinism!" cried Jeffrey in a rasping, boisterous voice. (She felt Miles' head turning ironically; but it was impossible to look.) "To hell with it! Glasses, Norah my girl. Preliminary round!"

Heads tossed up in unison, throats and hopes tentative on the receiving line. "Down the old hatch!" said Jeffrey. Margaret thought her "hatch" (how everything that Jeffrey said repelled her now) would never take it; when there was a sharp repeated ringing of a bell. Four glasses lowered. "It might be Bruno," Jeffrey said; and Norah ran to press the button. In the interval of waiting (Margaret prayed it might be Bruno) she slowly gathered courage: her eyes began their painful journey up the room toward Miles. She thought her heart stopped beating. For a mad moment she hoped he would leap at Jeffrey's throat—or at her own—to show he loved her; and then her eyes arrived. But Miles was carefully blowing upon his glasses, his cocktail waiting, peacefully, beside him; and the whole of her scene with Jeffrey lost what validity had lingered as she felt it had not entered Miles' consciousness. Steps sounded on the landing. There was a heavy rapping on the door; and Norah flew to open it. "Bruno?" Margaret wasn't sure who said it; it seemed the whole room wanted him.

"Of course it's Bruno," Bruno said; and stood in the door with bottles under both his arms like a huge and jovial Mephistopheles. "And drunk as hell, thank God." The room heaved a sigh of relief.

6.

The Bruno Leonard Circus

"But children!" he cried, stopping short as he ran counter to an air of doubt that floated off their little circle—their glasses poised, their faces lifted, as though like Elizabeth they floated rudderless in space, a chorus waiting for the maestro. "Children! you closely resemble a wake! what is the object of the game? sitting out the fall of Rome? acting a charade? or is it, mes amis," here he crossed his bottles piously, became the French for Sherlock Holmes, "that you plot the revolution?" But he must come in, come in, cried Norah; and he was just in time, said Margaret Flinders wistfully; Bruno's *always* just in time, cried Norah; and Miles ground out a greeting from a hollow granite shell.

The acoustics were bad; their voices stopped short of his fog. Only Norah seemed clear-cut, rich and deep in her mysterious private womanhood, which neither fog nor liquor could obscure. "Ah but wait, wait," he cried, reeling with his bottles in the doorway, "wait till you're all as drunk as Bruno!" (He was *not* drunk; he was God damn miserably far from drunk; but *shout, you fool, bluster you bastard—drown that damn cablegram! life goes on!*) "This way ladies and pseudo gents, for—" Come on in, you idiot, have a drink, cried Jeffrey. "Fellow-victims, I salute you," Bruno concluded, "from a full heart and a full bladder." He advanced, proffering his bottles for handshakes. "Pardon my stumps," he added courteously.

And yet at his utter nonsense, their faces brightened—from sheer relief, he supposed, at the spectacle of one more cynical than they, able and willing to present himself as a clown. But his own personal fog lay like ether on his senses; the fog that started from his inability to touch Elizabeth whose outstretched hand (the cable clasped within it) glimmered blurred before his tired eyes. "You're better than a show, Bruno," Margaret Flinders softly said; and eyed him with peculiar wistful brightness, inviting him to fraternize. "You flatter me, Miss Banner-Flinders," he replied; and moved off uneasily, evading her, for through his fog he felt obscurely sad for her tonight. "A pretty rotten show," said Miles, as Norah took the bottles from him—and Bruno was in a hyper-egotistic mood to think she touched his hand deliberately. But he must take his *coat* off, Norah said; and Jeffrey ordered the second round of cocktails served at once. Almost too cordial Jeffrey was, as though he feared the revelation of the Filing Cabinet (which now lay buried deeper than Elizabeth in Bruno's self-obliterating fog); flicking his fingers restlessly as though he longed to get them into something: sex or politics. "Or would you rather take yours straight?" Norah gently asked him. "Oh I'm thoroughly democratic," he touched her through his fog, wondered if she felt the deadness in his fingers, "I'll take the same as everybody else."

"Better than a show?" He turned indignantly to Miles. (Have I clowned enough for their benefit, he thought. Have I lacerated myself enough? have I parodied myself enough?) "Better than three shows, my good man," (yes, he had clowned enough, he had talked too much—a terrible weariness lay over his brain; but something drove him on), "I'm the Bruno Leonard all-purpose one-man three-ring self-kidding self-perpetuating exhibitionistic circus divided like all of Gaul into partes tres. One part sour grapes, one part wish-fulfillment, nine parts subconscious. And the greatest of these, according to the antediluvian Chinese, is the subconscious. This way, ladies and pessimistic gents, for the J.J. stream-line crooner, for old Doc Leonard the campaigning fool, watch him frisk, watch him scamper, watch him catch his fleas in public. Don't feed him peanuts feed him opiates, buy your tablets at the gate from Miss Diamond who has given many years of service, who sacrificed her vacations, her virtue, that this firm might go on." He subsided, to his own relief; collapsed in the chair that Norah drew up for him. "To sex and its many ramifications," he said; and raised his glass.

But he had wanted to find the Blakes alone. For coming to the Blakes' when one had the luck to find them by themselves was like stepping beside them into their eternal conjugal bed; he had the feeling that they never lost the aura of a recent love. They were the only pair he knew (he remembered telling Miles) who lived together, undisguised, frankly as man and woman, their quarrels and he supposed their loves, on the genuine, primitive basis. Jeffrey scattered his ideas and his hypocrisies outside his home, conceding Norah only his emotions; Norah, if she *had* ideas (one never knew, with Norah) left them folded at peace inside of her; he liked to picture Norah, not accompanying Jeffrey on his mental peregrinations but trudging absently after with his mending and his lunch. They took the struggle straight, in other words: substituting no fake intellectual battlefields, no fake intellectual beds. A little, he had admitted then to Miles, whose puritanism, ruefully offended, shrank from perceptible warmth—a little, perhaps, like living on roots and berries in the midst of the machine-age. But wholesome, vicariously refreshing to himself; who leaped (his muddled memory sighed) from one woman to the next just as Jeffrey did (but never lightly, never casually: cumbersome, rather, dragging all of his ponderous bulk instead of a satchel-full of light-weight week-end charms), but who had no placid harbor such as Norah was to sail serenely back to; and standing out in his mind, like Jeffrey's novels, as a miracle of simple, undiluted, inferior yet pure, un-Jewish success. But finding the Flinders present when he had meant to bask in borrowed Blake felicity sent a coldly intellectual draught through the blanket of his fog.

"Hell with the ramifications," cried Jeffrey happily—and held his glass to Margaret's. "To the spirit of St. Lawrence," she answered dryly; she wore an odd, accusing look as though against the whole male sex she harbored some unwilling grudge. "To cuts and castrations," Miles bowed bitterly; "and the little women all over the country who send their husbands back for more." (Clearly the Flinders were bound together; but by a string, it seemed, of sour negatives.) "Thank you, thank you," Margaret's brows made little tortured crescents in her forehead.

"Why not to the Magazine," said Norah, comfortable, and possibly obtuse. One never knew with Norah whether she was canny, or whether, like some placid stream she found her way instinctually in the dark, flowing simply where she had to flow. Whatever quality she had he found a comfort in it, felt his dampness warmed; and turned to her from Margaret—who was too unfulfilled, too wistful, to be endurable tonight. But Norah stood beside his chair, offering him her toast.

He had his defeatist laurels to protect. "Magazine? what Magazine? *is* there a Magazine?" He peered suspiciously about the room; lifted a corner of the rug; glanced briefly and salaciously under Norah's skirt. "No; I don't see any," he sighed with relief. He lifted his glass (*here's to you, Elizabeth darling, have you really gone and married someone? then here's to your God damned husband too*): "Your imagination, Norah, touches me; here's to the Magazine, to the existence of the non-existent, long life to the still-born."

"Defeatist talk," said Jeffrey blandly. "Oh, take another drink, your field is sex," cried Miles in irritation.

Bruno groaned, his memory rather than his mind aroused. "Trespassing again—and whose vocabulary have you muscled into this time, Jeffrey? Whom did he have lunch with, Norah? and was it in a cafeteria? In what phase do you find your husband at the present, madame? And by the way. A Mr. Harrison called on me today. A nice man, a lovely man; a pale man, with a splendid goiter. He dragged a large thing with him, which he referred to as a four-star pip; he insisted on garaging it in my study."

"Why, I just happened," Jeffrey said, "to be passing an office-equipment place." "Next time drop in at a pet-shop," Bruno said, "they have some cute things there."

"No, but really, Bruno, it really is high time . . ." "We're speaking of a Filing Cabinet, Miles, you ought to know, since you're its business manager." "A what?" said Miles; "what for?" "That's what I wondered; maybe Mr. Harrison is starting a Magazine." "If it isn't too much to ask," said Miles, "since I'm step-father to a Filing Cabinet."

Jeffrey's hands mysteriously flickered, as though engaged in secrets with himself. (Norah watched him anxiously.) "The time," he said, "I think the time is ripe." He narrowed his eyes; and widened them; frowned into obscure and mystic futures; then smiled, his fingers picking harp-strings in the air. Spinning, thought Bruno, in reluctant admiration, on his own axis, the volatile Goy.

"The time," Bruno said, "is always ripe." "No, but seriously, Bruno . . ." "And think how much riper it will be next year." "But the predicament of the intellectuals" "what predicament? intellectuals are always in a predicament, if there were no predicaments there would be no intellectuals" "and just what party," Miles asked icily, "is our mystic lined with this week" "Oh politics," said Margaret Flinders bitterly; "and Magazines; you talk and talk but I'd like to know what any of you *do*." "When I come into power," Bruno reassured her, "there will be a tax on words." "What child is ready for another drink?" said Norah like a blissful deaf-mute. She walked among them, offering friendship skillfully distilled: friendship in a bottle—tempered by her own dumb warmth.

He couldn't let her pass. He was seized with a need to touch her, to see if he could reach her through his fog. "And how does it feel, Norah, my girl," he said gently, "to have your life an open book? did you pose for your husband's racy demonstration chapter? Come here, darling; let Bruno see."

She came and stood like an obedient animal in the circle of his arm. He sniffed at her shoulder, not daring yet to touch her; looked up with an air of imparting a confidence to Miles. "Not a tang," he said, bewildered; "as little like soil as possible; ploughed or unploughed; she smells to me for all the world of soap and vegetables." He wanted to lie like a little boy in her arms; to let her friendly womanliness impersonally embrace him. The audience of friends lent a faint, perverted sanction. His arm about her waist, he felt his head sucked gently, irresistibly against her breast. He could have closed his eyes at last and slept. But his friends were waiting. He moved his head slowly, investigatingly, like a doctor's; and reluctantly lifted it. "As I thought," he sadly said; "nature-faking. Apples indeed! I'd sue him for libel, Norah." His head sank softly back. Norah laughed her rich, warm laugh; he felt it throbbing in his ear like quiet milk. "Apples! don't you know apples from manna, Blake?"

"The merest euphemism," Jeffrey said.

"Mistaking apples for such lovely, luscious euphemisms," Bruno murmured from his soft warm nest. "And I never knew I had them," Norah said.

"I'm sure," said Margaret Flinders, "that Miles' prole*tar*ians would never be guilty of such a mistake." "Not if they were hungry," Miles said coldly—(how Miles hated talk of sex!) "But I think I'd rather play post-office than fruit-store," Margaret said, the trace of tartness vanished from her voice; her words trailed sadly.

"But this is literary criticism, Maggie," Bruno lightly said. She nodded gravely, conveying that he (like Miles, like Jeffrey) were somehow failing her. There was something tonight aloof, pathetically ironic, unfulfilled about her, as though she preserved her little-girlhood unwillingly beyond its time; as though she waved it back for her protection; a strange defence—bred of the city perhaps (or bred of Miles' inadequacy)—but not, he thought, inherently her own: the thing had grown over her like protecting moss, her soft parts vulnerably projecting. Faintly she reminded him of Elizabeth. And he tried to think of Elizabeth, to fix her through his fog. But he could recover little except the sensation of a memory: of a delicate little boat headed toward him which he firmly shoved away (loading it the while with Chinese adages concerning independence for a woman); and he could feel it floating pluckily where he had pushed it—yet with a backward glance, a tremulous keel; he felt the hollowed imprint in himself from where it floated off. He moved his head on Norah's shoulder; there seemed to be room there for Elizabeth as well.

But life, his circus, must go on. "Now I don't get you writer-fellows," he used his petulant-pedantic tone. "Why can't you take anatomy unadulterated? Apples!" he shuddered. "There never was a woman with breasts like apples, thank God," he enjoyed Miles' bashful misery. "Reminds me of my late lamented bourgeois past, where ice-cream was dished to resemble skyscrapers and poultry disguised as pastry. . . . Now if I were a writer," he concluded modestly, "I should subscribe on this vital issue to the school of the absolute metaphor: 'he placed his head against her breast and it felt like exactly nothing in the world but a woman's breast.' " He closed his eyes in drowsy peace. "And it feels very nice, thank you, Norah."

His touch, he thought, did not excite her. But she sat on his knee, utterly pliable, utterly acquiescent, like a female animal being stroked. He was perfectly certain that she would have sat so also if they had been alone (as certain as he was that, had they been alone, he never would have touched her) ; and sure that in the same dumb, kindly, acquiescent way, she would lie down and let him make love to her. He wondered if it were her simpleness, her total lack of coyness, which left him now, not cold but cool, pleasantly stirred and at the same time appeased, desiring nothing more. (Or was it drink, or was it anaesthesia?) Or was she, as he sometimes thought, lacking in all but maternal passion?

"You might define," Miles seemed pressed to shut out from his vision the unit Bruno made with Norah, "tell us what in hell you mean—predicament" "a four-star word," said Bruno, "from an old four-letter man" "Why, predicament," Jeffrey wove in his joyful daze, "I mean predicament of course, the economic impasse, the function of the intellectual" "but the intellectual," Bruno said, "*doesn't* function—your boy has delusions of grandeur, Norah" "his immediate problem" "Ah, I have the solution to that," said Bruno: "let not your left wing know what your right wing doeth, and lie to your neighbor as you would to yourself" "lie *with* your neighbor," Jeffrey amended peaceably and looked to his Norah for approval. "All the same," said Miles preparing to chew the intellectual cud.

"Now, comrades," Bruno said (for the scene hit him with the dead force of something often played before), "let's get back to sex and euphemisms. All euphemism," he collected the disrupted circle by a mockery of his own professorial tone, "all metaphor, must spring from decadence. To an unjaded mind a metaphor would not enhance the quality of a thing but halve it. It's only the bored roué who calls for sauce with his meat." Just as, he continued, less professorially, to himself, Norah by herself does not excite me, but my own words and the reflection in the eyes of my friends, may begin to. Have we grown so civilized that we are more excited by the *idea* which represents the fact, than by the fact itself? We must be afraid of the fact! and so we substitute apples—or adages—to make it kosher. Was that puritanism or satiety?

"Your lousy book," said Miles (his quarrel, Bruno felt, not directed against Jeffrey, but springing from some plaintive inner need), "of all the un-classconscious tripe" "still, certain factions of the Left Wing," Jeffrey said, "I have it on pretty good authority" "I suppose you *felt* their message *mystically*" "no, I'm in pretty close contact, it's confidential, of course, a certain Comrade Fisher" and "Fisher, Fisher," Norah murmured, "I can't remember cooking dinner for a Fisher" "My God!" said Miles, "I never knew if I was reading about millionaires or travelling salesmen" "and now it turns out," Bruno said, "it was just Fishermen—I wouldn't trust even a comrade named Fisher, Jeffrey; sounds to me suspiciously like a Jew" "it happened, that in that book, I wasn't primarily *concerned* with class-lines" "an artist," Miles reiterated most severely, "ought to *be* concerned—with everything" "but my book," Jeffrey said, tapping invisible keys with his fingers, "my book is about men and women,

I don't know myself if they're farmers or millionaires or horse-thieves. I don't even care."

"It's barely possible," said Bruno in his scholarly tone, "that people feel a little different, necking in the back-seat of a Rolls or fornicating in a hay-rick. I don't know of course, a girl feels just as good to me in either. But the 'ploughing,' Jeffrey, that's what's hard for me to swallow. Is that euphemism? or just plain nasty sadism? Me, I'm an old-fashioned southern gentleman, I treat my women according to the books, resting twenty-five percent of the weight respectfully on the elbows. I have, so far as I can see, absolutely no ploughing instincts."

"Oh, ploughing," Jeffrey said. "Ploughing's fun." He rose and lightly stretching as though in fine voluptuous retrospect, crossed the room for Bruno's gin. The miracle, incredible, of human beauty, especially in a male, held them silent for a moment.

They sat thoughtful and withdrawn, all single vessels headed for the dark. His hands upon Norah, he longed like a dead man for sensation, envying in Jeffrey a purity of desire that he knew could never be his own. The dumb virility of the extrovert, he thought; needing no Idea to quicken it; whose sex-urge served no purpose but its own; Jeffrey's virility an absolute, an entity, a thing untouched, uncomplicated, always lightly functioning. (So he had instructed young Elizabeth: the casual, the light; avoid the awkward depths, my dear. A tiny germ of pain pricked through his anaesthesia.) His own need seemed a thing belonging rather to his ego than his body; a thing tonight which he longed to create by force to establish some contact again with the living.

"Make them strong," he called to Jeffrey; "I have my psychopathic difficulties, I can't do justice to your Norah's charms." "Perhaps I haven't got enough," said Norah in her husky voice. But any other girl, he thought, amazed, would be insulted. She curled her rich body to one side on his knee. Was she unconscious of her own sensuous movements? of his hands attempting sly and intimate possession of her? For if she were unconscious, then his own faint pleasure must die a shameful death, like a sensitive youth perceiving himself unrecognized at a party; so intellectualized was he, he thought, and sighed, that he could no longer feel even sensation unless it were accompanied by a smile or wink to show the stimulus aware. Idea again! (and he had trained Elizabeth to thoroughly ignore it, preaching purity of sensation!) Deliberately he opened all his pores for Norah's warm invasion; but they seemed clogged with some forbidding consciousness.

"Predicament or no predicament," Miles walked the room's length restlessly, turned and paced it back, "if we're ever *going* to have a Magazine" "who said we were," said Bruno "If any of us is ever going to do anything in fact" (Miles paused and kicked a chair as though it were himself) "it's now or never," he addressed the chair; pulled its leather seat to torture it. "Cigarettes and gin," he muttered. (Margaret sighed.) "We talk and talk like an old Russian novel," Miles cried bitterly; "I'd like to know what any of us *do*." "Personally I don't do anything," said Bruno; his fog closed over him; he felt that he was dead; "and you?" "I don't do a God damn thing," said Miles; "I don't do a God damn thing but talk." In the quick silence they turned their heads from one another.

Like a play too often played before, the whole revolved in Bruno's brain; a play with faulty continuity. What ailed them all, he wondered; and saw them, each in his separate groove, traversing parallels in an endless treadmill; a chorus composed entirely of temperamental first violins. Their energies combined would make terrific force, a powerful and vital symphony; but they seemed each to prefer being first violin in a small puddle to throwing in his lot with the common orchestra. So the strength of each, turned inward on himself, bored like a cancer in the tortured brain; his music, bursting and swelling, remained milling and unexpressed in his own private head. The women barren; the men dead; their common factors being negatives, rebuttals, refutations. (Perhaps Elizabeth was right? to go careening off in space, in any part of the world but home; attempting no rhythm but her own.) And himself? oh, loyal to the code, to the last defeatist ditch. He was dead.

But Norah, gratuitous remnant of an outworn wish, sat like a lump of dough on his lap. Norah, as an opiate, had failed. Tonight his mind forbade his body to react. He tumbled Norah off his lap.

"The investigation," he announced, "is closed. The show is over. Poor Miss Diamond wants to go home. You may take those figures of speech away now, Norah." He watched her cross the room, plodding, oblivious, through their dead desires. Poor womanly fool, he thought; she's the only one that doesn't know she's dead; who goes on with her mild and meaningless andante while the rest of us (tongue-tied prima donnas, small-puddle first violins) hold our bows and wait to die.

The silence was suddenly terrible.

7.

Why Can't We Have a Magazine?

HER head was simply spinning! *did* they all know what they were talking about? "I wish I had it down in Braille," she said to Margaret Flinders; and passed on looking for glasses to refill and pondering the shortage of cookies. And what did they mean, "not a God damn thing but talk"? didn't they eat, sleep, make love—God knows her Jeffrey did! (But life, for people who were clever, was no such simple thing.) Norah liked talking over gates. The best talk she had ever known was hanging over her father's gate and greeting villagers passing down the road. Short; friendly; to the point. "Hi there, Alice May, how's that new puppy of yours?" "Just fine, thank you, Norah, she's doing mighty nicely—the mother too. Have you seen Mary Pickford's latest?" "Why no, I guess I'll *be* seeing it though, before the week is out." "Well, I'll have to be jigging. So long, Norah." "So long, Alice May." Then swing back on the gate with no thoughts in your head but who will come next, the mailman maybe, or old Man Tilton or the Grierson's little girl. Not that there wasn't plenty of talk too, in the Meadows' household; at supper, for instance—she didn't think theater-hour in Times Square could hold a candle to the Meadows family sitting down to one of Mama's stews. I can't hear myself *think!* the Captain used to roar. What a school of them there were! Two big Meadowses (and I mean big! thought Norah proudly) and seven smaller ones; with Norah second to the oldest. And whatever had become of them all, Norah couldn't imagine, stopping to think, was it Johnny, was it Sebastian, who had earned them all a fine Spring holiday with the whooping-cough? She'd scarcely heard (they were a large family; but not what you might call a letter-writing family) since they wrote to say that John had married Fanny Stillwater from Cupper's Road. The scab! thought Norah, chuckling; could he have forgotten how the Meadows brood had boycotted Fanny for going on with her hair down her back in curls after the rest of them had looped their braids three times back and forth from ear to ear. . . . Well anyway, she thought (and wondered what had happened to make them leave off talking?) anyway, talk back home was plain; maybe nobody ever said much worth remembering; but down to the baby everyone spoke to be understood. But they were cleverer than she; and of course, if they didn't talk the way they did, they would come to the end of talk too soon. But this silence was peculiar; it must be twenty minutes after something . . .

Well then, thought Margaret, they had been for so long silent that they might have taken root in silence. It welled from all of them. It beat upon her ear-drums. Echoed in her blood.

But this silence was not death, Bruno knew. It was not so much a case of life must go on; but on it went; there was no stopping it. And there was no silence. For if they did not beat their drums and draw their bows across their violins (his old triumvirate!), there was a fearful throbbing in the air, of all their muted instruments; of pallid wings upon the windowpanes; of fear; of death; of life itself.

She was tired, Norah was, after the long day of work; after washing up in haste to make ready for their friends. But she wouldn't let herself drift off till she was sure that Jeffrey didn't need her. Every time the weather changed he started something new; and here was Fall and Jeffrey needed watching. Her eyes wandered back to her handsome Jeff (they never left him long), sitting wrapped in his complacent secrecy; his fingers fitfully fluttering, keeping time to the rhythm of the silence. She knew that he was playing games he loved, dashing about doing mysterious things so rapidly that in the end they mystified himself. He never explained things much to her of course (indeed, why should he? she was not clever like the rest, like Margaret, who although she was a woman, often entered conversation with the men—and then, they had sweeter, more wordless things to say when they were alone); only, when his activities collided or contradicted each other, when people called him on the mat for things he had forgotten, then he brought her home the whole mess to untangle, laying it like a broken toy in her lap. Then was her sweetest time; then he cast off the cleverness he wore before his friends, shook himself free of his mysterious games (alone with her his hands were often quiet), and lay like a happy child in her arms. And somewhere in him, though he might ignore her before the others, he never forgot that it was Norah whom he needed most. She never forgot it either. The knowledge was a soft melodic undercurrent to her life. She *was* sleepy, Norah was. But this was not the stillness of the barnyard, this odd, protracted silence; it was not a respite; the pillow was soft to her head, but the silence kept her from sleep.

Time was passing over Miles' head, whirling in his brain. Silence was unendurable. He felt himself on trial. For with his admission to his friends that he did nothing, absolutely not a God damn thing but talk, he felt that he had laid his cards implacably on the table; and not merely before his friends but in his own eyes and the eyes of something like his Uncle Daniel's God. It must be in such a period of concentrated, coiled-up tension that a man would spring to life if ever he were going to. He wanted to leap from his chair and cry to his friends that now was time for action (now!); he felt that if he did not, he would condemn himself to sit in that chair in silence for the rest of his mortal life. The minutes sped and dragged. The silence stood over him like his Uncle Daniel, like the justice of his conscience, exacting promises.

The day was longer than the year; one hour held more minutes than the day held hours; a minute was interminable. And so with life, thought Margaret. The whole flew by. But each step, each tiny interlude, must be swallowed with pain like a mountain. The silence was crossed and criss-crossed by her thoughts; the silence was a thousand cancelled voices; the din was pounding in her blood.

Fumes of silence rose up from the rug. Bruno thought: already through my fog I cannot touch my friends. A day will come when with my own tongue I shall not feel my palate. Has that day come? is this the endless silence? The wildest symphony could be no more terrible than this; the silence died and cried across his nerves.

Jeffrey's watch said twelve o'clock. He flexed his muscles restlessly. The silence was like the Sundays of his childhood spent in church; he could pray better in the school-yard; in church he dreamed of baseball. Now he tried to think. But his eye fell on Margaret's fine long legs. Something had surely gone wrong between himself and Margaret—what was it she had said? He thought of his book; his mind flew to the Filing Cabinet; to Margaret; to his watch; and Comrade Fisher . . . His fingers jumped. He thrust his tell-tale hands deep in his pockets.

She had seen that look in Jeffrey's face before. She must wait till after the others had gone, for that look to turn to her. She had seen it first when for the first time he had said to her, out under the trees in her father's orchard "I am something of a lone wolf, Norah" and she had immediately taken his face between her hands and laid it on her breast. But it was not her breast which he was seeking, not hers which could rest him forever; and soon he would be up again, frightened and eager, a child who having found his wish must seek to find and lose it endlessly. But what had happened to them all? Had they come to the end of talk at last? They seemed, each one, so far away. And Margaret Flinders with her hand stretched out, her eyes a thousand miles away, reaching and reaching . . . (Oh!) Norah gently pushed the cigarettes within her reach.

But after he had let his cry go ringing to the corners of the room, cutting like a sword across the silence, after that, what then? It was now or never, now or never, Miles grimly told himself; and continued to sit on in the silence.

She met Norah's eyes. Something valiant, utterly compassionate there; and sterile; offering a cigarette. Once women gossiped with pins sticking out of their mouths, bending over garments and mending, slipping their fingers in and out with knitting needles and darning eggs; with care, with purpose. Now our laps are empty, our bodies upright, our foreheads broad and scrupulously bare, our fingers lift, not needles, but cigarettes, cigarettes which we hold to our lips competently, puff competently, draw reluctantly out of our mouths. The moment must be swallowed, got down someway. But Margaret sat with the matches in her lap. To the silence she added her own vindictive emptiness; and heard it slap and wash against the walls.

They must have quarrelled, Norah thought; this evening; before they left their house, perhaps. She and Jeffrey never quarrelled. She slipped back deeper in her cushion; closed her eyes.

Elizabeth would draw her, Bruno thought (turning with relief from the men's sharp faces, from Margaret's odd accusing look) as a beautiful female animal, perhaps haloed like a saint, with little inadequate men clamoring to be suckled. Elizabeth? There was a quick tightening joy in his chest as for a swift, involuntary second he touched her through his fog. The muffled band played on in silence; but a fine brave piping sounded through it; off-stage, perhaps; from the marrow of his bones, it might be; from memory, from hope. It was Elizabeth.

Suppose that afternoon he had stood up to Mr. Pidgeon: said be damned to you and your dirty job, take it, keep it, I don't want the stinking thing. What then? What could he turn to? Follow the stony furrows, with his nose close to the ground? let the ache in his back press out the torment in his mind? At least each Fall there would be something, something he had planted, helped to grow. It might be sickly; meager certainly; but something. To tend, to watch, to hold to.

One minute after twelve, said Jeffrey's watch. He looked at Norah. Like a contented cow she looked, he thought. Everything in him warmed and relaxed. There was no wooing Norah, and no need to: she was always there and always his.

Then Mr. Papenmeyer was right; no change; no thread; it was all to do again. The match in Margaret's fingers struck bitterly across the box.

Miles went cold with terror. He had forgotten Margaret.

The pale glow held all their eyes. Norah moved her head; Jeffrey creaked his chair. Bruno felt a quickening of the tempo; the faintest concentration of their powers. Through the silence and the fog the clear note sounded. He remembered the carriage-step; and Elizabeth—what was it she had said, her braids going coolly down her shoulders? They had sat, their seven years between them, and looked into something terribly deep; had longed to plunge; had held their breaths; till he had pulled them (from his pinnacle of more years) safely back; a Chinese adage for their consolation prize. Pain filled him and he took it in with gratitude. The soundless notes were closing in; the silence gathered harmony.

Her lips puckered; the cigarette was too dry suddenly for their hunger. She held it in her lap and twisted it like something she was done with. Her sigh trembled in the silence.

Like a terrible, a deliberate, reproach to him, Miles thought.

My God, said Margaret Flinders to Margaret Banner-that-was; we are sterile; we are too horribly girlish for our age, too mannish (with our cigarettes, our jobs, our drying lips) for our sex. Was this what you intended, Lady Mary Wortley Montague? rolling your fine eyes about the drawing-room? Was this what my mother meant for me, sending me off to college, a book of Ibsen under my eager arm? O Economic-Independence Votes-for-Women Sex-Equality! you've relieved us of our screens and our embroidery hoops, our babies and our vertigo; and given us—a cigarette; a pencil in our hair.

She had that look, Miles thought, of a woman retired to count her injuries. His fists clenched in despair.

He heard the tuning-up; the gradual gathering of their separate forces. Something new was in the room. Bruno braced himself to meet it. The air stirred with the frantic wings; the din at the heart of the silence grew in volume and intensity: an awful stream.

Norah, why don't we have children? she heard her own voice piercing like a fine horn through the din, battling its way through her pounding temples, cutting through time and space and clearing the air of confusion and wrong. And gazing straight at Norah as though the truth were out at last, she saw that the words had never been uttered, that her piercing voice had sounded nowhere but in her own astounded brain. "God damn it," Margaret Flinders suddenly said.

Miles' nails bit deep and frightened in his palms.

(Norah, in her peaceful slumber, stirred.)

The note had sounded bravely. Bruno looked up,

startled, the words, the tone, were so unlike her. But apparently no explanation was forthcoming; she seemed already to have disowned her words. She was sitting looking down; he had an instant's odd illusion that she held a baby in her lap, she curiously (and for the briefest moment) resembled a madonna; a cheated madonna, he thought next (his brain stirred gladly as it shook itself awake) when he perceived the cigarette, twisting, twisting, on her modern knee.

"Why Maggie Flinders," Jeffrey said; and could have kicked himself for a blundering ass, so withering was the look she gave him.

But this was unreal, thought Miles; this was the bottom of everything. Margaret giving up; Margaret disloyal before their friends! Margaret, the calm, the cheerful; "balmy," demanding so little of life—and that it should have been Margaret after all (the blind, the mild, the seeker after "happiness") who had broken through the whirling time while he sat on in silence! Margaret voicing protest!

Sword upon sword they laid on each his separate note; Bruno felt the clashing steel and heard the band awake. His brain grew sharp and clear. "Speaking of euphemisms," he said thoughtfully.

There! they were off again, thought Norah peacefully. Right back where they started from. Shuttlecock and battledore. Jeffrey wouldn't need her now. She drowsed; she dozed.

Margaret sat like a naked woman among her friends. She looked at the floor, the common pool where she had thrown her clothes. Wave after wave of blood rose and fell in her temples.

"Speaking of euphemisms," Bruno said (and felt his brain emerge from adages, from sarcasm), "male writers lay too much stress on women's secondary parts. The point about a woman, the salient point," (they held their bows in marked suspense) "is her womb." He held his note till it should soar above the others. There was a bar of rest; in its midst he felt Margaret turning as though she knew herself compassionately addressed.

Something new was in the air. Miles distrusted it. When people *showed* emotion . . . He had seen his Uncle Daniel, after all, kill his dog without the flicker of an eyelid.

"Sure," Jeffrey said; "and by and large the better the woman the bigger the womb." And Norah's, he thought, proud, affectionate, must be the size of Jonah's whale.

Battledore and shuttlecock, murmured Norah's sleepy mind. Shuttledore and battlecock. Struttlecock. Struts the cock. Battles shuttles struttles.

"Of course the modern woman" (Bruno felt the interplay between himself and Margaret; a click, a contact, something human, real), "the modern woman has a pretty shallow model." He thought of Elizabeth, whom he advised at such a tender age to throw hers out an attic window; live like a man, he said; be light, be free. "But still, it's there, it's not to be denied. The melody lingers on." He thought of rainy attic afternoons. (Now that you're in de-part-ment-al, Betsey. . . .)

He eyed Margaret with resentment; covertly; with suspicion. A womb (unpleasant thought!). She had never told him she possessed one. Was that where women went and sat, to brood, to count their injuries? Miles vaguely hated her.

"I think," said Margaret slowly, "that that's what men are scared of—what they haven't got." Her smooth forehead was pained but enlightened; her eyes were sober, keen; in such a clear-cut moment, Bruno thought, her little-girlhood left her, she stepped out bravely, older than her years. "They resent it," she said courageously.

Miles feared her. Sitting in their secret chambers, looking out the windows of their (he couldn't say the word!), what couldn't a woman see? were all things grist to her—again he denied himself the word.

"Desertion," said Bruno lightly, "in my presidential day" (and watched Miles close his eyes as though he left the conversation), "will be on grounds of womb-neglect." Lightly but emphatically he wove his theme across their themes.

(Were they on the Magazine again, thought Norah, drifting peacefully. Funny they couldn't decide one day, whether they wanted one or not. What was the name of that book that everyone was reading? point counter point counterpoint counterpointercounterpointcountercockpoint-ercount.)

Wombs, Jeffrey thought; that's it; wombs, not souls—that's what women have, that's what Norah has. A lovely, brown—a great big comfortable home-like womb, a one-room womb; with room for me. A man's life went from womb to tomb. (Make note next novel; Blake's genius grows; wonderful insight; even the comrades admit.)

But they were lined against him, pointing fingers at him, Margaret and Bruno, building this thing against him. It was unspeakable. Miles could bare his chest to cuts; could turn his back for blows (receiving them with agony, with thanks). But this—this shaking emotion in his face, this dangling the personal before his eyes. A puppet, they called him. A marionette. But his shell was cracking; his own shell turned and with its splintered points dug sharply in his guts.

"I think we'll add," said Bruno cheerfully, "a happy womb in every home to my political planks. That'll bag the women's votes." And sustain the men, he thought; for barren women meant the men were sterile. If their bodies lay fallow, perhaps the men's brains too . . .

"You have my vote already," Margaret said. She felt that she was groping, groping through a long dark tunnel; Bruno pointing the way. The light was farther on.

"And how about Norah's?" said Bruno tenderly.

What? Had someone called her? Did someone want something? No; it was one of Bruno's jokes. She *did* think Jews were geniuses; but sometimes Bruno acted like a fool. She smiled and nodded tranquilly. And closed her eyes again.

She smiled and nodded, as though his talk were child's play, or something purely male, at once beyond and beneath her. Bruno smiled. "Now Norah," he said; "take Norah, for example—"

"For God's sake!" Miles' cry was genuine. He couldn't bear another word. His nerves were frayed; his shell was splintered; he had reached the bottom of loneliness and fear.

Had Margaret Flinders sprouted wings? Bruno watched her moving in her sudden radiance. She was beside Miles in a second, her arms about his neck. Something had taken hold of Margaret, filled her with triumphant storm; and Miles, allured, bewildered, stood like a moon beside the sun.

He was frightened of her as he had been that afternoon, coming at him like a mountain. But he was smitten with joy and pride in her. And this was something different; she was altogether radiant now; diffused; she was glorious; she was . . .

"Beautiful," cried Jeffrey (by God, she suddenly was!); "your girl is beautiful, Miles."

"Not beautiful, just balmy," Miles said, shaken. But she was beautiful. Her arms about his neck were beautiful. Her rapid, joyous breathing. He timidly put out his hand and patted her. The gesture was ridiculous; like patting God. But her hold tightened as if she knew.

One didn't make decisions, Margaret knew; one bore them—out of pain and fear and dark. Her own now was a shining light. "Darling, let's go home," she whispered; "I . . ."

He was afraid of her. She poured something in the air, something that filtered from Bruno to her, that came from her a large and awe-inspiring light. But he was in love. Miles had fallen in love again with Margaret.

Whatever it was that he had given her, she returned it to Bruno ten times over now. We need women, he thought; we can't go far without them. (I need Elizabeth.) "This way, ladies and gents," he said; "this way for the sleeping human volcano, the Rip Van Winkle of volcanoes." (Allegro, boys, all together, faster, nearer, play for all you're worth!) "I have a startling proposition to lay before the house."

December, January, February, Margaret thought.

"I propose," (the thing took all his strength) "oh what the hell," he cried; "what's stopping us? I propose we *have* the God damn Magazine."

March, April, May, thought Margaret.

"Magazine? what Magazine? is there a Magazine?" said Jeffrey in Bruno's most satiric voice.

"Comrade," said Miles; "is it that you think the time is ripe?"

Faster and faster the music played. Now there was free give and take. Bruno was bursting with strength, with love for his old triumvirate supplemented in their second youth by women, he thought of Elizabeth . . . "Defeatist talk," he said, "that's defeatist talk, my friends. The predicament of the intellectual today demands . . ."

(Norah dozed; she half-dreamed. She was out scattering corn to her mother's chickens. They ran picking and cackling about her skirts. Hush, hush now, she told them; there's plenty more in Norah's pockets.)

June, July. . . . Why, it might be in August! Margaret thought. Almost in the Fall. They would have Winter, Spring, and Summer; and surprise Mr. Papenmeyer in the Fall.

"Are you serious, Bruno?" Miles stood straight, his arm on Margaret's shoulder.

"We'll be on the newsstands by Christmas and in the public eye like a moat the morning after."

"Publicity," cried Jeffrey, "I can get us free publicity. And left-wing advice—Comrade Fisher."

"an office" "printers' estimates" "the size" "how often" "contributions" "advertisement" "the policy" (Faster and faster Bruno's music soared) "how soon" "meetings" "discuss" (the chickens continued to scramble and squawk, plucking at Norah's skirts) "politics" "criticism" "open forum" "and money . . ."

"We'll need money," Miles said; "plenty of it."

"There's Merle," said Bruno, "mother of Emmett, my young guinea pig. I'll tackle Merle."

"I'll tackle Merle," cried Jeffrey; "I hear she's a beauty—"

"A glandular beauty, I'm afraid she's frigid, Jeff."

"I'll tackle her anyway, I'm no snob, I'll tickle her, tackle her, plough her—I'll make her pay and *like* it."

(Norah woke up, startled, the rooster crowed so loud.)

"Then we'll meet" "no, sooner" "and decide" "I'll arrange the printers" "then Wednesday" "Saturday" "so by Monday at the latest" "and by Christmas" "surely no later than January" "How late is Western Union open . . .

"because I've got to send a cable," Bruno said.

"And we'll go with you," cried Margaret in a ringing voice. "I want to get out, in the air! Darling, look!" She flew to the window and flung it up. Night blew in. "It's Winter, Miles!" Outside Mrs. Salvemini's snow was softly falling.

TWO

I.

Elizabeth

"WHY it's snowing!" she did not exclaim with joy as she flew to the window for a first fresh breath of morning. "Why it's my first Paris snow!" she did not cry out as she threw back the curtains and let showers of snow-reflected sun spatter Denny and the bed in glory. "O it's snowing and maybe this is love and I don't want to leave you," she could not help not saying again not not once but not numberless times as she ran about the room looking for stockings without holes.

"Oh but I like it here with you, Elizabeth," he did not reply although he heard plainly every word she had not spoken. "I like it lying here and watching you with your shy merry eyes set slanting in your sad little hard little face. You are something that I desperately need to make me into a whole man and I would like to lie here every morning for the rest of my worthless life and watch you running around the room looking for stockings without holes."

"We might add a year to our three months together, Denny my darling," she did not say thoughtfully as she found the hole she had been expecting in the ankle of the gray stocking, "we might tell la Frump we're staying on, we might stay home nights and get up mornings. And before you could say *deux Pernods sec* there we would be together the two of us, living as fine a life as you please," she did not add as she flapped a sound stocking in triumph.

"Get up, get up, lazybones," she cried. "You've got to sit on my trunk, you've got to phone about my tickets."

"There's time enough," he said and flounced irritably beneath the covers.

"Elizabeth, I love you," he did not cry out in terror as she tossed the stockings like long braids over her shoulders and hurried off to the bathroom. "Don't leave me, don't go!" he did not dare to cry after her for he knew she was a girl who craved tenderness so deeply that when it was given her she was smothered and must shake it off to emerge sleek like a seal from water.

"I could learn to mend, I could learn to cook," she did not call to him as she stood sadly under the shower-ring and held out thin beseeching arms to the faucets. "I could make us chocolat with so much whipped cream we would never drink Pernods again," she said aggressively as the water poured like rain from a cloud-burst. "I would be your lover, I would be your sister," she could not resist not sobbing as she turned off the hot and let the cold water fall in a chill down her back. "I would be your wife," she did not murmur as she turned and held her breast to the stinging icicles.

"Will you never get up, will you never get up and help me," she said crossly as she came back bathed and wearing only the stockings rolled at the knee and fastened with an old pair of his garters.

"I have had nothing but unpleasant words from you this whole morning, our last day," he said harshly as she came and stood scowling over the bed. And so he pulled her down beside him and they lay on the bed together and caressed each other angrily.

"Last night," she did not confess as she lay for a moment remembering, with her face against his shoulder, "I woke up suddenly and you were lying with both your arms, even in sleep, tightly round me. For a minute I was so exquisitely happy that I thought I would die, I thought we both ought to die."

"Oh gosh, Elizabeth," he did not whisper back, "where's the sense in your leaving me, darling? We have left people before, both of us! Ah, stay with me, Elizabeth." His arms went tight about her.

"Denny, you're smothering me," she choked. "But I lay there darling," she did not continue, "and then I thought I was going to suffocate. No matter how I moved your arms were there. As if you were telling me over and over again, unbearably, that you loved me. I was smothered. I was coralled. Denny," she did not cry as a spasm of loneliness shook her by the shoulders, "I want to be loved and desired and possessed but I cannot stand it when it happens. Are you trying to break my neck," she said grimly.

"Elizabeth, I love you, love you, love you," he did not boldly whisper.

"But it is only in sleep, with your arms," she did not answer, moving her head in gentle recrimination on his chest, "that you dare to tell me. Ah," she did not repeat bitterly as his black hairs stirred against her cheek with her own breathing, "if only you were not as scared, as sceptical, as I."

"Elizabeth darling, if this isn't love," he did not whisper, frightened, in her ear as he moved to kiss it, "then what the devil is it, darling? Isn't it all we're capable of, after loving other people? And what will happen to us darling, if we go on leaving people?"

"Save me, save us both, my poor Denny," she did not answer as she looked him ironically in the eye.

"There are moments, my dear madame," he said guardedly, "when I am inclined to regret your untimely resignation. Might you be persuaded, do you think, to take a later train and a later boat and stay on another month maybe so I could show you Paris at Christmas? and Spring in Florence, Italy?"

"Thank you so much," she said politely. "I have enjoyed my stay here, Mr. Kirby, and the quarters are delightful. But I do not think it advisable to remain too long in one position."

"You have a lousy disposition," he said. "You might wait another month. A year. If my memory doesn't play me tricks, I believe I invited you to marry me last week. Why don't you reconsider, my dear young lady?"

"Because I have got my hair cut a new way to ravish the men on the boat, because to hell with modern marriages, because I've cabled Bruno and my mind is made up and I'm going. Because life goes on," she said gayly.

"Ridiculous," he said; "there's nothing to go home for."

"My country needs me."

"So does France."

"My country's on the breadlines, the headlines, the deadl—"

"Stop quoting that damn letter," he said sharply. They held each other close. "You are either stupid," he said looking about the room for a word and finding it on the lid of her bulging trunk, "or crazy. If you feel so swell about leaving me, then what makes your eyes so hard today, like nasty little stones?" He pushed his hands savagely down her back which was arched like a bow to her waist which was too narrow and her hips which were too lean and every line of which his fingers knew by heart.

Her laugh clinked out like little shells, falling from a child's tin pail. "Get up, you fool, Madame la Frump will be bringing our chocolat and finding us in bed again."

"And why do you have a hysterical laugh today?"

"Do you think it would be tactful of me, not to put on some sort of show?"

"I hate you," he said.

"I know; and One day you will kill me," she said wearily. "Only I won't be here. And someone else will be. . . ."

"I really hate you now, Elizabeth."

"Then let's get up."

"But you choose just the time when we are growing close, when things are growing warm, when things are growing real," he said, advancing warily as though he meted out just how much sentiment she could take.

"Ah that's just it," she said tracing with a finger the lines in his cheeks that were like commas as though she would forever memorize them. "I hate real things, I don't believe they're true. I can cry at a play but nothing in life can bring a tear to these old gray eyes."

"Is it because of that cablegram, that drunken Pernod cablegram, that you are leaving my bed and board, cherie? Would that I had never left your name at Cook's."

There was a sharp rapping at the door and they huddled together as if they were in hiding. But the voice of la Frump came relentlessly through the crack. "Is it that M'sieur-dame desire une cup chocolat?"

"Is it that you desire a kick in the pants, Madame?" shouted Denny, outraged. "Is it that you don't know tragedy when it's going on in your only suite-with-bath? No! Food will be served when the curtain has been rung down and not a minute before!"

"Pig of a Frenchwoman," he sobbed. "Chocolat! What does she think this is, just any old God damn day?"

Their bodies moved imperceptibly till they lay like old friends side by side. Their bodies, she thought, were better friends than they; better able to face the cloying drug of familiarity, changing their shape peacefully to fit together. But they were tired too; they needed something more now, those tired bodies, some psychic approbation from the higher mental spheres, some sanction from the heads. They were tired of this endless contact without benefit of soul, without benefit of love. "What I said to you was true, my dearest Denny," Elizabeth did not quietly tell him, "the real things are too strong for us to grasp. We haven't time to catch them, we haven't strength to hold them. We are scared till the blood in our veins runs thin and we must hop from one person to the next because to stay is too unbearably exactly what we want."

"Anyway you are a useless girl," he said tenderly. "No use to any man, not after three months when one's socks have begun to wear out. You are a fay, you are a sprite, you are not a woman at all."

"My hero!" she said derisively. "Then you will do

very well without me. If all that you wanted was a darning-egg."

"You are a nasty, cruel, mean, tough, hard-boiled little bitch," he said, pushing her away, "and your resignation is cheerfully accepted."

"Then the hell with all this," she cried, rising from the bed. "All this banter, all this epilogue stuff. Epilogues are out, didn't you know that?" "Life goes on," she said brightly after a long moment spent in looking into each other's eyes and not saying What damn fools we are, the pair of us! what poor damn fools! and standing above him she added "From an old Persian adage, my good fellow."

"And I thought women were home-lovers," he said ruefully, and sighed with relief and misery as life began running again and she threw open the lid of her suit-case where it sat waiting on the bidé. "I thought they were supposed to be lousy with maternal instinct and all that sort of slop. I've been cheated. Here I've got me a wench who's built like a boy with no hips at all and turns out to be a home-wrecker into the bargain."

"Oh we keep up with some of the folk-ways," she said, lining the inside of her bag with books. "We've forgotten the words but the melody . . ." She stopped, frightened; and remembered the carriage-step; and cousin Bruno clasping his knickerbockered knee in fright as she said (swinging her pig-tails) *Probably love is all that counts.* "And that's from the Orientals too, the good old Orientals," she said; and stuffed handkerchiefs into the toes of her shoes.

He sat up straight in the middle of the bed.

"Elizabeth!"

"Mr. Kirby! how you startled me."

"Why are you going away, Elizabeth?"

"Get up and help me pack, you fool."

"Why are you going away?"

"The bloom is off the peach."

"Elizabeth."

"Dennis!"

"Why are you going away, darling?"

"Because we're all washed up, darling."

"Elizabeth, why are you going?"

"Change of venue, darling."

"Elizabeth."

"You're just a parenthesis, darling, in life's long dreary sentence."

"You think you're funny, don't you."

"No. I think I'm a world cruise, a round-the-world cruise, and I've only got time for short parenthetic stops."

O God, she thought, is it Denny questioning Elizabeth, or Denny questioning Denny . . . or myself dishonestly cross-examining myself!

"Elizabeth! Could you possibly talk sense?"

"No."

"Elizabeth. Is it because of that cablegram?"

"What cablegram?"

"That cablegram, you know what cablegram."

"No," she said shortly, "no it isn't." For if Bruno's cable had *not* come she would have left Denny for that reason.

"Then, my darling idiot Elizabeth—"

"It has been a pleasure to know you, my dear Mr. Kirby, and it is an exquisite joy to leave you."

"Listen Elizabeth."

"Why are you going away, Elizabeth," she mocked him. "Because I hate you, sir, she said. Why are you going away, Elizabeth? Because I love you sir, she said."

"Do you love me, do you think," he said, curious and wholly disinterested.

"Will you kindly help me pack."

"No. Do you love me, do you think?" he asked, critical and calm.

"Oh—I sort of love you, I guess," she said.

"Then why . . ."

"Because you love me too much and I can't stand it."

"But suppose," he said excitedly.

"Oh then, because you don't love me enough," she said wearily. "Because neither of us gives a hoot in hell for anything."

"Listen to me, Elizabeth."

"I have tendered my resignation."

"No but Elizabeth! as an experiment! Why should we leave one another? We get along well, we're fond of one another. I put it to you before. Say we stay and each go his own way, leave out the romantic twaddle-twaddle, we're both hard-boiled. We understand each other, Elizabeth."

"The understanding that passeth love," she said coldly. "But if I ever should slip up and get married, I'd want a relationship and not an arrangement. And that's not from the Chinese, you God damn fool. You can take that one straight."

"I suppose you want me to get down on my knees," he said bitterly.

"Just what I want," she said. "Now will you kindly get up and help."

She moved feeling light as air, feeling heavy as lead. Humming she moved about the room not seeing it, and dropped little things of her own into the open bags. Somewhere there was a terrible little pain. Perhaps it was her heart? Perhaps it was too full? too empty?

He put one foot reluctantly out of the bed. "And what will you do when you have left me, Elizabeth?"

"Sit on top of the world cracking peanuts," she said angrily. "Draw caricatures of the new president's family. Get a permanent wave maybe."

"Alone, my dear Elizabeth, if I may make so bold to ask?"

"Not Elizabeth. Life goes on. The first brute that comes down the pike. Offering me understanding."

"I don't care, you're a sloppy wench, your stockings always are wrinkled."

"Good."

"You never told me it was snowing, you never told me how beautiful it was," he said bitterly standing in the cold keen light, his pyjamas eddying sadly about his ankles.

"Hurry, hurry!" she said brokenly and pushed him toward the bathroom; "and bring my toothbrush, I forgot my toothbrush."

Now there was nothing not to say and nobody not to say it to, so she walked slowly round the room saying aloud "Goodbye, walls, goodbye, window." She walked to the waste basket filled with orange peels and broken bottles and gave it a swift kick and said to it, "So long old thing, I'm up to the ears myself in the same kind of God damn waste." She walked to the unmade bed and stood looking down into it and said "Goodbye, bed. I'll miss you, I will. You were a good bed to me." And then she burst into passionate sobbing with her head buried in the bed's warm depths and whispered to the hollow left by Denny, "Oh darling, grab me round the neck, kick me in the pants, throw Bruno's cable down la Frump's old garbage chute! make me stay, Denny, hold me, hold me! I'll mend my fingers to the bone, I'll let you strangle me at night, I'll . . ."

He found her sitting on the trunk with her hat on the side of her head, jabbing petulantly at the overflow which prevented the lid's closing.

"There's a book in the way, my idiot-child," he said and lifted her off the lid. "Ulysses!" he cried. "Trying to sneak off with my copy of Ulysses! Have I harbored a thief in my bosom? Give it to me, you thieving wench!"

"It's mine," she cried, tugging at it.

"It's mine, you little bitch."

"Mine, you Indian-giver."

"Mine."

"Mine, mine, mine. I chose the binding."

They were silent.

"Do you remember the day, Elizabeth."

"The bridge, we were on the funny bridge."

"The man fell in love with you, darling."

"It was the day you tried snails, darling."

"Do you remember what the waiter said, darling. . . ."

"Yes, yes, yes, I remember everything, darling," she sobbed.

"Take it, take the book, Elizabeth. It's yours, my dearest, my darling, my darling Elizabeth, it's yours."

"No, yours, Denny, yours please, darling Denny, I am a nasty terrible girl, let it be yours, from me, Denny. You have it, Denny, you keep it forever, Denny, keep it forever, darling, I can't bear it. . . ."

The book in its fine red binding slipped to the floor as each one gave it to the other.

"You dropped my book," she said and cried as if her heart would break.

"You dropped my book," he scolded and his voice shook. "Elizabeth, we can't! Our book! We've only one of everything. Elizabeth! we're lost! we're saved."

The book looked up hopefully from its ribald red cover.

"Stay, I dare you," he whispered.

"Darling, I'm practically on my knees," he whispered.

"Elizabeth, tell me you love me, don't hide your face," he dared not cry.

"I, I think we could probably make a go of it, darling," he said unhappily.

She lifted her face at that and laughed with the tears rolling slowly down her cheeks. "Give me my toothbrush, Denny. And hurry, darling, hurry."

"I'll throw it out the window," he said like a defiant little boy; but did not. "Do you dare me to throw it out the window, Elizabeth?"

"Yes, I dare you to throw it out the window," she said grimly.

His hand shook with guilt before them both as his fingers, in spite of him, convulsively clutched what they held. "Ask me to, ask me to, Elizabeth," he pleaded.

She took it gently from his hand and laid it in her bag.

"At least we've two of those," she said.

"Maybe you will come back," he said, frightened.

The red book that belonged to both of them burst into passionate weeping on the floor as over it they gravely said goodbye.

2.

Bruno and the Black Sheep

"TELL him from me," Bruno shouted to Emmett through the door of his living-room which had turned overnight into Filing Cabinet headquarters, "that his stuff is sure-fire sale and sure-fire manure and we're not having any in our stable. Tell him to shovel it under someone else's door and get to hell out of our way—we're busy; we're a man of action, a man of Magazine. Besides we've got to meet a boat next Saturday." (He drew a deep and happy breath of memory.) He turned complacently to the Six Black Sheep squatting on window-sills and tables, like a young army too restless to take to chairs, their bright undergraduate sweaters like scattered parts of a flag at rest; and met the ultra-critical eye of their lean and undernourished Chairman as he sat swinging his feet against Bruno's grand piano. "Nothing," Bruno added, chiefly to irritate young Firman, "stinks quite like a bad writer. Unless it's the slightly foetid odor of a bad writer gone phoney propagandist. . . . Tell him we're not running a dirty propaganda sheet, Emmett," he roared, "we keep open house and open forum and if he can't take it slam the receiver in his propaganda face. . . . But what's the matter, Comrade Chairman? what have I said that isn't kosher?"

For Firman, perched like a young Jewish owl on the

music stool, had kicked the piano disgustedly, while his eyes behind his glasses gleamed with intelligent dislike. "Oh nothing," said young Firman coldly (did that lad exist, thought Bruno, returning the look and the sentiment irresistibly, only to remind him that he must have been just such a conscientious bore himself fifteen years ago?). "Nothing, only that the open forum policy is untenable from the ground up. Every written word," said Firman, hitching the glasses higher on his nose, "is propaganda." Six Sheep bowed in a haughty phalanx of assent; their sudden sway putting the flag together for a moment.

"I see you know your catechism," Bruno said. "We will proceed to the next step. How about poetry? One at a time now, children."

"An opiate," said Little Dixon briskly.

"Propaganda for spending your life sitting on your ass reading it," said Cornelia Carson promptly. Bruno failed to place her counterpart in any of the girls of his own day; she seemed an exclusive twentieth century product, half-boy, half-girl, born yesterday, of movies, radio and matter-of-fact class-consciousness.

"For forgetting what's wrong with the world and getting all tangled up being lyrical about the birds," said one of the Maxwell brothers.

"I'd have all the lyric poets jailed for counter-revolutionaries," said Firman, gathering the comments of his committee and fitting them precisely into his dialectic nutshell. He spoke with jagged edges to his speech but when he came to revolution he slipped it out with the U sound round and slippery as a peeled banana.

"And intentions?" Bruno began, thinking how the

pleasant sophistries of his own day had changed to dogma in the mouths of this younger generation; when Emmett Middleton came sidling through the door like an uncertain deer; paused and looked about him for a place to sit as though he weren't sure whether to cast his lot with his contemporaries or with Bruno. "Has our maiden contributor bit the dust, Emmett?" The boy smiled gratefully, as though Bruno's notice decided him; he chose for his seat at last the corner of Bruno's desk where he sat enthroned on Bruno's right and above his fellow-classmen. "I thought propaganda was intentional, deliberate?" Bruno quirked an eye on Firman, aware sheepishly that he had bought Emmett for an ally.

"In Russia," said Cornelia Carson in her dry two-tone, boy-and-woman voice, "intentions don't count." "Only results matter," said Kate Corrigan, commonly known as "Irish," laying the next step. "This is the age for objectivity, the subjective went out with individualism." "Everything in the world," Firman mounted the ladder and intoned from the top rung, "is propaganda. A tree is propaganda. Propaganda for cutting it down and making it into guns. For reforestation. For pulp magazines. . . ."

"And just for lolling under counter-revolutionarily, I suppose, to the fat professors like myself," said Bruno; perceiving that a superior form of Blake's disease had taken the youngsters by storm. "Oh who will come and lie with me, under the propaganda-tree. . . . Pardon me, Firman, I have a touch of horse-blood." He met Firman's eye ironically; saw in them a reflection of his own look and drew back startled by the felt resemblance. "But you asked for an interview, Firman. Let's get on with it,

I'm a man of action this week, ask my secretary. . . ."

"Yes, Doctor Leonard hasn't got all night," said Emmett in the tone of class monitor; "make it s-snappy, Firman."

"Nor yet all week," said Bruno happily. Five days to Elizabeth's boat; five days to seeing his earliest friend, to tearing down the walls of fog that they had let be built between them; to reaching out, touch hands at last, beg for forgiveness, beg for love. . . . "Now what's on the Black Sheep's mind?"

The Sheep scrambled out of their silence and clattered eagerly for his attention. Only Emmett, diffident, kept still, dissociating himself from his colleagues (Bruno wondered what weakness in himself had made him choose the weakest of their number to befriend) till he saw which way the land lay.

"The point is, Doctor Leonard" "and they won't give us a column in the Campus Pilgrim" "open forum is all very nice" "but like all open forums" "it's only open to one side" "try and slip in one intelligent thought, one protest" "I wish you'd all shut up," said Arnold Firman vigorously; "how can he hear if we all yell at once like a damned cheering-squad."

Their enthusiasm for whatever it was that was eating them touched him but it made him feel a hundred years old or more. It had been so long, so many years, since his own contemporaries had gathered like an army behind him. "I gather that the Black Sheep are even hotter under the collar than usual," he said dryly; "but my senile brains, you know . . . Firman, the ancient mariner looks to you."

The boy approached his desk with an air of timid impertinence, as though to show he dared be at home in the enemy's territory, as though despite embarrassment to himself he claimed his rights. "Doctor Leonard. Before we go any further . . . excuse me for getting personal—" the lids fell half-way over his eyes—"but we've been hearing about your Magazine for so long now; rumor whispers—and yet . . . *is* there a Magazine, Doctor Leonard?" He raised profoundly sceptical brows.

From behind their glasses the two Jews in the room glared at one another with what (Bruno was certain) must be the identical look. "Your scepticism, Firman," he spoke coldly; but he could never avoid a faint intimacy when he spoke to Firman, "does you credit. But the Magazine," and he felt stronger at once, as though he had needed his own words for re-conviction, "the Magazine, to my own surprise, is rapidly becoming a fact. Great trees from little shoe-strings grow; but our Magazine was founded on a Filing Cabinet. Behold, children! The first instalment's paid—and Emmett's mother's going to meet the next. Although, I think, she doesn't know it yet." Emmett blushed with pride.

"Well then," young Firman said; and stood as though he planted his thin chest against invisible but omnipresent enemies impersonated momently in Bruno. "The Pilgrim is supposed to be the mouthpiece of the whole student body. 'Open forum' it says on the title-page; and some drivel about inviting all opinions. But it turns out that it's only open to the opinions of the conservatives, the football heroes, the stinking-fascists."

Football! Was that the worm that gnawed that hollow intellectual chest? Bruno felt a wave of nostalgia, the strange and nauseating kinship, binding and repugnant, which a cripple feels when meeting a fellow-cripple on the street. Jew on a window-sill! When did not a smart young Jew turn his back with hate upon the football heroes of his world—and pinch his heart at night with longing to be one of them? One batters on closed gates begging for admission; and when the gate stays fast, the battering turns imperceptibly from pleading to attack.

"Why?" said Arnold Firman rhetorically. He spoke with the relentless persistence of one climbing endless ladders toward an unwavering and unforgettable goal. "Because of football politics. Because of fraternity politics. Because the same stinking-fascism that rules the board of directors runs the student-body too. Because, as I said before, the open forum principle is untenable, because propaganda is inherent in every written word. Now—when the Black Sheep resigned from the Campus Club last year in protest against the fraternities. . . ."

"Can the Roberts rules of order, Firman, and get to the point," said Cornelia Carson briefly. She was a small girl, taut and tightly drawn on strong dry wires; it occurred to Bruno that she might not have enough to eat.

Firman pulled himself up short. "Objection sustained, sister. I thought for a minute I was on the soap-box. The point is, Doctor Leonard, that the Pilgrim's pages are so filled with football drivel that the Black Sheep can't get a word in edgewise. Last month we sent in an article on the Scottsboro case—from the youth angle, you know. They sent it back. 'We haven't room,' they said, 'for anything but collegiate topics.' And it's the same with everything we write."

The Black Sheep nodded like one man. They all reached boiling point, catching heat from their leader, at once.

"We think the student body has a right to know the facts" "whether they want to or not, the dumb yeggs" "if we have to ram it down their throats" "what's education *for*" "we're sick and tired of being told to shut up like a bunch of God damn kids," cried Cornelia, summing up, "when the Scottsboro boys are younger than we—and they're going to hang them like sure-enough adults."

The telephone cut like a barbed wire through their unity. They dwindled angrily into silence; drew together whispering and gesturing in their bright wool sweaters, the parts of the flag almost fitting together. Emmett jumped up—"I'll take it here," said Bruno grimly; he wanted respite from the mounting fire. Jeffrey's voice came like a thin thread sounding the note of his own contemporaries. Behind his back the army of the future milled. He heard Jeffrey through. "I don't give a damn," he shouted back, "Fisher or no Fisher, Comrade or no Comrade, I won't print lies. And badly written ones at that. Stop acting like a God damn procurer. Alienate, hooey. If literary conscience alienates them we'll start a lefter wing. Tell your Comrade Fisher that a truth in the hand is worth twenty propagandist lies in the bushes, from the early Esquimaux. . . . And don't buy any more pen-holders. All we need now is an umbrella stand and a spittoon. Goodbye, you God damned fool. See you on the barricades. Yes, I'll speak to Emmett. Yes, sometime this week if his mother can make it. Goodbye, goodbye." He slapped down the receiver with vigor. He would have to wait for Elizabeth; his friends were mad. "See, Firman?

Man of action. Brusque. Determined. Editorial sense combined with courage. . . . But I think you were saying something. All of you at once, if I'm not mistaken."

The flag broke up as Firman rose again; behind him the woolly parts waved as though the same wind blew them all. The pose of angry unconcern fell from Firman's face; the very lines that made it ugly made it, for a moment, fine. The eagerness in those lidded eyes, unaccustomed as they were to holding light, was singular and moving; Bruno warmed despite himself. An ugly Shelley, the boy stood, raised by some inward urge, forgetful at last of a world forever hostile; and behind him his small army stood solid.

"Doctor Leonard. The Black Sheep need a mouthpiece of their own. We want a chance to speak. Not on such little issues as football—that's just a symbol, so far as we're concerned." (Take that, Leonard, Bruno told himself; these kids are smart; maybe they *apply* their lingo.) "And not just to the students of this campus. We feel that college students don't live in glass houses, the campus is a miniature fascist state, run by the same lousy factors that the outside world is run by. We want to open students' eyes. We want to talk to all the students in the country. . . ."

Excitement mounted among the Sheep. They leaned forward, their eyes alight on Bruno. Firman at their head looked like a tough little Jewish Napoleon—Bruno felt himself drawing back from their concerted onslaught. Young Emmett squirmed, his eyes swinging like a nervous pendulum from Firman's face to Bruno's.

"We'd like to strike a bargain with you, Doctor Leonard. We'd like to volunteer to work for you, free, do all the dirty work, the grubby odds and ends, on your Magazine. If you'd let us, in turn," here Firman's passion made him shy; "if you'd let us—I suppose you think we have a hell of a lot of nerve—if you'd let us have one department in it. A student forum, run by students, you see, run for them. If you'd let us run it," he concluded bravely. He fell back and became a private in his own army again.

The Sheep leaned forward, their eyes big with their daring and their hope, and shouted.

"relate collegiate topics" "apply Marxism" "correlate" "emphasize" "denounce" "teach" "explain"

Twelve years had passed since Bruno and *his* friends had grown so heated. Twelve years since Bruno the valedictorian had remained behind to be instructor, then professor, in their hated Alma Mater; since Elizabeth had said (she was fifteen then; precocious but sentimental; impelled trustfully to always speak her mind): I hope you won't get glued behind that desk, I hope you won't grow fat and jowly and sad like our fathers. No, he had not got glued; this he told himself sternly now; and all this week he had been feeling in himself (since his cable to Elizabeth, since her quick response) the strength stored up in all these dozen years.

He suddenly resented Firman and his devoted army as though they threatened the twelve-year dead triumvirate of Bruno, Jeffrey, Miles; as though they eagerly dug graves for the generation fifteen years their senior. Into their smug united strength he felt impelled to hurl a knife.

"Spare my aged ear-drums," he dropped his words heavily on the bold and budding flower of their zeal. "Sheep in wolves' clothing I call it—you want to get in on the ground floor, do you? and buy the old man out?" But his irony was heavy, without meaning even to himself. In young Firman's fierce pale eyes was coldly marked acceptance of the fifteen years which separated them. The army of the younger generation, led against him by his counterpart, the bitter Jew. He longed for autonomy of contemporaries; for Elizabeth, so close a reflection of himself. He resented Emmett, the boy's imagination fired, hanging between two armies, between two generations.

"But I don't know, you see—" He found himself hesitating; but he discovered that he knew he would accept them; to include them was peculiarly fitting, ironically just; but also he felt vaguely apprehensive. "You might all get kicked out of school," he threatened them lightly.

"We don't give a damn," the younger generation cried. He could see Emmett barely suppressing a smile of pride for his colleagues.

"I'll have to think it over," he said; he knew he sounded like an irritating and unreasonable parent; but his mind was made up. "I'll have to put it to the others too. There's plenty of time anyway," he said uneasily.

"There isn't plenty of time," they shouted back. "We want to do something—NOW." They stood, a half-dozen lean and half-grown children; but Bruno saw their banner waving; their numbers multiply.

"All I can do," he said firmly, "is put your suggestion before Flinders and Blake;" but he knew the Black Sheep must be voted in; they would lend a life and a fury and off-set the tired-radical element.

"Thanks, Doctor Leonard." "Three cheers!" "Hurray!" they cried, accepting it as a matter settled in their favor; and rose like a triumphant army moving on to conquer further fields. The parts of the flag sprang together; moved in a swirling mani-colored block toward the door. "We'll work like hell, Doctor Leonard," said Cornelia Carson in her boy-and-woman voice.

Emmett had leaped off his perch to the floor; stood hesitantly beside the desk; for a moment Bruno thought he made an odd gesture forwards, incomprehensibly, perhaps from habit, as a child automatically rises and follows its class out of assembly, to join his generation. Bruno touched his arm; he fell back quickly. "If you can put up with my company, Emmett—we might go over the manifesto again; we might even play chess." Emmett brightened; smiled ostentatiously at the backs of the departing Sheep.

The little bastard Firman, Bruno thought; the smart wise-cracking little Jew; *is there a Magazine?* the nerve of the little devil. But *was there?* It was up to Elizabeth. The door closed on Firman's army; the room was ten shades darker. "Get out the masterpiece, Emmett," he said; "it's filed under something or other. We'll go over it with Jeffrey's red pencil."

3.

The Fast Express

OH have another drink, Elizabeth! Thanks Elizabeth, I will. "The same, please," she said to the riddled steward who like a eunuch moved indifferently to serve desires he no longer felt; and did not add "And hurry! hurry! for God's sake hurry, between drinks one falls to thinking —and thinking, from the old Chinese, my boy, is a viper in the chest." And a cigarette, my dear, can I tempt you? And another lover, can I find one quick enough? Chain drinker, chain smoker, chain lover, chain rover—let the chain sag somewhere and you will have a pain in the lung from cigarettes, a pain in the brain from pernods, and God knows your soul will ache from undigested unloved lovers. But the steward has forgotten pain with joy, if he ever knew it he's lost the need for quick oblivion; the God damned steward doesn't hurry. My good steward you are a stranger to me but I must tell you all: only this morning he gave me the sack, the gate, le congé, he gave me the bum's rush steward, he gave me back my own tooth-brush, he gave me all he had to give and all he had was a bright red copy of Ulysses and my own American tooth-brush. Life is the longest distance between two points my good man (even on board my fast express, my rollicking jittery fast express, my twentieth century sex-express), the bar is filled with strangers, all non-lovers, and

Denny, my parenthetical Denny, is gone, gone, gone. Close parentheses bravely on the poor little unsatisfactory detour-amour. . . . *Steward a drink for the lady!*

You find yourself in the middle of the ocean, mademoiselle? Between two continents so to speak? A case of sink or swim at twenty-six? What is the object of your game, sister? Why have you left one island, why are you crossing madly (all aboard the fast express) to the other? Why will you eagerly seek on the second what you eagerly bid goodbye to on the first? All over the cockeyed world you have carried your tough little American body and your lamb-profile (so like Bruno's)—and what has it got you, Elizabeth, if you will pardon a personal question? what have you today at twenty-six as over and above the ambiguous hopes you entertained six years ago when you left the first gay gent (name of Ferris, good old Ferris, good old art-colony Ferris) and trekked with your toothbrush to the second? Why, I am an emancipated lady, Elizabeth, I play the game like a man, Elizabeth—you donkey, you sentimentalist, you cry-baby, you sissy—what in hell do you want, every damn thing that's going? The answer is Yes, Yes, Yes! But choice involves sacrifice, is largely a matter of elimination, Bruno pedantically said—oh quite some time ago, some years ago in fact, certainly before one started this endless chain, this fast non-stop express, of drinks and unloved lovers. Elizabeth your mind is a slop-pail, all odds and ends and floating twisted orange peels (goodbye, my dear Denny, we're all washed up), orange peels and broken corks and busted truisms—from the damned Chinese—and you tell me my eyes have grown hard, my poor Denny—(*steward will you hurry hurry hurry*). And the only thing you've saved out of the fire my dear is your nasty destructive beloved wit, he said it was sharp as a razor-blade (who said it, which one said that to Elizabeth, was it Brownlow, good old Brownlow—what! mixing your drinks and mixing your lovers, Elizabeth!), he said I was Delilah going around stabbing men with my sharp razor-wit. Ah, here comes my double Scotch!

Set it up, my boy, my riddled ancient eunuch steward, your desires are dead but the melody—oh let's not quote, Elizabeth! Let's not quote and let's not think, let's never do anything but drink. Here's to you Denny my darling, you can't hold your liquor and you can't hold your gals. Maybe if we had an understanding, he said politely, you know, hell with the romantic twaddle-twaddle, do you want me to get on my knees you fool, let's have an understanding. Ah yes, the understanding that passeth love, arrangement instead of relationship—thanks darling, I'd rather have the toothbrush. So long Denny, so long France, so long Florence, Italy—hold everything, America, your wandering daughter's coming home. Home is where you hang your hat and drop your skirt, my dear by the time I'm thirty I'll be at home anywhere in this cock-eyed world, I speak the universal language, the twentieth century snappy dead language, of no-love loving, of lust without love, I belong anywhere and nowhere (self-pity is the lowest form of wit), a gal without a country, a ship without a port—never mind America, I'm coming back to stay! Love without lust and lust without love, kisses don't touch you, without them you're lost. . . . Ah stranger, I see you, at yon corner table, give me the glad eye, the sad eye, the mad eye—professional glad girl, hysterical sad girl, the old army game is beginning again. Hold off a bit stranger, where's your technique?

In the strange half-gloom of rainy attic afternoon, now that you're in de-part-ment-al, Bruno said—and of course it was raining that day so they couldn't go out to the carriage-step, so they sat there (are you sure your mother's out? why yes, she went shopping with yours) sat there and talked in the strange half-gloom. Now that you're in de-part-ment-al, Bruno said—and didn't he just tell her what men could do to girls. But can't the women do it back (*steward one more of the same*), she said: if I were a woman I would. But Bruno said no, oh Bruno said no, he said it was up to the man. But the girl can say no if she wants to, Bruno? That floored him a bit, he squirmed and scratched. Then he shot out, She better not—no one might love her and ask her again. So probably love is all that counts (she asked it then and she asked it again). She said would he do it to her; he said no. Of course not, he said. You're crazy, he said, growing angry. She said there was nobody else she loved, no other man except her father, nobody else she knew so well. Bruno said she was practically his kid sister and everybody knew that cousins didn't 'love' that way. She grew mad and indignant, she reminded him bitterly how he sneaked into the nursery at night and tried to scare her, telling her she was an adopted child and not her own mother's baby at all, not his cousin, not her own nice uncle's niece; if she was adopted surely it was all right? And Bruno said if she told anybody what he told her in the strange half-gloom of rainy attic afternoon he'd pull her damn braids out and he said further that he'd tell how she had shown him where women were different and then he ran downstairs and she ran after him and he jumped on his new two-wheeler and pedalled fiercely down the street and she ran a little way after him and then stopped and stood crying before the house.

Probably love is all that counts (in the long slow days of the carriage-step, in the gently rolling endless days before one boarded the fast express) probably love is all that counts? It took him seven years to answer that one, by that time my hair was up in braids, yes Bruno I know it's high time I know I ought to go off the deep end but all the boys I see are stupid, I don't like any of them, it's true I'm going to be an artist and I have to be free to be an artist, but what can I do if the boys are all stupid? The sooner you get rid of sentimental notions, kid, he said; you're not in de-part-ment-al any more, he said; don't be obsessed by inhibitions, don't be possessed by superstitions; you've got to be free, my dear, free, as free as a man, you must play the man's game and beat him at it; read the books Betsey, you'll see, it's a matter of health mental and physical, a small fact of science, of scientific friction; romantic frustration—the hell with all that; be light, be free, be casual; why don't you try an art colony, kid? no use postponing, no use frustrating, freedom's the password the byword the slyword, don't get possessed, cruise around kid, see what it's about; listen to me Elizabeth, I'll make a man of you yet! Love without lust and lust without love, poor haywire play-girl, drink-sodden gay girl (stick around stranger, have patience, stranger) —hell with it, steward—*one more of the same!*

Steward a drink for the lady—the lady is lost, the lady has boarded the fast express, all aboard ladies and gay modern gents, try an art colony first, all aboard, no stops no halts no brooding there, all aboard the twentieth century unlimited, hell-bent for nowhere, the only non-stop through express, try and get off it kid once you're on board, no peace for the young, no rest for the restless, the rollicking jittery cocktail express, nothing can matter so wear down, you nerves, no brakes, no goal, no love, on we go glittering jittering twittering, try and get off it kid once you're on board, it'll rattle you shatter you, if you jump out you're lost, stick with it girl, where's all your masculine guts? The smart young adages race down the tracks, the train runs on theory, the passengers' nerves, the train roars on no stop no change, no love just lust, goodbye home and hello France, goodbye France, I'm coming, home—love without lust and lust without love, the country's on the breadlines, the deadlines, the redlines, have a heart America, I'm coming home to stay.

Listen steward, so I went to the art colony, don't you see, he put me on the train, he put me on the fast express and filled my pockets with quotations from the old Chinese. Throw out the notions that possess you, outmoded superstitions of a bygone day. We're not the children of our parents, we're the parents of the new. Shake yourself free, Elizabeth, step out boldly like a man. So I went with too much rouge on my lips and I met Ferris and we had a drink and he said why don't you move over into my studio, my girl left Saturday. But isn't it, I said timidly, but isn't it, I started shyly—isn't it—please tell me—a little bit cheap? Cheap, that's a good one! cheap! that's a hot one! he roared till the blood burned his face. *Cheap*—what you see around here isn't *cheap*—why it's better than that, he said, laughing and laughing—it's *free! Steward you can see for yourself the lady needs another drink.*

(Why stranger, you are growing bold! Is that a smile mixed up with your moustache? Moustache like Ferris, eyes like Brownlow, nothing like Denny—will I never know a whole new man again? just carbon copies, slightly blurred? Hold off a bit, stranger, let me get my bearings, stranger, I'm tired as hell, mister, and I can't find my lipstick . . .)

Oh artists, artists, I said I was tired of artists going about with their tongues hanging out of their mouths bored wanting a woman not wanting a woman, what kind of men are they talking so freely to girls about how hard it is to make a girl how easy it is to make a girl, how long do they think a girl can listen to that with her mouth open politely smiling, politely sympathizing, politely laying bets on sorority-sisters and all the time the sex in herself drying up and sitting like a ball of rotten cheese in her lap. Something's the matter with sex these days, these twentieth century rollicking days, either there's too much or too little anyway it's too easy (free, not cheap, that's a hot one!) sitting up finding yourself in bed with a man you don't like and yet there you are both tired both a little sick with too much intimacy sitting up in bed and talking about how good a ham sandwich would go with a bottle of beer and if only we were in good old Paris. Well I've been in Paris, Ferris my friend, and it's the same thing there, *"I'll show you Florence, Italy."* Oh artists, artists, I said I was tired of artists—and anyway you've got to play the man's game, Betsey-Elizabeth, the man runs fast, the girl must run faster, look sharp Elizabeth here comes your train, pack up your toothbrush, your hard-bristle toothbrush, wave him goodbye, all aboard, all aboard, all aboard ladies and gay modern gents, all aboard the gay twentieth century, hell-bent for nowhere, the sex-express. *Steward something tells me I will have another drink.*

Listen steward, I'll tell you the story of my latest, the latest notch in my belt, this arty, helpless newspaper reporter, my Denny (I wish he were here.) I'll make a story of it for you, steward my dear, a twentieth century three-month detour, rollicking parenthesis on the sex-express. Her wit almost abandoned her, mister steward, as they sat forgetting the others at the little round table in the café while the plates piled up at their elbows. On the third pernod she discovered that cleft in his chin which promised weakness. Out with the scissors, Delilah, out with your good sharp razor-blade wit. Leaning toward him, leaning toward the stranger Denny, she took a shot in the dark at that cleft in his wavering chin: So at thirty-three you're still reporting for the newspapers, Mister Kirby, incoming boats, outgoing boats, what did she wear, whom will he marry—well, well, well, wouldn't your old high school English teacher be just too proud? Would you mind, Mister Kirby, lowering your head a bit, I am doing a drawing of you, one of my nasty satiric caricatures; your head must be lowered as though you were about to buck the world, but you and I of course will know better—have another pernod, Mister?—we will know all along, and keep it between us, that you hold your head down because you would be ashamed to look your old English teacher in the eye. He narrowed his eyes and hated her; but then he lowered his head (exactly as that nasty girl was drawing him) as though he were ashamed to look *her* in the eye; and smiling with charm and sheepishness, the cleft in his chin going in as though weakly receiving her thrust, he met her eyes with a look of recognition; they smiled and they knew they would be lovers, unloving lovers on the fast express. (*Steward do you see that impertinent gentleman at yon corner table? that look in his eyes, it's familiar, he knows, . . . try and get off it kid, once you're on board . . .*)

The first month steward, we laid serious plans for his breaking away and doing a novel; he leaned on me utterly; bowed his head; reached out to what seemed my superior strength. But the girl couldn't take it, it looked like love. Good old Denny, grovelling in the dust, Elizabeth will join you and grovel too. Have a pernod, Denny, what's it all about? what's the object of the game? suppose you did write a novel, it would be a rotten novel, what have you got to say, what matters enough to write about? And look at my drawing, my poor defeated unloved lover, look at my lousy, phony, stinking-cynical drawing. Caricatures! Destructive, defeatist, escapist—but let's not go highbrow, let's take up drinking again, la Frump will serve us pernods with our chocolat. He ought to have yelled at me, steward, throttled me, burned our damn bridges behind us, he ought to have shouted that we strike out together and aim at decency in art and life. But why? what for? and what is decency? these things are pleasanter discussed in our cups. He liked finding his girl as weak as himself. His lovable weak smile was for both of us now. In the second month we went back to drinking pernods; in the third month we barely held our jobs for sleeping the pernods off. Delilah conquering? Delilah triumphing? Why not at all my dear steward, I should have thought you keener—I feel like hell, while with my sharp phony-razor-blade wit I cut out his strength I cut out my own as well. What will become of us, Denny my dear, my lost abandoned unloved lover, weeping together over Ulysses we wept because we could not weep, we wept because we could not love, we wept because we loved before, we care about nothing, believe in nothing, live for nothing, because we are free, free, free —like empty sailboats lost at sea . . . *and Bruno withheld his consent to our marriage.*

Bruno, Bruno, help me out, catch me careening in my mad pace, let me rest for once and catch my breath. "We are scared till the blood in our veins runs thin and we must hop from one person to the next because to stay is too unbearably exactly what we want." Bruno, we're unhappy. Bruno, we're mad. Bruno, explain it to me, tell me the object of the game. You've told me what to turn my back on; what, my darling, can I face? Tell me why I went away, tell me why I'm coming back. Tell me if there's an end to my endless journey, why did you put me on this fast express. Where am I going and why, is there no end but more pernods and men? Probably love is all that counts? and love is not to be found these days, or not to be looked in the face when it's there? What do we hide from, Bruno, what do we seek? I'm so gay, I'm so light, I bounce here and there like a bright rubber ball; and yet the look in my eyes is hard, is hard, my wit is like a razor-blade, I use it to wound before I can be wounded, my wit protects me like a glittering twittering barbed wire fence and no one can come through and touch me. Each year I shrink smaller, I huddle together, and the barbs on my fence grow sharper and brighter, I am gayer and harder, my voice grows brittle, my laugh grows harsh. Love, don't touch me; love, keep your hands off this proud modern daughter; happiness girl, no brooding there, it's a matter of friction, of scientific friction; if you go sentimental you have only yourself to blame, don't be obsessed by inhibitions, don't be possessed by old traditions. (*Ah stranger, I see you, at yon corner table, you know me, you know me, as if I were naked.*) Haywire play-girl, drink-sodden gay-girl, self-pity is the lowest form of wit, wit is the purest form of self-pity. I was tired of artists, artists, I'm tired of unloved lovers, *Bruno what is the object of my game?* Hell-bent for what is my fast express, my jingling jangling cocktail express, lust without love and joy without joy, we pound down the tracks on our sex-express, no stopping, no loving, no time to take breath. Goodbye Ferris, give me my toothbrush, hello Arthur Brownlow I'm not stopping long—my toothbrush, my toothbrush, my fast train is leaving, I must run, I must catch it, no I won't forget you, I'll chalk you up, I'll put a notch in my belt to remember you by. . . . Bruno, Bruno, another gent has bit the dust. What am I, your father-confessor, Elizabeth? No darling, you're something else again—I don't know what, procurer, vicarious cousin; my dear, you're my only stop, you're where I climb down and take breath, my link with the past, the peaceful past . . . before I change trains and jingle jangle along again on my fast express, the non-stop, non-loving twentieth century unlimited, the haywire cocktail express, the gay and happy sex-express, hell-bent for nowhere. . . .

Steward, the stranger approaches my table. The eye of a man, the eye of a man, looking down into hers, it's the old army game, the train's roaring again. "Can I sit here," he said. But why did he ask. He was sitting already, his knee touching hers. Two drinks on the table, two knees underneath. A Jew too—medical student perhaps? haberdasher? son of a cobbler drifting toward socialism? All Jews look like anything, all Jews look like Bruno, all Jews are not Denny. Welcome, stranger! sholom aleichem, my poor fellow-passenger! I give you the glad eye, the sad eye, the mad eye. You steadily give it back. Know the rules, do you, my boy? Know how the game goes on, steadily, stealthily, know how to play it with languor and skill? "You're sure you don't mind," he said brittley, bitterly. "I have whiskey in my cabin," he said, sly easy gent; "want to come down awhile"—carelessly, casual. "You talk quite a lot, I see," he said, lonesome and human.

"I beg your pardon," she said (oh Bruno, please help me). "If there's anything I hate it's whiskey," she said. (Goodbye France, wait for me, America, your wandering daughter's coming home, coming every step of the way on the fast express, jingling jangling on the whiskey express, eggs without salt and lust without love, joy without joy and motion without splendor, the express careens, it rolls faster and faster, it's rolling down-hill, it's hell-bent for what.) "If there's anything I hate it's cabins," she said. (Try and get off it kid once you're on board—with *your* help, Bruno, with your help, Bruno, you put me on, now lift me down, now stop this train, oh Bruno I need you.) "If there's anything I hate," she said, "it's strange gentlemen in strange bars, I beg your pardon, but I wish you'd go back to where you came from, no, we've never met before I'm sure." (Oh Bruno, I love you, it's love without lust, oh Bruno you sent for me, forbid me to marry, I'm coming home Bruno, the short-cut home, no detours Bruno, no harsh parentheses, I'm coming straight and you must catch me, save me, flag my train. . . .) "Good night, of course I forgive you, a perfectly legitimate mistake I'm sure."

(*Steward, the lady wants her check.*) The lady feels good, the lady feels sure, the lady looks forward, she's headed for home!

4.

Miles and His Wife

IT was like bending to lift the customary stones and finding them lighter than air in the hands.

It was like peering down the difficult road and seeing it miraculously straighten before him; wide and smooth and simple.

It was like trembling before God and finding God sweet and genial.

It was like a God damned honeymoon, Miles thought.

It took strength to face, to bear, such joy; it took room inside him to receive it. Some golden touch had fallen over everything; his breakfast coffee tasted like no coffee in the world; the sunshine filtering on their wall was a personal, bewildering gift, exclusive decoration for their home; and Margaret deftly sliding toast was a being that caught and held his eyes as though her slightest move were marvellous. She moved with a new vigor; a purpose; as though there were some backbone now to her soft balminess. And then—withdrawing her hands from the toaster and clasping them on the table, her eyes floated into space above his head, beyond his ken, with a curious and complacent languor. What is it, he thought of saying to her, what is it that makes everything one's lover does appear so *apt,* so perfect, so proper, so fortunate, in the other lover's eyes? Do you ever feel this way about me, he thought of saying to her. Is there anything else in the world that matters, he wanted to say. Can you keep us forever on this light-filled island, he almost cried. Aloud he said, with difficulty, "We'll both be late as hell, my dear. Look out, you'll burn the toast."

She started and smiled; moved her strong fingers about the toaster. "What do we care," she said. *"We're* going to have more coffee," she said. Her eyes were luminous above the percolator. "Mr. Pidgeon and Mr. Adolph Worthington—let them wait; let them whistle; let them write their own silly letters."

And let Bruno fall in love with manifestoes; let Jeffrey flirt with Magazines, with meetings, with the whole Left Wing; Miles—his fences down, his shell forgotten—was engaged in a passionate love affair with his wife. "I see by the morning papers," he dutifully began—and stopped; dropped the paper to the floor; took the coffee she held out to him; "hello Margaret," he said weakly; and felt himself smiling like a fool.

"Hello," she said back and smiled. They sipped from their cups and flirted over the rims. "I love mornings!" she cried and stretched her arms and grew like a tree across the table from him.

"And afternoons—don't you love afternoons," he said; "you balmy wench, don't leave out the afternoons, they'll be hurt—and you love evenings, don't you, and rainy days and sunny days and nights with moons and nights without moons. . . ."

"I love everything," she said. "The whole blooming works." She had grown careless about her dress; it was shabby—he remembered it when it was new, fine wine-colored wool, fitting closely to her shoulders. It was much more beautiful now, faintly worn, slightly darkened under the arms; the collar limp about her neck. It looked like her.

"I love that dress," he said.

"This old rag." She laughed. "I love it too." Her eyes floated again, that absent look shining brightly in their depths. "And no new ones this year," she said in a ringing voice.

"Maggie, I forget: are you supposed to be a beautiful girl? I can't seem to tell any more. You've got such a great big light where your face used to be."

"Idiot, balmy idiot," she said. A happy, volatile film rose in her eyes. He took her hand. "We *will* be late," she said, almost as though even she could bear no more, was frightened. "And what did the papers say, darling," she mocked him tenderly. Her laugh reached him like the lapping of small warm waves. Smoke rose from the toaster. They sprang apart laughing as though the toaster had caught them out; their eyes parted slowly. He watched her rise and carry the burned slices competently to the sink. Every movement fascinated, comforted him. He had an excited sense that he was living in a house with a woman, his own private woman.

"That will teach us," she said, turning on faucets, turning them off, wringing her hands in the strange gestures of a woman rapidly cleaning house. "Teach us to be balmy at breakfast, my love. If you will hand me the cups, my good man; and the butter in the ice-box, please. My hat, my gloves, my handkerchief—has Mr. Salvemini been for the garbage yet?"

"Five minutes ago," he said. "We're late! But *we* don't care—let Mr. Pidgeon and Mr. Worthington burn in hell." He found her a little absurd, a little beautiful, in her last year's Empress Eugénie hat. "Margaret, before I go to Mr. Pidgeon," he said; and hovered like a small boy with a confession to make, watching her pull the wool sleeves down over her wrists, hold them in her fingers as she slipped into last year's coat.

"Margaret, there are times . . . Margaret," he said uncertainly. But she would not help him out; she had grown sure of her joy and stood there laughing at him. Well, well? she seemed to say; come my New England lover, come my little wooden boy, come all of the way by yourself, I'm betting on you, darling. He couldn't make it. She turned to go, still smiling. He was miserable, stood rooted in his New England tracks. "Margaret, wait a minute, I love you," he said painfully. He had said it before; but never, he knew, from such binding necessity as he experienced now. He kissed her till her ridiculous hat perched on the back of her head; till it fell on the floor; till his hands trembled and his voice broke and the world tolerantly stopped moving and the irrelevancies fell off and there were left only himself and Margaret and whatever it was they dared to bring into the world together, out of their love and joy, their sequestered island of light. There was a rumble and clatter from the world: Mr. Salvemini had returned the garbage pail and left it, with a fine Italian delicacy, outside the door.

5.

The Pivot

THE web, thought Jeffrey (smiling into Mrs. Middleton's eyes) was growing closer; the bloods of antipathetic persons forming (through him) into a nucleus, one fine comprehensible kernel; the loose strings (he thought of the old triumvirate) tightening, gathering together, the separate ideologies (Merle Middleton kissed him with aristocratic restraint) all beautifully merging; himself in the center, at the political switchboard, at the pivot (he thought of Comrade Fisher); the strings in his hands, the tactics in his head; intellectual, aristocrat (he grew drunk on Merle Middleton's perfume), merging, clasping hands in his own personal brain, their common meeting-place his heart. . . . "I think I hear my husband coming," said Merle Middleton fearfully.

They sprang apart and picked up papers pertaining to the Magazine, knotting their brows and moving their lips as they glanced over the typewritten lines. "I am very much interested," said Mrs. Middleton primly, one hand on her hair—but it was only March, the butler, entering with the Middleton canary who had just returned from a bird-hospital where it had sojourned for a week. "I am a fool about that bird," said Mrs. Middleton, abstracted; "I know he gets as lonesome as a human."

"He looks very well, Madam," said March kindly; and before beating a butler's retreat he uncovered the well-appointed cage with a name-plate on the gate. He passed from the room and Jeffrey's consciousness like a fat and ancient sleuth.

On a swing which was supported by a pair of miniature tropical trees the Dickie-bird sat wearily, a convalescent smile upon his face. "He knows me, he knows me," cried Merle Middleton softly, and gave him her finger to dodge. "Doesn't it know its mother," she crooned—and blushed girlishly: "oh Jeffrey, if Doctor Vambery could hear me now!" She turned and smiled; and Jeffrey caught the wistfulness, the loneliness, what he interpreted as an appeal of some kind to himself.

He kissed her outstretched hand. "Santayana," he said (a throw-back to his pre-Bruno, pre-classconscious youth) "reduced everything to a common denominator, to different numbers of atoms floating democratically—all of equal importance—in the general life-stream." He was faintly puzzled by his words, as he was often puzzled by his writing; wondered if he attributed them rightly to Santayana, or whether he had made them up himself. "You are like me, Merle—unconsciously a mystic; the canary means as much, a part of life, a part of happiness. . . ." He was lost. He found himself by taking her in his arms and kissing her. "But my husband *will* be here soon," she whispered reluctantly against his chest.

He was unaccountably relieved. "When will we ever be alone," he said tragically—and renouncing her, his hand upon his own moist brow, felt tragic. He paced the floor in circles round the Dickie-bird. "This bourgeois substitute for love, this unwholesome play which is never finished, this is a sin, Merle, a sin, when we feel like this about each other." She abandoned the bird again and came and pressed his hand with ice-cold fingers. "I am something of a lone wolf," he said pathetically.

"Next time, next time," she whispered with the timidity of a virgin, assumed, he felt, to tempt him further. "Let us talk more about the beautiful project, the Magazine . . . did you say it was to be translated into several languages abroad?"

He nodded, thrilling to his dream of Foreign Offices —his own the French branch, situated on the Seine. "But we are crossing bridges," he said, smiling. "Naturally that may not come about for some time—for six months, or a year." The months skimmed by like so many days in his excited mind. "Meantime we have America." He rose to go. "I have a number of things to attend to," he said. His hands began to twitch as though they counted. When he had seven things to do, they came so often rushing through his mind that they multiplied to seventy. And now he remembered Comrade Fisher; and the fragrance of Merle's expensive perfume suddenly pricked his conscience vaguely. "I *must* go," he said with dignity. Tender and reproachful, he gazed his farewell into her really lovely, frightened eyes; she smiled back; and he straightened the tie that Norah had chosen that morning for him to wear.

He came out on the street, and in the sunshine the seventy things in his mind multiplied gayly to seven hundred. His fingers wove constructively as they ran over the rest of his day. Meanwhile the sunshine was a blessing; passersby were friendly; the city was his own. Life was too short, the day was too short, his heart was too small—for all the merry and important things his hands conceived. He knew he must hurry. For he was between books now; he was luxuriously and unbearably energetic and ambitious—what Bruno called his "manic" period. He was building things in his mind so rapidly that he was tearing them down to replace them with larger things before he had completed the plans for the original. He must work fast; for he knew in some distant portion of his brain that Spring might find him, as it had before, gently living with Norah again and starting another book.

A telephone booth was what he needed next. He found one in a drug-store on Madison Avenue, and quieted his nervous fingers with a pencil. The innumerable telephone calls he had felt he had to make dwindled miraculously under the pencil's matter-of-fact touch, to two. He telephoned to Bruno and reported on his successful transaction with Merle Middleton. He listened impatiently (tapping the pencil on the sides of the telephone booth) to Bruno's report of his labor on the Manifesto; Bruno—or anybody—on the other end of a telephone wire was so remote, unreal, that Jeffrey resented the normal responses which interfered with his own. "Come *up?*" he said incredulously to Bruno. "Come up to *your* place? *Now?* You're crazy! I've got seven thousand things to do. I haven't had time to *eat* all day. The Manifesto? I know, Bruno, but good God! these other things have got to be attended to!"

A little irritated, he inserted his second nickel to call Comrade Fisher. (Damn these women anyway, he thought, humorous at his own expense; they've all got offices to be in just when I want to see them.) "I've had a most successful meeting," he said to the distant Comrade Fisher, incredibly taking dictation for her living, "I've just come from Mrs. Middleton. I've persuaded her . . . she will give money . . . she's very much interested." He wondered with chagrin what Bruno would say when he learned that Comrade Fisher was a woman. "I'm so tired, Comrade," he suddenly said (the operator asked him for another nickel); "and worried; it's like selling my old friends, a little," he said, aware that he voiced an atavistic bourgeois sentiment, "planning things that they don't know about."

"Your loyalty, Comrade," Comrade Fisher spoke grimly over the wire, "is pledged to something bigger than personal friendship. Your friends, the Magazine, may be useful weapons. If not, you'll have to chuck them overboard, if they've outworn their usefulness. . . . You stand in a most strategic spot, Comrade, I've told you: the pivot . . ."

The pivot. Again he felt his blood go round, rising proudly to meet the boast. The pivot; around him the drug-store, the world, turning, women dancing, political movements revolving. His hair might go gray; he might rot in jails; he might lose his friends, his livelihood—before the world would know him for a Comrade. "I know, I know it, Comrade," he said, grateful to her for this piecing together of separate parts of himself. "I know that I must keep my finger on the bourgeois pulse." A ribald joke possessed him, about the delicacy and charm of the very bourgeois pulse of Mrs. Middleton; but this kind of humor was foreign to Comrade Fisher, who once passed a night in jail. "And you ought to see me in action," he said as much as he dared, "I am developing into a first-class strategist." He flexed his muscles in proud retrospect. The telephone booth was too small to hold him.

"I notice you never take me along, on these strategic adventures," said Comrade Fisher faintly over the wire. "Remember, Jeffrey, there's such a thing as capitalist consciousness, this Middleton woman is playing some game of her own at the same time you are. You've got to distrust them every time . . . class enemies . . . Mrs. Middleton is an upper-class whore. . . ." It cost him another of Norah's nickels.

"Of course," he murmured back, remembering that extravagant perfume. But there was something feminine in Comrade Fisher's fears. It turned his awe for her into something faintly condescending; as Merle was ultimately a small item in his important schemes, so some day Comrade Fisher too, her usefulness outworn . . . "I'm awfully sorry, Ruthie, about this afternoon . . . I did think I could stop by for you, but I can't . . . too much to do . . . I'll see you when I can. . . . I've really *got* to say goodbye." He hung up, left her to take dictation at twenty-two dollars a week.

He observed with a feeling of gratitude that the drug-store clock had travelled thirty minutes. It left but two more hours of the too-short day. He strolled to the counter and bought some cigarettes. "Give me some nickels in change," he said to the clerk. Two minutes had gone by. He paused at the door of the drug-store; it was pleasant outside; it was pleasant behind him, in the drug-store. He was a little irritated, in retrospect, at Bruno's peremptory command to come on down to his place—as if Bruno belittled his duties and thought they could be dropped at any moment. And then his hands began to worry again.

For how was he to explain to Bruno that not merely was Comrade Fisher not a man, but she was also not a comrade. Not properly speaking, that is. Comrade Fisher was no strait-laced communist (so she had told him many times, lying on her narrow cot beneath the photograph of Lenin); she despised what she called the "American movement" as it was and lived chiefly to reform it, to bring it to its senses, to remind it of the principles of Lenin which it had forgotten under the rule of Stalin. Comrade Fisher had learned it from the inside; she had been to Russia on a six-week tour; she had been in prison for a whole night while the police made certain she was not a member of the party; and above all she had been secretary and lover to two young party leaders. After which, ironically, ridiculously (after a trip to Russia! after twelve long hours in jail!) the party had refused her membership unless she went and studied at a Workers' School! (Jeffrey turned and ordered himself a malted milk.) "It was this," Comrade Fisher had explained, "this hide-bound bureaucracy, that finally made me suspicious of the party." After that she had made investigations, rounded up a group who had been treated by the party in the same ridiculous way, and together she and her new friends had made a study of the party's defects. They termed themselves "sympathizers," "fellow-travellers,"—amusingly enough "outsiders"; but actually, she had explained, they were on the inside, the inside of "the real thing," the inside of what Lenin and Trotzky had meant to bring about and which now they saw perverted in less immortal hands. He finished his malted milk with vague dissatisfaction. It was clear enough to him, but Bruno was often as hide-bound as Ruthie Fisher described the communist party.

He felt at home now in the friendly drug-store, where one ate and smoked and telephoned; and leaning over the counter he engaged in whimsical banter with the soda-clerk—and wondered if somewhere, perhaps in his next book, he might use that banter; with an angle of class-consciousness. When at length the soda-clerk, as skilled as himself in whimsy, shot with a brief apology down a trap-door in his alley, Jeffrey felt he had lost a friend; and he sat for another moment, really puzzled now, on the customers' side of the counter, before he reached a rapid new decision. He moved back to the home-like telephone booth, which reeked of his own tobacco as his study did at home. Down went another nickel. Poor old Norah, he thought; she always worries so.

"Hello dear." "Why *Jeffrey!*" Poor simple Norah! she was always where he expected to find her. He thought briefly but with no pain of the tedious office where she spent her days; with no pain because she didn't mind it, Norah never minded anything. "A hellish day," he said, "but damned successful . . . tired? my God yes . . . my dear Norah, what do you mean, do you think I can just knock off any time and go home to sleep? I don't even know if I'll be back for dinner . . . oh possibly Comrade Fisher . . . bring her home? well maybe . . . a *sweater?*" he said, delighted; "you've started a sweater for *me?* Oh darling . . . you're such a fool, you never think of anything but sweaters and things . . . what color? well, I'll see it later, dear, I haven't time to listen now. I've got seven million things to do . . . goodbye, don't work too hard—I may be home, and then again . . ." Down went the receiver on Norah. And Jeffrey, feeling glad that he had made her happy, stepped out of the telephone booth (the good-natured clock had knocked off another twenty minutes) feeling as though he set out on adventure, with both the blessing *and* the cake from loving Norah.

He rummaged through his pockets and found that he had still a dollar from the two that Norah had given him; for his books of course scarcely made him anything. One dollar and approximately one hour left to spend. He bid the drug-store a brisk farewell; stepped out on the street in pleasant indecision, and hailed a taxicab and told the man to rush. To the Herald Office Equipment place where he had once spent a happy week selecting a Filing Cabinet; where now a quite delightful salesman (really almost a character out of Dickens) would stand him a drink and show him the respective merits of any number of . . . of . . . adding-machines, perhaps, or perhaps an electric fan against next summer's heat.

6.

Emmett Middleton

"By God we've almost got a Manifesto, Emmett," Bruno said, speaking in the man-of-action voice that Emmett dreaded. "We'll have to do some piecing though—" he tapped the papers of the many-drafted Manifesto; Jeffrey's corrections and Miles' interpolations and Arnold Firman's religious dialectic, Bruno's rewritings and Emmett's retypings covered the surface of the desk. "Can you spare another thirty minutes, Emmett—or will Merle withdraw her support if I make you late for dinner?"

Emmett nodded happily. Thirty minutes, thirty years, or thirty lifetimes—Emmett prayed that they would never end; that night would never fall; above all that Bruno would not suddenly remember, as he sometimes jovially did, the existence of some woman, that strange importance in his life. It was the one aspect Emmett could not reconcile with the Bruno he knew and loved, that only to imagine filled him with hollow after hollow of loneliness as though he lost his friend. He would have been content to wait, the door to Bruno's home securely locked, forever. Alone with Bruno he let himself forget that dinner awaited him at home, that Merle would raise a minor nervous hell when he arrived. For a strange thing happened to time in Bruno's presence; it lost validity as the world outside lost substance. Emmett's own life, when Bruno was not contemplating it, was nothing; these days he brought his life daily to Bruno, holding it in abeyance overnight, whisking it smugly past the eyes of jealous classmates, waiting for it to come real on being beheld by Bruno.

Emmett was disturbed by the new régime; by the influx of printers, machines, collaborators—his own colleagues, the Black Sheep, lifted to the rank of partners; by the unprecedented hurry in which Bruno had begun to move. He felt by instinct that his strongest hold on Bruno lay in Bruno's moods of inactivity. Of the Magazine he was profoundly jealous (he had liked it better when it lay in the realm of theoretic Project) ; yet, because Bruno suddenly and unaccountably wanted it, he urged his mother's help. But it wasn't just the Magazine that worried him; something underlay it; something which Emmett, spending his evenings alone in brooding, laid to the mysterious cablegrams, to the steamer whose progress home across the ocean Bruno followed in the daily papers.

But this was Bruno's *home;* where he retired by himself each night to live his secret, private life. He looked about with awe, with sadness; for though he had always known that Bruno must live somewhere, he had never visualized him except behind his familiar college desk. Now strange vistas opened out before him—how little he knew about his beloved friend; how little he might ever know. He took refuge in his favorite dream: himself and Bruno (Merle and his father become memories, or, if more convenient, dead)—himself and Bruno sharing an apartment, waking in the morning to chat like equals over coffee, the difference in their ages cancelled out by friendship. . . . If Bruno ever marries anyone, Emmett thought with sudden calm conviction, I shall kill myself.

"Something pretty damn funny," Bruno shook his lion's head, "about me running around starting things. . . . Can this be Bruno Leonard? as his public has been taught to picture him? Don't tell anyone, Emmett—but I've caught myself *hurrying.*" The boyish something in his voice that frightened Emmett! spoke of something in Bruno's life, of how little he needed Emmett.

"Probably it's the influence of the Filing Cabinet," said Emmett eagerly; and paused for adulation, feeling that he must have scored, speaking in Bruno's own language. But Bruno's eyes remained abstracted, intent upon the Manifesto. And Emmett, sensing with a pang that he was quite forgotten, withdrew respectfully into silence, his pencil searching errors in his copy.

But it mattered very little, as long as the door remained closed on himself and Bruno; as long as the telephone (filling him every time with chills of apprehension lest it be a woman calling Bruno) didn't ring; as long as Emmett wasn't dismissed to his home that had never been a home, where he never knew whom he might find, what man, ingratiating himself before his mother. His eyes went up in gratitude to Bruno's face, the safest harbor he had ever found. The heavy shaggy eyebrows, with their air of rising diffidently, marking to an infinitesimal degree the finest shade of meaning; the eyes which brooded bottomlessly or suddenly went opaque, shallow and brilliant like stones; and the long nose which wandered indiscreetly, only to lift unexpectedly at the end of its journey, stopping short as though stopping to sniff what it had come all that way to find.

"This business of decision," Bruno said, and sighed; his eyes hung suspended like brooding lamps so that Emmett, in rapport with his slightest gesture, felt them to be hollowing tunnels through mysterious depths of thought. "Firman's death on art, Jeffrey's platform is sugar-coated propaganda as opposed to Firman's hammer methods—and Miles is death on anything that sounds like fun. We've got practically six different Manifestoes here," he said bewildered; and lifted his eyebrows in ironic delight at the hopeless tangle before him.

"Your version," said Emmett shyly, "is the best."

"My boy! you must have overheard me talking to myself. Or else you've an infallible instinct for brewing the wine from sour grapes. . . . God damn this perfectionism of mine—or is it moral constipation? The Magazine to end all Magazines—or no Magazine at all; the Manifesto to end all Manifestoes. . . ." He shook himself into the man-of-action again; the new Bruno tossed off paper-clips and shuffled manuscripts and sent the terror into Emmett's soul. "Run along home, Emmett, indecision's bad for growing boys. Go home and keep our financiers in order."

Emmett sat tight. He wanted nothing but to sit on in Bruno's presence. He wished that time would suddenly stop, that the Magazine would not emerge from the safe realm of Project, that the home-coming steamer would pause in mid-ocean forever. "Soppy," he was, about Bruno. The Black Sheep (but they were jealous!) said so, termed him "Boswell;" called him Leonard's Shadow.

It was Al, his father, first discovered what he called his "case" on Bruno. His mother's Hungarian psychoanalyst had termed it a "transference"; Emmett had blushed with rage at the ugly implications. Maybe he *was* soppy. Maybe he *did* have a "case." But he had never had anyone in his life before to whom he had come so close. One could not belong to an extravagantly beautiful and modern mother who insisted on being called Merle, whom one half-suspected (but how Bruno had eased *that* pain!) of having an affair with Dr. Vambery (and only yesterday, he had seen her serving a cocktail tea to Jeffrey Blake!); nor to a father who was nothing but a lecher and cared more for his business than his life. Not until Emmett had sat in the front row of Bruno's freshman composition class and found Bruno's bright eyes falling rather more in his direction than his classmates', had Emmett known anyone he dared be soppy about.

"We would favor," he read from the paper before him, *"a policy based on science and Marxist materialism . . ."* and then his eyes, his thoughts, began to wander, back to Bruno again, the harbor of his loneliness. The evening merged with that day last Spring which he would not for the rest of his life forget, when Bruno had abruptly become his friend. Emmett had come with the newly organized Black Sheep (he had hoped for an end to his loneliness there, but the Sheep distrusted him because his father was rich) in the midst of the famous fraternity controversy. After the Sheep had won Bruno's promise of help (and Firman had pinned him down unmercifully!) and filed slowly out of the study, Emmett had found himself somehow going on sitting; Doctor Leonard merely nodding, as though he tacitly confirmed

the rendezvous their eyes had made in class. Emmett had discovered for the first time the now familiar campus landscapes that hung marking the seasons on Bruno's wall; the perpetual restless throb of his nerves (which Dr. Vambery, to Emmett's infinite shame, attributed to adolescent sex) had gradually subsided, time had ceased to matter. He sat brimming with repressed confidences. But as their talk progressed, his need faded; it was clear that Bruno understood—how lonely a boy could be, on his own campus, in his own world, in the heart of his own family—and understanding, hedged; played delicately with allegories, never probing deep enough to wound. And to make them equal Bruno talked about himself, telling Emmett of his own dream, the Magazine, which last year was referred to as the Project; so that they parted, even that first afternoon, it seemed to Emmett, friends. Something had been released in Emmett's chest, as though he had found what he was always looking for and found that it was not, as he had told his father angrily, Poetry; nor, as he had beautifully written in his freshman themes until Bruno begged him not to, Beauty; but just a friend; just someone to talk to. . . .

"This stuff, my colleagues' contributions," said Bruno in bewilderment, "is all so *positive.* It would take a microscopic scale to weigh it, to maintain an open forum. How in hell can anyone be so sure, so downright? When I read such positive statements, even—or especially—when they illustrate my own point of view, I begin to squirm and doubt, dodge around till I'm almost siding with the opposition." He paused and rubbed the furrows in his brow as though they ached. "But this is retrogression, Emmett; Leonard atavism. Word salad blue-plate, by Bruno Leonard, constipated Chinese four-star chef—dash of Firman, touch of Miles, oil of Jeffrey, shake them all together they spell mother; m for soup, o for mustard plaster, t for umbilical. . . . Umbilical reminds me, Emmett; how is your private life these days? how are your parents behaving?"

"They're pretty awfully stupid," Emmett said. He would gladly sell his family short for Bruno's entertainment. "Dr. Vambery's practically moved in now Mother's 'graduated'— and he and Al aren't on s-s-speaking terms. As long as Al is home, Dr. Vambery plays Hungarian solitaire in a corner. . . . But Al is never home for long, I think he's got a new s-s-stenographer." Remarkable how these things, for years so painful, sank to the level of comic relief, under Bruno's tolerant gaze.

"And no more 'business'?"

"Father's given that up." Emmett had hated the word "business" since he was three years old; it came out of his father's mouth tobacco-stained and dry, slightly nasal; the combination of the zz sound with the n went the wrong way up his nostrils like burning sulphur off a kitchen match. "He s-says I look too much like a girl scout for his racket anyway." He thought with relief how since knowing Bruno he had relinquished the vain attempt to gain his father's approbation.

"And how does your father regard Merle's latest flyer into the angel business, supporting the Magazine?" Bruno's eyebrows pointed in delight as they always did at anything ridiculous.

"He says he's glad she's given up supporting opera

stars, he hopes the r-r-revolution will be quieter. Last night Dr. Vambery said it would be a fine sublimation for Merle's creative instincts, so Al said the Magazine ought to be called 'Mother's Outlet.' " He grinned sheepishly.

"Al's all right, you know, Emmett," said Bruno rather seriously. Like the side of him that went with women, his friendliness for Emmett's father hurt. "He's got some damn thing the rest of us haven't got. Thank God he's not an intellectual. Of course he'd cut his competitors' throats behind their backs; but in some ways he's a singularly honest guy—he's got some funny integrity; he's somehow no phony. But Merle! Merle's dangerous. In the first place she's too beautiful for a man's mother, seems indecent somehow. And if there's anything tougher than being born with a silver spoon in the mouth it's coming into the world with silver apron-strings about the neck—and every one of Merle's marked sterling at both ends. You'll have your job unsoldering, my boy. My own mother's umbilical," he confided grimly, "was made of noodle-charlottes, I had to gnaw my way to freedom." He made a gesture of impatience, as though someone were talking on and on and he condemned to listen. "But where is this getting us with the Manifesto to end all Manifestoes, my boy, or the Magazine to—*is* there a Magazine? I thought I told you to go home, Emmett," he said sternly.

Emmett didn't move.

"Is it better," said Bruno quizzically, "to have a half-thought-out Magazine and produce it? or the perfect conception that can never appear?" He sat looking this conjecture in the eye. "Too much knowledge after all," he answered himself in a puzzled tone, "is death. If a baby knew all that was involved in sucking its mother's milk it might be a total abstainer till it died. . . ."

Bruno's words had lost their meaning to him, but he sat straining every nerve to listen as he would have listened had God sounded suddenly over the radio. Perhaps, he thought, it would go on forever; perhaps Bruno would invite him to stay all night, and having enjoyed each other's companionship, they would discover, at breakfast, how indispensable they were, Emmett to Bruno as Bruno forever to Emmett. . . .

". . . on the other hand, if an inventor stopped to think, how many people will be put out of work by my patent, how bad will it be for the sum total of humanity to freeze ice-cream mechanically . . . a little ruthlessness is necessary, to accomplish anything. . . ."

Oh, let it go on forever, Emmett prayed.

"Oh hell!" cried Bruno boyishly and suddenly was some other person, some eager non-professorial Bruno that Emmett didn't know; "my God! I've been forgetting the man-of-action—sitting and weighing abstractions as it were last week! back in the Chinese pre-Magazine pre-progress age!" He was curiously joyous, curiously alive; and cruelly indifferent to Emmett. "I've forgotten the human volcano, the Rip Van Winkle volcano. Run along home, Emmett, and let me erupt by myself. No, I really mean it—beat it, my boy, I want to be alone. I'll knock this out if it takes me till tomorrow morning—let's see, the meeting with your mother Friday, a boat comes in on Saturday . . ."

"But can't I stay and help," said Emmett miserably; but he was standing, he knew he was beaten.

"No, no, you've done enough, get the hell out and

rest," said Bruno; and waved him away; and drew his chair closer to the table as though he were already by himself.

And so he was dismissed. Emmett sadly crossed the room. Home again, home to loneliness, and terror. For Emmett knew that without Bruno, out of Bruno's presence, he was *dead,* he belonged nowhere and to nobody else. The evening unrolled before him like a coma that must be got through somehow before he could come back to Bruno in the morning. He squared his shoulders for his end. But turning he saw that Bruno had forgotten him already; was rummaging (the unfamiliar man-of-action) over the littered table-top. Emmett's sadness turned to sudden hate (his only friend was keeping something from him!); hysteria mounted—an inexplicable mingling of his fear and hate and painful love; and as coldly as he could he said good night.

He shook the reproachful Emmett from his conscience. For he must not encourage Emmett, Bruno thought; neither for the boy's sake nor his own. Product of luxury without warmth and leisure without direction, Emmett would cling to anything to prolong his baby-state and turned to Bruno like an unweaned pup. And Bruno knew he had permitted it, allowed the boy to grow dependent, through a shameful corresponding weakness in himself. The thought of Emmett was distasteful now, tinged with a faint perversion. But he was done with meddling in younger, weaker lives, done with doing his living at cynical second-hand. He turned with vigor to the tangled Manifesto.

The symphony resumed its happy swell. The old triumvirate revived—Bruno, Jeffrey, Miles, each playing his assigned part in the heroic whole; the Black Sheep the youthful drums, quickening the tempo and sounding impatiently throughout; and Elizabeth the top part, the high part, the thin and soaring melody. Without the Sheep he knew the old triumvirate would weaken; he knew too well Jeffrey's straw-in-the-wind quality, Miles' too-rigid rules of thinking—but he loved them both, he loved the thing that the three of them together still represented in his mind: a bold minority, taking their stand (when they were just the Black Sheep's age) against the strong in brawn and numbers. The three standing together again brought back youth as Elizabeth did, injecting Bruno with a sentimental faith.

The important factor was Elizabeth. Small part of an ocean lay between them now, a matter of days, of hours. As she crossed the sea to come to him, he made loyal journeys through a clearing fog to her; and found her where she always must have been, in the very center of his life. Happy nostalgia swam over him because he knew they would rebuild together all that they had deliberately thrown away, the last movement of the symphony would commence with their first sight of one another. He bent determinedly over the Manifesto. He felt his old friends (however they split on small points, however impelled each of them still was to listen chiefly to his individual self) nevertheless on the main points solid behind him: that there was to be the Magazine, the culmination of all they had thought through and lived through since their ardent college days.

7.

Before the Fast Express

ELIZABETH knew that she was waking and she swam laboriously out of sleep: she knew that she would not know when she opened her eyes in what bed or what stage of life she would wake to. Not in Paris with Dennis Kirby; for a moment she felt him on her breast, his impression lay lightly like a shadow, and then was gone; not in Paris with Denny. Not in a studio smelling of turpentine; not in the little coffin-shaped room at college, with the library chimes ringing out clear and false across the campus. She knew she would not wake to the nursery at Longview with the sun coming up out of Lake Michigan, with Fräulein drawing back the curtains—she closed her eyes more tightly as though sleep might take her back; held them shut and prayed that when she fully waked some miracle would have taken place, and there she would be, back in that white iron bed, that light-flooded room; a child with pigtails scattered on the pillow—the rest, the other rooms, the subsequent beds, a fevered night-mare. Behind her own closed lids she lay safe and could *feel* in that deliberate dark the dimensions of the familiar nursery; she could feel the white-painted bureau on her right, the snap-shot of Bruno in his sailor-suit, riding his first two-wheeler; the collection of eleven dolls with which she would not play because Bruno called it sissy; the heart-shaped locket which she wore even to bathe and sleep in, that Bruno's father gave her for her seventh birthday: the walls, the windows, Fräulein guarding them, pushing out the outside. Emptiness crept from her chest to run with a vague ache through her body, as though all her limbs were hollow. It was nostalgia; the strongest, most painful, the only real nostalgia: nostalgia for childhood, for oneself as one started to be.

Whatever bed I wake in I shall not belong there! I shall not be there! the ache compellingly taking over her body informed her. *I want to go back, to go back,* to before the fast express, go back twenty years and more to that era of timeless peace, to the days without end, the wide sunny days, each issued like a coin to be squandered recklessly; to be saved forever; each one a lifetime in itself, encompassing a thousand births, a thousand deaths, with a fine wide stream of warm brown family, a thin strong thread of happy Bruno, running through. Bruno explaining to a pair of pigtails the mysterious nature of time and eternity; where God lived; how babies came. Time rolling always out of a gigantic spool which unwound itself ponderously like syrup round and round before the window so many child's paces from a child's bed; jumping each morning like the hands of the school clock, giving out another day. Terror of being alone through the long, long nights: would daylight ever come again; had that afternoon of shooting marbles with Bruno in the back-yard been their last (the world ending every night when one was only seven)—then leaping with joy to find Fräulein at the windows; the time-spool jump: another day, a *day,* a day-long day, in which to live with Bruno.

But time narrowed, time conformed; the wide days were pressed into service, became so many units in a week; a week was recognized; one day it would be Summer and the next day Fall and seeing the bare branches emerge even a child knew that special Fall would never come again. The day came wide and beautiful; but as its hours progressed they narrowed, then flew; and were lost down a dwindling funnel. There was a quick week of packing, of holding one's breath; the heart beat faster like the clock, the time-spool spinning negligently; and Bruno was gone, to prep-school.

Bewildering days, a foretaste of life without Bruno, dry and cold, no longer precious to wake to; time rolling faster, less important, from the great spool grown smaller, spinning quicker. Good that night came now; good the first snow, because Spring would be that much sooner; and after Spring Summer and the thought of next year's Fall more endurable by far than this one. *Give away my dolls, I'm not a child any more,* she told Fräulein, told her mother. How they laughed and cried over her. *Eight years old and not a child,* they cried, *why you're our baby, Betsey*—jealous and frightened that they could not live forever in their child's slow rhythm. *I'm not a child,* she firmly said. *Our melodramatic baby,* they laughed and cried. *Bruno's coming home, coming home for* CHRISTMAS, *they said; but aren't you glad, Elizabeth? Why, what a child! your only cousin coming home and—I believe the child's forgotten* BRUNO. They laughed and cried; they cried and laughed; the mothers, the fathers, the uncles and aunts. She closed her mouth and closed her face; she broke her bank to buy Bruno a present.

He's downstairs, Elizabeth you funny child! your

grown-up cousin's come to see you! come and see Bruno in his first long pants. She hid in her room; she hid his present; she brushed her hair standing consciously before the mirror for the first time in her life; she undid her pigtails, braided them all over again. She rushed down the first flight; she stopped dead on the landing, the window framed a picture she would never forget, her eyes large and trembling to receive it; she crept down the last stairs as though she had been summoned for punishment. *Doesn't he look handsome, Elizabeth?* they all cried and laughed, and stood like vultures in at the death. Strange Bruno stood there firmly planted on the carpet, his legs going down in their fine long pants, his face a yard above them, disconnected; beside him another boy, a stranger-boy, no stranger than Bruno, standing and laughing in triumph because Bruno had brought him home. *And look, he's brought you a friend, the Davidson boy, a beau.* She stood stock still on the bottom stair, a mile away; she thought of the safety of the landing, twenty steps above; her patent-leather feet refused to move. *Why you funny children!* cried the mothers, the fathers, the uncles and aunts, *you funny, funny children! don't you know your cousin any more, Elizabeth? don't you know your cousin, Bruno? How quickly children forget,* they all sighed, and smiled, and touched their eyes. The room stretched a mile between them, lined with strangers, poking fun and laughing. The strange boy continued to stand, obstinately, beside Bruno; his triumphant smile a ghastly challenge. *Ah, ah, she can't look at Bruno because he's brought home a friend, ah, fickle Elizabeth, your cousin's fickle, Bruno.* At last Bruno revolving slowly through the space, a prep-school man, a long-pants man; the boy beside him moving like a shadow smiling his strange triumphant smile. *Hello kid, meet my kid cousin Arthur, doesn't she look like a baby-lamb?* Shocked grown-up silence, amusement filtering through like pepper in her nostrils. *Show him you're a lady, Betsey, set him an example, tell Bruno how nice he looks in his new long pants, shake hands nicely with the Davidson boy, tell him you're glad to meet him.* The stranger-boy with the stranger name held out his stranger prep-school hand. Bruno's long, long pants were stilts, sending his head a mile above her own so their eyes could never meet again; he stared like the stranger out over her head. *Bruno looks silly, I think,* she said. They stood there flanked against each other, pitted against each other, like hostile, stranger children; she ignored strange Arthur's hand. *And they used to be so devoted, inseparable, almost too much, we used to think,* moaned the mothers and fathers, the uncles and aunts; *children are so cruel,* they smiled and touched their eyes; *she's flirting with you, Arthur, don't mind if she doesn't shake hands,* they laughed and cried. But Bruno was climbing through the window with the stranger Arthur after him toward two bicycles which stood against the porch. Christmas died before it came; Bruno was gone before he had come home. The spool spun fast and brittle.

He called Tommy Spencer a fat-head when she asked Tommy to take her to the high-school dance; he said Jerry Marks (when she hung over the balcony of the gym to watch Jerry shoot baskets) was a matinee idol; he said Dick Hyams whose fraternity pin she wore for six months was a sissy, a jack-ass, a small-town sheik—and when Easter vacation came she gave Dick back his pin. Well, why don't *you* take me to the dance Bruno, she said; he laughed his superior laugh. You've got no sex-appeal for me, Betsey, he said; he was running around with the town's wild girls, hitting the high spots all around Chicago; and then he was writing letters from New York, all wise-cracks and adages, no news about himself; and briefly home again, sitting restlessly next door, unbearably dipped back in slow family life. *Get out, get out of it, Elizabeth, as soon as you can get out.* Off down the block on his bicycle, off down the block in his roadster. She couldn't stay home and get his letters; couldn't stay home and watch him tearing down the street, around the corner, out of her life. She could ride as fast as he. She could run like him banging the door behind her, she could leave the family sitting growing old with the safe mahogany chairs they sat on. She could step forever on the accelerator, she could sit a restless prisoner on the fast express, by his advice, with Bruno's sanction; she could go twenty times faster in her direction than Bruno in the other, she could fly, she could spin, she was casual, gay, she dropped him letters from way stations, he wrote back that men-artists were generally fools, that Wheelwright sounded like a ninny, she wrote that it wasn't Wheelwright any more, she had moved her toothbrush to the next one, he wrote back saying he hadn't raised his girl to be a travelling salesman, she stepped on the accelerator and met him for a mute three days in New York, then sprang on the train again, rolled on again, sped away again, faster and faster, careening on the downhill special, left him on the station platform with all they had to say and could not say standing like a spectre beside him, waving like a spectre after her, *don't forget to write,* she cried rapping on the window-pane, and *life goes on but you're ahead of it,* he roared above the roar of the train gathering motion, the train gathering noise and stood there looking after her with her own expression in his eyes while she bounced on the dusty straw seat and hurtled down the singing tracks.

Through the pounding and the pulsing in her ears there floated up some feeling, faint, some straw to cling to, wake for; something to flag the fast express; some memory she could not place. The high speed slackened; this day was not like other days; the bed rocked, swayed: she was on some boat, no fast train this, this slow and gentle motion. She lay there trying to waken, trying to remember; like trying to capture some name which, lost in memory, becomes the keynote, the important cabala. Perhaps when she found it, it would be some name like White; or it might recall associations in no way satisfying the urgent need. Yet it would remain a fact; and though one could not conjure with it, it must be endured, accepted, forever after faced. She tossed on the bed as the train moved slower. The memory came up clean and shining; *Bruno, she was going home to Bruno;* the brakes ground noiselessly; she was awake with a new wide day before her. Something of the joy of waking in the Longview nursery shone in the wavering stateroom. Bruno next door; Bruno waiting at the pier; in twenty-four short hours.

8.

Margaret and Her Husband

"NO, YOU go, go without me, darling," Margaret said absently; "you can represent us both, I'm tired."

December already, she thought, the middle of December; leaving only January, February, March . . . the months stopped on her fourth finger, the ring finger; August on the finger that wore the little marriage band. The doctor had laughed; he couldn't be sure, he said, as long as the months counted so many ahead, up to his own ring finger; ah you eager young women, he said, and wagged the June index finger playfully. But Margaret and Mrs. Salvemini were perfectly certain. It didn't take a doctor, Mrs. Salvemini said, to tell *her;* she knew it; had the feeling; a heaviness in the eyes, a lightness in the heart—it was she who told the doctor. And I always ask God, said Mrs. Salvemini, I always ask God. Go ahead, said Margaret, her eyes shining with her heresy; go ahead and ask your God; for me, Missis Salvemini, she said. God, snorted Mrs. Salvemini; I'll ask the Mother of God, Missis Flinders.

A heaviness in the eyes, a lightness in the heart—let Miles wait for scientific confirmation from the doctor; Margaret Flinders had it from Mrs. Salvemini and Mrs. Salvemini had it straight from the Mother of God. And be sure and take it easy, Missis Flinders, Mrs. Salvemini said; it's the first two months you have to look out for; one I lost, she said, I lost because I didn't wait for Mr. Salvemini to come home and beat the rugs; you take it easy, Missis Flinders, she said, scolding in advance.

"You're such a funny girl," Miles said, bewildered, and followed her from room to room; "staying home from politics—to take a *bath."* But being in love with her again, she reflected, he was in love with her eccentricities too. She glowed complacently; dropped the last shred of her clothing and stood before the mirror screwing back her hair. "Don't you want to keep up," he said; "the Magazine, don't you want . . ."

"But I'm definitely not the *au courant* type," said Margaret placidly. She enjoyed Miles' faint discomfiture on beholding her with sails full-set, naked at an unexpected hour in the day. "I'm a political moron, dear, we know that. Besides, I don't *want* to be courant—with anything but you." She turned with one hand guiding her long hair to a ridiculous knot on her head and blew him a kiss with the free one.

"It's too soon after dinner," he said, disconcerted, "it's too soon after dinner, to take a bath." She knew what he was telling her: it was too soon after dinner to catch him unawares, surprise him with love. He hovered like a shadow while she pulled her hair into a ridiculous plume on the top of her head. A heaviness in the eyes, a lightness in the heart—she moved with the special consciousness of a woman grown suddenly beautiful, a woman loved; she felt proud and secretive, gathering towels and flying to the bathroom to watch the quickly spouting water, Miles slowly coming after. He took his puzzled dignity and sat with his hesitant grace on the laundry hamper beside the tub.

"And you can tell me," Margaret said, "everything that happens; all about Jeff and Mrs. Middleton, and Bruno and his pet lamb Emmett—and of course the machinations . . ." She swished her hands with pleasure through the soapy water; gravely handed him the brush.

"You know I won't see any of those undercurrents you specialize in," he said with his sheepish reluctant grin that told her he knew more, in his inarticulate way, than she would ever know, about himself. "I'll hear the wrangling, I'll come away wondering if Jeffrey can be trusted, I'll have my philosophic doubts, my conscience will prick—but none of it will look like melodrama, as you see things." He floated the brush absently over her shimmering knees. "But you, Meg, aren't you interested, don't you care—don't you care for anything, but being *happy?*"

Some day she would cure him, Margaret thought, of saying the word in quotations, as though he borrowed it from some foreign language, speaking it faintly with an accent. "Of course, if you prefer *la type courante—*" she raised her soapy face; eyed him with mock archness through sleepy lowered lids (if life held anything sweeter, she swiftly thought, than the luxury of flirting with one's husband—then Margaret didn't want it).

"No, I prefer you," Miles admitted awkwardly. "Even with your face all soaped—even with that crazy top-knot dancing on your bean—" he tried to pull his shots, inject his caustic New England—but it failed; his voice fell into tenderness; "I suppose you looked like that when you were Mrs. Banner's little girl, Maggie?" He examined the back of the brush minutely; focussed his eyes on a spot on the laundry hamper; cleared his throat with embarrassment.

The heart could grow so light, she discovered, that it nearly flew out of one's chest. But Margaret Flinders had grown canny; gently she tempered her love and her joy till they were something he could take; his New England tract was small. "Getting late," she said calmly; "Bruno will be there by now." She had a sense of deliberately dimming her lights.

"I ought to go," he said reluctantly. "I really ought to go. I can't announce at the Middletons' that I was late because I stopped to watch my wife take a bath. My wife," he repeated, surprised. *"Wife,"* he said again. And paused as though the word, the fact, were something new; *"wife—"* he examined the effect on himself and faintly smiled. She saw the tremulous moisture gather in his eyes. Be strong! she told herself; not all at once; it mustn't come too soon and frighten him. "I'm getting positively balmy myself," he murmured, smoothing the bristles of the brush. "You're seducing me, you soapy wench! with your balmy wiles, your top-knot guiles . . ."

Darling beloved, she swiftly thought, let's die now, quickly, in this bathroom. The world holds nothing greater.

"Old softy," she said; "if your New England aunts could see you now!" For a little grit must always be thrown in his joy; a little sand preserved in her own voice when she spoke to him. O Margaret was taking no chances now! "Get along, darling, to the meeting of the world-revisers. One of us must be *courant.*" For he must not stay, for both their sakes. Margaret must be alone with the lightness of her heart, alone so she could shamelessly enjoy it. And Miles must run away from too much joy, so it would not drown him, choke him. But more than that. The Magazine and Margaret—they made a cycle for him; maintained the balance in his conscience; each made the other possible. The Magazine restored his faith, his long-lost God, gave life a forgotten validity; and so he earned his personal joy, a joy made valid by religious satisfaction.

"But I don't want to go," he said incredulously. (Feeling took him by such quaint surprise!) "I want to stay home and take baths with my God damned *wife.*" He trailed his fingers in the water. "It's much more fun at home." He shyly winked.

"Counter-revolutionary," she mocked.

"All those schemes and Manifestoes," he said recklessly; "let Bruno and Jeff be the commissars—I want to make love to my wife."

She grew grave. "But Margaret—your scheming wife—has plans too, darling, a life-ahead plan, Miles. You aren't forgetting, Miles . . ." She could not resist the pleading; the lightness of the heart was not to be belied. She drew herself back with difficulty from telling him what she and Mrs. Salvemini between them knew. Happiness was too precarious . . .

"I'll stick to my side of the bargain," he said courageously. "But—it does worry me, darling. My salary—I'm sure to be cut again, or fired."

"A smoke-screen, darling," she said carefully; "not what you really mean, Miles. Come clean, my dear."

"The Magazine," he offered; "the movement, revolution—these things mean more to me than to you." He played vaguely with a lock of his own hair.

"Come cleaner, darling." She was playful, but hard. "You're mixing your mind with your emotions, Miles—a common New England fallacy." She watched him gravely.

"It does worry me, Margaret; it—I think it *embarrasses* me. As if I weren't ready for so large a step." His voice was husky. "I can't seem to—seem to—imagine it somehow, believe it. I don't cotton to it, as my aunt Martha used to say. I—maybe I'm jealous, Maggie; but I can't seem to see myself, quite, in the rôle . . ."

She laughed vigorously. "Quite natural, Mister Flinders. Missis Salvemini says—until he saw them with his own two eyes, Mister Salvemini never gave a damn. She says that men are like that. Very dear and very, very stupid."

"Are you taking up with the Salveminis," he said, bewildered. "We might call him Daniel, Maggie," he said suddenly. They were quiet with the vision. "And will you look like Mrs. Salvemini, Maggie, when . . ."

"No, the Banners don't run to so many bosoms, not even 'when' "—she mocked his puritan reticence. "I may be a bit more billowy," she said proudly. "I may look older," she said firmly. "I may look a little on the full-bloom side—like my mother looked before she died. Do you remember my lovely mother, Miles?" She paused, moved; and shaken with wonder that they both instinctively went backward in their minds when they contemplated going forward; the thing made the thread, the meaning. "We mustn't let ourselves forget her, darling." She recalled her mother's astonished acceptance of

Miles; her loyal explanation, in the terms of the only thing she had ever understood, that the lad was young, the lad had never had a childhood. "Do you think I look the least bit like her, Miles?" she wistfully asked. But she was not like her mother, with her head filled with recipes for calming men and scalloping potatoes; or was she? "My forehead, I think, my eyes?"

"In your balmy moods," he said, with one of his quick, rare flashes; and he put his hand on her forehead so that she felt it round and high and beautiful beneath his touch; "in your balmy moods you look exactly like Mrs. Thomas Banner; telling her son-in-law to take life easy, to be happy with her daughter." He smiled, the recollection filling him with tenderness. He could face Mrs. Thomas Banner and her ultra, rich-developed balminess, thought Margaret, more tenderly now she was dead; and could transfer his fear of it to the strain of the same thing in her daughter. She was deeply grateful for his tribute to her mother; felt it ironic but inevitable that only death had bridged the gap between the two she loved the most. *Do you see, mother, do you see what's happening to your daughter? she has a real live husband now, a man of flesh and blood, of tenderness; a man who dares to be a father.*

"Mrs. Thomas Banner," she said softly, "wouldn't need to tell you now."

His lips (so bitten in against emotion) trembled. He looked as he had on that dear morning when he marched across the kitchen to say, "Wait, I love you, Margaret." He looked at her—then quickly down. "It needs a lot of strength," he said, "to take so much. Even to look you in the eyes these days. It's almost blinding." He ran his fingers on the rim of the tub. His eyes he held carefully lowered; and suddenly, as though he were hiding the motion even from himself, his hands shot out toward her and reached with the despair of a child.

In a flash Margaret Flinders forgot all she knew, all she had carefully schooled herself to remember—and was in his arms, all wet and clean and naked, all of her pressed and gathered to his frightened heart that beat so painfully under the clothes he wore to hide it. He sobbed against her shoulder. Again she wished that they might die, that minute, so that their joy would last forever. But they would not die. And through her unbearable love for him, her grateful, overwhelming love for this moment that was like the end of all her aims, her new-found wisdom slowly filtered back. She held his head like something infinitely precious against her. But over his head her mind conferred with Mrs. Salvemini's Mother of God.

As when a thousand people gather in a square, an enigma called "mob" is born, so two people cannot live together without giving birth to a third entity, at once a part of themselves and greater than the whole. This entity, so Margaret thought, was a thing to be reckoned with, wooed, its presence constituting the aura in which lovers must live. They are never alone. This thing that is born of their being together is a censor, a chaperon, made of their separate consciousnesses meeting, not quite merging, wavering in a pattern they never can see, which nevertheless (dancing on the bathroom walls, the ceiling over their bed at night) dominates their life together. Ignored, it stretches forth an icy hand and claws their joy to death. Wooed, it hovers like a blessing on their heads.

Margaret, born with the knowledge dumbly in her soul, having had it simply nourished by her mother who was born for nothing else, lived to court its blessing. Margaret could hold her breath forever in its service. But men, she thought, need something more; something at once more and less. So Miles, just dimly conscious as she felt he must be, would fight it even against his will, because it threatened death to him of those parts exclusively his own. *She* became whole (she knew it shamelessly) only when her self was merged. But Miles feared drowning.

So over his head she studied minutely the stern and beautiful face of this thing that ruled their lives. She weighed and measured, her body and senses became the most microscopic thermometer of Miles' emotional strength. She was superstitious, as though some god of love must be placated. The moment came (did she feel Miles infinitesimally withdraw? or did she merely anticipate and did the anticipation immediately become the fact?).

She lifted his head and looked with cool tranquillity into his pleading eyes. "I shall catch cold," she said lightly. His face looked hurt. Don't you want me, he seemed to say. "You must go to meetings and things," she said. (She couldn't stop the bells from ringing in her voice.) Wouldn't you rather I stayed home with you and let the meeting go to hell, he as much as said while he stared at her with his eyes filled and glowing. "Immediately, at once," she murmured; and held him close against the lightness of her heart. "So that you will be back sooner," she said, and firmly withdrew her arms, reaching bravely for the towel.

He nodded as though he understood. The world came back as he looked at his watch. "My God, I've got to run! Jesus, how *could* I have hung around so long—" He caught her eye and smiled; handed her the towel as though he must do one last thing for her—and ran.

"My love to Bruno," she called as if to establish some contact between herself and the place he was going; "don't let Jeffrey run away with the meeting darling, hold out for what you believe . . ." But he was gone; and she put his gift of the towel about her shoulder and it warmed her like a blessing. *Middle of December, she thought; the old hat will surely do; work till June for Mr. Worthington; be careful till the end of January; January, February, March, April, May, June, July, and August on the wedding-finger.*

9.

The Inquest

"MRS. MIDDLETON," said the butler with gravity and finesse, "sends down word she is binding the canary's leg—the little fellow broke it; Doctor Vambery is with her."

"Now what is your honest opinion, March," said Al Middleton, button-holing him, "do you think Dickie's leg is broken or that it's just a compound complex, needing psychoanalysis. . . . Well, tell her," he said, sighing, "that the whole left wing is waiting for the outcome. Personally I'm betting on Vambery. Tell her her husband is fighting off a counter-revolutionary stroke himself, and that if she isn't down soon the radicals in the parlor will be so many grease-spots on the rug. Now: what are you going to tell her, March?"

"That you hope she will be down shortly, sir," said March and wheeled his abdomen about to carry it before him like the banner of his admirable profession.

"A man is never a prophet in his own pantry," said Al; swallowed his drink and made inquisitively for the library which Merle had "opened" for the reception of the plotters. He stood for a moment listening outside the door; the buzz came out pleasantly like the growing roar of the Stock Exchange when something was brewing. But no sound like the one he wanted most to hear: his own son's voice raised and bold like the voice of someone who belonged somewhere. The buzz went on; but Emmett played no part.

He opened the door stealthily. "tactics" "I say tactics be damned, Jeffrey" "but boring from within"—"Pardon me!" said Al loudly—and noted with malicious amusement how the steady mumble of voices died down at his entrance; saw with a touch of irritated sympathy how his own son looked up in fear; "pardon me for just stepping right in as though I lived here. My wife is upstairs having a love affair with a sick canary and I got to feeling a little lonely. Ah there, Leonard, glad to see you. So this," he said with a quick look round, "is the Revolution. Glad to meet you, boys."

"Please Al, we're having a d-d-discussion," said Emmett miserably.

But Bruno Leonard was crossing the room with the swift tact of a woman and took his arm. "Since you're buying a stake in revolution," he said genially, "you ought at least to meet the dark horses, Mr. Middleton. Miles Flinders—between the fireplace and sofa, he's marking it off for firing—Norah and Jeffrey Blake, Arnold Firman and Cornelia Carson, classmates of your son's—and your own son I think you know."

"My own son I think I don't know," said Al advancing briskly. "Pleased to meet you all." He swung the hand of each in turn. He was amused at the silence, both hostile and embarrassed, which greeted his appearance. "Well. Have you come to blow me up," he said pleasantly. Still no one quite reacted. He felt the show was his. "And what a lovely female decoy," he said, bending to the one called Norah Blake who sat on a hassock knitting peacefully; "Madame Defarge, eh?" he said, patting her—for she seemed deliberately planned to rest the eyes. The other girl, the Cornelia one sitting close to the angry young Jew, affected him like so much sand-paper, an insult to his generous welcome to the female sex. Male and female created He her, thought Al, vastly pleased with his wit.

"Please, Al." He heard Emmett's agony; slapped his own hand on withdrawing it (though God knows there had been nothing but friendliness in his gesture, and the fair one's smiling nod reciprocated nothing else), and put it firmly in his pocket. "We were talking, dad, I don't know if you'd be interested . . ."

Take that, Middleton, you plain tough guy—from your own son! that'll show you—marrying an orchid and producing a pansy. (It hurt him nevertheless.) "Nonsense, my boy," he said with cheerful cruelty, "I'm only doing what the medicine man told me—taking an interest in my son's activities. Can I help it if my boy likes revolutions? Papa'll get right down on the floor and play along." Vambery called him a sadist, explaining it in terms of four-syllable words from the Latin; but Al slipped into bullying his son because it was the only way he could talk to him, because time after time he hoped he would kick the lad into being some kind of a man. "Go right ahead, boys," he said genially, drawing a chair beside the knitting one, and crossed his legs to listen.

There was silence, the young Jew and the female-impersonator whispering impatiently. "They're taking your number as an upper-classman, Mr. Middleton," said Leonard pleasantly (a nice guy for a professor, Al had thought from his few visits); "the younger faction, the

Black Sheep, or Red Lambs as history will probably call them, I suspect are reverting to Alice-in-Wonderland: the off-with-his-head chorus. How about it, Cornelia? are you playing the Red Queen over there?" Trying to bridge the gap, thought Al, between the high-brows and the low-brow—good-natured devil.

"We've merely been betting," said the sand-paper acid voice, "on the chances of this meeting getting anywhere." "We figure if we just came here to spend the evening" "why it's a nice warm place to sit" "but we had rather thought"

"They won't talk," Emmett again, in his wretched, sissy voice, "as long as you are p-p-present, Al."

"Why not?" Al said coldly. "I'm the step-sugar-poppa. If your revolution's borrowing money from Middleton's MidTown Essentials, I don't see why I can't buy my way in; I want a ringside seat when the fight comes off." "*If* it comes off," said the tight-faced Yankee lad (Cinders? Flinders) who continued moodily to mark time on the carpet. Al looked them over coolly. From the young Jew perching defiantly with his shoes (and what shoes!) resting on Henry the Eighth in *petit point* at he had forgotten how many francs the square inch; to the handsome Jeffrey incredibly clad in a costume replete with wind-breaker; the nice plump knitting decoy duck; to Emmett, poor kid, stretched on the rack by his uncouth father. "How about it, boys? can I tune in on the inside dope? I want to deal in futures. When's the opening? But please," he said amiably, "don't pull it off on a Saturday; it's my only day for golf." A pretty solemn bunch, he thought; all but Bruno Leonard.

"We've been discussing a paper, Mr. Middleton,"

said Norah kindly; "some kind of a paper Bruno wrote; to go in the front of the Magazine." Thank you my dear, he said; and patted her warm hand; and is that a sweater you're doing? Yes, for Jeffrey, she whispered back; I'm turning the sleeve.

"My girl," said the blond Jeffrey (and hadn't he caught sight of him, clicking glasses with Merle last week; yes, he remembered the wind-breaker lying over March's puzzled butler's arm), "my girl has trouble with the English language. What we're discussing is a Manifesto, a statement of policy, drawn up by Bruno, naming the issues."

"Evading the issues," said the young Jew quickly "not a positive statement in it" said the dry male-and-female "cowardly" said the meager Jewish captain "hypocritical" said his sidekick immediately "wishy-washy liberalism" "pacifistic bellywash" "pink" "soft" "emasculated" "mugwumpery"

"How many of them are there!" said Al, bewildered; "my God."

"Of course what you youngsters don't understand," said the wind-breaker conciliatingly (jumping his hands on his lap like a baby) "in your eagerness to go the whole hog, is that the intellectual has a definite function *as* an intellectual, a place of his own . . ."

"On the side-lines, according to you," said the minister's son Flinders, pausing sternly in his walk; "a box seat, a loge, where he can reach for a drink if the revolution bores him. This thing is beyond a game, Jeffrey—even the Sheep know that."

"No game," said the blond Jeffrey eagerly, "of course not; but it must be played like one at first. It's a matter of tactics, I've just come from a conference with Comrade Fisher—"

"So that's where you were," said Norah chuckling; and skillfully drew out an amber needle to start another row; "and there I was with all that lovely pot-roast."

"I bet you're a swell little cook," said Al turning to her with pleasure. She smiled complacently.

"The revolution," said Bruno Leonard lightly, "has taken a slight turn for the worse, ever since I learned that Comrade Fisher was a woman."

"And I," said the caustic Firman, "have begun to suspect that it isn't a revolution at all, since I learned she didn't belong to the party." "Her record," said Cornelia, "would take some looking into."

"I told you smart kids," said Jeffrey patiently, "that she's even been in jail. . . ."

"Now would you question her, you hard-boiled cynics?" said Bruno with delight.

"Ruthie's a nice girl," said Norah simply.

"I really think," said Emmett, distressed, "that if mother doesn't come soon, I mean we're wasting so much time . . ."

"My son," said Al dryly, "counts on his mother's arrival to drive me out. My dear boy, would you have her neglect a canary for a revolution?" My God! tears stood in the youngster's eyes. Father to a sissy—I'd rather have a gangster in the family! "Do you really want me to go, Emmett," he said gently.

But Bruno laid his hand on Emmett's shoulder. "Suppose you play umpire for a little, Emmett," he was saying; "I'll indulge in a little reactionary banter with our right wing." Emmett calmed as he might beneath a mother's hand—and never had, reflected Al. "Well! what do you think of my circus, Mr. Middleton?" He came jovially and sat between Al and Norah. "How would you like to place an ad in my Magazine? guaranteed to reach nobody with the cash to buy your product?"

"I figure," said Al, "you're up against the same thing I am with that Magazine of yours. You've got something to market nobody wants: Revolution. As a business venture it interests me. I deal in luxuries and call 'em Essentials. You deal in destruction and have to put it across as construction." His eyes wandered to the little group, where the buzz was flaring up again. "Say, one thing I advise you; if you're going to peddle your dope in the sticks, get some appropriate salesmen—these four-syllable boys can't touch the American market."

They had turned it on full force again, the young Jew and his echo leading; he wished that Emmett would join in. They were pretty crazy, Al thought; but no crazier, possibly, than a view of the Exchange to an outsider looking in; their own language; their own gestures; their own particular mode of high-brow yelling—he was sorry for his boy, and ashamed, watching him sit with that nervous look upon his face.

"I don't get it," Al said patiently. "It's a funny line to handle, revolution. When I was a kid . . ."

"But times have changed," said the professor smiling. "Get used to it, Mr. Middleton, I'm afraid you're going to see plenty more. In your day it was each man for himself. But nowadays . . . well, get an eyeful of those kids; they were born to band together. They know it's no use bucking it alone. . . . But hell," said Doctor

Leonard boyishly, "I'm not trying to sell the revolution to you. The revolution needs the income from the non-essential Middleton Essentials . . ."

The tight-faced Flinders paced the floor; the wind-breaker talked like a deaf-mute with his fingers on his knee; the kids came forth like a trained Greek chorus. But where on earth did Emmett fit?

"Worried about my kid," he said telegraphically. "Poor Goddamn forlorn little bastard; what's the matter with him anyway. Can't be all his daddy's fault. Sometimes I think the poor kid's dotty like his mother." Funny thing about Jews: you met them downtown and wanted to cut their throats; you met them at home in the evening and found yourself telling them your troubles. "Too many private schools," Al said succinctly; "too many lectures on sex with the shades pulled down; too much Vambery—altogether too much of something that the poor kid got from his mother and not enough of plain red blood from low-brow papa. . . . Say Leonard, you're a high-brow," he said: "do you think the Vambery's right? he says Emmett pulls that stuttering stunt half on purpose, making tracks for a kind Freudian home-plate. . . . Jesus Christ!" he said disgustedly, "a stutterer in the family! Is that why he can't get in under the wire any place, make friends?"

"I used to be a Jew," said Bruno smiling. "And I thought that was pretty tough, at Emmett's age, I mean. But a Jew has an easier time than Emmett. You might be a sort of outcast, but you always have a sense of fraternity with the other Jew-outcasts. But you can't expect Emmett," he raised his brows in almost delicate sympathy, "to bat around the world looking for the rest of the boys who stutter. . . . But the trouble lies deeper than that, Mr. Middleton. Emmett suffers from a form of social disease that strikes only the sons of rich men. He was brought up with too much of everything to think that anything mattered. And he was brought up to be the only pebble on the beach. Plenty of others like him, of course; but they can't get together because they were brought up religiously to be separate—individualism, my colleagues would tell you. The kid was practically born in solitary confinement."

"He's had all the freedom—"

"That's what I mean," said Bruno; "he told me his chief ambition a few years ago was to be sent to military school."

The storm was brewing in the room. Al turned his attention from the problem of his boy. "Jesus Christ, Leonard, do they always go on like that?" Excitement had mounted; arguments rose and clashed like boxers chasing each other around the room.

"Why they're tuning up for action," Doctor Leonard said easily. "Wait till you hear them when they've learned to play together. I admit right now it sounds like a community sing . . ."

"A funny racket," said Al conclusively.

It was a funny sight for a man to see in his own library, those sprawling kids who treated *petit point* as though it were a bench in the park. In all his years of living with it Al had never felt at home enough to sprawl. Funny thing for a man to bring down on his own head anyway; a man who didn't give a damn for the kind of house he lived in or the kind of wife he kept, to spend his life working like the devil to keep the house going and the wife (and her canary) more elaborately preserved. Of course the point that nobody admitted was that it was the making of money that held the kick; after that the *petit point,* or diamonds for Merle, were nothing but the chalking up of extra credit. But there was nothing the matter with it, nothing was the matter with anything, as long as you didn't take too much time to slop around and think.

"The Vambery," he turned to Doctor Leonard, "gets a good fee and a living to treat my wife. Do you know what really ails her, man?" He spoke in a low voice. "She's *bored.* That's a terrible thing. Do you know how terrible that is? My God! *bored!* that's the only God damn thing the matter with her. Why she's got endless, infinite endurance—to stand things that would knock me to hell-and-gone: permanent waves, fittings; massages that make holy rolling look like nine-pins. But give her a plain day to go through—and by God dinner preys on her mind all day, she can't decide what dress to wear, she goes mad wondering if she ought to have asked the Whitmans, she counts her jewels to make sure of the new maid . . . and by evening she's ready for the Vambery again. . . ."

The butler heaved his ponderous belly through the door. "Mrs. Middleton will be down in five minutes," he said; bunched his size together and carried it considerately away.

"Her Majesty," Al said grimly; "prepare to kneel." He remembered the comfortable Norah squatting on her hassock. "And what do you think of all this, Miss Norah?" he asked.

"I think I've made this sleeve too tight," she said, stretching it gently.

But he heard Merle's step upon the stairs. Slow; tantalizing; perfect; she had not had a moment of being at ease, of being herself, of making a natural gesture, since they had taken to separate rooms at her request . . . or the Vambery's expensive advice. . . . His boy looked tortured; sat on the edge of his chair much as Al felt he must have sat, some twenty-odd years back, calling on the aloof Miss Emmett with flowers in his trembling hands.

The buzz died. Here's where a pair of hips, Al whispered to Bruno, knocks your revolution for a goal. . . .

Merle stood in the doorway, the Vambery behind her like a shadow. Wait till she issues The Voice, Al thought maliciously.

If he could keep his eyes down, Emmett thought, if he could fasten them on the mobile safety of his dear friend Bruno's face (who was meeting a boat tomorrow!); if he could think hard then of the Magazine, of Russia; of the proletariat . . . But Merle drew him irresistibly. The damnable little Vambery behind her stuck in his eye like a grain of sand. Over and over he could kill the pain; and over and over it swept him like icy bands around his heart. "Too beautiful for a man's mother," Bruno had said. It was a terrible thing, her beauty. She lived inside it, Emmett thought, like a woman caked in ice. Terrible to look at one's mother and perceive her as ice; as beautiful, slippery, treacherous ice; as a creature of no blood with himself, or even of no blood at all. And to think then of the grotesqueness of one's father . . . cigar in hand (did he ever put it down? could he ever stop reeking of it?) approaching that terrible whiteness, spotting it, polluting it . . . and out of such pollution he was born!

How she had planned her entrance! Bruno thought, amused. She stood in the doorway; diaphanous; pained; gracious; a cross between a crystal-gazer and an advertisement for too much perfume. She hovered in a "poignant" way, her fine-drawn brows the only moving lines in her pallid, careful face. The effect upon Jeffrey, he noticed, was that of a baby having the soles of its feet tickled.

Isn't she horrible, vulgar? murmured Firman behind his hand; spot the diamonds, Corny. I want to put in my application, darling, Cornelia whispered back; I want to see personally to her slow dismemberment.

She issued The Voice and Al sat back to watch. It came, low and sad; each word formed and formulated in pain; with a brave effort; exquisite; poignantly cracked; the accents shaped by Benvenuto Cellini. Each word worth its weight in gold, in subtlety. "I am proud to meet my boy's friends." Stage silence. "I am sure you will forgive me for being late, the poor little fellow was in agony; stupid little beastie, he always eats too much and then of course his leg breaks when he stands on it." Al loved the kids for standing in their still hostility—all of course but Jeffrey Blake, who came forward eagerly, his fingers signalling to his inside-man.

"Meet the wife," said Al brutally. "And how do you fancy the diamond crown, comrades? my gift to the little woman to wear to the revolution."

She fluttered like a bird and turned with a martyred-humorous look toward the heaviest of her crosses (the Vambery eyed Al with satisfaction: checking off his categories, placing Al where he belonged, neatly filing him under "sadistic"). "I thought you had gone, my dear." She extended her hand and Al was God damned if he was going to kiss it. But the blond finger-waver pinch-hitted for him and seemed to like it thoroughly. They stood there doing a tableau out of Candida.

This is more than tactics, Firman whispered; or tactics makes strange bed-fellows. Upper-class sex, Cornelia snickered back; I bet she conceived Emmett by letting fairies kiss her hand.

This, thought Jeffrey, inhaling the perfume for which he had already conceived, in its absence, nostalgia, is playing the game; but he felt guilty, not toward Norah sitting there, but to the memory of the loyal, scrawny little Comrade Fisher, sitting tonight on her little cot and planning campaigns under Lenin's picture.

My God, thought Miles, the whore of Babylon! And is *this* the mother of our Magazine? My God! If only Margaret were here, to show him the joke, to make him laugh!

His father and Jeffrey and the Vambery swam in black nausea before Emmett's eyes. The light tremor in his mother's voice, the easiness of her extended hand lingering in Jeffrey Blake's, froze him as nothing else could ever freeze him. Why didn't Al . . . But it was Merle's fault; for Merle permitted men, Merle encouraged them, Merle wore pale silver-white clothes that fell from her pale silver-white shoulders . . . He hated her, he hated her.

"I am so flattered, so honored," said Merle (speaking,

Bruno thought, with an expensive, bewildered air, as though English, as though language itself, were foreign to her), "that my home, this library, will see the beginnings of what I know, I know . . . Dear Doctor Leonard, how lovely to see you again."

He hated her, he hated her. And then he closed his eyes. Her perfume was in his nostrils; her hand upon his head. "My son. At last you have brought home your friends, Emmett, to meet your poor old mother."

But she was like an actress, Norah thought, enchanted; and put her knitting down to watch. The sort of incredible lady whose hose were never wrinkled, whose powder never caked, whose girdle never rode above her hips—who had, in fact, no hips at all. Marvellous to watch her moving, like an actress on the stage, greeting, pausing, moving on, stopping to touch her son. And Jeffrey standing up to her, kissing her hand as though he did it every day. "Thank you for coming, my dear," she was talking to Norah herself; bending and fingering the wreath of diamonds in her princess hair, her head faintly weighted as though the wreath were too much for it; "thank you for coming to a dull old woman like myself." "Why not at all," said Norah quickly; and looking toward Jeffrey to share her delight saw that she had said again, apparently, the wrongest possible thing. "You lovely child," said Emmett's mother soothingly, "you lovely peasant—isn't she a lovely peasant, Vammie?" The little dark man bent and nuzzled Norah's hand. Norah loved it all! She sat back on her hassock again and took up the knitting; settled as though she were in the theater.

"Well—" Al rose. "This is no place for me, this hotbed of revolutionaries. Don't forget to protect the Middleton interests, my pet. For every cannon you donate, sell 'em a ton of Middleton's Essentials. Good night folks, good night, I look forward to seeing the red flag flying from my roof when I come home. Good night, good luck. . . ."

Well, Cornelia murmured, if we don't get down to brass tacks now I'll start the revolution myself, without the God damned Magazine. Corny, poor kid, you must be tired—checking out at the library, all afternoon, and hungry too, I see it in your eyes, Cornelia.

He had sat back long enough, Bruno decided. The elements were restless, impatient to be drawn together. Merle's presence was embarrassing (ludicrously clear how Jeffrey had won her support, and a little disconcerting too)—and yet it made their group more real, less isolated. He glanced over the scattered parts, from the bombastic Black Sheep to the decadent Merle sitting with Jeffrey and the Vambery at her feet—and took heart; he had assembled this conglomeration, he had given them something to come together for—and now he must piece them together into a whole, as he had pieced the Manifesto, and make them a working unit, a practised symphony: that he could present to Elizabeth in the happy morning. He felt solemn with responsibility, and a little bit ridiculous, as he must always feel when himself in connection with sentiment or achievement stared him mockingly in the face.

"If you don't mind, Mrs. Middleton," he addressed her curtly, "we'll be getting on with the Inquest."

"Oh please," she said, with her vague foreign air of absent humility, "oh please go on. Don't pay any attention at all to me. I shall feel so privileged . . . Vammie, you must explain it all to me. I am very stupid," she said appealingly to Jeffrey. "My son is always telling me . . ."

"I suggest," said Miles, seating himself with determination at last, "that we speed things up a bit, after all the Manifesto isn't everything and if we're going to have a Magazine . . ."

"Oh, isn't it," said Firman sharply. "The Manifesto is the keystone, we have to sail under its colors; and this one," he flung his eyes contemptuously toward Bruno's well-marked sheet, "is cowardly" "pink" said Cornelia quickly "emasculated"

"Mugwumpery," said Bruno, bowing. "That, I think, completes the circuit." The younger generation, he uneasily reflected, was going to be no cinch; perhaps he had been rash in admitting them—and yet, as he looked around him, checked up on all the faces, they were necessary, valid: provided some sort of backbone, ballast (dogmatic though it was) to the old, revived triumvirate. He could scarcely imagine this meeting, the Magazine itself, existing without Firman, without the dry Cornelia sitting by his side. "If an open forum, inviting truth, is counterrevolutionary, my honorable students . . ."

"Revolution," murmured Merle, lifting her ringed hands in ecstasy, in deprecating ardor. "The very sound is beautiful."

Sit tight, Firman, muttered Cornelia; you've got to swallow this, I s'pose we need the bitch's money. Of all the slop, groaned Firman.

"This life we lead," said Merle, her hands descending in little graduated jumps as though the rings were heavy on her hands, "no life at all," she said to Jeffrey.

She bravely smiled. "Doctor Vambery has the most brilliant explanations. Relating everything to frustrations, to disappointments, to tiny little psychological factors . . ."

"Look, let's get on with the business," said Bruno firmly, "before Miles wears out the carpet." For Miles had taken to pacing off the floor again. "We seem to be editing at least six different Magazines. We might at least give Mrs. Middleton her choice of which to support. Myself I'm frankly after two things: truth, regardless of propaganda; and art. . . ."

"Art," cried Jeffrey, "art *as* propaganda! of course! Art as a weapon . . ."

"No, art as art," said Bruno grimly. "I've always been in favor of it."

"But we've got to change our ideology," cried Firman, "to fit the times." "Aesthetics were all right in *your* day," cried Cornelia impolitely; "but this is war-time! we need ammunition, not poetry."

"If there's any such thing," Bruno was aware of the heavy sentimental sincerity of his words, "as intellectual integrity, if art was ever valid, then it still is. It would be a fine thing if intellectuals altered their philosophic concepts according to the headlines in the papers or stock market reports. . . . Being an intellectual," he brought this out with care, "surely implies something else, to some extent the power of rising above individual or immediate circumstances . . . the privilege of bringing to the conflict something abstract, something resembling a universal truth—something else beyond the status of his private person and his bank account. . . . Why must a depression put an end to art?"

"Art can't make a revolution," cried the Black Sheep.

"Revolution," murmured Merle. She held her hands to Jeffrey as though she implored him to tear the rings from her suffering fingers. He caught her hands and kissed them whimsically.

"What makes you think," said the little Vambery slowly in his patient, foreign delivery, "that revolution is superior to war? Are they not both killing? Are they not both fruit of the same psychological germ?"

"Oh my God," said Cornelia. "The revolution," she patiently explained, as one addressing the very young or the very old, "will be the last war, the end of bloodshed." Of them all, thought Bruno, Cornelia was the only one in whose mouth the word rang clear and simple, like any other word, as though she were neither afraid of it nor in awe of it, but quietly accepted it as one of the inevitable facts in her vocabulary.

"War," the little Vambery intoned prophetically, "will be on the earth for as long as men are born of mothers. War is an enlargement, so to speak, of the inner, basic struggle. It is blood to avenge blood; sin to avenge guilt. . . ."

"Fascinating, the different points of view," Merle clasped her hands before her. "Are you a Freudian, Jeffrey?"

"I am a Marxist intellectual," said Jeffrey simply. "I am a gentleman farmer," cried Miles in disgust; "I tell the hired man where to shovel the manure. If you're a Marxist intellectual I'll eat my shirt—last week you were in favor of something else, like nature it sounded to me. . . ." "I'm in pretty close contact with the left wing, Miles—" Jeffrey's fingers wove self-consciously. "Why don't you join the party and get in closer then," said Firman irresistibly. "Because," explained Jeffrey kindly to the Sheep, "my job is on the outside, I've got to keep my finger on the bourgeois pulse." "I'm a little fed up with compromise," Miles started coldly—and there was Norah standing sweetly by her husband, docile but persistent, pulling at his sleeve. Hold out your arm, dear, she was murmuring, stretching her knitting around Jeffrey's wrist; and Bruno understood that she was saving him.

"Comrades, a little autonomy!" said Bruno as the peaceful interlude closed and Norah with a reassuring nod resumed her seat. "Is this a united front?" He permitted himself to grow serious: "A little trust, a little tolerance . . ."

"You sound like a Goddamn Christian Socialist," cried Firman fervently.

"It's my Jewish inferiority complex," said Bruno coldly; and looked his fellow-Jew ironically in the eye. "But look here, Firman, you are the strongest against my manifesto, suppose you tell us all how you would draw one up."

Firman had his way of commanding silence. He spoke like one admitting no doubts. "I'd cut out all the pseudo-clap-trap. I'd take a definite stand, the only stand: Revolution; no more dialectic humbug. A Magazine's for propaganda. A revolution is for a full belly. There isn't anything else. You've got a full belly or you haven't. You're in favor of them for everybody or you're not." (He remembered Firman a spindly freshman, borrowing Veblen and borrowing Marx from Professor Leonard's shelves. Something struck him now about the Black Sheep; it was not merely their youth that set them off, that blinded as it fired them, it was their poverty. Perhaps poverty, undercutting everything else, removed them a priori from the class of intellectuals.)

"Man's desires," the Vambery stated with a complicated smile, "are unfortunately not so simple." *Say, did you have anything to eat tonight, Cornelia? you look damn white.* "Man's wishes have gone beyond the need for food alone. . . ."

Certainly, thought Bruno, if one conceded the necessity of the full-belly fight to the exclusion of everything else (of philosophies, of tolerances, of poetry and concerts at Carnegie Hall) then argument of the kind they were indulging in was forever ended; then dispute, except in matters of strategy, of "tactics," was ruled out; then the mind (like Firman's) would narrow to a single course, pursue a single aim, ruthlessly shove overboard whatever interfered. It was unfortunate that all sides held truth, that sanity to him consisted in a constant balancing. For he agreed with Miles, agreed with Jeffrey, agreed with the Black Sheep; and weighing their opinions, he agreed with none of them. It was most unfortunate that at the moment he agreed with Vambery; and that his sentimental war-time notions of free speech compelled him now to admit it.

"You heard the Herr Doktor, boys—man does not live by bread alone." He grew reluctantly serious again. "But the fight for full bellies—that can't mean everything to *us;* we come of a long and honorable line of full bellies—most of us," he added; "and we know damn well it's not enough; it's not the final object of the game." He thought with repugnance and pain of his father; reared in poverty and piety, his father had come to America to fight for a full belly for his family—and in the fight had dropped the piety along with poverty, in favor of a paunch: for himself, to pass on generously to his son. His father had turned from Jehovah to Mammon; and on his face for the rest of his life he wore the pitiful sign of his sacrifice—something left out, something wistful, defiant, something that undercut the growing ugliness of his fat and prosperous jeweller's jaws. "The intellectual," he continued, "is a scientist; whatever field he's in, he's looking for the truth—it's the eternal values he's after. The full belly—we've got our eye on something higher, granted the full belly must come first. . . ."

"Those higher things," interjected Firman, "are going to fall pretty flat if they fall on empty bellies" "or on half the world dead of starvation" said Cornelia.

"I said the full belly must come first," said Bruno impatiently. For that all bellies, being created equal, should be equally full, was an axiom; it needed no more thought. Someone should see to it—economists, efficiency experts, agriculturists; but it was a small and specialized, almost esoteric, realm of life. "Don't you see," he said confidently, "someone's got to take the long view, someone's got to keep his eye on what comes after . . . Once all the bellies are full, what then? We—the intellectuals—have to step in and show them what else there is; keep them from aiming at a fuller and fuller belly to the exclusion of everything else." And he thought how he had turned in disgust from his father's full-belly pursuits; had reached (dragging Elizabeth with him) for a world in which only the intangibles were goals. He grew strong again with the memory. "There's danger in this war; there's danger that the new god may become efficiency, that though the aim is different, the results may resemble a sort of belt system, even under communism. . . . The intellectual has to climb the sign-posts, ask himself at every step of the way, What is the object of the game? are we achieving the proper object? or are we being carried away, destroying, and forgetting what we mean to build. . . ."

"Now that," said Firman, "is a specious, bourgeois argument" "and sentimental" "because obviously your 'higher things' can't happen" "until efficiency is so far along" "that the business of canning for instance is mechanical"

Firman's fight, he thought, was not (except in some inevitable underlying realm, some inescapable Freudian sphere), like Bruno's father's, for himself; not even restricted to the full bellies of his race; ostensibly it included all the world. Grant the necessity (he ruminated, while the talk burst out again around him). Grant the justice (which sometimes, in a mood of scepticism, one could doubt) of keeping a world alive, of nourishing every single individual in it, the underdog Chinese, the starving Armenian, the slaves in French Guiana; the living dead scattered now on the redlines, the deadlines, of America. Let us grant (he thought, observing the angry Firman, the pallid Cornelia, pressing their arguments upon their seniors' ears) that all these aching bellies must be filled, blood pumped upward to the brain even if that brain be so much sterile gray stuff. And then suppose the feat to be accomplished. The world populated with fat people sitting on complacent backsides—the world with a paunch, in short, with a sad fat face like his father's.

He knew the dialectic rebuttals, that efficiency, materialism, were the means and not the end; recalled a paragraph that ended Trotzky's book, in which the future's average man, having mastered canning, building, mining, rose head and shoulders above the Goethes of the past. But (his mind as ever restless till it provided not only the rebuttal to itself, but furnished also the subsequent rebuttal *to* the rebuttal) had not his father promised as each year added to the lines in his face and the thousands in his bank, to retire next year and live, as he timidly put it, "the life of Riley"? And had he not been carried home at last, forced to retire (having grown too old to enjoy the life of Riley earned him by his bank account) by nothing short of death? Despite his careful reading of the communistic bibles, Bruno's inevitable scepticism rose to point a world in which trees were torn down for bigger factories, other trees planted in organized rows for factories of the future. . . .

"The point is," Jeffrey said complacently stilling the Black Sheep, "that even though you're right, we've got to step easy; you can't knock the bourgeois intellectual on the head with a blackjack and expect him to like it; we've got to approach him warily. As a matter of tactics," he said, and drew the fingers of one hand down the hand of the other as though he whittled the revolution into shape.

"What a dinner with Comrade Fisher," said Bruno. "Everything from soup to tactics. Go on."

"As a matter of tactics we don't want to come out—in the beginning—too frankly as left-wingers; we're sympathizers" "camouflage, sounds dangerous to me," said

Firmin. "compromise, sounds lousy to me," said Miles. "Only for the beginning," Jeffrey said; "we'll be fellow-travellers."

"Fellow-trav-ell-ers," said Merle ecstatically. "Oh I never knew that politics could be so *beautiful.*" "P-p-please for God's sake, Mother," burst from Emmett.

"Fellow-travellers," continued Jeffrey calmly, "is what they call intellectuals, you know, who aren't joined up exactly. . . ."

"Yes, we've all been to dinner with party emissaries," said Miles dryly. "And it's nearly twelve o'clock," said Bruno.

"Anyway, I discussed our policy," said Jeffrey patiently—

"We had no policy at eight o'clock this evening," said Miles. "And we still haven't any," Firman pointed out. *God kid, can you hold out, are you terribly hungry? My stomach's upset so badly by all this tripe, Cornelia said, it wouldn't hold a meal—do you s'pose we'll be like that when we're old? We'll never be old, baby, don't be dumb.* "Nor is it precisely," Miles said crisply, "your place to discuss without consulting us."

"I acted," said Jeffrey quietly, "under advisement."

"Visions from Moscow, comrade?" Miles asked him coldly.

"There are circumstances," Jeffrey said, "you may not be aware; currents; cross-currents; certain repercussions . . ."

"Oh it all sounds like a play," said Merle softly, "a fascinating Russian drama."

"Are you by any chance suffering from repercussions of the brain?" said Bruno wearily at last.

"The party wants to establish relations with the intellectuals." "A marriage of convenience," Bruno said, "surely you won't assist at such sordid opportunism?" "support them from the outside, don't you see," Jeffrey pleaded with the bored Black Sheep. "sounds like compromise to me," said Miles uneasily. "sounds like flying buttresses," said Bruno grimly—for his own tribe must not be seduced into alien territory.

If this keeps up, Cornelia, I'm going to ask for something for my girl to eat. Ask them to borrow from the bird-cage, Cornelia whispered back, my legs are stronger than the Dickie-bird's.

"and don't you see," Jeffrey went on, nervous, his fingers interlacing, "the Magazine can be a useful weapon—"

"A weapon," said Bruno elaborately. "Ah yes. But what war are we fellow-travellers off to?" The thing was getting out of shape; he wished the triumvirate were as single-tracked on their own level as the young Black Sheep.

Jeffrey's hands went carefully over his sentence. "Why the class war, of course," he said, puzzled with himself.

"Ah yes, the class war." Bruno scratched his head. "But it's hardly our war," he said calmly. "You don't fancy yourself a capitalist, Jeffrey. And as for being a proletarian, I'll bet your Norah changes your typewriter ribbons . . . No, I'm sorry, Jeffrey; it's not our war; we're not eligible. We're neither fish nor flesh nor good red herring. Just lousy intellectuals." He was aware that he was sentimental, that he drew a gold line around the intellectuals and put them in some holy place beyond the economic; but each man for his class; each man for the preservation of his own kind, his own fraternity; and intellectuals engaged in a property war would lose their identity as intellectuals.

"It's everybody's war," burst from Firman.

"Of course, of course," said Bruno. "But the intellectual belongs on the sidelines—where he was born."

"That's stalling," said Firman angrily. "That's sitting on the fence," said Cornelia.

"But what's a better place to look on from? Doesn't the world need an umpire?"

"Consider the intellectual," said Firman: "he toils not neither does he spin . . . to hell with that." "Economic determinism," said Cornelia, "has bitten the intellectual in the pants too."

The Vambery cleared his throat for action. "My dear young people: economics most surely plays a part. But it is not, you cannot believe it is, a basic human motivation. Not a fundamental. Investigate your earliest memories: they are not, surely, either of too much or too little money."

"My earliest memory," said Cornelia dryly, "is my mother throwing a kettle at me."

"What?" cried Merle. "How terrible, you poor child! —was she—'nervous'?"

"Worse than that," said Cornelia cheerfully; "she didn't have anything to give me to eat. I'd come home from school and said I was hungry. So she threw the kettle at me." "But why, why," wailed Merle. "Because she was angry at the kettle for being empty," said Firman shortly.

"To get back to the subject," said Bruno impatiently (these damn youngsters! they had such concrete illustrations of their simple point!) "Religions and civilizations,

Firman—built if you will, on propaganda, and by those in the thick of the fight—have flourished and died; but the art depicting them has lasted. It seems to me quite right, quite just, inevitable in fact, that the intellectual stand on the sidelines, fiddling while Rome burns or what have you; our fiddling produces the records for posterity. . . ."

"Unless, professor," said Firman, "the intellectual happens to fall in the flames himself; and his worthless record with him." "Your position, Doctor Leonard," said Cornelia, "is an anomalous one." "Anomalous," Bruno nodded approvingly; "I thought one word was missing; now they're all checked in."

"I want it born, inaugurated," cried Merle, "in a burst of glory, the Magazine!"

"What Magazine?" "*Is* there a Magazine?" "What is your mother talking about, Emmett?"

"Defeatist talk!" cried Jeffrey. "And what in hell else have you contributed," cried Miles—but Norah stood between them.

"You'll have to take your coat off, dear." She stood like a very stupid woman (which Bruno was sure she was not) until Jeffrey swallowed his rage and rose with a sigh—more like a spoiled child than a plagued husband—and slipped on the sweater she was knitting him. The room was calmed; Jeffrey emerged from his fitting with spirits soothed and temper cool. (Bruno thought of Elizabeth.) "Go on, tell them, Merle," said Jeffrey—and gave Norah a little pat as if acknowledging his debt to her.

Merle faced them graciously. Bruno observed how Emmett writhed with filial embarrassment. "Jeffrey Blake and I," she said, "have planned a party to inaugurate . . ."

The room broke into discords. "A party?" "What has a party to do with a Magazine?" "A combined party, we thought—proceeds to be divided between the Magazine and the Winter Hunger Marchers." "Hunger Marchers!" Bruno heard Miles, sounding his stern worry through the dissonant fugue: "It's compromise, no good will come of it, a Magazine baptized in gin, will there ever be a Magazine?" *Listen darling, for God's sake, do you have to go back to the dormitory tonight? Dixon doesn't mind sleeping on the floor at our place. If this meeting ever ends, Cornelia whispered back; darling, I am so tired.* "A revolutionary Magazine," said Miles, "inaugurated by a drunken party—I don't like it . . ."

"A Hunger March Party!" Al had come back and stood maliciously surveying them. "I'll donate the buffet —nobody will go hungry at *our* Hunger March Party, shall they, my pet? Caviar, lobster, nothing's too good . . ." *Sit tight, Cornelia, if this meeting ever ends we'll beat it over to Dixon's. . . .* "And how have you gotten along, my dear," he said placing himself beside Norah; "did you turn the sleeve?"

"Baptized in gin—" said Miles unhappily.

"Hell, no, champagne," Al interposed. "The refreshments are on me. I want 'em to cost more than the whole Hunger March expenses, otherwise I won't play."

I want to go home Arnold, let's beat it now, to Dixon's, I feel as though I'd be sick any minute all over this carpet. Hang on kid, we can't let them run themselves into the ground like this, can you stick it out? All right darling, but break it up if you can, I feel damn funny.

"Of course you realize," Firman broke out of a huddle

with Cornelia, "that we haven't settled on anything resembling a policy."

"Nonsense," said Bruno, "we've settled on no less than six." "Oh we can have a meeting to decide that," said Jeffrey easily. "I thought this was supposed to be a meeting." "I know, but we can have another." "A drunken party," Miles said bitterly; "I don't like it."

"Not a drunken party at all," cried Merle, "it will be beautiful, dignified, we will have speeches and banners, music . . . Run up like an angel, Vammie dear, and see if the Dickie-bird's all right. . . ."

"It will be," stated Jeffrey firmly, "a party on the surface, and concealed strategy underneath. . . ."

"Ah, spies in dinner jackets!" said Al Middleton with pleasure.

"Dinner jackets!" burst from Miles. "In R-r-russia," Emmett began. "but tactics," said Jeffrey "selling out" said Miles "what the devil does it matter, it's no costume party" said Bruno angrily "real democracy" said Merle ecstatically, "the perfect party" "when the R-r-russian ambassador attended the conference in Paris" "we will have posters, we will have speeches" "there'll be a party, but there'll be never be a Magazine" "dinner jackets and there'll never be a revolution"

"Anyway there'll be caviar, sceptics," Al shouted into their midst. "I guess you'll have that sweater finished pretty soon," he said to Norah. "Yes, I don't like to waste my time," she said, "I mean," she added blushing, "I like to keep my fingers busy, I'm not clever like the rest."

O darling I do feel sick. O darling hold out a little longer.

"And the R-r-russian ambassador was criticized" "what can it possibly matter" "because clothes are a symbol" "if you start to compromise you're lost" "so snobbish not to attend a charity ball dressed in your best," said Bruno bitterly. "It will be a party no one will ever forget," cried Merle.

"How do we know there will be a Hunger March this year," said Al. "Maybe nobody is planning to be hungry enough to march. . . ."

But there was a small cry, a timid crash, and Cornelia lay in a heap on the floor. Norah, awakened miraculously, was as quick as Firman to reach her side. Deftly she and Firman unloosed the collar of her blouse. "My salts," moaned Merle, "ring for spirits of ammonia, Emmett. Ring for March. Where is Vammie? oh I sent him to look at Dickie. . . . What could be the matter with Miss—Miss—"

"Over-eating," said Firman briefly; and shook his girl with a fierce tenderness by her slender shoulders.

Al hurried with his whiskey bottle, Miles ran for water, Jeffrey flung the windows up—Merle was busy with her heart, her hands, her moans. But Bruno couldn't move. *The fight for full bellies . . . a property war . . . that can't mean anything to us . . . you're either in favor of them for everybody or you're not . . . they had reached, he and Elizabeth, for the world in which only the intangibles were goals . . .* Philosophic truth, artistic integrity, open forum . . . all the precious things that glimmered with a sudden cheapness, brought suddenly face to face with a vulgar staring empty belly. *B-b-bruno, Bruno!* Emmett shivered beside him, as helpless as himself. Bruno stood there paralyzed.

Cornelia's eyes were slowly opening. "Fainting," she muttered angrily. "Pulling a Goddamn 1870. Sorry, everybody." She grabbed her side. "Oh Jesus."

"But what is it, what is the matter, Miss—Miss—" cried Merle, wringing her hands in anguish.

"Nothing at all, my pearl," said Al; "the girl has no manners, she has had the bad taste to faint of hunger on the *petit point*."

"Oh oh," sobbed Merle, covering her eyes with her hands, "I'm going to faint myself. I never can bear the sight of someone suffering, I had to hide my eyes while Vammie bound Dickie's leg . . . perhaps she'd like some food, would you like some food, Miss, Miss . . ."

"No thanks," said Firman. He was busy picking Cornelia up, putting her together tenderly. "She really fainted out of spite—just to end the meeting. A mean girl." Her eyes had closed again. He shook her by the shoulders. "Cornelia!" He slapped her briskly. "Cornelia. Pull yourself together. We're going. You won. You broke up the party. Very effective strategy." He laid her head against his shoulder and rose. "Come on darling, show them you're hungry enough to march." No one spoke. Al fell back to let them pass. Miles stood with his head lowered as though he were taking part in a religious ceremony, as though the prostrate Cornelia were some Christ who had died for him. At Bruno's side stood Emmett, his shoulders shaking like a sobbing child's. Bruno couldn't move. Young Firman stepped proudly down the aisle they made for him, his girl's arms going weakly round his neck; Norah fell calmly in the rear of their procession, carrying Cornelia's fallen few belongings.

And so, he thought, the room stood still, lined with corpses as though a multitude of living people had taken up their lives and carried them away to some more fitting place. It seemed to him suddenly that he and his friends were ridiculous, doctors who had passed examinations in a correspondence course; that when suddenly they were faced with a suffering patient, the patient had more concrete knowledge than they, for all their learning. The uncomplicated physical had no reality for them; its unexpected presence had one chief effect—while their busy abstract minds worked to reconcile it with some preaccepted doctrine, some maxim of their own, their emotions were stricken in a harsh new way which argument would fail to solace; their bodies (his own was numb) were paralyzed by this sudden failure of their minds, this wretched cancelling of emotions they were unaccustomed to. What they had seen was hunger; deep as was his own tortuous unwilling scepticism, Bruno knew that before the last ten minutes he had been sceptical even of hunger. Nor was there any place for it (now that he perforce accepted it) in the academic scaling in his mind. It didn't fit. It was irrelevance. It was some other language than his own. But all the time through the numbness of his body, his own belly ached with a fierce imitation of Cornelia's.

They were turning aimlessly to go, afraid, because each one knew what his fellows were thinking, to look each other in the eye. Miles was white as though he had experienced some awful revelation. Jeffrey's hands were feverishly trying to weigh things, to balance things, to put this new idea into a decent resting-place; for once his fluent tongue was failing him. The whole thing, the meeting, the Magazine, this roomful of ghosts, his own whole life, seemed to Bruno farce. "B-b-bruno, Bruno, take me with you, don't leave me here," sobbed Emmett; and his weakness was only putting into words the wretchedness that all of them were feeling. It took all of Bruno's strength to reach out and put an arm on Emmett's shoulder; it would have taken more than he possessed (despite a shrinking in himself) in order to refrain. "So perfectly awful," sighed Merle; "I felt all evening—since the Dickie-bird's little accident—that something awful was going to happen, I'm a little psychic that way. . . ."

"Curtain," said Al. "Shall I ring for March, my angel, and order up some sandwiches?"

10.

The Conscience Ticks

HURRY, Miles wanted to shout at the man in the subway change-cage; and hurry, he wanted to scream down the empty curving tracks to the next train sliding so coyly into the station; hurry up, I've got to get home to my wife.

For the thing that had happened at the Middletons' had frightened him, startled him, like some canny premonition of his lurking guilt, the end of his illusion of joy. He knew he dared not travel far from Margaret, not and keep this strange new peace he had submitted to. Now he closed his mind to what had happened and pinned it ahead to Margaret. She would be asleep; he would gently waken her, thrust a lighted cigarette in her sleepy mouth; she would open her eyes wide, glad to be awake, glad of him, glad (eternally glad she was, grateful for such simple things) that they had "each other," her consciousness returning like some joyous gift she had forgotten—and he would talk, endlessly perhaps, through the dawn, into the next morning if need be; he would never let go of her, sitting in her rumpled nightgown with her tipsy cigarette, until she had eased the terror in his vitals (that anyone was hungry, that anyone fainted in his sight from hunger, was a personal, a damnable reproachful fact), until they had given each other strength and more strength, separately, together, until they were the strongest two people in the world.

His own street frightened and reproached him, empty and baleful in the early morning light; one beggar drunk or sleeping on the curb, the lamps ironically glowing over his head; Mrs. Salvemini's window dark and gaping, the curtains blowing, shrinking, in. He took the stairs in a frightened leap, and his heart pounded until he stood quietly by the side of the bed where Margaret lay sleeping, her face gray and beautiful in the cold dawn, her hand curled on the empty pillow beside her own.

His peace, his warmth, his only chance for happiness lay waiting. But still he stood there looking down, his bones growing dry, his heart contracting. That was death! that was surrender! cried the part of himself that to this day held out against pillows. Save me! cried the little boy who turned from love as Uncle Daniel turned from drink; save me from plunging like a coward into that warm oblivion. Margaret lay waiting; his bed lay waiting. It was too easy. It brought back the Magazine to be baptized in champagne, the world struggle fought in dinner jackets. He drew back sternly.

Womb versus world, he thought, silently removing his shoes, his clothes, in dread of waking her. For Margaret, women in general, lived in their wombs; put their womb before their wits; all things grist to their wombs, all the time drawing their men to those rapacious female caverns, striving to make them forget the world, their rival.

A part of him wanted to go and fling down at Margaret's side, crying that he wronged her, crying that he had come from the world outside and nothing there was palatable, that nothing was worthwhile but that they two hide and hide in ever smaller corners until at last they had hidden themselves from any onslaught from the world; then they could creep beaten but unashamed into each other's arms and curl still smaller until at last they would be utterly, shamefully safe, for there would be nothing left to breathe but each other's flesh. For a passing second he felt nothing for her but tenderness and compassion, as though she were a day-old kitten curled for comfort, that would never dare open its eyes and see the world. A man could devote his life to shielding such a kitten, to guiding it down safe paths to safe bowls of milk, and in doing so could forget perhaps his tortured longing to be of meaning to the world, to work out by giving his life the sentence of endless guilt pronounced in childhood. No, no! he cried to himself, and it was as if his Uncle Daniel stood above him, exacting promises again. Margaret, he thought in a flash of insight, has wisdom, more than I; but she has the intelligence only of a homing bird.

He climbed unwillingly into the bed beside her. She stirred like a faithful watch-dog ever on her guard; he knew that he could wake her easily. But he lay with his head (on the pillow, his childhood's symbol of unmanliness) turned from her and closed his eyes to shut her out. For if he let her wake, if he acknowledged her, she might reach and touch him, might soothe and lull him, might carry him back to that shameful world-obliterating peace. Her end was peace and his was truth and they must be enemies (he discovered it again as a fact he would never in future ignore) as their ends were enemies. They could not both win. In the bottom of her soul

Margaret wished him to lay aside his restlessness and his fine nervous seeking (though they might be the very things she loved him for) and in exchange she offered him oblivion, an entirely personal world of vegetables; in which only a vegetable could endure. She wanted him to surrender.

Like his aunts, he thought, she wanted to frame him, to shame him. Afterward she would in her soul despise him, she would have crushed out the man in him and subdued him to merely the father of her child. Outwardly he would seem then more of a man; he could bow and smirk in public; he would be gallant, flying to pick up her handkerchief—he would be the puppet of a man and she could pull his strings, dangle him this way and that. Inside he would be nothing. And she, having narrowed their world, having furnished it with a baby's crib, flooded it with soothing syrup, would sit back satisfied.

The larger fight went on without her. Being a woman she was capable, he thought, of only a personal revolution, a sex revolution, having its boundaries in her own air-tight world. She offered him a sop, a compromise; permitted him to play with Magazines and politics; and stayed herself plotting at home, preparing a downy cage to catch him in. So he had stepped out, tonight, without her, into that larger world, gone with his faith and his eagerness; and found it lacking, found his friends scarcely nearer than she to the reality of one empty stomach that had sent them all reeling home to defeat. And here he was, on the brink even now, with her female body curved so close to him, of seeking consolation (he thought with horror of Jeffrey), of hiding in a woman's insides from a world he couldn't face.

A world where friends did not trust friends (but it was a sinking ship, the ship that the intellectuals were afloat in, and perhaps it must be a case of each man for himself?) The terrible compromises, the endless postponements . . . his mind went over irresistibly into the rutted treadmill of the evening's happenings. It struck him with full force for the first time that all their arguments were loaded; they were engaged in continually proving to themselves that activity was futile. And the evening, the constant meetings, the Magazine itself . . . were they not all of them rationalization, an elaborate plan on his part and his friends' (the old triumvirate! he bitterly thought) for postponement of some stand? For clearly if they felt a common cause (like the Sheep who knew what it was to go hungry) they would sink their differences and act in common. He saw them suddenly, coming together less from their belief in revolution (did any of them really believe a revolution would take place?) than from some terrible inner need in each of them to lay out his own personal conflicts in terms of something higher, to solve his private ends camouflaged as world-problems, secretively in public. Had Bruno or Jeffrey or himself listened to each other, except in a desperate sort of way, for reassurance, for purpose of identification with some other human, some stick on which to pin a banner? The Black Sheep came the nearest to his notion of what revolutionists should be; but he thought with distaste of their taciturnity, of their coldness, their matter-of-factness . . . Miles was looking for something higher (higher even than Bruno's search for what he called "integrity"), something that would sweep him, lift him, as nothing had done since the look on his Uncle Daniel's face when he killed his own dog without flinching: some faith, some belief that enabled men to act sharp and decisive and know the reason why.

And he himself, Miles Flinders? He loathed his daily job; he kept his job. He talked bitterly of what he hated, righteously of what he favored; and bought his tobacco of a communist. He condemned Bruno, condemned Jeffrey, couldn't swallow the hard materialism of the young Black Sheep; and threw up smoke-screens between himself and himself so that he could never come to action. He longed with all his heart for Mr. Pidgeon to fire him so that he might be prodded to life again against the jutting rocks of reality like the stones in his childhood's earth. Let the world struggle be brought to his door, injected in his veins; let him come to grips with that struggle, let the struggle be his own. Let there be but two sides, without this intellectual's no-man's-land in between, let him believe in one side or the other as he had once believed in God (as the youthful triumvirate had believed in pacifism), let him fight for it, live for it, die for it, with all his Uncle Daniel's strength. . . .

The pillow was unbearable beneath his head. He remembered Margaret's cry, in the early days of their marriage: *I'm going to make you so happy, Miles, I'm going to teach you to sleep with pillows, we're going to be so happy darling.* Happy! his Uncle Daniel always said his *pigs* were happy. And now she planned to soften him further, melt him down further, provide him with the irrelevance of a child. Ignore the lumps in the mattress, lay a pillow over them; ignore the world and bring forth a child to hide it further from their consciousness. The world at which she never looked, a world where people starved, where friends did not trust friends, where nobody believed in anything—into such a world she would dare to bring a child: to satisfy her inner physical needs; to compromise; to veil; she would bend and stoop and take what was not the real thing and feed it and nourish it and take it to bed with her and never know (with her blind passion for peaceful ignorance, for living what she called a personal life), that it was not the real thing, that she had brought forth a counterfeit planted in filth, to grow stunted and unwholesome in the tainted air. The pillow underneath his head was hot and soft, a bribe, a snare, reeking of the feminine . . .

He turned from Margaret, from her generous warmth (her body stirred lightly as though even in sleep she was conscious of him); and felt again the fervor, the high hope, with which, a frightened, stoic child, he had locked away his pillow in the closet. More joy in those early nights of unaccustomed hardness than in a thousand pillows, more valid peace than in a thousand women's arms. He moved away further, and her arm followed him out; he slid away until his head, leading the way back to loneliness and courage, to the endless search for God, had left the pillow quite behind, till it hung like a severed fruit upon the edge.

II.

Bruno and Emmett

"COME on," said Bruno sternly; "one for mama, one for the Dickie-bird, and one for mama's psainted psychoanalyst." He took the bottle from his own lips and held it to Emmett's, tipping it so the whiskey ran like tears down the boy's white cheeks. Emmett gasped and choked, spluttered like a helpless baby. In a pair of Bruno's large pyjamas he looked about five years old and faintly girlish. "Are you tight yet?" said Bruno grimly.

"Not m-me," said Emmett, wavering proudly. "I guess I inherit a cap-p-pacity from my . . ."

"All right, keep going. One for Commissar Jeffrey. One for the Reverend Miles" (the memory of Miles' stricken face was something, like Cornelia, which Bruno wanted blotted out), "one for Uncle Bruno, the tiredest radical of them all. And one for poor Miss Diamond." He raised the bottle and saw that it held just one more swallow. "And one to bigger and better opiates;" he forced the last drop between Emmett's laughing lips and crashed the empty bottle against the filing cabinet: which remained blind and impervious, and though shattered a little, though ringing metallic and insulted, righted itself at once and went on doing its duty. He remembered its duenna, the patient Mr. Harrison; and remembered how though he had denied to Mr. Harrison almost the existence of filing cabinets, Mr.

Harrison (because the cabinet was his living) had gone on quietly unwrapping it; just as Cornelia, to whom he had carefully expounded the non-validity of hunger, had quietly and insolently fainted from it.

Emmett shook with laughter as though someone had blasphemed in church. "If he *is* my f-f-father," he stuttered with a kind of lewd irreverence, and shivered like a dissipated baby.

The boy filled him with loathing and pity and a keen sense of his own depravity. He didn't know what urge (conquering repulsion, conquering a half-wish to be alone), had let him answer Emmett's cry and bring him home. His mind leaped forward to Elizabeth. But he discovered himself, now that so few hours remained to their meeting, totally unprepared for it; a bridegroom who had rehearsed, who had dressed himself, who had got ready too far in advance—so that when the hour was at hand and his mind, like his tie, impeccably in place, some extraneous event served to shatter his composure. Take Emmett home? when Elizabeth was coming? Preposterous! but why not, he thought the next moment, in defeated relief, in drugged tranquillity. The symphony he thought he heard had died; Elizabeth had been a part of it—when he thought of her now he thought of her as he did of himself and his old triumvirate, as static, as ironic ghosts, as dead beyond recall. Why not? he thought (glancing with a pang at the room he had with childish pleasure got ready for Elizabeth; the flowers shaking in a vase; her own brand of cigarettes scattered liberally to make her feel at home; even the piano, long unused, was open for her)—why not? and with an unhappy knowledge that he took Emmett not so much from pity as for his own protection he put his arm around him, and loathed the boy and loathed himself.

"Drunk yet?" he said. He wanted the last vestige of anything human wiped from Emmett's face as he wanted the last concern for Elizabeth violently removed from himself. He wanted to see Emmett weak and helpless, he wanted to destroy him for the reflection of his own despair.

The smile was frozen on Emmett's lips but suddenly his eyes grew wide and frightened again, he shrank away in Bruno's large pyjamas. "Bruno . . . I can't forget . . . Cornelia . . ." He buried his head pitiably in his arms and sobbed again.

"None of that now," said Bruno abruptly, rose and found another bottle. "You're slipping up. Remember you're not supposed to be human, you're an intellectual. Humor is the intellectual's favorite opiate and rationalization is his strongest virtue—an old slogan, my boy, from the early Roman days. Pour it down, Emmett. Good ole whiskey. Prove that Al's your father." He drew the boy's shoulder against his and held the bottle for him.

Emmett swallowed obediently, sank back mollified with his head against Bruno. "So terrible," he murmured sleepily; "hungry—in my own house, I've never been hungry, but I felt it, I felt so funny in my insides, Bruno. Bruno, you know what it felt like? It felt to me like loneliness, like the way I used to feel when I f-f-found myself away from home; and l-l-lots of times when I was in it. Bruno, do you think hunger could feel anything like l-loneliness? is that silly, Bruno? . . ."

His head lay so helpless on Bruno's shoulder; so easy to reach out a hand and gently stroke it. Bruno's hand shrank back as though identification with Emmett meant identification with final defeat. He took a drink himself (of Elizabeth's welcome home bottle, of a mellow Bourbon that he knew she loved) and watched with disgust a few drops fall on Emmett's head; his hair was childishly thin and soft, the scalp shone through vulnerable and fair like a baby's; the drops of whiskey glistened.

"Can't be compared, Emmett," he said. "Hunger is a crude thing any fool can feel; loneliness is subtle, refined, complicated pain—only a sensitive, well-bred palate can feel it. . . . Good God, Emmett, what's upsetting you? Can't you take an object lesson?" He loathed himself. "Take another drink, Emmett," he said roughly.

"Must I?" Emmett stirred, his lashes fitfully fluttered. He drank again, wiped his mouth with the back of his hand, and settled more heavily on Bruno's shoulder. "But Bruno—" his voice came troubled, reminding Bruno of Elizabeth so many years ago, asking him to bound eternity. "Bruno, if hunger doesn't really count . . . what *is* the object of the game? I mean . . ." He paused, unhappy; frightened as Bruno was, at what he said.

"I really do not know." Bruno let his words fall coldly like clots of earth against a coffin. He was filled with unholy satisfaction. "When the intellectual gets intellectual *enough,* my boy . . . *is* there an object? *is* there a Magazine? *is* there such a thing as hunger?" The boy was quivering. *Is* there, Bruno asked himself, myself? Elizabeth? is there anything? he thought and looked about a once-familiar room, doubting suddenly its existence and half-expecting the walls to fall in, the piano to fade . . . "Scepticism," he said comfortingly to the top of Emmett's head, "is the vile retreat of the weak stomach; the intellectual steals a peep at reality and can't take it . . . so he begins to question its existence."

Emmett was trembling. "Why did you m-m-make me get drunk, Bruno? Why did you, Bruno? I feel so sick, I want to die. . . ." Again his child's accusing voice reminded Bruno of Elizabeth. His head was so close, so vulnerable; as easy to crush, as to caress it. . . . Murder, he thought, must be a cowardly projection of the will to suicide. He put out his hand and rested it gently on Emmett's head. Beneath his fingers he felt the vulnerable sliding scalp, so like a baby's, so like a girl's.

"Better?" he said, and was surprised to hear his voice as gentle as a mother's. "You want to sleep," he said tenderly, "you don't want to die." You don't need to die, he thought; you are dead, we all are. If we were a jot less cynical, if we believed a jot more in life, we'd kill ourselves, he thought. But since we aren't alive, we have no need to die. We're shades. We don't matter anywhere. We don't even produce waste, like Emmett's father. "Sleepy-kid," he said, "say the word and I'll put you to bed."

"Why do we bother then," said Emmett sleepily. "Why do we bother with anything, if nothing makes any difference, Bruno? I mean, why do we start Magazines and r-r-revolutions and things. . . ." His voice was the voice of Elizabeth asking for more about the Three Bears.

"Oh we don't really, we just pretend to," said Bruno lightly. "There are no Magazines, there are no revolutions," he said as though he explained away the fear of lightning from a child. "From the early Normans," he added soothingly; "and now it's time for growing boys to get their sleep." He struggled to rise, but Emmett, laughing sheepishly, clasped both his arms about his neck.

"Don't *want* to go to bed," he said petulantly. "Want

to stay up all n-n-night and talk with the grown-ups. *Won't* go to bed," he said with sly impudence; "can't make me," he said, growing bolder. His mouth was weak with liquor, strong with some half-felt sense of his own power over Bruno.

They struggled lightly. Bruno rose, and the boy rose clinging to him. "Here, here, this is disrespectful, you damn baby," Bruno feebly said. Emmett tightened his hold; drops of perspiration stood on his broad baby's brow. "Let go, you young idiot," Bruno muttered; but the arms were comforting. "Won't, won't," the boy crowed; "car-ry me, carry me, Bruno," he said in a triumphant nursery sing-song. "We'll get this over with," said Bruno grimly. He lifted the boy roughly, his hands on his fine vulnerable ribs, and felt his body like a frail triumphant leech against him. He swung him round, Emmett's bare foot caught the whiskey bottle and he laughed with his head close to Bruno's as Elizabeth's home-coming drink formed a rapid pool on the middle of the floor.

In a swell of repugnance he carried him and deposited him in the bed he had meant for Elizabeth. He laid him down, settled his lolling head against the pillow. Emmett lay back smiling like a cat. As though he knew himself instinctively for a usurper. "Goodnight, goodnight," said Bruno briefly. But Emmett's hand shot out and clung to his.

"Don't go, don't leave me, Bruno," he pleaded, his mouth still curved in that triumphant baby-smile.

"I've got to get some sleep, I've got a boat to meet to-morrow," said Bruno cruelly.

Emmett gripped his hand; the smile ran off his face, his eyes grew large with terror. "You b-b-brought me here," he almost sobbed, "you made me drunk . . . now you want to desert me, like my mother and f-f-father, like everybody. . . . I'm dead when I'm alone, when I'm not with you," he sobbed, "I'm as good as dead, and you're going to meet a boat, you're going to desert me too. . . ."

"Nonsense." The suddenness, the sureness, of his own voice startled him. Whatever it was in men, he thought, that drew them toward each other rather than sent them posturing after women, was in him irresistibly now. The root of the thing lay in fear, in defeat. Before a woman one must wish to be a man, to be strong, to strut, to maintain some permanent impregnable masculine dignity in the very act of melting. With a fellow-man, a fellow-frightened-man, one was reduced without shame to a common denominator. Beaten, he was not fit for Elizabeth. He had run the gamut of indifferent women and couldn't face the highest. It was another thing with Emmett; Emmett was beaten at the start, before the line-up, the only woman he would ever see was Merle, his own forbidden mother. "Nonsense, you're drunk, I'm not deserting you," he said crisply, and felt the feverish grateful pressure of Emmett's hand. "I won't leave you till you've fallen asleep," he said, and drew a chair beside the bed.

False dawn entered at the window and Emmett with his hand still clasping Bruno's, fell asleep. The first milk-wagons rattled archaically up the street and still when Bruno tried to free himself, Emmett held on tighter to his hand. He was touched and indifferent in separate layers of his mind and he sat on thinking of the futility of Elizabeth's morning home-coming, of the impossibility of conjuring her up in three dimensions. From the distant river came the wakening cries of boats. Elizabeth, he thought, signalling vainly across the small stretch of ocean that lay between them now, through the blanket of impenetrable personal fog. Emmett lay sleeping in Elizabeth's bed, his head triumphant on Elizabeth's pillow. He tried again unclasping the lax sleeping fingers; but Emmett's hands awoke in fright, gripped his like a convulsive little child's. Bruno gave in; despite himself there was comfort, as if in love of any sort there was something which he had to have. He drew his chair softly close to the bed and bowed his head till it lay on the pillow beside Emmett's and the boy's fluttering whiskey breath blew ironic solace on his cheek.

12.

Under Comrade Lenin's Eye

HE lay beside Comrade Fisher (Merle Middleton's perfume still lingering, although forbidden, in his nostrils) and drew comfort from her dry, authentic voice. On the steps of the Middleton house he had paused, uncertain, watching his friends go off with scarcely a word to him, as though—incomprehensibly—they blamed him for the thing that had broken up their meeting. Restlessness seized him, a bewildering suspicion that nothing that he touched was real; he felt briefly a victim, alone and scared, a political lone wolf. But he could not go home with his bewilderment to Norah; he was not ready for Norah, he was at the middle of his cycle, outward bound, away from her—the charm of lazy fidelity was a luxury he seldom dared permit himself. And so, his own hands jumping, pulsing, fluttering in his pockets, fantastic strangers to himself, he had thought of Merle and thought of Norah; and come, because it seemed more fitting, direct to Comrade Fisher.

He knew that although she was ugly, although her body was all scraps and joints and angles, he must find her beautiful, he must love her; because she had been in jail; she had been in Russia; because she had loved two revolutionists and their blood must pass through her to him. He could feel the spirit of his predecessors throbbing in her temples, entering his nervous finger-tips and flowing secretly to his head and heart. He lay lightly touching her, listening to her voice; and memorized the details of her bare and pitiful room, the only decorations posters—and the newspaper photograph of Lenin (like a picture of a young girl's father) sitting dynamic and patient behind his desk, waiting, it would seem, for Comrade Fisher to interpret him, or for a second coming.

He had come prepared to talk about Cornelia, to describe the strange feeling of utter incredulity he had had (and still had) when without a word of warning Cornelia slipped to the floor and ended their discussion. He supposed that he ought to feel (as Miles had looked) as though he wakened from a dream and saw reality; but he felt the opposite; he felt that he had been living eagerly all evening (in the center, at the pivot) and then was forced to witness melodrama. Yet it must have *been* real; he had seen Norah rushing up; mechanically he himself had opened windows—and felt that he was taking part in theater. Now his head was spinning, his hands trembling. "I love your hands," said Comrade Fisher. (Merle Middleton had called them sensuous.) They stilled with pleasure. "I put the party idea across," he said—and feeling quieted refrained from telling her about Cornelia. "Of course, our difficulties are the Black Sheep—as orthodox, as hide-bound, little religious fanatics, as you describe the average communists." And yet he was taken again (it was so clear his old triumvirate looked down upon him, didn't altogether trust his strategies) with the longing to announce his machinations to the world, to wear some badge across his chest, to hold innocent and quiet hands to the accusing public (to sit for hours on end, watching Norah sew or knit or cook for him)—to be one thing or the other; he remembered Bruno's disconcerting "neither fish nor flesh nor good red herring, just lousy intellectuals." Was that the matter with him? Was that why he, who could weep at a book, weep at sight of the Hudson River unexpectedly blue at the end of a street, had felt nothing but incredulity for Cornelia? He raised himself on his elbow, looked Lenin eye-to-eye where Lenin went on writing in his photograph over Comrade Fisher's bed. "I'd like to join the party, Comrade," he resolutely said. To belong somewhere, he meant.

Comrade Fisher sighed. "I've told you, Jeffrey, over and over again. The time isn't ripe. Boring from within . . . I've told you." He let himself be soothed. Both Comrade Fisher's words and the picture of Lenin (a dead man, after all, a photograph, all his accomplishments behind him) rested him, comforted him. "I love your hands," said Comrade Fisher, and lay stretched in her strange kind of agonized silence beneath the head of Comrade Lenin; "the hands of a future revolutionary, a leader . . . whether the *party* knows it or not," she said contemptuously. But he wished they could rest, those hands of his, he wished their complicated secrets didn't itch so painfully in their bewildered palms. He felt that if he carried more secrets in his hands, more tactical plots in his brain, he would burst. "I know," said Comrade Fisher definitely; "because I've known the leaders." He looked into her eyes and saw the memories of many lovers, famous revolutionary leaders; himself the latest. He kissed her passionately.

This then was real, a woman's arms around him, early

morning blowing in the window, the day ahead, the sun in the sky, Norah at home with breakfast waiting for him. Real too, when he beheld himself rebuilt in a new woman's eyes. "Tell me again, Comrade," he murmured, and pillowed her head on his shoulder, "tell me again about Comrade Turner, how you sat up all night with him in jail, waited for the strike to break. . . ."

He lay and listened peacefully to the revolutionary bed-time story, his hands at rest on her head as though her story, her former loves, the spirit of Comrade Turner, the spirit of the strike itself, passed through her and into his fingers and strongly fed him. The experience became his. He was Comrade Turner lying with Comrade Fisher in his arms and planning the tactics of the strike. He was the raw-boned mill-worker who led the strike. He was the many mill-hands singing the International. He was the successful lover of Merle Middleton, the messiah to his friends. He was the personal medium for the strike, the interpreter of Lenin, the battlefield for revolution. He was the strike. He was the revolution. His blood rose; his fingers grew tense as claws; gratitude toward Comrade Fisher overwhelmed him like love. He threw off the hot counterpane and made love to Comrade Fisher, Comrade Turner's Comrade Fisher, under Comrade Lenin's sightless eyes.

13.

Hello America, I'm Home!

A ROUND brown cylinder of sound snorted out of the funnel, gave way to billows of smoke which darkened the sky; smaller cries echoed from the smaller fry all over the bay, fretful shrieks of ferries, one deep groan from a lumber barge; Elizabeth's great home-coming ship let out another roar of pain and submitted, gigantic tamed beast, to being led by the nose by a score of anxious little tugs. Elizabeth stood pressed against the deck-rail. The sea-gulls hovered, shouted overhead; the worried little pygmy-passengers scrambled like the sea-gulls' shadows on the deck. She saw how her great ship moved reluctantly toward its harbor; the nervous little tugs manoeuvred briskly, straining and pulling on their incredible leashes. The ship bungled, fumbled; pointed its blunt nose obscenely toward the arm of the enormous slip. There was a moment of drifting with the Hudson tide; when the passengers wondered if they must put out to sea again; and then the ship was beaten, pinned; little men armed with fluttering sheets of paper sprang nimbly, exultantly, over cables as large as their legs.

She saw him at last. There was his face again, Bruno's face, among the faces of the strangers swimming on the pier. Bruno's face, a family face, an inside face, so vibratingly near and dear that it was almost unfamiliar, so that she felt a rush of embarrassed blood beat in her temples, like terrible stage-fright, as if what they were doing there should have been done behind a bolted door. It seemed to her infinitely pathetic that he should have dared to bring so vulnerable a thing as his face down here, before the public gaze, to greet her. She was afraid for his face; it was so real, alongside the indifferent stranger faces, so blurred, so soft, how had he dared to bring it here, how could it exist, how could it hold its own in a world of faces belonging to people not related to him. It was so courageous and yet so frightened, she wanted his arms to wash around her and send them both back to the long childhood days, to purge her of the last taste of Denny and the fast-express; she wanted to melt into him and tell him that she knew forcefully that they were of one family and the same blood, that never again would she hurt his softness, his blurriness, his peculiar caustic tenderness. That he stood there patient on the pier seemed to her the bravest thing she had ever seen.

He moved nearer the edge of the wharf and his eyes were patiently searching for her. They skimmed her twice as though they were evading her; and suddenly, sliding along the deck-rail, they acknowledged her. She experienced a distinct physical shock; she was paralyzed, blood rushing down from her head and settling in legs grown numb and painful; for a tremendous second neither of them moved. Then their arms shot up in the family salute, straight and grave, from the temple out into the air with open palm, the same thing always used for greeting or farewell. Scarcely smiling he gave a series of stiff little confirming nods as much as to say ah there you are, so you are back are you, well hello. She ducked her head as though assenting. Slowly across the chasm they smiled their old familiar smile. A terrible joy burst open in her, a spasm of excitement too painful to be borne; her pulses pounded, the blood leaped back, as if it were the moment before her marriage, the one still moment left her before their raised hands would be joined. In embarrassment she lowered her shining eyes, her hand fell back on the rail. She leaned over and looked down the sheer shining side of the ship sliding steep to the moat of black water that still lay between them. The boat-side and the side of the pier made a tunnel. She could feel the weight of her head and shoulders suddenly over-balancing gravitation, she could feel her body hurtling down the deep black well; in passing she had time to witness Bruno's face asking her to stop it please, to come on back, to cut the melodrama—and she gave him a fleet wry smile in return; then as she would strike the water a surge of terror came and shook her so that she stepped back violently from the rail and stood clutching the suitcase and shaking, examining Bruno's face for signs of his grief and fear.

There was a quick and violent silence, the boat was wedded to the harbor. The gang-plank went out gravely.

The gang-plank is a thing that lends every man a moment's dignity, a second's distinction, as he moves slowly and majestically, passing from a super-world, pauses at the end in doubt as though he might turn back, and steps down giving up his chance irrevocably. Each as he takes the first step feels himself alone and responsible, deeply grave and joyous, as though he ushered in a personal New Year.

Elizabeth could feel her two suit-cases flanking her as importantly as bridesmaids by her side, as she modestly, with this strange sense of her own value, took the first steps. She stood straight, she walked proudly; she would never for the rest of her life huddle or shrink, she could conduct herself always with this sense of her own importance that she found on the gang-plank, marching austerely home to Bruno. He was waiting; now he revolved embarrassed through the crowd; and waited again, for her to come the rest. Down, down, she came; soft music playing; marching to the rhythm of her own calm modest senses. Her foot shrank from the commonplaceness of the dock; she stopped dead for the fraction of a second while her senses whirled, while nausea circled; stopped dead as she had on the landing twenty years ago and saw Bruno standing in his first long pants again, a mile between them, distance lined with strangers —*don't you know your cousin* BRUNO, *you funny, funny girl*—he came a step toward her apologetically, and then she saw that he had brought *the Davidson boy* again to guard him from her, she saw the prep-school stranger moving like a shadow by his side, a thin triumphant smile upon his face; she hurried forward sarcastically.

They stood together, Bruno and Elizabeth, smiling the same embarrassed smile; the strange lad lined with Bruno. Then they shook hands, vigorously, sarcastically, like visiting mayors at a baseball game. "Well fancy meeting you here," he said as their hands suddenly withdrew and their smiles grew sharp. "This *is* a surprise," she said lightly, brightly, harsh and false. "Meet Emmett Middleton, meet my kid cousin Emmett, doesn't she look like a baby lamb?" he said as he whacked her on the shoulder. *O Bruno for God's sake, I've come all this way, I've come all these years, I've come all my life,* she did not say, as she coldly pumped the hand of the stranger boy; *we're scared till the blood in our veins runs thin, oh Bruno, Bruno, come bravely through the fog,* she did not cry as she said instead, "You can't fool me, it's *the Davidson boy* grown up."

"Cold for a landing isn't it," she said merrily, warily, smartly and tartly; "it's always cold when cousins meet," she said bitterly, brittley; "from an old Chinese adage," she added tardily, hardily, neatly and sweetly, snappy and dead; and met the strange boy's hostile eyes with answering hostility as Bruno bent to lift her bags, his head going down before them both, apologetic and abject.

THREE

The Party

PERHAPS, thought Arturo Teresca of Art Terry's Prosperity Boys, perhaps if he had really had the "stuff" his gift would have pushed itself someway to the fore, drowned his need to earn more money, killed the fear of poverty—and he would be today (instead of the leader of a party-band) what his promise of twenty years before had hinted. Yes; that must be it; he was a second-rater, born a second-rater, born a minor artist in the field he passionately loved. A one-symphony man, he reflected (jogging his knee at the party raging behind him, indifferently conducting the semi-classic they had asked for as an opening number); and remembered with bitter pride his "Symphony of the Seasons" composed while he was still at the Music Academy. But the Boys would play it shortly, play the Rearrangement he had made for his wife's last birthday. Poor Mary. She had married him with reservations, fearing a marital continuation of the poverty to which they both were born; accepted him with hope that he might prove a musical exception and manage to grow rich. He was a tremendous success, outshining her farthest hopes. And Mary had bloomed and blossomed, wore fur coats like a queen, bore him three fine fat sons every one of whom sang like Caruso and roved the streets like petty gangsters—and never knew she was married to that greatest of all tragic figures, a frustrated artist. Arturo sighed and waved his head (a gesture caught from Toscanini) ; he stared somberly till he caught the eyes of all his band. "Anything the matter, maestro?" said the cellist from behind his smiling party-mask. Maestro! Arturo smiled his melancholy musician's smile; he was never certain whether the Boys were kidding him: the smile played safe. He jogged the well-known Prosperity knee and performed a minor Toscanini over his shoulder at the party.

For at ten o'clock (despite—as Merle was saying at the bottom of the stairs—all manner of confusion) March had raised a disapproving portière on Merle Middleton's Hunger March Party. For the first time in an honorable private life March was stationed at a door to *take in tickets;* to dig in the presence of company vulgarly into his pockets and bring forth change; to admit as guests persons obviously, even frankly, beneath his own gold standard. God knows what it did to his formal butler's soul; but it made no difference to his peculiar butler's stance which remained proud and indifferent by the portières like the monuments over a hero's grave. March resembled a Czarist Duke, a Hoover banker, a Wilsonian war-profiteer far more closely (so thought Al, pausing to salute a passing guest with a drumstick at his temple) than he resembled his step-brothers the ascetic or pugnacious, anaemic or bull-necked, Polish or hundredpercentAmerican Working Classes ranged ("I suppose because they couldn't come in person," Al explained to anyone who listened) in life-size banners all about the ballroom. Service was March's motto; loyalty his slogan; let them station him at a door to take in tickets, let them crown him with a crown of thorns: March would stick his belly out and vote republican, feed beggars at the backdoor and throw away the rag with which he wiped their crumbs; "and if the revolution came," said Al, "March would send it up the backstairs to wait while he announced it. Such is the kingdom of habit, Miss Powell honey," he said to the Daughter of the Confederacy selling drinks for the benefit of the Hunger Marchers, "and a fine old kingdom it is." He sighed, pointing his drumstick derisively at his heart. "Playing angel to a revolution, me, at my age. What *are* we coming to, Miss Powell honey."

"I thought," said Merle Middleton—light, charming, fluttering, at the bottom of the stairs—but significantly retaining Mrs. Stanhope's hand; "that at a party of this kind . . ." She pressed Mrs. Stanhope's hand intently, tested it as one might a barometer, tentative, deprecating (at the same time guiding her gently toward the ballroom to steal a look herself), not certain whether to line herself up on the side of her party or to go on condescending to it. For one never knew; one couldn't always judge ahead; what made a party smart or not smart depended so much on the unpredictable moods arising out of nowhere—and a party of one's own could be so cruel! "And Graham Hatcher is, well he is just *too* . . ." She lifted her shoulders crucified by ecstasy; but her eyes narrowed like a gauge, peering past March at the portières to the brilliant room beyond torn in many colors by the banners, by the incongruous garb of the early guests: her own friends correct and puzzled pushing in startled sequins or emphatic black-and-white through the motley ill-clothed younger set circling bar and buffet—or holding their heads decently to one side as they stared at the posters self-consciously, like cousins of the artist at his opening, forming no opinions because the critics, the Majority, had not arrived. "At a party of this kind," she clasped Mrs. Stanhope's hand, "just *one* Negro," she begged Mrs. Stanhope.

Mrs. Stanhope whinnied. "As many as you like, dear Merle. Wh-hy! don't be a fool Merle, you always think you're being a pioneer. It's been smart to have one Negro for over three years now. I must say your decorations are superb though—the banners—reminds me of the Stables on racing days." And Mrs. Stanhope who spent all of her life that mattered on the back of a horse, whinnied again and entered the room past March. . . .

As though March were a hitching-post and she had broken loose, thought Al, who faintly liked her. "Look, Miss Powell honey, Black Beauty has checked in; easy canter across the old corral—my God!" he groaned, "the old mare's headed our way. Will she make it, no she's licked, by God she's coming on." Mrs. Stanhope however, loped by them, shieing perhaps at his drumstick; peered down a bridle-path that wound among the clumps of guests and spied her side-kick Mr. Merriwell; and started for him at a conscientious trot. "Now that the rodeo is settled," Al sighed with relief, "how about shaking me up another glass of that altogether lousy charity punch—before your colored suitor makes his next advance?"

"What a stomach," said Miss Powell rolling a pair of unbelievable violet eyes framed in Junior League eyelashes that must, Al decided now admiringly, have started life on one of Mrs. Stanhope's thoroughbreds—and pocketed his quarter aimlessly.

"What a *heart,*" corrected Al piously. "Remembah our stahving boys, Miss Powell honey." He pointed to the banners behind the bar and crossed himself with the punchglass and the drumstick.

The buffet girls sneered classconsciously.

Merle scanned the room in haste, seeing (through March's injured eye) too many ill-dressed strangers; approved the laden buffet; looked in vain for Emmett (who surely ought to be here soon!) and located Graham Hatcher a little too stiff by the wall, his face a black pearl above impeccable evening dress, pausing (she observed with horror) directly beneath a banner in which Elizabeth Leonard had portrayed the evils of a colored chain-gang! God keep him, she prayed, from bearing down too often on Miss Bee Powell, Daughter of the Confederacy—but there was Al, bending solicitously above her naked back, who would too willingly serve as southern womanhood's protector. A wry little twist of pain inside her branched out into worry again about her party. Her friends were standing about the edges like a border of transplanted trees. If Jeffrey Blake would only come! She retreated, flinching, with an apologetic smile, past March's loyal pomp (she had not recovered from the hurt in March's eyes as with a dog-like questioning look at his mistress he had taken the colored gentleman's ticket, suffering him to pass in with the rest), and resumed her post at the bottom of the stairs.

The music quivered shyly. Bunched in a corner of the room it could command or be commanded by the party. But Arturo Teresca, thinking of his wasted life, deliberately pulled his shots. He knew that music should not talk without demanding answer; he could not bear to make music that would stand around the room ignored like decorations; and so he reserved his strength and muffled his sound and held the Boys in check—only remembering to jog the Prosperity knee every ten bars or so. He could feel the guests behind his back, their numbers growing, swimming without knowing it in harmony with his tentative rhythm; puzzled, unsettled, as he was.

A segment of the Hunger Marchers strained in menacing red paint along the wall behind the Brobdignagian refectory table, too well-bred to creak beneath its weight of six whole Virginia hams, two sliced turkeys, six platters of devilled eggs, sturgeon and salmon, a tray designed in canapés of caviar, cheese and anchovies, bowls of olives (the Hunger Marchers lifted angry feet above the plate of celery lined with cheese), and so on up to where ferns eked out the scantier fare of sweets and nuts and paper napkins, the fragile climax of the table as the tottering white-pastry Capitol was the fragile climax of the banner just above. Behind the buffet two thin young girls dressed alike in red turtle-neck sweaters popped olives into their mouths contemptuously and glanced with hatred at the bar and the Daughter of the Confederacy. Their own business was to slice ham and put paper napkins on plates for the eaters; but the eaters, beside being quantitatively more feminine than the drinkers, were perfectly able to slice ham for themselves and perfectly ready to do without paper napkins.

"I thought Blake said," began the first one, "I thought *you* said *Blake* said, that we were absolutely to have the bar."

"He did, I did," her twin snapped back, "but after all it's lady Middleton that runs the show and what does she care for a promise? a typical, bourgeois, snobbish trick."

"Anyway Fish," said the double conciliatingly, "the blond will make more money than we ever could at the bar."

"Speak for yourself, Lydia," said Comrade Fisher witheringly.

"All right, it's hotter than hell," said Lydia obediently.

The early guests continued to be shy—this party had no definite precedent somehow—and so they wandered, looking for signatures so to speak, harking for familiar signals; wondering if the Ballisters would deign to come; if Mrs. Fancher on the other hand would dare—and how did one treat Emily Fancher these days anyway, as a grass widow or *what?* and Hatcher, Graham Hatcher, what had Merle said he was? in musical comedy perhaps? Some of them passed in slow approving judgment before the hams and paper napkins, picked over the nuts dispassionately (it was too early to take eating seriously) and glanced in polite consternation at the angry turtle-necks behind the table. At about the tray of sturgeon each eye brightened, quickened, each owner moved with more composure, doing double-time to the still slow-motion of the music with which Arturo appeased his artistic conscience; past the rickety baby rescued by the Hunger Marchers, past the platters of celery stuffed with cheese, past the tottering Capitol and on firmly toward the brave familiar note, the happy combination which made a party a party and life a respectable repetition: the bar, a Daughter of the Confederacy, a large Wedgwood bowl for coins. Society, Liquor, the Poor: faith, hope and charity revived; the guests began to recognize the party. There seemed no reason why the Ballisters should *not* come.

Up with wraps and down with gleaming shoulders, with solid stiff white shirt-fronts; here and there a costume odd and dated, designed in all humility for modest daytime wear—the obscure proud owners dodging Merle as though she were hostess in a restaurant! For her house was like a theater tonight, anyone could come for the price of a ticket, her home was public, her hospitality for sale. (And her own son! Emmett, where was Emmett? what were they doing with her boy?) Merle had searched her wardrobe for a fitting dress; and been driven to buy one, a strange thing neither in the mode nor out of it, Greek in its simplicity but distinctly French in the details. (A Rabelaisian puritan, Vammie had said, bowing before her beauty; taking back with the left hand what the right hand giveth, Al had said in his crude crass way—but of course Al was terribly jealous of the little Doctor.) "My dear, so *glad* to see you, yes isn't it unique, no not my idea entirely, my young friend's, Jeffrey Blake the novelist—oh yes, I *invited* Emily Fancher but whether she will *come,* well Mr. Crawford, well well, you'll find Al somewhere about if you're lucky, ah Marion, ah Laura, now don't be *too* startled, I did think *one* Negro . . ." "We can take it," snickered Laura Titcomb vulgarly, "if *you* can." "A bit of local colah eh," said Mr. Crawford who fell short of being an English lord only by birth and a monocle; "oh jolly, jolly, jolly;" and passed on as best he could under the double handicap to March's more competent guidance. Vammie floated up like a straw in a wintry sea and Merle gratefully took his arm; stood watching the backs of her friends floating toward her party to make or break it, and thanked God for March standing like an old and faithful habit by the curtains.

And jolly, jolly, jolly, continued Mr. Crawford rapping with his knuckles on the sloping forehead of March's belly. "Quite a circus in the old homestead tonight," said Mr. Crawford handing over his ticket good-naturedly. March bared his teeth. "Quaite a circus," Mr. Crawford improved on his accent and March slipped his teeth back into his head again and raised the velvet portière in the rôle of a Christian ushering fellow-Christians to the lions' den.

"Well pretty jolly, pretty jolly, pretty jolly, Middleton," said Crawford advancing like a good fellow, a prince of a good fellow, a jolly old egg, good old bean. "All the er banners and pretty jolly the music and what not, the wife's notion, eh Middleton, and what ayah you doing with that tuhkeystick, a bit under ayah you, Middleton, ah jolly jolly jolly." "What ayah you doing here, Crawford," said Al sternly brandishing the drumstick, "why aren't you battering at our Capitol side by side with our . . . the least you can do, my good fellow, is ruin your stomach for charity." "But whose benefit," began Mr. Crawford puzzled. "For mine, I'm trying to make the girl that makes the punch." And jolly jolly jolly, Mr. Crawford continued, first to space left by Al Middleton and then to the astonished glass of punch in his own hand and at last less vaguely to his pinochle chum

Bud Chapman who was under the distinct impression that the Negro was a part of the entertainment which had got in too early by mistake or else was an Abyssinian prince; and both of them reckoned that their old third, Jim Fancher, wasn't doing much in the way of pinochle *now* . . . more likely solitaire!

"Are you masquerading as laryngitis, my good girls, or is it just the latest craze for teasing bulls?" Al Middleton leered down above the buffet girls, foreshortening his creased lean face till it resembled a gargoyle sardonically adorned with gold-capped teeth. "Thought you gals were communists?"

"Sympathizers," they answered in their quick defensive chorus.

"Ah sisters." He surveyed them sorrowfully. "What kind of sympathizers do you call yourselves! why aren't you down there in Washington D.C., marching, starving—sleeping, with our boys." He leered through his gold-capped teeth and tapped Fisher on the head with his drumstick; "heh heh heh" he said wearily and passed down the table from them, firmly wavering toward the bar.

"Oh!" breathed Lydia, swallowing her giggle and drawing indignation from her comrade.

"Oh!" breathed Ruthie Fisher in genuine disgust; and felt forlorn, abandoned, as though Jeffrey had exposed her, left her out somewhere, a prey to anybody.

Arturo was giving the Boys a rest and looking over the growing crowd approvingly. Pretty fine folks, he thought, at this house. He took a drink from the bottle the host had brought up for the band and swallowed reflectively. The drink was mellowing. The crowd was beautiful. Arturo began to feel pleasantly sorry for himself. It might be that he had indeed that divine gift his teachers had spoken of back in the Music Academy days; it might be that he had never got the breaks. Married too young, for one thing (Mary was a ripe, rich-blooded girl and eighteen none too soon for her) ; the kids came right away; living costs plenty—was it his fault altogether that he had turned his back on creative music and earned his way as the leader of a little party band? Arturo sipped steadily. He didn't join in the talk of the Boys who liked parties and used these intermissions for spotting the beauties. "Nifty crowd," said Frankie Teener, tightening the pegs on his instrument. Arturo smiled sadly and tossed his head for the Boys with Toscanini's borrowed gesture.

"But I do not," Mr. Hatcher was saying unhappily, "represent anything in particular, Miss Titcomb; at least as I am here tonight; perhaps you have confused me with someone else. . . ." "Ah *that's* impossible," Miss Laura Titcomb gayly shook her finger (but hadn't she said something rather funny there?) ; "and Mrs. Middleton assured us," she went on by way of covering up, "that you are a ve-ry interesting person, so we think you're hiding your light," said Miss Titcomb merrily—and stopped; and blushed; and floundered; and said there was her uncle and she must go and greet him because there he was and he was her uncle.

"Oh Christ, here comes your Negro again," said Al; "a black fate, Miss Powell honey. I'll tell him off, we'll have no raping at *this* bar. . . . Good evening, kuhnel," he greeted the impeccable Graham Hatcher advancing behind the cheery vanguard of his smile.

"Who—" began Lydia.

"I really don't know," said Fisher, crestfallen. Both of them stared at the Negro. "I wonder," said Ruthie Fisher, "if he might not be the communist candidate for vice-president; he must be *somebody*."

"Have you ever—" began Lydia.

"No, but I do think they're awfully attractive," said Fisher thoughtfully.

"*Would* you ever—" began Lydia.

"Of course, I'm no bourgeois," snapped Fisher; and thought she saw Jeffrey Blake at last; but no, it was a tall bald man who stooped, who bore no resemblance to her handsome Jeffrey; her heart beneath her turtle-neck sank painfully.

"Whoever said you were," said Lydia placidly.

Decidedly, thought Mrs. Stanhope, organizing her equine faction about herself and Mr. Merriwell, if Emily Fancher had any guts at all, she would appear. And I'd like to see any of you, she threatened them with her high-drawn mustang countenance, cutting her; just try and let me see you.

"This party," said the little Doctor, smiling and bowing and kissing hands at the bottom of the stairs, "is society psychoanalyzed, all the cross sections exposed as in a tree. . . ." Oh Vammie was doing his best for her, Merle gratefully knew, but this was agony! why had she not given her usual New Years' Party and let it go at that? and where was Emmett (whom she had seen just once since that awful night of the meeting, since Doctor Leonard had carried him off)? and where was Jeffrey Blake? . . . "Oh go right in, how nice to see you" (and the Ballisters hadn't come!) "oh very Bohemian, Emmett's young socialist friends you know, oh good of you to come Bianca, why yes I really *expect* Emily Fancher, so embarrassing inviting her you know, whether to address her Mrs. Jim or Mrs. Emily, no not the guest of honor there really *is* no guest of honor, just one of our more distinguished Negroes. . . ."

She studied their quizzical looks with alarm and weighed their reactions in her minutest social scale. One thing was certain: her party could not be less than a magnificent failure, if a failure it was destined to be. Sensational—no one could deny it: the banners, the speeches planned for midnight, even the guests' quixotic costumes; the orchestra, the food—somehow the recollection of the bills was reassuring. . . . "A noble experiment," said Al's lawyer bending to kiss her hand; "and a gorgeous experimenter," said the efficiency expert treading in his wake; "a study in contrasts," said the efficiency expert's wife who was so clever that they all suspected she was a Jewess.

"Do you see," the little Doctor had hit on something new to sell Merle's party, "*they* want to blow us up; but they come here and enjoy our company. Also we *know* they want to blow us up; yet we enjoy theirs." The little Doctor fairly glittered, polished his moustaches with delighted fingers. "And why?" he asked of himself in his brilliant pedantic Hungarian manner. The Whitmans and the Drapers stood still in their tracks. "Because we are decadent. Because they are decadent. Destroyers and victims drinking to each other from the common bowl, perversion." The Drapers and the Whitmans bridled in a kind of flattered amusement.

"A study in contrasts, do you see," Merle plagiarized

from the efficiency expert's wife. Lucius Whitman smiled; thrust his wife toward Henry Draper and ludicrously embraced his old friend's wife. "Since we're all decadent," he said; and led Violet Draper laughing toward the party; "since it's the end of the world anyway," he tossed to his own wife over Violet's shoulder; "why here's to it," he said and waved his noble cinema-banker's head, winked to his wife and gravely escorted Mrs. Draper as his own.

Vammie had brilliantly struck the right note. His words went to everyone's head like little drops of Tokay. Merle's own head grew light and gay. The party would be a success, she knew it now, by her proper hostess' instinct. If only Jeffrey Blake would come! For Merle had a promise to keep to herself. (Not again would she succumb to cowardice, holding her finger to her lips and pretending to hear her husband. . . .) She grew a little reckless; smiled too long at Mrs. Stanhope's brother-in-law; fairly writhed in charm before the oldest member of the New York City bar; laughed uproariously at Mr. Thayer (who was a wit she generally rebuked) for his suggestion that they act toward Emily Fancher (if she came) as though Jim Fancher were enjoying a rest-cure in the South. . . . "Just as in our fashionable magazines," Vammie was keeping up a steady stream, "the cruelest caricatures are of society . . ." "idea suggested, do you see," Merle helped him out, "by my young socialist friends . . ."

"Communist," said a stern voice coming down the stairs. "Communist, Mrs. Middleton, not socialist." It was young Flinders (but Jeffrey was not with him!); his wife, Merle supposed it must be, on his arm—a pretty, shabby girl. "Ah Mr. Flinders," Merle brightly cried and extended her hand, "does it matter, does it really matter, I mean aren't we all drifting toward the same goal anyhow. . . ."

"Watch them high-hat the Negro," said Comrade Fisher indignantly; "race-conscious snobs."

"Just the same I wish," said Lydia, "that *I* had on an evening dress cut down to my middle like the bar-keep's; I'd sell more ham and God knows I'd feel cooler."

"Upper class steam," said Comrade Fisher viciously. "They turn on all they've got to show they can afford it." They drew their hair virtuously behind their ears in deadly contrast to the fluffy Powell's.

"Fish! Will you promise to pinch me the minute *he* comes in?"

"God I'm tired of you being a virgin," said Ruthie Fisher scornfully; and longed with all her heart for Jeffrey Blake.

"I can't help it if I live at home," said Lydia humbly.

"What are you doing here," Al said sternly (Graham Hatcher blanched); "why aren't you storming our nation's Capitol where men are men and women hungry?" (Graham Hatcher revived.) "Aha Mr. Middleton," he vented an operatic gesture and smiled effusively at Miss Bee Powell, "I am not—" "What, you're not?" said Al; "then I suppose you are a Duke." "N-no," said Mr. Hatcher renewing his smile. "Well then, a commissar," said Al impatiently; "everybody here is something if it's only a God damn fool, we've all got titles of some kind, haven't we, Miss Powell darling?" The Negro had French manners or else some pullman porter blood, Al reflected (suddenly anxious about that fool son of his, why the devil wasn't he here?); he accepted his drink in exchange for his money, bowed, saw that his presence was no longer required, thanked them for something and vanished backwards leaving his smile like the cheshire cat's in the air behind him. "Makes mah southern blood boil," said Al. (His eyes roved the ballroom looking for Emmett.) "Well, he don't mine," said Miss Powell wittily; and gave him a Junior League flash from the incredible violet eyes. "One more look like that," Al said firmly, "and I'll forget that I'm just an impotent old man and ask you to meet me behind the potted palms." "What, sell my beautiful white body," said Miss Powell rolling her eyes. "Remembah our stahving boys," said Al wearily; (it was two weeks surely since he'd seen his boy); "I wonder where in hell my son is. . . ."

"There ought to be a special machine," said Bruno returning from the telephone and pulling his suspenders over his collarless dress-shirt, "for filtering Comrade Blake's enthusiasms. . . . That was your classmate and peer, Emmett—young Firman, who apparently sleeps with both eyes open and has gone into the detective business. . . ." He stood before them lost in thought for a moment, looking at his watch and not perceiving it; started as though it suddenly came to life and exclaimed: "My God! it's half-past ten! Climb onto the Remington again, Emmett, and help me remove the Fisherisms from my speech"; he swayed and rolled his eyes like a Harlem blues-singer; "for Fisher isn't kosher an-y mo-o-ore." Emmett, who loved being Bruno's amanuensis, and more than ever now because it was something Elizabeth couldn't do for him, asked no questions; he snapped up the lid of the typewriter and sat with his fingers at the keys, a righteous example to Elizabeth, his eyes upturned to Bruno.

But Elizabeth—sitting in her party slip with Bruno's smoking-jacket pulled about her shoulders—burst into gleeful laughter. "I thought Fisher and Jeffrey *owned* the revolution!" (What the devil right had she—wearing Bruno's clothes—to sit in as though she were a man on their last-minute conference!)

"That was last week," Bruno told her. "The latest bulletin—according to young Firman who has crashed communist newspaper headquarters, the only true organ of the holy church. . . . God knows what honest mischief that kid's up to! Well, anyway, he ran into somebody who knew somebody who slept with somebody else who states that Fisher is nothing more than an ex-camp-follower, a hanger-on. It seems that the 'fellow-travellers' are a little band of disgruntled off-shoots who didn't get elected commissar . . . oh, I don't know; the whole thing begins to look like playing mud-pies. . . ." That look that passed between them (filling Emmett with the pain of being left out)! they laughed the same laugh, Bruno and Elizabeth, raised the same eyebrow; broke off short on the identical note.

From the first he had seen how those two fitted together or almost fitted together, like the jagged halves of a coin torn apart and facing one another. Elizabeth could finish Bruno's sentences; Bruno could cap Elizabeth's; sometimes it was not even necessary to finish a sentence in words. They laughed uproariously at jokes he couldn't see; they grew suddenly silent as though they knew, as though they shared, some secret thing between them; and they resembled each other like a large and a small branch growing from the same tree.

It seemed to rouse them now, that identical laugh, to some high pitch of mutual glee and understanding. For Elizabeth jumped up with Bruno's smoking-jacket flying (Emmett tried not to see her shoulders shining bare under the straps of her party slip), seized Bruno as her partner, and the two of them went whirling round the table, singing in the same falsetto: "For Fish-er is-n't kosher any mo-o-ore." Round and round laughing they flew as though they had forgotten Emmett, forgotten everything but themselves, as though they would never stop. . . .

"If she doesn't go and dress," cried Emmett pettishly, "we'll all be hitting the b-b-bathroom at the same time again." They stopped short like two children rebuked by their elder, their arms dropped, their song died instantly.

"Tell the bottle-baby," said Elizabeth, drawing the jacket soberly about her shoulders, "to mind his business—don't I live here too?"

"Don't mind me, children," said Bruno wearily (a little gray, thought Emmett, as though the dance had worn him out); "I don't count, I'm not a man, I'm just an interpreter . . ." but he sat down, to Emmett's relief, and picked up the red pencil again. "The boy is right, Betsey; when in a madhouse do as the mad-men do: take yourself very seriously. All right, Emmett: take out that line, fifth from the bottom, about fellow-travellers. . . ."

But she had spoiled, again, his peace. She was always

doing that, stepping in to make her presence felt, disturbing the harmony which (he had known since that one remarkable night with Bruno, before her boat arrived) could exist between himself and Bruno. "Won't be bad, will it, kid," (so Bruno had apologized for her appearance) "to have a woman in our house?" But it was bad; it was terrible; it was agony.

She was the first woman beside his mother with whom he had lived intimately in the same few rooms, whose half-clad person he had seen, lounging, fussing over things, as women did in the privacy of their home. Even more than he hated her standing as a barrier between himself and Bruno, he hated her persistent feminine presence. There was no escaping her, or some suggestion of her; the bathroom bore her scent; in the living-room her drawing materials lay scattered possessively day and night, occasionally too some article of her clothing; from where he slept he could now and then hear her sigh or move or laugh; her voice was the first thing he heard in the morning. Once Bruno had left the apartment, leaving Emmett alone with Elizabeth; she had stayed quietly in her room—her indifference to him was patent—but even so the whole place was so pervaded by her that after twenty minutes of restlessly trying to forget her presence, he had found it necessary to leave the house (slamming the door behind him) and paid his only visit to his parents. . . .

"as intellectuals," Bruno was dictating; Emmett fell with more content into the rhythm of the keys and Bruno's voice, "it's time to take our stand; it is our belief that this Magazine, providing . . ."

"Bruno!" Her voice was shrill—they jumped, all three

of them; even Elizabeth, Emmett observed, as though her own voice were a shock to her.

"What is it, Betsey?" "I c-c-can't work with her in the room," Emmett burst out, almost against his will. "What *is* it, Betsey," Bruno said.

"Nothing," she said, laughing. "Only tell the bottle-baby to pass the whiskey my way."

"She's been drinking since three o'clock this afternoon," said Emmett, loathing himself.

"Since ten o'clock in the morning three weeks ago," Elizabeth corrected without a glance in his direction.

Bruno reached patiently for the bottle at Emmett's elbow. "Sure that's all you wanted, Elizabeth?"

"What more could anybody want?"

"Good ole whiskey," said Bruno and Elizabeth in the same breath, the same tone, the same inflection. And laughed; withdrawing from each other as the whiskey bottle passed between them as though by sulky mutual consent.

It was this deadly similarity, he thought, that hurt him most. He remembered having thought once, clearly, that if Bruno ever married, he would kill himself. But this was worse; Elizabeth was closer than a wife. With a wife, Emmett vaguely felt, there would be at some point in the day a climax from which Bruno and a wife would then retreat, becoming their separate selves again. This thing had no crisis; there was no union, hence no separation; they bent along together closely parallel, following each other's devious routes—and how then could it ever end?

They were most, he thought, like a brother and sister; yet not being brother and sister brought them closer still. The mystery of their belonging to each other in the same *family*—that was it. He was a child who had grown from the beginning feeling no sense of belonging to his father or his mother; surprised, he had discovered as early as his nursery days, that both seemed strange to him and strange to one another. He had spent his lonely childhood dreaming of a brother or a sister, someone to whom he could, most intimately, belong: belong mutually, on equal terms. No one came; and he had tried, in various chronologic stages, to establish a relationship with Merle. But she treated him alternately with indifference and with the detailed passion of a woman for her lover, and both things froze him out, left him passionately indifferent too, or passionately jealous. . . .

"but the time has come," Bruno dictated, "when it is no longer possible to hesitate. . . ."

Between Elizabeth and Merle there had been no other women in his life. He didn't really hate Elizabeth, he thought (glancing briefly at her, avoiding contact with her slender shoulders) ; he played at hating her; it suited his dignity best to fly into a rage when she spilled her scented powder over their common bathroom; because he could find no unembarrassing relation with her it became necessary to assume hostility—and since that day of her arrival they had not spoken two words directly to each other, preferring to use the medium of Bruno. No, he didn't actually hate her. He hated her only because she spoiled the only place that might have been a home to him. Again, as in his childhood, he was a third person, living in a place where two should be. . . .

"are we, as intellectuals," dictated Bruno, "to remain in the middle, on the fence, or are we . . ."

He pictured his mother suddenly (wondering if she were missing him), coldly playing hostess at the party; asked himself what gown she might be wearing.

But what man was a failure, thought Arturo strongly (the whiskey was good; the crowd was excellent) who had even one symphony to his credit? It might go unpublished; it might be played only at parties where no one listened to it; but it was music, it was eternal, it added to the sum total of beautiful music, to the unheard vibrating stream of perpetual music that surrounded the world, that would one day subdue the world to all its concerted rhythm. The memory of his Symphony of the Seasons flared up in his heart. He rose, lifted his baton to the Boys. "The Symphony," he said imperiously—he always referred to the Symphony of the Seasons briefly as The. The Boys rose respectfully and took their places. Arturo's nostrils expanded with love and pride. He gave a little nod to the Boys, tapped with his baton on the music stand, and started in on the Allegro, Spring, the first movement of his latest Rearrangement of The Symphony.

"Beethoven, isn't it?" said a Miss Hobson raising her brows at a Mr. Terrill whom she hoped to marry. "Ah I never can tell right off," said Mr. Terrill (playing safe) but beginning to wave uneasily with the music.

"Ah what difference does it make, Mr. Flinders," said Merle stretching her arms in voluptuous generosity, "socialism, communism, true democracy—it's surely the fraternal *spirit* that counts, these petty distinctions, what *difference* can they make?"

"No difference at all," said Margaret Flinders, laying a restraining hand on Miles' arm, "especially at a party." As papier-mâché as Miles had said perhaps, thought Margaret with amusement, but much more beautiful and much more touching; a glacier that tried to melt, a toy doll that wanted a heart that would beat instead of just eyes that closed—but she was seeing people so differently these days, Margaret was! either as they really were (she secretly believed) or, as Miles insisted, through rose-colored spectacles. The little Doctor bent to kiss her hand; and Margaret, standing proudly in her last year's best, surveyed the gathering with pleasure. Their own friends of course would not have come; but Miles, bursting with plans and latent indignation, had insisted on regarding this party as a meeting (so he explained his presence to his conscience) and arriving scarcely half an hour late. She enjoyed his stiff reluctant gallantry, his utterly unconscious grace as he coldly greeted Mrs. Middleton. His tuxedo he had left righteously at home, bedded forever in moth-balls; but his bearing, his ascetically rigid jaw, left him, she thought, as well-dressed as any there. "So anxious," Mrs. Middleton was fluttering them toward the ballroom, toward the music lightly starting, "to have you meet Mr. Graham Hatcher, I thought a Negro, I thought the perfect party ought to have *one* Negro," she strained delicately for their understanding; "if you would seek him out, perhaps?" she smiled like a gracious sorority sister, initiating Margaret in the facts of life.

"I'm sure," said Margaret, blandly smiling, "that we'll have no difficulty; since he's the only Negro present." The ice was broken; the little Doctor chuckled; and taking Miles' arm Margaret led him toward the ballroom.

"Dear," she whispered irresistibly (for she felt very merry, very handsome, very much of a wife leaning upon her husband's arm and making her entrance at a party), "could you manage to look less like a tortured saint, do you think?" "Could you manage to lend me your rose-colored spectacles, do *you* think," he answered; and consented to be led.

Tears stood in Arturo's eyes as his body swayed to the first movement of The Symphony. It had always seemed to him, that first movement, with its gentle crescendos, its crooning melody, its mild and lovely allegro ripple, like the tune of his own youth when music was a promised land and the teachers at the Academy had praised a young man's progress. Spring; snow-streams melting down the mountain-sides; buds were bursting. Arturo was humble before his own youth, his own music, beauty created by himself; he played in his heart to Mary.

They advanced arm in arm and Margaret thought how beautiful it was that everything good in this world started from two people walking together from choice. For a lovely moment they were Miles and Margaret walking shyly toward her graduation dance (the music fine and sentimental), the campus alight with magic lanterns; they were Miles and Margaret walking yet more shyly to the wedding-march, her mother standing before them beautiful in large white tears; and then they came to where the major-domo guarded the ballroom entrance: lifting back a velvet portière so all the world could see Margaret Flinders standing proudly with her husband. He hung back faintly and she strengthened her clasp on his arm. "But it looks like the Tower of Babel," he said, unhappy, as the noise and the brilliance burst upon them, washed up at their feet and bore them in with the backwash.

"I am asking you, Mr. Tevander," Mrs. Stanhope was leaning forward piercingly in the midst of her little group, "what you honestly thought of Minerva."

"Minerva," said Mr. Merriwell, hurt. "I should have thought I had known every horse in the Stable, but Minerva! Minerva's a new one to me."

"How did you know, Mrs. Stanhope," Mr. Tevander faltered, "how did you *know* I rode Minerva?"

"I am asking you, Mr. Tevander," Mrs. Stanhope repeated, her nostrils aquiver, "how you *liked* her?"

"Minerva," said Mr. Merriwell dispiritedly, "is certainly a new one to me."

"Ah they've been holding out on you, G.F.," screamed the merry lady in velvet trimmed with ermine-tails.

"How did you like her, Mr. Tevander?" said Mrs. Stanhope sternly.

"Why I liked her all right," said Tevander guiltily. "I liked her, yes I liked her."

"You *liked* her!" cried Mrs. Stanhope bridling like a war-horse. "You liked that blind-in-one-eye, spavined, consumptive creature with a rotten gallop like a Ford, *wh-hy!*" She whinnied in her horror.

"It's a funny thing," said Mr. Merriwell gloomily, "I should have thought I had known every horse in the Stable. . . ."

"Of course you wouldn't know Minerva, G.F.," cried

Mrs. Stanhope loyally. "She's the Stable's Sunday School nag, they only keep her because . . . It's men like you, John Tavender," she said bluntly, "who pull down the whole reputation of the Stables. Minerva! Wh-hy!" said Mrs. Stanhope blowing out her nostrils.

"Whut did they say this party was a benefit *for,* G.F.?" The merry ermine lady tapped Mr. Merriwell on the arm.

"Minerva! my stars and heavens!"

"I'm not just sure," said Mr. Merriwell conscientiously. "I believe it to be for someone's relief or other, perhaps some organization, very likely something that the Negro gentleman represents."

"Nonsense." Mrs. Stanhope used her spurs. "The Negro is some celebrity Merle picked up—a pity she couldn't find one among the whites, less glory to us. Mr. Tevander, I wish I could impress you with the *importance* . . ."

"Ooooh, I wonder could he be Paul Robeson," said the merry lady squeezing her ermine tails one after another with love and cruelty.

"Why yes, I think so," said Mr. Merriwell kindly; "I don't see why not," he added out of personal bounty. "Very likely that's just who it is," said Mr. Merriwell magniloquently for he had known the ermine lady's father and dandled little miss Ermine-tails upon his knee.

"Well anyway, I liked her," said little Tevander miserably; and wilted under Mrs. Stanhope's bitter eye.

"Ah no," said Miss Hobson wagging her finger like a metronome at Mr. Terrill; "no, I know my Beethoven too well for *that.*"

"You know it's possible it's Brahms," said Mr. Terrill

suddenly, bending his head in a musical position; "I wonder if Emily Fancher will have the nerve to show up."

"If she does I am not going to speak to her," said Miss Hobson firmly.

"Really?" said Mr. Terrill; and moved back with alarm for he saw that Miss Hobson had the kind of morals one married for. "She, after all, had nothing to do with it."

"No, but it's touching pitch," said Miss Hobson. She began to weigh the music in her hands. "Not Brahms, certainly, not enough melody, ah this is a disgrace, Mr. Terrill, I'm ashamed of us both."

"Well, if we need a cheaper grade, stick different labels on the same stuff," Al said testily to his efficiency expert; "and for God's sake don't talk business to me, this is a charity brawl and I'm looking for my God damned son." And what's more, he continued (rapidly walking away) you wouldn't be here at all if it weren't that anybody could buy their way in tonight. "Really my dear," said the efficiency expert's wife who being under suspicion herself always checked carefully on her husband's movements, "you might have been more tactful."

"That's enough now, my dear," said Mrs. Whitman playfully; "a joke's a joke but—*there are limits.*" "Do you mean you're *jealous?*" Lucius Whitman smiled. "I must say," said Mr. Draper ruefully, "it's not very flattering to *me,* my dear; and look at my Violet." Look at his Violet; she had had too much to drink and was leaning heavily on Mr. Whitman's shoulder. "Since it's a party to celebrate the end of the world, my dear," said Mr. Whitman gayly; and suddenly went sober: "My God, I wouldn't want to be in Jim Fancher's boots tonight." Violet straightened; in a crisis she wanted Draper, her husband for so many years of ups and downs, of living on Park Avenue one year and not having enough to go to the country with the next. "No, I wouldn't want to be in Fancher's boots," Henry Draper sighed. The wives joined glances. "Pretty hard to tell," said Mr. Whitman gently, "what another man would have done in his place." "You mean," said Henry Draper, "what you would have done; or I." Wives looked at their husbands like nervous wolf-hounds, scenting danger. "It's hard to tell," said Lucius Whitman after a conscientious self-investigation. "I know," said Henry Draper. "Of all the things to talk about at a party," said the wives reproachfully. "You just don't know," said Lucius Whitman heavily, "until you've been there." "That's a fact," said Henry Draper and pulled on his cigar as if he hoped that it might tell him.

"Bach, perhaps?" said Miss Hobson tenderly. "But you could tell us, Mr. Hatcher. I'm sure," she said gracefully, "that you are an expert in 'things musical.' "

"No, I am not," said Mr. Hatcher irritably. "I assure you I am not, everyone seems to be under some misapprehension about me. . . ."

"Perhaps," said Mr. Terrill nervously, "Mr. Hatcher's field is the theater."

"I assure you I never go near a theater." "Then perhaps" "or perhaps" "I think I've heard your name in connection with" "Oh I wish," said Mr. Hatcher unhappily.

"I am going back to thinking it *is* Beethoven after all," said Miss Hobson wrinkling her eyes which were her one good point. "I flatter myself I know my composers."

"She knows her onions," said Mr. Terrill coarsely, growing a little tired of music and high standards.

"The upper-classmen," Miles said, sweeping the party with his gloomy look, "are certainly in the majority. I'm not going to like this party, Meg: it looks to me like a freak-show." "Now darling," said Margaret placidly, "just remember to say how-do-you-do nicely to everyone and not to over-eat. . . . Darling! get ready to smile; isn't that our host?" "Oh God," said Miles. *"Smile, darling."* "I'm smiling," he said stoically, "but it's for you and not the party." And he smiled down into her party face; she could wear the same dress every day for all of him and still if she had that tingling thing inside of her she would be the most beautiful woman at any party he could take her to.

"A brilliant girl, that," Al sighed and shook his head; indicated Miss Bee Powell; "would you expect a girl with all those looks to have brains besides?" "No," said Miles Flinders. "Ah, it's Flinders—well, she hasn't," Al admitted. "Your wife? congratulations, the party's looking up. How about a little drink in honor of our thirsty marchers?" "No thanks," said Margaret happily, "no drinks for me tonight." "No *drinks?*" "Doctor's orders," said Margaret cheerfully. (Damn it, thought Miles, uncomfortable, airing our most private life in public!) "I doubt," he said, "if the Hunger Marchers can be making half this noise." "Course not," said Al indignantly; "it ain't worth while, howling just for a bowl of soup; it takes caviar to make people really bloodthirsty. I told Bruno Leonard he'd have to hold out something if he wanted to put across this communism. . . ." "But Bruno," said Miles, "is not exactly . . ." "You don't say?" said Al in great astonishment; "and how about yourself?" "Well no," said Miles reluctantly; "if you mean in the sense of *belonging* to the movement." "A rose by any other name," said Al, "but ah the difference to me. But where *is* Bruno Leonard? and where has he hidden my son? If you happen to see him," he said; and moved on, saluting with his drumstick. It was two weeks surely since he'd seen the boy. If the professor turned out some phony kind of Oscar Wilde then professor or no professor . . .

"I wish you'd stop refusing cocktails, Maggie; it sounds so damn affected." "But I didn't want one, darling"; and that was the nearest he had come, she thought, to making an allusion since the time he said to call it Daniel. "I don't belong at this kind of shindig," he said, contrite; "I don't believe in parties." "Isn't that Jeffrey's Comrade Fisher?" Margaret said. "Yes. . . . I wonder what *she* thinks of us, she must despise us!" "She does look," said Margaret, peering, "as if she were despising *something;* but maybe," she added, "it's only herself."

Summer—the second movement, lush and fruitful—Arturo forgot that he was a small Italian gentleman with a neat and rounded belly; he grew tall and broad, the melody grew heavier, like a richly flowing stream. The second movement had been strongly influenced by the Germans, Arturo acknowledged that; and he thought of the happy Heidelberg days before the class broke up to go to war. Come to think of it, wasn't the war responsible, perhaps if he had stayed on in Heidelberg . . .

"Who—" began Lydia.

"The kids—Doctor Leonard's students," said Ruthie Fisher half-contemptuously; being three years older she hated them for being at once fresher and more stupid than herself. She had heard from Jeffrey of their dogmatism, seen for herself their orthodox approach to politics; and though she must despise them, she envied them a little—how short a time ago had she lived too in such unquestioning belief. . . . She watched their entrance, all together in a bunch, like some invading youthful army, and felt a thousand years between herself and them. "Just kids," she said; and saw that they had not brought Jeffrey with them.

March lifted up the curtains. "Here—comes—the Bride," Little Dixon whispered as the music opened in the air and six Black Sheep crossed the desert of the ballroom sticking together like a jaunty little caravan; "believe me I'm glad I won't have to sleep on the floor any more." "Who said you won't," said Firman laughing backward to his army. "I didn't notice the judge handing out any extra beds," Cornelia said, addressing her lone bridesmaid. "None of your fainting acts tonight, my good girl," said Firman taking her arm; "my God is this a skating-rink we're walking on—because we'll need you conscious." "Damn right," said one of the Maxwell boys, "this reforming of our elders is going to be no cinch." "*What* a wedding-party," said Cornelia; "I've surpassed my mother's fondest hopes." The music picked up joy. "She looks terribly different," whispered Kate Corrigan to Little Dixon; "I didn't think she'd make a decent bride but begorrah if she didn't surprise me." "My God, your Irish bridesmaid's gone romantic," said Little Dixon dryly. "You were crying this afternoon, Kate," Cornelia slowed the procession to accuse her bridesmaid tenderly, "right smack in the Municipal Building." " 'Tis a dirty lie," said Kate. "I'll smack you both," said Firman, "you sentimental bourgeois hussies, beginning with you, Mrs. Firman, I've got the legal right." "She was too crying, Arnold," Cornelia said; "as a matter of fact, I was myself," she said complacently.

"Now by my long gray beard and jittery eye," said Al Middleton jovially, holding them up like a bandit with his turkeystick (how many of them were there? only six? they marched as proudly as a hundred), "what are you proletarians doing here? why aren't you storming the portals of our Capitol. . . ."

Their procession broke up and their hundred became a thousand as they surrounded him eagerly and answered, in their fashion, all at once. "God damn faculty" "we asked could we go investigate for our sociology class" "but they want us to stick to the mummies in the natural history museum" "said they'd kick us out if we went" "so Doctor Leonard persuaded us not to" "suppose we've *got* to be educated while we've got the chance" "Firman was in favor of some excitement anyway" "so he got married instead" "this afternoon" "shut up, you fool, that's a secret" "no politics, no sex for undergraduates" "but we're juniors, we've only got another year"

"Children," said Al, surprisingly touched, "aren't you forgetting something? You're treating me like a human being. . . ." "Oh we're celebrating tonight," they shouted boisterously, "we're breaking all the rules." "Don't be idiots," said Cornelia curtly, "Mr. Middleton's a good guy, we'll like him until we have to shoot him." He humbly bowed his thanks. "Have you any idea where my son . . ." "Oh yes, we spoke to Doctor Leonard on the telephone" "they'll be here soon" "they're going over Doctor Leonard's speech" "we told him" "Say, don't you kids even telephone singly?" Al asked. "United front," they shouted, roaring laughter; "but Firman's the only one that married Corny." This pleased them so that they broke into peals of laughter which made him sad because he knew his son had never laughed like that. "Well, move on, kids, and celebrate. Wait. May I kiss the bride?" They were no more surprised than he as he bent and kissed the blushing Cornelia chastely on the cheek.

The wedding-party proceeded, a little shy; settled near some palms, grazing close for mutual protection. "The music's pretty," said Cornelia.

Arturo swayed and thought of Mary, Mary in the late summer of her life. Everything, at this moment which was the high point in his life, while he lived and played his music, mild and certain again with the promise of his youth, was worth his Mary, worth her dark and healthy beauty, her lush late-Summer limbs, the little black kids that sprang out of her every few years. His Summer music ran like liquid down the hollow of his legs, became the same as his desire for Mary; this was the poignant moment, the moment before his Summer ended, when he knew with every drop of his blood that he was a man who lived and who loved.

"We want cav-iar!" the wedding-party chanted. "Oh let's not," said Firman; "I think I'd rather starve than eat their food—look how they've got it lined up, like dangling grapes just out of the Hunger Marchers' reach." "I'll faint again," Cornelia threatened him; "no reason why we can't have a wedding supper, Arnold—that's sentimental pride in you." "I've got plenty of room, God wot," said Kate. "Why not?" said the Maxwell brothers:

"we want *cav*-iar, we want *cav*-iar." "Go ahead, Little," Cornelia urged Dixon, "go steal us all a sandwich. And none of your God damn fripperies, my good man, get something a bride can sink her teeth in." "Maybe you'd like to be alone with your husband," Kate said, giggling; "come along, you tactless lads—hey, wait for me, Little, give me a hand across the ice." Little Dixon crooked an elaborate elbow and Kate minced off like Eliza with the blood-hounds after her; the Maxwells scrambled to their feet and followed. "And bring some caviar," Cornelia called, "I've never tasted caviar." "Jesus, honey," whispered Firman brokenly, "I'm cockeyed crazy about you, I think you're swell." "I'm cockeyed crazy about *us,*" she whispered back; "I think we're the best thing going." Their hands shot out and clasped secretly between their chairs. "I wish I could take you on a swell honeymoon," said Firman, "a trip to Russia for instance." "I don't want to make pilgrimages to the holy land," Cornelia whispered back; "America's big enough for me, and I love you terribly." "I love you so much it hurts," said Firman bluntly. The music swelled with a fine sense of its own power.

"But I am not, I assure you," said Mr. Hatcher in his unhappy Harvard voice, "representing anything at all." "No, why should you be," said Margaret easily, "we're not accusing you of that. We just stopped by to rescue you, we'd like you to meet some friends of ours." "But I have been most distressed all evening," said Mr. Hatcher, mollified, "because everyone expects something of me that I am not. . . ." "It's that kind of a party," Miles said grimly; "everybody expects something of everybody else so nobody does anything but sit back and wait . . .

if they manage to come at all; here it is nearly half-past eleven and Jeffrey with the opening speech to make, and Bruno probably lying drunk in a ditch somewhere." "Oh come, darling," Margaret said, "there are the Sheep; and they look as if they could run a party or fight a revolution without Bruno. I'm sure Mr. Hatcher would enjoy them." "I will enjoy them," said Mr. Hatcher firmly, "only if they do not expect me to be something I am not. Because I, really . . ." Margaret piloted her two disgruntled boys, one white, one black, across the floor. "And there is Norah!" she exclaimed; "and so you see, my dear!"

"It's his wife, Lydia."

"His wife, Fish!" Lydia scarcely breathed. "You never told me he was married!"

"All the best men," said Fisher grimly, "were either killed in the war or are married."

"His wife!" repeated Lydia happily. "Does she—*know?*"

Ruthie Fisher tried to calm her beating heart. She didn't understand, quite, about Norah. She was used to men with wives; but she was not used to wives who cooked in blissful ignorance for three—or *was* it ignorance? Ruthie didn't know. She was not certain of anything about Norah; but she knew she lost all composure in her presence. Norah was again the girls in high school, the girls who had beaux, who went to all the basketball games; while Ruthie Fisher who was as bright as any of them, who liked boys as wildly as the most attractive of them, who could (but only practising in the privacy of her room or flirting with her father) look as arch, as soft, as aloof, as any of them—while Ruthie Fisher broke her handsome father's heart by sitting at home and developing a love for study that ended in passionate hate: because she wasn't pretty.

"Oh what a silly question," she snapped at Lydia. "I don't know if she knows and I don't care either."

She had learned long ago to be sharp when she felt like crying. Now she hardened her mouth and balanced her cigarette in the corner, pulling her red jersey stoically tighter round her waist. She felt miserable and sick (the students looting her buffet table seemed to glance her way contemptuously). Never since William Turner had she loved a man as she loved Jeffrey. And William was her first; from one strike to another they had gone, to prison they had gone together; and then, as Ruthie put it, they had "busted up." For even William, and perhaps now even Jeffrey . . . oh Ruthie had cleared out from home when she was twenty; the pitiful look in her father's eyes who could do nothing for his only daughter drove her out: but leaving home had never made her pretty. . . . But where was Jeffrey?

"I left my husband," Norah said in her gentle voice, nodding and beaming like a pot of acquiescent honey on his arm.

"Fine," said Al.

"No, I left him with Mrs. Middleton," she explained.

"Then that makes everything perfectly lovely," Al said drily.

"I mean," said Norah laughing, "I don't want to get completely out of sight, he might come back and want me. What a grand lovely party, Mr. Middleton," she sighed with pleasure; "reminds me of the movies, I never get enough of the movies."

"And you," he said, surprised gently out of his wooing instinct, "remind me forcibly of something I faintly remember, life I think it was called." She laughed warmly; and settling beside him patted her hair with modesty and joy, waved to her friends, and looked frankly past his shoulder for her husband.

"There's Norah," said Firman; "well thank God for that." "It's no assurance," Miles said, gloomy, "that Jeffrey's anywhere about." "But he goes on at midnight—isn't he to start the speeches?" "We've got to get hold of him," Cornelia said excitedly, "before he starts to speak." "Have you heard yet, Flinders, about Fisher?" "But that's terrible," said Miles desolated; "that's simply terrible—whom is one to trust?" "You say you've been to Spain?" said Margaret absently to Mr. Hatcher. "No, I said my grandfather was born there," said Mr. Hatcher shortly. "But it doesn't mean she's necessarily dishonest," Margaret said, "perhaps she really believes in the fellow-traveller idea." "Effect's the same," said Firman; "see, she belongs to a group that roots for Lenin but is thumbs down forever on Stalin" "and Lenin was a great man in his day" Cornelia said "but he's dead" said Firman indifferently. "Whoops, is *that* caviar, Dixon my good man?" cried Cornelia as four more Sheep skidded to their group.

"I am worried," to his continued surprise Al found himself letting his conquest slip, "I am worried no end about my boy, Miss Norah." For Emmett hadn't come; nor was there any sign of Bruno Leonard. "What do you think of this Bruno Leonard, is he a great friend of yours?" he said.

"Oh yes," said Norah vaguely, and her eyes looked

frankly round the room for Jeffrey. But had she ever thought him funny? Al softly asked her. Oh yes, Norah said, very funny, very, very funny indeed, the funniest man she had ever seen, kept them all in stitches. He didn't mean quite that, Al said; what he meant was—you know, "funny."

Norah burst out laughing. " 'Funny'—oh good heavens no! Oh good heavens, Mr. Middleton, everybody goes around thinking everybody else is funny and really I wonder sometimes if anybody really *is*. But Bruno—Emmett could tell you about Bruno, Mr. Middleton, I do wonder where my husband is." Relieved, he bent a little closer and told her she had been deserted, told her of the excellent non-charity whiskey upstairs—but mildly, from a sense of habit; all he wanted was to sit with her and rest; and no thank you, really, was all she would say, and that she preferred to wait right here till Jeffrey came and fetched her.

"And take out Jeffrey's line about economic fate," said Bruno; "because that's slop, it's poetry, and poetry, as young Firman rightly says, is dangerously ambiguous. . . . Now, it should read: The world is up a tree; fundamentally there are but two sides . . ."

"Bruno!" How shrill Elizabeth had been all day! Twenty times her voice had run across his nerves like a knife; twenty times today had he told her, if there was anything she wished to tell him, save it for after the party. *"Bruno! please come here!"* Lent distance by the door which closed her room, her voice wailed, pleading, like a child's; it held the quality for him that the cablegram two months ago had held, weeping across a sea. "I'm coming, Elizabeth," he called in the teeth of Emmett's hurt distress. "Listen Emmett," he said conciliatingly, "we won't go over it any more, I'm nervous enough as it is. Besides, my chief job, coming after Jeffrey, will be to refute his speech. . . . Just put it in the envelope and finish dressing, we'll have to hurry anyway."

He caught the look on Emmett's face, pitiful as Betsey's voice. Damn these children! "You've been a great help kid," he said perfunctorily and paused to tousle Emmett's hair. And then he crossed to Elizabeth, afraid to look back at the brooding child he left behind him. He opened her door; and finding her standing dejected, her party dress drooping off her shoulder, he closed it rapidly having some baseless sense that it must be wrong for Emmett to see her so.

"What is it, Elizabeth?" He was really frightened. She was cowering, peering at him from behind her naked shoulder; her eyes large and fearful—terribly like the child at Longview. If she had been the child she looked he would have gone and put his arms about her, comforted her. But he couldn't touch her now unless she dropped a word of needing him; and she wouldn't utter that word unless he took a step in her direction; and he couldn't take a step unless first by some special look. . . . So he remained against the door, embarrassed, troubled, looking at her, the space between them impenetrable as fog. It was like this always: when he thought of her, when he couldn't see her, she touched him unbearably; but face to face with her she somehow put him on his mettle, on his guard, made him feel guilty and therefore defensive, so that *in* his sight she was farther from him than when an ocean stretched between them. "What is it, Betsey," he said again.

Her lips quivered, her eyes filled with tears. It occurred to Bruno coldly that his little cousin must be drunk again; but it made no difference—so was he; and her distress was genuine. For two pins (if she said the word) he would have sent Emmett on ahead to the party and stayed to talk things out; for two pins (if she said the word). . . . But she would never say the word if she wanted to; and torture would not have made him take the step alone. "What *is* it, Betsey?"

"My dress," she said, suddenly grinning like an imp. "My Paul Poiret dress, I can't hook the God damn thing."

"My good Elizabeth! is *that* all? have you ever heard of the boy who cried wolf once too often?" He did not altogether believe that that was all; but their time-honored code was to consider the unsaid things unheard. And his relief at having nothing spoken to deal with was so great that he approached her and put out his hands good-naturedly to be placed on the difficult hooks. "And if there's anything more you want to say," he added, gay, a little uneasy too, guilt dictating that he recognize at least the existence of something she might anyhow never say, "it will have to wait until after the party." She turned her back and flirted with him over the shoulder of her Paris dress, pouting, smiling, through her actress tears. "That won't go down with me," he threatened her, "you've got no sex appeal for me, spoiled baby, too thin," he said, washed with pity for her transparent shoulder-blades.

"Dear me, these Poiret gowns," she said, satirical; "made for ladies with lovers—no consideration at all for the deserted damsel who is also not double-jointed." He struggled with the hooks. "I miss Denny," she mocked him over her shoulder; *"Denny* could have done it better."

He felt the twinge of pain go through him that he had felt so many weeks ago on receiving her cablegram, as though he were still not certain that it was between Elizabeth and Denny that the ocean now was stretching. "What do you mean," he said sharply; "do you really mean you miss him? What kind of brute was he anyway, you've never really told me. I mean, how close did you really come in your mind to marrying him?"

"Everything must wait till after the party," she said derisively; "my dear Elizabeth, can't you see I'm starting a Magazine, I've got things on my mind?" He watched her with distrust as she preened without him, expertly. She had left him a little girl and now, come back, was a woman who could alter miracles by a deft twitch of a bow, an infinitesimal touch to her hair. She swung round like a conscious mannequin. "How do I look," she said, standing out in her lettuce-colored dress trimmed with flounces, looking very much, he thought, appeased, as she must have looked when he refused to take her to dancing-school. "How do I look," she said posing, teasing, swaying like that heart-broken little girl.

"Like a nice little salad," he said, flung back to the days when his adolescent pride forbade him to give her any satisfaction. "Too thin," he said, again, touched by the childish collar-bones which rendered M. Poiret's artistry naïve. "But since you refuse to answer the district attorney's questions, we'll go—in fact we've *got* to go. Don't you know I'm making history tonight," he said with a grimace.

"*Bruno*—no! wait a minute. I'll answer anything." Again that shrillness in her voice; again the quick change from woman to imp that mocked him. "Prepared to tell all, she stood with her lips trembling bravely, her Poiret gown revealing every line in her slender little body, the earrings from the Galeries Lafayette that *he* had given her shaking with emotion—it was a crime passionelle, she sobbed, and the judges broke down and cried like a baby."

"Oh you poor damn fool," he said, admiring her, "will you never grow up and talk sense?"

"Ah, just what they all say," said Elizabeth sagely, and lifted to her ears the earrings (from the Galeries Lafayette—which *"he"* must have given her, thought Bruno, instantly disliking him). "Just what Denny said when I told him we were all washed up."

"What made you think you'd marry him, he sounds like an idiot," Bruno said.

"Oh—I wanted love," she said, her eyes cast up, teetering demurely with her hands clasped at her throat.

"You wanted what?" he said, incredulous.

"Love," she answered cheerfully. "L-o-v-e, love."

"Say, I send you abroad and you come home with a foreign vocabulary," he said, troubled. "Put it in English—you mean you wanted *amour?*"

"Sure, I know," she said airily, "when I lie everybody believes me. When I tell the truth they think I'm lying. It's my theatrical technique . . . Maybe I *am* lying," she said calmly; "how do *I* know."

"You're drunk anyway," said Bruno shortly. "Come on, sling a wrap over those shameless naked shoulders, have you forgotten the Hunger Marchers?" He turned to go.

"No, but *you* have."

"Go to hell," he said.

"Listen. You haven't asked me why I *didn't* marry Denny."

He stood puzzled with his hand on the door-knob. "All right. Why? Make it snappy. 'Intellectuals postpone political party for talmudic discussion of love.' Go on if you have to."

"Bisecting love," she said, contemplative. "Do you remember the two boys in Chicago—our heroes, how we read the papers!—who bisected their young cousin to see what he was made of?"

"Are you going to tell me or aren't you? Why didn't you marry the man?"

"Because I wanted love."

"Well, didn't he love you?" In spite of himself he grew gentle.

"Oh sure, I guess so; à la mode, at any rate. But I wanted to love somebody myself."

"And the gentleman in question didn't make the grade?" In spite of himself again, he felt pleasure.

"Too weak," she said nonchalantly; and after framing her face with the weak one's earrings tore them off indifferently and thrust them back in their box.

"What makes you always pick weak men?" he scolded her, relief restoring his superiority.

"I don't pick them, they pick me."

"You always," he continued wisely, "land the kind

that need mothering, and then they have to put up with your kicking them all around the lot." He thought with distaste of her procession, the unfortunate Wheelwrights and the Ferrises. . . .

"Kicking is a form of mothering," she said, considering. "And maybe I don't pick weak men at all," she said defiantly; "maybe all the men there are are weak. Or weaker anyway, than any woman who's strong."

"What is this," he said to her quizzically, "an amatory championship?" And what had happened to women, he wondered, looking at her. Once a woman had built up a man, lent him whatever she had; because his glory was hers, because then a woman was only so great as the monument of her man. But these strange days, when women were out in the world, on their own, competing with men on the men's own level, they seemed temporarily to have got ahead, to be going still farther while man, surprised, exhausted in the fight, sat down with open mouth in a stopping-place in the road. But that the women weren't satisfied with their victory he could plainly see, reading something hollow in Elizabeth's pained, triumphant look. Where once they fought their men because the men were stronger, now they seemed sworn to continue the fight in bitterness because the men were weaker. She stood tough and straight as a soldier, a brittle tin soldier sticking defiantly out of some child's Christmas stocking. He felt sorry for her, standing in her lonely strength, wondered why she felt it necessary to tilt her chin at such an angle, why she grew thinner and somehow younger each time he saw her (between her strange adventures) as though the years were giving nothing to her. "I guess it's all right, Betsey," he said anxiously, "only I didn't raise my girl to be a soldier."

She returned his look, ironic, and he had the odd impression that himself was looking reproachfully at himself. " 'You've got to be free, my dear, free as a man, you've got to play the man's game and beat him at it.' "

"Check," he admitted ruefully; "hats off to the elephant's sister; do you remember all the stupid things that everyone has said to you . . . Only," he said doubtfully, almost to himself, "half the fun to a man is having a woman a little weaker than himself. It's easy enough," he said, "for a man to grow indifferent to a woman he thinks is his equal; being weak is a woman's strongest weapon in the old sex struggle." He thought with clarity of Emmett. "Virility, after all, is partly a matter of vanity. Dependence, of a sort, is what endears a man, what binds him. . . ."

"You are thinking of the other part of your *ménage à trois,*" said Elizabeth; and smiled so certainly that he had to take his hand off the door-knob to deny it and in denying it admitted it, and admitting it discovered that he wished he could deny it. "The *ménage à toi,* I should say." She stood smiling that still smile so awfully like himself, daring him to go in to Emmett and daring him to stay with her, so that in the end he stood there helplessly. His mind was torn as it always was faced with the smallest choice; and he felt inside him Emmett's agony as he must sit staring at that door remaining closed so long before his eyes.

He had caught a glimpse of Elizabeth as Bruno had gone to her room, standing with her dress falling off one shoulder; he had seen with what terrible swiftness Bruno had shut the door. What might go on between a man and woman behind closed doors was still a mystery to him. Afraid to guess, afraid to put his scanty intellectual knowledge into images, the possibilities although remote were infinite and black. He sat drinking from the whiskey bottle and staring at the blankness of the door until suddenly staring at the door (however blank it was) became stupendously indelicate, making him a party to what went on behind it. His blood beat in a terrible way; he pressed his hands over his eyes to shut out the images he had forbidden and on his eyelids as on some awful screen the figure of Elizabeth was repeated, a green dress falling from one shoulder.

"Can I help it," said Elizabeth, lofty and bitter, "if I have as much guts as most of the men I see about town."

This Bruno accepted somehow as a personal blow and bowed his head to its validity. He moved nearer to her (feeling he abandoned Emmett with every inch he departed from that door), thinking that what strength she had could complement his weakness, almost as though they must have changed places somewhere until he almost became the woman and she might be the man. He lifted his eyes. She was strong and staunch, suddenly brave before him, like some very truthful, clear-sighted child. Her chin was raised to a forbidding angle like a soldier about to strike or a little girl trying not to cry; but there was also a hardness, a brittle something about her that frightened him back, repellent almost to whatever there was left in him of manliness.

"Guts," he said. "You've got more guts than any man.

You've got so much it's disgusting. When a woman goes in for having guts," he tormented her (as well as himself), "she has no sense of delicacy, she goes twice as far as any man."

Her chin went higher, her face went colder with a clear purity of outline that cut through the air like a knife. "Somebody's got to have the guts," she said, shrugging. They eyed each other across the space that she had rendered crystal-clear and sharp. "I've got plenty of guts," she said, "guts to endure anything. But I haven't any nerve, I haven't got the nerve to *do* anything about it." Her face was like a cruel and delicate steel blade.

"We'd better be going," Bruno said quietly.

"Why yes," said Elizabeth, "the bottle-baby must be champing at the bit."

He ignored her, taking out his watch to lend naturalness to their going. "My God! it's almost twelve! Jeffrey will have made a fool of himself before we get there." He felt miserable and hopeless, as one does in dreams, wandering round in circles and never quite catching the bus. The worst of it was that the party had lost importance in his consciousness; he was a man going mechanically to do his duty. "Will you hurry, Elizabeth," he said, feeling that he must wait for her, that he could not go out and face Emmett alone.

She collected her gloves and handkerchief with the coolness of a much older woman of the world than twenty-six; it hurt him to see her child's face gaze with no pleasure for a last perfunctory glance at the mirror; to see her childish slender arms swing the wrap about her shoulders with the air of one accustomed to doing things for herself—and a little too as though she were in the habit of leaving places.

She stood on tiptoe again in her silver slippers, leaning toward the mirror, running her little finger over the red of her lips; he could see that her eye was not following the finger's journey. *"We are scared till the blood in our veins runs thin and we must hop from one person to the next because . . ."*

"What?" he cried, astonished, frightened.

"Oh that," she said, laughing, turning (and he saw her lips were much too red); "that's a quotation from a musical comedy in good old Paris. Off to the party!" she cried, swinging her long black gloves. "Off in a cloud of dust! My ears hurt," she said querulously, "there's a ringing in them."

"Too much alcohol," he said. He took her arm and felt that her skin was ice-smooth like the icy purity of her face. He went out with her, feeling the comfort that attends walking naturally in step with another person, even though it might be walking to a funeral; and he had the feeling, part relief and partly fear, that they had left something or other in the room behind them.

The third movement, the scherzo, Autumn—the gayest of them all; dry leaves circled by the wind, branches crackling on the violin, birds escaping pianissimo, even the cello grown playful as a cello can, the melody skittish and bright. . . .

"My uncle," said Mr. Tevander with the defiance of the weak, "was a *very* fine rider and he claimed that he was never run away with."

"There is no good rider," said Mrs. Stanhope severely, "who has *not* been run away with."

"My uncle," continued Mr. Tevander desperately, "was a very fine rider and he always said that it is not a runaway unless the rider tries to stop his horse; and my uncle," he met Mrs. Stanhope's eye brazenly, "never tried to stop one."

"We would have," said Mrs. Stanhope acidly, "to ask the horse about *that.*"

Miss Ermine-tail's laugh was a hearty yawn, remnant of the days when she had bothered with the whole process rather elaborately. Nowadays she omitted the details, merely opened her mouth wide and gave the concluding yelp. She yelped now and plucked at Mr. Merriwell's sleeve. "Did you hear, G.F., did you hear what Mrs. Stanhope said, we'd have to ask the horse about *that!*" Mrs. Stanhope complacently snorted and Mr. Merriwell who remembered when he had dandled Ermine-tails upon his knee patted her very very kindly. "Oh look," said Mrs. Stanhope in a hushed and reverential voice, "the Ballisters; God bless them." They all sustained a moment's silence like the moment after grace, and Mr. Tevander felt himself forgiven for his uncle.

And March (remembering his coachman days when he drove Merle's father over Brooklyn Bridge and both of them wondering if the Bridge would hold, yet even then aware each of his given place in an ordered world and holding no converse from their distances) humbly and happily drew back the portières and would have scattered roses if he could: for the Ballisters were all that were left to him of blizzards and top-hats and silver-headed canes.

"Oh look, the Ballisters," said Mrs. Draper, coming to.

"The Ballisters," said Miss Titcomb and Miss Henley-Star, Miss Cracken and Miss Milliken.

"My God, the Ballisters," groaned Al.

Someone tapped Arturo on the shoulder. For the smallest fraction of a second Arturo closed his eyes and admitted a dazzling flash of dream. For he never played The Symphony without a faint belief that at its end some connoisseur would recognize it: some party would burst into applause behind his back: 'Bravo, bravo, Teresca!' He snapped to attention and threw over his shoulder the melancholy smile that could be photographed as anything; to the last that smile played safe. "Mr. Terry, sorry, would you mind playing old New York songs, you know, 1890 vintage, someone's just come in . . ." The smile turned smoothly commercial; Arturo broke off the Autumn movement in the middle; he gave the Boys a signal and wound up his knee for action again. "Af-*ter* the Ball was o-over . . ."

(Thank God for that, Mr. Terrill whispered; I never really cared for Debussy anyhow.)

Having bowed themselves under the portières and crouched themselves onto the ballroom floor, the Ballisters stood, like royalty. Envoys were quickly sent from all the separate groups. Mr. Whitman and Mr. Draper both hurried forward at the instigation of their wives, Mrs. Stanhope despatched Mr. Merriwell; the efficiency expert's wife insisted on accompanying her husband (contact with people like the Ballisters was always reassuring), Mr. Bud Chapman had to drop his mental pinochle hand because Mr. Crawford scraped back his chair and said there were the grand old Ballisters; a Mr. Harrod whispered to his brotherinlaw that the Ballister house had eighty-seven rooms and can you imagine that grand old pair keeping it up even though the rooms were no longer in use and they were both too old to walk up stairs, that's true aristocracy for you, Mr. Harrod explained to his brotherinlaw who was from Pennsylvania and not expected to know; farther on down the room gentlemen laid their sandwiches on plates and wiped their hands carefully before starting for the Ballisters; and in a corner by the music a man by the name of George Hervey Junior tried to look unconcerned while the male members of his party rose and left him sitting with the ladies, all because George Hervey Senior was a self-made man self-made so recently that his bank-account had scarcely had time to jell—and more than ever Junior was convinced that Socialism was the best way out.

"It's people like the Ballisters," Violet Draper murmured, watching her husband's course across the room, "who restore one's faith in life." "They make all the sacrifices well worth while," sighed Mrs. Whitman; "even a tragedy like poor Jim Fancher's." "Standards," said Mrs. Draper, nodding, "it's all a question of standards—and poor Jim Fancher had them too." "In a broad way of thinking, yes," replied Mrs. Whitman; "but principles—" "Standards are stronger," said Violet Draper; and both ladies fingered their pearls and began to sing through closed mouths: "mm hmm hm m" to Af—ter the Baaall.

Upstairs in the library Merle whispered, "The Ballisters must have come. We really ought to go down." But because Jeffrey answered nothing, she protested for him: "But not yet, not yet, in a moment." Af-ter the Ball kept floating up.

"But look here, Firman," Miles was saying, "what classes *is* the Magazine supposed to reach, that's the point, the whole point." "I think personally," said Cornelia laughing, "that your Negro was a house-detective." "No, he looked too much like one," said Margaret; "a dark horse if ever there was one!" "only two classes," Firman said "and no use trying to bridge them over" said a Maxwell "nor inventing smaller classes in between" said Little Dixon "because in a war after all," said Cornelia leaning forward, "there can only *be* two sides" "the fellows in No Man's Land in between are shot from both trenches" said Firman, taking Cornelia's hand. "But intellectuals," said Miles. "I think you're very brave," said Margaret, "to face a life like that; but what are you going to do about a *personal* life, Cornelia?" "Oh I'll grant you that the intellectuals were born on an island of some sort, Flinders," Firman said; "but is that any reason," said Cornelia eagerly, "for never crossing over to the mainland? . . . Why I don't know what you mean, Mrs. Flinders, Margaret, what exactly do you mean, a *personal* life?" she said, absently stroking Firman's hand.

"It begins to look," said Al, "a bit like the last round-up taking place around the Ballisters. . . . So this is a revolution party, Miss Norah, is it? Well, I think it's a pretty nice party because *you're* at it."

"I do wonder where my husband is," said Norah politely smiling; "I hope he won't forget to make his speech." Al put a brotherly arm about her shoulder.

Ruthie Fisher caught her eye. Norah was absently smiling; but as she smiled her eyes seemed to make a quick decisive tour to every corner of the room; and returning, calm from their vain trip but still watchful, they encountered Ruthie Fisher sympathetically. At once the knowledge leaped in Ruthie's heart: that Norah, like herself, awaited Jeffrey; that Norah's heart beat just like hers; that Norah too, beneath her mild composure, knew that solemn anguish . . .

"Of course she knows about me, Lydia!" she said indignantly. "She's no bourgeois, Norah and I are the greatest friends. Oh Norah's swell," she said in a burst of love, of loyalty, for Norah; "sometimes," she added, feeling the solace of their combined pain and love, "sometimes I think I like her better than I like Jeff . . . if she weren't a girl," she finished honestly.

"Gosh! Fish!" Lydia said. "Doesn't she *care,* I mean how can she be friends with you, I mean . . ." But for Ruthie Fisher there were in that room for the moment only two people, herself and Norah Blake; and in the whole world only three, herself and Norah waiting hand in hand like sisters, and beyond, somewhere elusive in space but still belonging vividly to both of them, their lover Jeffrey Blake. The nearest thing to peace that she had known all evening filled her.

The court of the Ballisters grew and the Ballisters came up to the shoulders of the first rank courtiers. The ancient Ballisters as they were called again although they were brother and married sister, had been wedded one third of their lives and widowed one third. This last lap that they were on was like a continuation of their childhood and it is doubtful if either remembered the married interim. They crouched and shoved through life together, equally in need of one another's arms and valiantly "kept up" the grand old mansion in which (some seventy years ago) the Ballister children had played Hunt the Slipper: though they could no longer climb its stairs. Old Mr. Ballister was considered especially valiant because despite his years he kept his hearing; old Sarah Ballister was valiant because though deaf (or else remarkably absent) she conducted herself without ear-trumpets. They bowed and crackled now; said things like "well well, how is your grandfather, oh yes, he's dead," that were taken away by the first rank as very precious favors. The next rank came up as the first group settled on the outskirts and the little Ballisters shrank a little more and licked at their turned-in lips; the third rank pressed in close enough to see the velvet band that held up old Miss Ballister's throat and then old Sarah Ballister murmured to her brother that she was tired and her brother said aloud that his sister was tired and everybody murmured of course, significantly and self-reproachfully, and sprang forward to lend the Ballisters arms across the floor. "It is not," whispered one member of the cortège, "that eighty is so very many years; but it is so awesomely near the end of them." And the band played Auld Lang Syne.

Arturo was not playing Auld Lang Syne for the Ballisters. He was playing it to Mary. He was lonely for Mary, he played to Mary sitting at home with a mending basket on her knee; or going in to change the littlest kid; or stealing a look at her fur coat hanging grandly in the closet. Very well, Arturo thought with dignity: let him be a minor artist; he was a major lover anyway.

The music went up the stairs in a slow crescendo, came and circled faintly in the library like a hurdy-gurdy sounding melancholy from the street. "I have always been" said Jeffrey (*be still, my trembling hands!*) "something of a lone wolf; even in my childhood." He had almost forgotten Merle, sitting with his head on her lap and letting Auld Lang Syne stop his ears and brain. Now he brought himself to look at her. He thought she looked a little drunk, as though her mouth had slipped, her eyes were floating; all of her swayed like a plaster cast of Venus—if that were passion, he thought fastidiously, then passion was not becoming to her; but it looked more like despair. What on earth was he doing here, he thought, waking with surprise. I don't want to be here. I don't want to be with Merle. He buried his hands in her hair to still them there. But his hands trembled, thinking of Elizabeth; his mind wandered, thinking of Elizabeth. (He recalled again how she had violently struck him.) It was like this always: when he was with one woman he would think of another. When he had lightly courted Margaret Flinders he had thought of Comrade Fisher; when he made love to Comrade Fisher he had lain and longed for Merle; and now that his fingers swept at will through Merle's lovely cloudy hair he wanted Elizabeth Leonard. And when the cycle was complete, when he had won his way again around the cycle, there would be Norah again, his Norah, waiting: with whom at last he was at liberty to be himself. "I have almost always," he said, "been lonely"; and heard his words mechanical and yet sincere, like the murmurous sentimental hurdy-gurdy from below.

The Ballisters were seated with care, arranged, refreshments brought them; ambassadors lingered, broke off and returned to their separate parties, Bud Chapman called for his friend and plucked at Crawford's sleeve, Mr. Harrod bowed himself back to his Pennsylvania brotherinlaw. "They didn't know us from Adam," the efficiency expert whispered witheringly to his wife as against no protests whatsoever they tore themselves away. But the Ballisters of course must never be left alone; and Mr. Draper who had been sitting closest to Mr. Ballister's valiant voice, straining for the end of how his sister had found cobwebs over their great-grandmother's picture in the hall, looked up to discover that his was the glory, the embarrassment, the fame, of "sitting with the Ballisters": for Lucius Whitman, laughing, had returned to both their wives.

"Now this," said Bruno tentatively, standing in the doorway with an arm about each of his protegés, "reminds one forcibly of Marx: that there might be a revolution; or there might be chaos." They stood blinking in the light, Emmett, Elizabeth, and Bruno, searching through the ballroom for their friends. "And here comes your father, Emmett, to tell us which it is."

"Say, your revolution's late," Al said. "It's twelve o'clock. Is that my son? Well, I'm damned. What? no shakee hands with revolution's sugar-papa?" Emmett hesitated; held out his hand and drew it back, perceiving that one of his father's hands was engaged round Norah's waist, the other held a turkey-stick. "What's this?" said Bruno. "This? Oh it's my lamp," said Al, brandishing it; "I'm Diogenes looking for a proletarian. But who is this," he said. "I'm Emmett's girl-friend," Elizabeth said, "I hope you don't mind, Mr. Middleton—and would you ask the steward please," she waved toward March, "for a little drink for the lady?" "Nice to see you all," said Norah; "Jeffrey's mislaid somewhere." "And where's my mother," said Emmett suddenly; "where's Merle, I d-d-don't see her anywhere." "She's upstairs, son, she got tired of waiting for you." Al smiled down anxiously into Emmett's face.

"I think I'll go and find her," said Emmett to his own surprise. He was home again. He wanted Merle. "I wouldn't, son," said Al with gentleness. And that was his God damned jealousy again, thought Emmett, his cruelty, his sadism as the Vambery called it. "Stick with us, Emmett," said Bruno kindly. But Emmett had turned against them all; a wave of pity for his mother swept him as he thought how she, like himself, was left out of things here, by his friends, by her own husband. He had a keen thrust suddenly of instinct: his mother would be waiting, lonely, hungry for a sight of him. "I wouldn't, son," said Al again. "Don't leave us, Emmett, I couldn't bear it," said Elizabeth coldly. "Look, we'll be needing you to help with the speeches, Emmett," Bruno said. Emmett turned upon them all. "What do you th-th-think I am, anyway," he said, "a God damned b-b-baby?" And swung round, brushing March's belly, to mount the stairs.

"In the library, I think," said the Vambery, directing him. From the stairs the party filled Emmett with disgust. He saw his father guiding Norah Blake, his arm about her waist; Bruno and Elizabeth following, arm in arm, step matching step. He went up the stairs more eagerly than he had for years. How many times, he thought, had he crept up them to hide away from Merle; and now he climbed them swiftly to find her and tell her he was sorry. He had very little notion of how to speak to her, even of what, precisely, he had to say; but words would come somehow. Reaching the top he grew exalted with a new impulse: he might tell her of what he saw below, tell how Bruno let him down as Al did her, he might offer to take her away—he had a fine vision of their going off together, Switzerland perhaps, "the young American and his lovely mother, what a beautiful relationship between them"; educating her; or perhaps merely pleasing her—he wanted somebody exclusively to himself.

The door to the library stood closed; light shone over the transom. He walked up gently, shy with faith. It occurred to him then that Merle would not be alone; she could not (however she had wanted to) have deserted the party to come up here and wait for him. He lifted his hand to knock—and saw how large and blank the door was. *What might go on between a man and woman behind closed doors was still a mystery to him . . . the possibilities although remote were infinite and black . . .* He remembered Al's face; thought now in retrospect the Vambery had looked peculiar too. His blood beat again in that new and surreptitious way and he went on up the stairs past rows and rows of blank closed doors until he found his own. He went in and stood with his lonely childhood until he burst into tears for company. When the first tears failed him he drew the pages of Bruno's speech out of its dog-eared envelope and looking at it, touching it, remembering how they had written it together, the tears came burning forth again.

"But we mustn't forget the party," said Merle again (dance music sounded from below), growing suddenly frightened—less, she decided honestly, at the sudden descent of Jeffrey's hands from her hair to her rigid waist, than at the simultaneous leaping of her heart. She had been happier when he had been tender and poetic, when he sat with his head in her lap, like Emmett when he was a darling little boy, like Emmett no longer and never again.

She could have left it so, only that this terrible fear of hers that men could not desire her had crept like a challenge into her memory; and she had promised herself, had promised herself . . . So she had stolen closer to him, bringing her perfume and her Greek gown and her show of warmth into the circle of his arm, letting them play substitute for what she felt she didn't really have. Till slowly his desire roused, till at last his hand went trembling round her waist.

Her heart leaped with the terror. And so it always was with her and so would always be (despite poor Vammie's bright advice and brilliant explanations) ; only for Al because it had been her duty had she sufficiently stifled the terror to mechanically submit; and resentment had regularly frozen her stiff (as though in shutting off the terror she shut out also all capacity for joy) so that what she endured with Al—in her younger days, when she was still divided between hope that she might thaw and yield, and pride that her being remained untouched by him or any man—was torture beyond words, beyond even what she had conveyed in confidence to Vambery.

"The party, we must go down to the party," she whispered, frightened. And the last time that he had so embraced her, this ardent youth as near her son's age as her own, she had murmured 'But I think I hear my husband coming,' and then promised herself that if ever again she came so near . . . For something whispered that where Al had failed her (he had meant to be kind; but his kindness was rough and uncomprehending) this gentle youth might well succeed. But fear was greater than desire for what she had never fully known, and fear as well that

Jeffrey, her last hope perhaps before she grew too old, would fail her too. "Listen to the music, we must go down," she whispered, trembling.

Her l's were not so clear as always, Jeffrey felt, her voice not quite so beautiful; he felt that he had done with her forever. He had no mind for any woman now except Elizabeth (who might have come, who might be downstairs even now with Bruno—who had slapped him on the first occasion of his meeting her); and yet he had to show Merle, had to play the gallant, had to protest against her protests. "You are so nice, Merle, your hair is nice, your lips are nice." He used the word "nice" with the double finesse of a mathematician and a poet. He used it, as a mathematician, as though it were an exact word, definite, as though he had chosen it scientifically out of all others to precisely bound his meaning. And yet he used it too, in his capacity as a poet, with deprecation, as though he stooped to it as to a common word because of his poet's fine sense of a better one being lacking in this our English language; it became delicate, apologetic; it carried an informal transcription of "words cannot express."

She went limp again for a moment at his third "nice" and his tired hands patted her sexlessly and felt nothing but the texture of her gown. The thought that Elizabeth might already be below was unendurable; and Bruno would be with her—with his unbearable air of handling her like a chattel. Ah, he was beginning to see through Bruno, Comrade Fisher had been right; Bruno was a bourgeois, his attitude toward woman, toward Elizabeth, proved that. He had a vision of himself and Norah and Elizabeth —and Comrade Fisher—starting their own Magazine, their own workers' movement. "Perhaps you're right, we'd better see about the party, Merle." He tried to sound reluctant.

"If you think so," Merle said sadly. Her heart went dead. He gave her up too easily. Now she would give her soul to win back the ardor to his voice, now she would turn herself inside out to regain the exquisite terror. But she had no instinct, only fear, only endless humiliation. She stood before the mirror and smoothed her cloudy hair. She saw herself there between two candles as a woman who had never tasted life at all, who might as well have been a picture chastely framed by the pair of unused candles standing all of their lives in helpless decoration on the mantel. If one could scream, if one could tear one's hair and beat with one's breasts against the walls! But she went on smoothing her hair till not one strand was out of place.

He watched her and thought again, Fisher is right; this woman, worse than Bruno, belongs in some other fraternity than mine. She is not honest. She is an upper-class whore. She swung toward him, blown and angelic; histrionics, he thought with disgust. "Vammie calls me a Rabelaisian puritan," she said. Archly, coyly, with all the bourgeois grace he had hated and must hate again, through Comrade Fisher's eyes. "Do you find me very, do you find me—like other women, Jeffrey, like your, oh like Norah for instance? do you think . . . ?"

"Like nobody else in the world," he said mechanically; and closed his eyes for a farewell kiss, his nervous hands longing for the door and for escape, longing for morality of his own kind, for Norah, for Elizabeth. Dance music greeted them in a rush as they opened the door to the landing.

This was sugar-coating the pill, Miles thought, as the distasteful jazz drummed its way into his ears, his blood, confusing his brain against his will, like some slow poison of the devil. What sort of Magazine could they build from such a base, what sort of movement could they serve if they must sugar-coat each step to suit their over-civilized palates. They had lured the upper classes here on false pretexts; now they gave them music, dancing, caviar—everything they could to fool them into swallowing something alien, into giving their tainted money for a cause in which they played no part. "Now if Jeffrey only would appear," said Bruno. "I am in favor," said Firman, "of more and more investigating" "not skating round," said Cornelia, "as we all are" "we are just as bad as Fisher's fellow-travellers" "on the periphery of things" "and intellectuals as a class," said Firman, "are dying out, their function's dead—nobody's left to support them" "But we haven't anything in common with proletarians," Margaret said, bewildered, "I wouldn't know one if I saw one." "Don't talk like that," said Miles too sharply; for she said, in her simple undirected way, what he hated admitting to himself: that with the far-off and somehow disdainful class of proletarians they had as little in common as the upper classes here foregathered had with them. "I had a hard job," said Elizabeth (how like she was to Bruno!) "drawing proletarians for the posters, I wasn't sure they didn't have horns or some distinguishing characteristic."

"If the Magazine," began a Maxwell brother . . . "What Magazine," said Bruno wearily, "I don't see any sign of the assistant editor who's supposed to start the works." "If the Magazine," continued the second Maxwell brother, "is to have any value more than just being a swansong for the intellectuals, it will seek to introduce them" "to the proletariat" "to the real movement" "to America" "to life, in other words, outside of books," said Firman winding up in triumph. "How in hell did I ever let myself in for this," said Bruno; "I could have stayed at home and gone on drinking."

"And what happens to the intellectuals," said Miles, "if our race is dying out?" He addressed the eager Sheep; Bruno's look was too disheartening. "Why we'll hold down regular jobs for a change" "instead of wearing caps and gowns" "instead of being figure-heads" "instead of writing useless books and having useless titles" "we'll use our brains where they are needed!" they shouted in noisy chorus above the raging music in his ears. "Anyway," said Margaret—placid, Miles thought, but worried too, as any sign of confusion or disagreement always made her, and following again his innermost thoughts and feelings and ready blindly to turn herself inside out to soothe him, "anyway I hope intellectuals, people in general, will be made happier." He looked her way ironically; they were people, he thought, with such different paths! "Pigs!" he reminded her gently, "pigs are happy." "Well then, I wish I were a pig, I wish we all were," she cried in one of her sudden bursts of revolt against him in which he could feel her live and powerful, ten times more than he, as though she deliberately made the contrast; "don't you remember, Bruno, what you said one night—" "Now none of that," said Bruno, "you'll have Elizabeth thinking I'm a God damn sentimentalist." And Margaret crumpled then; "Norah, Norah, let us get some air, some water, Norah wait—" Miles thought her cry was piteous as she rose to join her friend. He watched her with compunction, remembering with embarrassment her condition; but he could not bring himself to say a word. "Will you come, Elizabeth," she said politely, "and have a change from the revolution-brewers?" Elizabeth shook her head. And Miles watched Margaret and Norah, very much women, both of them, move off together arm in arm, floating in their women's world.

No, Elizabeth would not join them. She sat with Bruno's friends and could not take her eyes off Bruno's face. Here she was home again, she thought, ironic. Here (with Bruno) she had meant to stay forever. But her trunk remained unpacked; her mind remained unpacked; Bruno postponed talking to her, put off meeting her eyes. She recalled that they had come near to a real conversation when he came to hook her dress; but what they had said and why they had not said more was not clear to her. "Our report," said Firman, laughing, "was that Fisher's only claim to fame is that she's slept with all the crowned heads of the left wing." "My God," said Bruno, "I wish I'd said that; nasty wit" (was he turning toward her?) "is the opiate of the intellectual." "An adage," she said, suddenly elated, "recently dug up from the tomb of Tutankhamen." They laughed simultaneously, the laugh they had used from childhood for jokes more valued for familiarity than wit. She caught in his look (as his quick smile died) some weight of guilt as he might look at a woman he had wronged. She looked back gravely as though some ultimate truth might suddenly spring to life between them. And then it was over, it was too late again. God knew, she thought a moment later, which had happened first: the wryly smiling downward curve of her own wounded mouth or Bruno's eyes flickering back to Miles.

"Let's have some water," Margaret said; "the crowd and the music are going to my head as though I'd drunk." "It's a nice party," said Norah, "only Mr. Middleton wants to seduce me and I've lost my husband." "He'll come back," said Margaret warmly, "he always does, Norah darling," she said for she wanted everyone to feel as happy, as secure, as she did. "But so will Mr. Middleton," said Norah laughing; "what, no cocktails, Maggie? only water?" "No cocktails," Margaret said, "because a Mrs. Salvemini told me—oh Norah listen; I've got the silliest thing to tell you: I'm going to have a baby." Norah dropped her arm in alarm and they stood stock still on the fringe of the dancers. "A *baby?* have you tried everything?" "Why Norah Meadows Blake, you *cynic!* I *want* it, I did it on purpose." Norah seemed to think a minute. "Well I'm damned," she said at last; "I thought there weren't any any more, I mean, I thought they'd gone out, like horse-cars." Norah's voice was dry, contained no lift. That Norah should not recognize her joy was sad; she had hoped in some way to make herself more secure by telling Norah—for Miles was clearly frightened, she would have to wait months (according to Mrs. Salvemini who had waited five times for *Mister* Salvemini) before Miles would share her feeling or dare to face his own; but then, she thought, the thing was *hers,* she could feel secret joy and secret pride until her friends could see. "But haven't you ever thought of it yourself," she said, curious, for Norah's eyes, as though she had forgotten Margaret's news, were roaming absently around the room. "Oh, yes." "Then why—" "Oh, we're supposed to be making some sort of protest against something, Jeffrey and I," said Norah cheerfully; "sometimes I forget just what." They walked slowly back toward Miles again; and Margaret knew that Norah was searching through the crowd for Jeffrey. "I suppose you think," said Margaret, "that Jeffrey couldn't stand the competition; but he wouldn't be so spoiled, Norah, if he weren't your only child." "Oh you're all too smart for me," said Norah; "I don't know, I was brought up in a barnyard, I was brought up to respect the rooster." "But Norah, is it fair, do you think, to *you?*" said Margaret anxiously. "I have everything in the world I want," said Norah primly, "and all I want is Jeffrey—oh look, Maggie, there he is, there he is! he's looking for me. Of course, I think it swell about you, Maggie, I wish you all the luck. . . ." Amused, Margaret watched the back of Norah forging through the crowd, taking a short-cut through the dancers straight to Jeffrey; and felt a warm urge herself to return to Miles.

"Lydia! that's Jeffrey now."

"Where, where? *where?*" Lydia craned her neck. "Oh he's simply *beautiful!*" she said; and her feelings for Ruthie in this crisis and for the mystery of lovers in general smothered her with joy.

All at once Ruthie Fisher grew quite calm. She discovered to her own surprise that she was proud of herself, of being in love, of taking chances in the world, proud even if it brought her suffering. She felt a dignity she had never expected to feel, a calm, a willingness to face anything that should arise, take anything that should be flung at her. For she saw clearly that Jeffrey's restless eyes were not seeking her behind the buffet; she saw (as he took Norah's hands in greeting) that it was not Norah either whom he sought. She watched them cross the room together, Norah's eyes uplifted and quiet, Jeffrey's roving like his hands. Not till

Norah pulled his sleeve did Jeffrey so much as glance toward Ruthie; and then it was a nod, a wave, the barest smile—and back went his eyes on their journey, seeking someone else.

Of course, Al thought, after twenty years of being married you didn't really love your wife; nor, after five years of not sleeping with her could you even remember her very well; all the same it was a little hard to see her entering her ballroom now, her hair suspiciously smooth, her expression frozen—and her Greek dress sloping off one shoulder. He watched her move across the room, with each step attaining more grace, more deliberation; past the group of Black Sheep she sailed without a sidewise glance and on, growing cooler, more collected, toward the double throne of the Ballisters. Changing classes, he thought ironically; and could have sworn that her dress lifted itself back on to be respectable.

"Well, we have a minyan," Bruno said as Jeffrey came at last. "Hurray!" cried the Black Sheep. "We thought we'd have to hold the revolution without you!" "Can't we," said Miles, "get on with the speeches at once? The party is getting out of hand, they'll never listen if we wait much longer." "Well, if our assistant editor prefers fornication to revolution," said Bruno (Norah was talking kindly with Al Middleton). "Just a minute, just a minute," said Jeffrey testily; "let me get my breath. Oh—Elizabeth: I didn't see you." "Ah, the lone wolf at our door again," said Elizabeth dryly. Jeffrey flushed. "But we haven't told him," Firman cried, "about the ultra-comradeliness of Comrade Fisher." "Fisher?" Jeffrey said, "I saw her." "Yes, but not in her true colors," cried

Little Dixon raucously. They told him. He was embarrassed; undecided whether to show surprise or attempt to protect her. "Fish-er is-n't ko-sher any mo-ore," sang Bruno and Elizabeth. "My God," said Al; "tell me, *is* there a communist party?" *"Is* there a Magazine?" said Miles with gloom. "Is there an object to this game?" said Bruno. *"Is* there another drink," said Elizabeth. "How about shutting off the band, Mr. Middleton," Cornelia said, "and *making* them start the speeches?" "My speech," cried Bruno, waking; "Emmett's got it, where is Emmett?" "Emmett," said Al, "didn't he find his mother, Blake?" And two Black Sheep were despatched to look for Emmett.

Fisher a worse-than-bourgeois, Jeffrey thought; Fisher a downright counter-revolutionary—the Black Sheep had it straight. He hated Fisher for letting him down; but in his heart he knew she had not let him down—she was a woman and had taken him for a man, but being the kind of man he was he had grown utterly tired of her, he needed something new, someone to look at him through fresh eyes, someone through whose eyes he could see himself. "Elizabeth," he said, "I've been wanting and wanting to see you."

"I know," she said. "You're a lone wolf and I'm 'nice' and everybody else in the world is neurotic and you're the only communist. You'll have to think up some other way of wooing me." Nevertheless he squatted beside her on the floor, his head against her knee; and after a moment she allowed him to hold her hand. Rhythms beat faster in her ears at the familiar touch of an unfamiliar hand (*the express train is leaving . . . oh Jeffrey, oh stranger, you know me, you know me as though I were naked*) ; all right Jeffrey, she thought wearily, you don't want me, I don't want you, and in the end we'll have each other. She felt a wan kinship with him, knowing him to be the same thing as herself, a weary Don Juan whose impulses having lost their freshness were the more compelling therefor. The ballroom buzzed about them, the whole of it in her ears. She thought she would never again be rid of the noise and confusion circling in her head. She looked at Bruno now, sitting a large and helpless man, abandoned both by Jeffrey and herself; even by Emmett who had gone to seek his mother. His blurred and kind face hurt her. The perennially bright and vulnerable face of the precocious child aging much to its own incredulous hurt. Long nose, grown for fifteen years in a sheltered society (oh Longview, dear childhood) where long noses did not matter; and then projected into the world where it longed to shrink and because it could not, grew sharp and disdainful, but humble, and—longer than ever. It was a predatory nose, she thought, reaching out bold and eager for its prey; yet its tip was suddenly blunted, stunted, as though it would never dare seize all it could reach. It was a noble nose, arrogant—and yet it was futile, impotent. When he wore glasses on its bridge its length was foreshortened, lending him a peculiarly benign and harmless look. The glasses tamed it, kept it in its place, caged it, and when it reached, angry but helpless, out of its cage, it resembled an elephant's foreshortened trunk, pointing madly toward his enemies the zoo-gazers; and forever deprived of its prey. But the pain of looking at Bruno bulged inside her temples and her breast till she had to look away, till to quiet her own nerves she patted Jeffrey's hand: and knew that it was understood between them; and understood too by Bruno though his eyes were turned away.

She reflected how little, at best, she had to do with her own destiny. She lived in a frame of men's reactions, building herself over from one man to the next; her character seemed compounded on what various men had told her she was. What Denny had said, what Wheelwright had said, what Jeffrey's look requested, what last year and this year and the year after next Bruno had said and would say. . . . She rose up each time, perhaps hurt, perhaps newly hopeful, presented herself each time as a target—and each time, it seemed, some accident, some small arbitrary fact . . . like a toothbrush clasped unwittingly too tight in a lover's hand, like the presence of Emmett (now slowly and fatefully approaching, between his Black Sheep captors) always with Bruno, like the fact that her eyes and Bruno's always, by the fraction of a second, failed to click. . . . But the accidents matched, the patterns matched; and much as she dreaded, she welcomed, the identical disastrous ends. In a sense one stood in line for all the kind of things that happened; one stood inevitably in one line or another. It was the same with Elizabeth's drawing as with separate incidents in her life: which started each time large and fine but which she never let go until she had spoiled it, apparently without volition, by some comic touch. Still one could ask why? Success perhaps was insupportable; somewhere along the line she must, she felt, have missed out badly and forever after would take no substitutes. And so she ran away or laughed accidentally at the wrong moments or stopped her ears with a roar when some truth battered for entrance; and so she would go on until she had laid the ghost of what she missed, or found the magic number; or else she would come face to face one day with the main issue, in some narrow passage, where she could not turn aside or make a joke.

"I'm sorry, Bruno," Emmett said; "I was m-m-mad for some reason, or drunk I guess, I almost threw away your speech." He stood like a pale ghost who has come to his senses again, and handed the envelope to Bruno. "And I'd like to ap-p-pologize to Elizabeth, I think I was very rude." "Well for God's sake," Al said, "if you were rude to someone, stick to it, I'm glad to hear it, Emmett." "To hell with that," cried the Black Sheep, "stop the music, Mr. Middleton before they discover something else to fight about. Come on, let's get front row seats!" "If you can tear yourself away from Elizabeth, Jeffrey," said Bruno coldly. "I'll s-s-stay with Elizabeth," said Emmett pleasantly, "and hold her hand; didn't you tell my father you were my g-g-girl, Elizabeth?" "Well, I guess the revolution's happened," Al remarked, bewildered, and started off to tell Teresca.

In spite of himself Bruno felt the solemnity again, and walked proud and firm with Jeffrey, toward the draped-off place beside the buffet where the speeches would take place. Elizabeth's painted Hunger Marchers formed the back-drop; already the Black Sheep, eager, had spread themselves before it, dragging chairs to the astonishment of the dancers. The speech felt good in Bruno's hand, the familiar envelope was reassuring—even its surface had not been spared: there were sentences and half-sentences scribbled in his and Jeffrey's, Miles' and Emmett's hands.

Al spoke briefly to Teresca. The dancers sensed nothing

because they were lost in each other's arms and rhythms; but the sitters noticed something, felt something in the air, wondered where the change would fall from. "Something's going to happen," muttered Mrs. Whitman to Mrs. Draper. "Something's going to happen," said Miss Titcomb and Miss Milliken. "Oh jolly jolly jolly," Mr. Crawford said, "the entahtainahs ayah assembling." Arturo closed off his music, jogged his knee, and sat, smiling to his audience, the Boys, himself, his absent wife. "Whut's it for, this benefit, Mr. Middleton," called Miss Ermine-tails, giggling, "whut's it for?" "The blind, I think," said Al; and moved on down the room. Mr. Graham Hatcher could bear it no longer: "I am *not* the entertainment," he exploded, "God damn it, I am Vice President of the C.F.S.U.S.—The Colored Folks' Social Uplift Society." "Some little Magazine they're starting," Merle explained to Mr. Ballister who could hear and old Miss Ballister who couldn't.

Jeffrey stood forward, handsome and nervous, and on the other side of the room Norah clasped her hands over her heart to still its beating, to send a message of help to Jeffrey.

"FRIENDS AND COMRADES":

(Ruthie Fisher leaned across the buffet to catch his eye, to smile, to encourage him with all her heart.) "All of us could not be present at the Hunger March today. We have our separate reasons, and all of them are valid. For one thing, thanks to our gracious hostess," he waved a gallant hand toward Mrs. Middleton, "we are not hungry." A pretty ripple of laughter flowed out from somewhere. (That kind of humor, said Miles unhappily, is what will sink us in the end.) "But the main thing is, we are not needed there; we are wanted on the outside, to lead, direct . . . keeping watch at the pivot, at the helm." (I'm going to be sick again, Cornelia said. Wait for Doctor Leonard, this doesn't count, Firman whispered back; Blake is a sop to the aristocrats.)

"The injustice of hunger," continued Jeffrey, "is something we can all appreciate . . . driving mothers to despair . . . fathers to militant objection . . ."

("When you come right down to it," said Mrs. Stanhope, "horses are more intelligent than people. Ever hear of a horse taking up a gun and going to shoot another horse? Ever hear of a horse marching to Washington because there were more oats in some other horse's stable? Ever read in the papers about *that,* Mr. Tevander? Wh-hy!" All her group politely whinnied.)

"and now the times are dangerously bad for everybody, we all must have our eyes open to the common suffering which tomorrow may be ours. . . ."

(*"That's* no joke," sighed Mr. Draper, "I've been thinking of starting a colony of ex-bankers in the South Seas on an island." "And think of poor Jim Fancher," Mrs. Draper said behind her hand.)

"I attach no labels . . . speak to no class-consciousness . . ."

("He says there are no classes in America," said Merle to old Miss Ballister who could not hear.)

"but to a sense of justice, of intelligence, and even, in the last analysis, of self-preservation . . . I ask for hunger-consciousness . . . before it is too late . . ."

("he says we've got to protect ourselves against the

lower classes," Merle said to Mr. Ballister who *could* hear.)

"it is not that the bins of this country are empty . . . that the houses of this land are full . . ."

("When you come to think of it, *why* should the Ballisters keep that big old empty house," said Mr. Tevander thoughtfully, "I mean, I wonder . . ." "Wh-hy!" said Mrs. Stanhope incredulously.)

"but they are closed, the food-bins, and the houses . . . to our unemployed . . ."

("A little serious, I think," said Miss Hobson, "for a party, don't you think?" "Still," returned Mr. Terrill—who had lost a fortune since 1929 and was living on half a one now—"it's a pretty serious problem, even *at* a party." "I know so little of these things," said Miss Hobson femininely; "art means so much more to me.")

"as intellectuals, it's time we took our stand. It is with this purpose that Dr. Bruno Leonard, whose liberal views have long made him an important figure at his College . . . who has espoused the cause of students who held minority opinions . . . who wishes now to aid the larger cause, not this time of a minority, but of the great majority: the working-class . . . is founding now this Magazine . . ."

("What Magazine?" said Ermine-tails restlessly; "I thought *now* they'd let Paul Robeson dance.")

"to establish a Forum for the radical intellectual, for the puzzled upper-classes, sympathizers with the plight . . . I have the honor to introduce to you: Doctor Bruno Leonard."

There was a scattered round of applause and heads were

craned toward Bruno. Humph, said Mr. Ballister who could hear. Oh very good, ve-ry good, said ancient Miss Ballister who could *not* hear; and when she clapped her hands together it could be seen that they did not meet or made no sound: as though whoever pulled her strings was very, very tired—after all these years—and couldn't be bothered any longer with making a thorough job of it.

"I'm going home, Lydia," said Ruthie Fisher suddenly through the applause; "I'm going home," she said, and was amazed at her own dignity. For Jeffrey was bowing and bowing and his bright eyes were never turned in her direction; she saw the object of his gaze, the girl in lettuce-green, to whom he looked (though Ruthie Fisher had composed his speech) for approbation now. It was all too plain. She had taken her chances and lost—lost again; and she must hurry, hurry home, hurry to where she lived for independence (so she wrote her father), where she lived for love—hurry to the little room and weep all night, for Jeffrey Blake, for William Turner, on that narrow cot under Lenin's eye. "Cheerio," she said to the astonished Lydia; and rapidly collected the man's wallet she carried for a purse; and a crumpled pack of cigarettes; and started (terrified lest bourgeois tears burst from her aching heart before she reached the end), started on her own private hunger march, an agony of bright self-consciousness, across the mile-long ballroom (begging the pardon of an iceberg clad in pearls who collided coldly with her) . . . under Jeffrey Blake's indifferent eye.

And Bruno rose, ponderous and very brave; the girl in lettuce-green rose with him. He lifted his hand to compel silence; and hers went up like its shadow. "Oh my God," said Emmett, next to her. "Don't be nervous, son," Al Middleton whispered gently.

The buzz was disconcerting; despite his lifted hand it did not die, it seemed, indeed, in some subterranean way, to grow. Bruno waited confidently (he looks Jewish, the efficiency expert's wife said loudly; the efficiency expert blushed with pain)—for here were the old triumvirate pulling together again; he felt the presence of Jeffrey solid behind him (whatever inanities there were in Jeffrey's speech he thought his own would iron out); he caught Miles' eyes, lifted to his own in steady faith. "FRIENDS," he said into the oblivious buzz. "FRIENDS," he said louder; and observed that face after face was turning from him, like an epidemic. A low murmur spread through the crowd.

"Well, I *admire* her," said Mrs. Stanhope boldly; "she's got my *admiration*." "I'm hanged," murmured Crawford to Bud Chapman; "pretty jolly *this* will be, I wonder if the Ballisters . . ." "Go on, bring her here," Mrs. Whitman and Mrs. Draper urged their husbands forward; "the courage of the poor thing, wearing Jimmie's pearls!"

"Look," said Miss Hobson, drawing herself up; "that woman *did* come, after all: Emily Fancher—if you please!"

"Emily Fancher," buzzed the ballroom as March stood solid behind her like a portent.

"Emily Fancher!" said Miss Titcomb and Miss Henley-Star, Miss Cracken and Miss Milliken. And *Doesn't she look stunning,* breathed Miss Milliken.

"FRIENDS, THE PURPOSE OF OUR MAGAZINE," said Bruno, plunging desperately into the middle of his speech

—when Al came rushing to his rescue. Over the Black Sheep's heads he spoke: "Better wait, Leonard, better give them their heads for a minute. Lady entering in pearls is our first prison-widow. Husband embezzled. Got five years. Damn shame. Best card player I ever knew." He retreated, winking sympathetically, and took up his former station at the bar.

Emily Fancher, as cool as her pearls, was too wise to show gratitude for her reception and passed among her friends a happy cynosure. "Why Jim's just fine, having a fine rest," she nodded to one group. "Oh certainly everything's all right," she waved her hand at another, "certainly: half the property had been transferred to my name." "Now that," breathed the efficiency expert's wife to her husband reverentially, "that's savoir faire—that's *born* in a person, the real thing," she wistfully concluded.

The Black Sheep grew furious. They were signalling to catch his eye, Bruno knew, urging him to stand and shout his speech if necessary. He looked out like a man of stone above their heads. He saw Elizabeth, standing in futile replica of himself. He saw young Emmett, pale and frightened; he tried to smile, but Emmett wouldn't meet his eye.

Like a little ghost of something human the Middleton boy sat beside her. "Why doesn't he start, what's he afraid of," he stammered in what Elizabeth conceived his strongest effort to be cruel. Elizabeth's eyes had somehow lost their focus; for the room had grown very large, incredibly large and terribly bright; and all the people in it were very small except Bruno, a large and helpless mountain of a man, crucified and hung before the world for ridicule. Jeffrey she perceived beside him as a Judas; and the Black Sheep waving in their anger at his feet were torn scraps of some flag struggling to rise and mend itself. "He's s-scared, that's all," sneered the Middleton boy. She did not strike him because seen through her anger he had too many faces; instead she held herself tall as she could in her lettuce-colored dress for Bruno.

"My dear, what *else* could he have done?" Mrs. Fancher asked her friends. "Just barely settled in . . . the walls of the living-room imported . . . Tudor house in England . . . imagine the cost of that alone . . . and the bedroom absolutely lifted" "absolutely lifted" echoed Miss Titcomb and Miss Henley-Star "from a Louis Sixteenth boudoir" "a Louis Sixteenth boudoir" echoed Miss Cracken and Miss Milliken ("Don't speak to *me* of bravery among your lower classes," Mrs. Draper said; "I know nothing to compare with Emily Fancher's courage in coming here tonight" "a question of standards," said Mrs. Whitman proudly, "when one's standards are at stake, culture, art—") "an onyx bathtub," Emily Fancher continued bravely, "gold faucets, oh gold fixtures everywhere, and the floor inlaid in marble, you know Jim, he had, he *has,* absolutely perfect taste" "absolutely perfect taste" breathed the efficiency expert's wife as though she were in church "and he always, thank God, wanted the best of everything for me" "the best was none too good for her" "and then the marvellous Gobelins to cover up the Tudor walls" "Gobelins" "and then the crash came . . . well! what *could* he do?" "what *could* he do?"

The buzz had risen in Elizabeth's ears until it was terrific din, of drums and music expressing finality like the Day of Judgment, parade music, music louder than the world, and through it all some quiet bell, some quiet voice, trying to tell her something. She turned and struggled, tried to hear, tried properly to fix her aching eyes; but her camera trembled, the world and Bruno shaking on its retina. "S-scared, that's what," said the Middleton boy in a shaking voice. "Oh be quiet!" said Elizabeth.

"Mr. Tevander, you are being deliberately obtuse," Mrs. Stanhope rallied bitterly; "Jim Fancher *had* to do what he did . . . what he did took *courage*. . . ." "I know," said Mr. Tevander restlessly, "all I say is, it oughtn't to be necessary, I mean the system, I mean, men shouldn't *have* to do such things as Fancher did. . . ." "Oho," said Mrs. Stanhope cunningly, "so you are a *Socialist,* Mr. Tevander; but have you ever stopped to think what would become of art, of culture?"

The Black Sheep were roaring out their anger.

This is hell, this is purgatory, Miles said to Margaret; and he wiped his brow on which angry sweat was bursting out. Bruno stood before him as large, potentially as noble as once his Uncle Daniel striding down a side of hill; but Bruno's hand was stayed, his strength was bottled—and Miles' faith was trembling. It's like a ghastly parable, he said. And she said nothing back to soothe him; she sat there beside him in the center of the maddening din and couldn't find a word. It's like a kind of sarcastic revelation from God, he said. I know, I know, she said, helpless.

"and not one square inch of tapestry will you return, Emily, he said to me; not one gold gadget, not one splinter of the Tudor walls . . ." "not one gold splinter" said Miss Ermine-tails, her kerchief at her eyes ("She *is* brave, you were right," whispered Miss Hobson, giving in to Mr. Terrill) "and his last words . . . before the reporters . . . goodbye, see you in jail, darling. . . ." This *did* affect Emily Fancher, brave as she was, in retrospect; she touched her eyes with a bit of lace and her audience solicitously looked the other way. "When you tell *me,*" concluded Mrs. Draper savagely, "about the sufferings of the poor—I'd *rather* starve than some things . . ." "I always say," said Mrs. Whitman tearfully, "remember—" and she nodded a sage, coiffured, experienced head, "the rich have their troubles too."

Bruno stood crucified before the Hunger Marchers that Elizabeth had painted. He thought with pity of the envelope shaking in his hands, containing little words by all of them, his old triumvirate, or little designs that each had absently made while engaged in the endless conferences to prepare the speech within. He could hear the Black Sheep, could sense their impatience; he knew without listening to their words that they were shouting at him, pleading with him to go on, to drown the whole flimsy circus to which they turned their lean strong backs, to restore their faith in him, in themselves, and even—because they were so pitifully young, because they were children and he their teacher—in life. And he looked away, out over their heads, until one person emerged, as crucified as he was; he saw Elizabeth still standing like himself and his head grew rigid, his blood changed, he was paralyzed with a sense of shame. He looked from her to Emmett, wavering now in a strange excitement, entering Bruno's vision of Elizabeth as though deliberately diluting it. He saw a look in Emmett's eyes that he utterly failed to read, ironic, bitter, challenging—and because he despised Emmett now as much as he pitied him, his look was more unendurable than even the Black Sheep's. He stared back, advanced to the extreme edge of the improvised platform and shouted into the swimming mass: "LADIES AND GENTLEMEN."

"S-speech, speech!" cried Emmett in a high falsetto. Glances shot his way. He was the son of the house. "Speech, speech!" he cried again in his high wavering shrill voice. The Black Sheep took it up, stamped furiously and roared for silence. Al Middleton put down his punch; never had he seen such violence in his puny son—he seized his turkey-leg and beat upon the punch-bowl: "Shut up, shut up, everybody! Doctor Leonard's going to speak!" "S-speech!" Emmett's voice broke into hysteria. The buzz died slowly.

The silence sounded. It was as though the congestion in Elizabeth's ears were pierced at last so that the voice which had been saying something to her for twenty-six years quietly, spoke quietly now and could be heard. It was final but not surprising. As a child she had waited two hours for a parade to pass a certain window; *it was coming! it was not coming!* (but all the time she knew it was); till there it came, rounding a corner and burning itself forever into her eyes. So now in her eyes this figure of Bruno (after twenty-six years of waiting), Bruno standing mountainous and mountainously weak; so now in her ears this cessation of sound, this cessation of doubt, this quiet voice, you love him, you love Bruno, you never loved anybody else, you never can love anybody else. Lucidly she saw that there could never be any exchange on this level with Bruno; not unless one of them lay on his death-bed. And now looking at him she could see again that look of guilt, as he would look at some woman he had wronged, to whom he could make no retribution. As though he had had a light case of some malady himself, and instead of hiding himself from her had drawn closer and infected her, recklessly, half-knowing, half-unwitting, with a severe case which would—which had—marked her for life. Never then could he see her without seeing those marks upon her face, which marked her sicker with his own disease, which must mark her ugly and yet a part of him, which marked her forever his victim and his possession, a possession which he wanted and which he loathed. I love you, she said quietly into the silence; and leaned against a pillar for support. But Bruno was raising the envelope which held his speech and her fingers moved with his. She could feel with the tips of her fingers the touch of the cord as rapidly he unwound it. *Oh my God!* said Emmett—and started forward weakly, *oh stop him, s-s-stop him, Elizabeth! don't let him* . . . With a strength that was scarcely her own she put the Middleton boy back in his place as Bruno with his peculiar delicacy of gesture ran his finger under the envelope's flap. *Oh my God,* said Emmett, trembling under Elizabeth's restraining hand, I wish I were *d-dead.*

"The time has come," said Bruno; and at least a thousand scraps of paper, torn and torn again, fluttered like confetti in his hands, inside his coat, hung on the edge of his pockets, clung like powder to his cuffs; and scattered at his feet and over them and lay, some with the white sides up and frightened, some with little dots of print. He stood in horror and continued to shake the envelope till it gave up its thousandth scrap. Then he stared gravely in for more, turned it in bewilderment, this way and that, and fell to shaking it again, without much hope. *Oh my God,* moaned Emmett, *I c-couldn't help it, I couldn't s-stop myself . . .*

The ballroom trembled with embarrassment, the people sat, shocked corpses, on their chairs. Bruno's hand continued to move monotonously; he shook the envelope up; he shook it down; he seemed to eye it with some morbid hope; and then the thousand-and-first scrap fluttered in bewilderment. Then someone laughed out nervously: Miss Ermine-tails—her mouth *would* open in spite of her, just as it did at accidents, just as it had when her father was brought home dead from a fall off his horse, and emitted its short yelp. She clapped her hands over her mouth immediately as though she had sneezed. But the germ got out; Miss Hobson caught it. Mr. Terrill, bored, was an easy victim. Then someone else; and then a fifth; Miss Ermine-tails, in terror at what she had done, squeezed the little tails, looked down, tried to look demure, and failed: was re-infected—the mouth opened again and repeated the theme-yelp. Oh very good, ve-ry good, said old Miss Ballister who could see as well as she could not hear. Oh jolly jolly jolly, Mr. Crawford yawned, a vodaville. The laugh ran round the room. It grew. Arturo and his orchestra awoke and craned their necks over their sleeping instruments to see the joke, were in time to spot the envelope shaking like a palsy in the speaker's hand, and added their cooperative employees' laugh. Mrs. Stanhope's crowd were softly whinnying. Miss Titcomb murmured through streaming eyes that she had thought all along he did it on purpose but was afraid to laugh alone; and passed her laugh to her friends:

Miss Henley-Star, Miss Cracken and Miss Milliken. The thing went so far that at last Mrs. Emily Fancher gracefully cast her vote, handed over the laurels and started a round of applause. Mr. Terrill took another look at Bruno covered with confetti, gasped and slapped Miss Hobson on the shoulder. Miss Hobson grew hysterical and abandoning more respectable desire became short-sighted and rolled in Mr. Terrill's arms: so fun-nay, so fun-nay, she cat-called. The laughter was enormous. Laugh collided with laugh; echoed; doubled; crashed; shrilled; shrieked; held its breath and burst again; and held its breath once more and waited, tittering, to be renewed. Al Middleton, shrewdly observing his son, was alternately shocked and pleased: such malice he had not suspected in the boy; but when he speculated on the *motive* . . . he grew ruminative and drank mechanically, reluctant to go nearer for an explanation.

Mr. Terrill, drunk, threw a wad of paper napkin which landed at Bruno's feet. As though it were a signal Bruno stepped up closer to the crowd and waved his arms till he was a large and frantic cloud above the Black Sheep's heads. "Pardon my dandruff," he bellowed at the crowd; and fastidiously flicked the thousand scraps of paper. They screamed again; he reared reproachfully and rapped with his empty envelope for silence. "FRIENDS," he shouted—but at the very sound of his voice they roared again; comfortable, assured; a happy audience.

"FRIENDS, INTELLECTUALS, FELLOW-SCEPTICS:" (Emmett's eyes opened wide in terror for this was not the opening they had planned). "I am with message." (*O I could die,* wheezed Ermine-tails.) "The world is up a tree. Three movements are abroad to lure it down, led separately by Einstein, Vambery, and Mary Baker Eddy; we will omit the communists because no one present ever saw one." (*O my God,* moaned Emmett.)

"To the future this era will be known as the great age of panaceas, of patent medicines, of Little Magazines. Friends, as intellectuals it's time we took our stand.

"Are we as intellectuals going to remain sitting on the fence, watching Christian Science fight with Freud? are we going to twiddle our thumbs and stew in our juices while the world is on the breadlines, the redlines, the deadlines? are we going to dope ourselves and stuff ourselves, intoxicate ourselves, anaesthetize ourselves, against all decent feeling—and meanwhile miss the bus?" He tottered, swayed; the laughter held itself as when the clown, hanging from a ladder too high above the audience, swings out and threatens the safety of the crowd. He recovered and straightened, bowed with a homosexual Tammany smile and waved his empty envelope to show them they, as well as he, were safe. "The answer is: WE ARE." The laugh broke out, relieved, the merry cocktail laugh, the self-indulgent, self-effulgent upper-class champagne laugh. *O my God,* moaned Emmett.

"But comrades! need I tell you" (he brandished the envelope with an arm emotionally aquiver) "we must have competent defeatist leadership; without it we are lost.

"Friends, it's time our party organized; I offer you a leader. My candidate stands on the slippery platform and the sliding scale, the only frankly anti-progress program in the country: the old barbed wire fence.

"Our party is of the intellectuals, by the intellectuals,

and naturally against them. Down with revolutions, resolutions, Magazines, and all attempts to put this country on its feet. We believe in nothing but aspirin and sex. The full bladder is our only goal. We sponsor: sublimation, constipation, procrastination, masturbation, prevarication, adumbration, equivocation, prestidigitation, moral turpitude, split personalities and rape; pornography, salacity, apostasy, hypocrisy, erotica, neurotica—in plain words, fellow-victims, anything that's phony or a fake."

"Leonard for president," Al Middleton cried—for he had caught a look of terror from his son (standing now, side by side with Bruno's green-clad cousin)—and the horror dawned upon him; a horror to be drowned, or drunk, enough to annihilate a father. "Second the nomination," cried Mr. Terrill recklessly. *O my God,* moaned Emmett. "Middleton for commissar of sex," Lucius Whitman (his hand on Mrs. Draper's knee) cried gayly. "I decline," shouted Al, mounting the buffet table and standing with one foot in a Virginia ham, "I'm no intellectual, I practise, I can't preach." He dragged Miss Powell up beside him; the merry olives flew.

"Fellow dope-fiends!" Bruno cried. "Observe your host in position one of a most important object lesson, proving that the greatest opiate the intellectual has ever known is SEX. There are those who will tell you that all activity is sublimation, a substitute for sex. Don't believe the lousy academics, gentlemen: TO THE INTELLECTUAL SEX IS THE SUBSTITUTE FOR ACTIVITY, THE HIGHEST SUBLIMATION, THE FINAL OPIATE."

"Hurray for opiates!" cried Mr. Terrill drunkenly. "What's position two, there, Middleton!" cried Mr. Draper. "What am I bid for this lovely pony?" shouted

Al, revolving Miss Powell on the buffet table; "
I bid for the Magazine in cellophane, unseen by human hand? what am I bid for one half-baked revolution, guaranteed not to bite, scratch, or come off?" Miss Powell laughed her dress half off her shoulder; Al reached behind the one remaining turtle-neck, pulled down the banner of the Hunger Marchers, and used it for a screen. "Position three," he cried, and disappeared behind it; laughing olives skipped from Miss Bee Powell's feet. Oh very good, ve-ry good, said old Miss Ballister feebly. *O my God, Elizabeth, can't you stop him? why don't you move? are you drunk?*

". . . for too long," Bruno was calling hoarsely, unheard, into the growing din, "for too long we have wandered unorganized, unwitting members of the lost tribe, the missing generation, the forgotten regiment; outcasts, miscasts, professional expatriates . . . accidents of birth—for many of our fathers were farmers or tailors or jewellers—we have no parents and we can have no offspring; we have no sex: we are mules—in short we are bastards, foundlings, phonys, the unpossessed and unpossessing of the world, the real minority." (Was she looking at him, thought Jeffrey, was Elizabeth's strange and beautiful stare for him? or was she staring still at Bruno? Never in all his life had his blood surged with such violence.) "We have no faith," cried Bruno: "we are scared till the blood in our veins runs thin and we hop from one faith to the next because to believe is too unbearably exactly what we want." (Oh Margaret, Margaret, let's go home . . . darling, darling, I am frightened too—perhaps he's drunk.) "We have no class: our tastes incline us to the left, our habits to the right; the left distrusts, the right despises us. Our race, one time the aristocrats, the philistines, the high-paid prostitutes, is dying out; our function's dead, our blood is blue. Have you read today's assignment in Pushkin, young men? 'Strike me dead, the track has vanished, Well, what now? We've lost the way . . .' "

"Oh he's starting on the Bible, Mrs. Middleton, can't we have some music," cried Miss Titcomb and Miss Milliken. The band was tuning up. Miss Hobson kissed Mr. Terrill passionately (and knew that he would never marry her), Miss Ermine-tails squeezed her fur pellets till they bled between her thumb and forefinger, Mr. Tevander felt sick at the stomach and didn't know why, Miss Powell screamed in sensual amazement and scattered more olives from behind the Hunger Marchers, Miss Titcomb permitted herself to smile with chaste pleasure at the 'Spaniard,' Graham Hatcher, the efficiency expert got rid of his wife to someone else and reminded Emily Fancher that she was a merry widow now, and Mrs. Whitman sucked her pearls on Mr. Draper's lap. The music blared out, as much under control as it would ever be—and Al and Miss Bee Powell kicked aside the Hunger Marchers and leaped down to dance, Miss Hobson sprang up with Mr. Terrill in her arms, in no time the floor was covered with dancers spilling out like beads from a box, melting rhythmically in one another's arms. "Dance!" cried Elizabeth, waking like a mechanical doll (she *was* looking at him, thought Jeffrey, with a sudden fear), "dance, Jeffrey, dance, partner!" *O my God,* moaned Emmett.

"Listen, comrades!" shouted Bruno in a fury. "Don't wait for the bandwagon to steamroller you, the ghost brigade is forming now, the corpse parade, the fellow-traveller charade; limp up and join us now, there's room on our fence for every individual straddler in your number. Are you a tired radical? are you a parlor pink? are you a political pansy? are you a morbid individualist? are you a victim of the twentieth century social disease? do you have singed or clipped left wings? then climb right up and straddle with us. . . ."

Bruno saw them moving, swaying (Elizabeth whirling in her stiff bright lettuce-green, her little-girl skirts flying gayly) one-dimensional figures on a shaking paper screen; but close to his vision and moving strong and sudden, their number multiplying, he saw six others, flesh and blood: the Black Sheep rising in a body.

He looked down, meeting Firman's eye, prepared to meet irony with irony or anger with anger. But to his endless shame and horror the eyes of Firman and of all the Black Sheep were lit with pity for him; as though like some youthful jury they had sat in judgment on him and grown mellow; sure of themselves and mature at last they were suddenly able to get on without him, able to endure with sorrow their master's vast defeat.

"Where are you going, you adolescent fools!" he roared; "didn't you hear your professor, Literature 71 with full credits, didn't you hear—'strike me dead, the track has vanished' . . . where do you think you're going?" He threw back his head as though they had struck him, and addressed his speech to passing, non-committal dancers. "There is a band of decadent optimists among us, traitors to their class—Black Sheep in fact—who refuse to stay drinking and dancing on our merry sinking ship. Like rats they will desert us. Very well," he cried with drunken dignity, "we can dance, we can drink, we can fornicate on our graves, without you. . . ." He resumed his lost professorial grace and spoke with a familiar mingling of his irony and sincerity. "My advice to all young rats and Sheep," he lowered his voice and spoke closely to the band of youngsters, "is to get out, here and now; go west, young men, go south, go north—go anywhere out of our God damned city. New York is the precocious head of the adolescent body of America. America is still growing—I presume it is, if it exists at all—still angles and painful joints, and it's too big for New York to coordinate. The city's got dementia praecox, and the intellectuals along with it. . . . Maybe as intellectuals we've got some part to play; but take it from the old Chinese: this army of the lame, the halt, the blind, will come to an end, will be wiped out from start to finish, before the workers' movement will be widespread and successful . . . if there *is* a workers' movement," he revived his cynical eyebrow with gallant insincerity. "The only way," he continued as though he pulled his finger from his verbal dykes, "to come to this cause is to come 'clean'—that is to come not in order to solve one's individual neuroses, but to come already free of them. My friends and myself are sick men—if we are not already dead. Our values were mixed in our intellectual cradles; we've muddled the idea of love and sex until we are psychically incapable of either; from being ashamed and afraid we have thrown out one and degraded the other to the level of show-window exhibitionism, or taking of twentieth century snuff. . . . You may think me sentimental; but the lie in our private lives is important, it makes our public lives unreal and fraudulent—a man can't do good work with an undernourished psychic system. . . . In each individual case a Vambery could give you valid special reasons—but when an epidemic's so widespread, it has a deeper basis than the individual. I suppose we're victims of the general social catastrophe in some way we're too close to to figure out. . . . So we come, each of us, believing in nothing and certainly not believing in ourselves, equipped with little but our private hate and the symptoms, each one of us, of our own personal disease . . . and play at making revolutions for a band of workers we've never even seen. . . . Our meetings are masterpieces of postponement, our ideologies brilliant rationalizations to prevent our ever taking action. . . . I think I'm talking life, not communism—all I know is myself and my friends have never had a good look at either. . . . Listen, you kids, get out of it, get out of it while you can, leave us rotting in our blind alley, we've lost the way, we've dug ourselves in . . . you kids get out. . . ."

"Don't worry about us, Doctor Leonard" (their voices rang with triumph) "we want to say goodbye" "and thank you" "gosh, you've done a lot for us" "please tell the Dean" "to hell with hot-house education" "we've started breaking the rules already" "Firman and Corny got married this afternoon" "and now" "hell with the ole diplomas if they won't take us back" (their voices rose in concert) "we're going anyway" "we're going to bum our way to Washington and see the Hunger March"

He reeled as though their flag were too bright for his eyes. They stayed a minute—he thought he saw Cornelia's eyes go misty—as though like crusaders on their way they might pause to succor the sick. He waved them savagely away. "Go on, go on, get to hell out of here, beat it—I don't believe there *is* a Hunger March—go on, why don't you, what are you waiting for, I'll give your message to the Dean. . . ." And as they still lingered, as though at the end of their childhood they hoped for one last sanction from their elders he shook his fist in warning, smiled like a very old professor over the top of his glasses: "Run, Sheep, run!" They smiled, Firman and Cornelia, Irish Kate and Little Dixon, both the Maxwell brothers—or were there more of them? were they all the decent children in the world? were they the vanguard of the newest intellectuals who, not remaining aloof with their books and their ideas, had strength to mingle with the living and bring their gifts among them? —and about-faced, marching from him, marching from the ballroom to "bum" their way to Washington, their flag one piece at last. *O my God,* moaned Emmett; and followed his generation to the ballroom door; but he was too weak, or else the Sheep were ruthless—for Bruno saw him turn and mount the stairs, like a lost child climbing to the nursery. He caught sight of Elizabeth, whirling, whirling, gay in Jeffrey's arms, he caught the look of pain in Miles' tortured face as Miles saw his second God killed before his eyes, he laughed to Margaret Flinders who sat, her beauty gray and troubled, he waved to Norah dancing bewildered and unwilling in a stranger's arms, turned his eyes from Elizabeth's merry glassy stare over Jeffrey's shoulder. . . . "Listen, fellow-bastards!" roared Bruno unheard at the punchbowl; "drink, drink with me! Up with your glasses, down with your hopes! TO THE REVOLUTION, FELLOW-LICE: THE MOST IN-

GENIOUS OPIATE OF THE INTELLECTUAL." *O my God,* sobbed Emmett, trailing up the stairs.

Faster and faster his arms went around her, the arms of the stranger, the lone wolf Jeffrey, the weak-willed Denny, art-colony Ferris, faster and faster their arms went around her, they danced and they danced and they swayed and they bent (Margaret, Margaret, I can't stand it), they danced and they swayed, they bobbed and they bent (Margaret, Margaret, won't you understand? how *can* we bring a child to this?) careening faster on the fast-express, the rollicking jittery cocktail express, nothing can matter—so wear down, you nerves, no brakes, no goal, no love, no faith, on we go glittering jittering twittering, *steward a drink for the lady!* Ah Jeffrey, my lover, my unloving partner, the eye of a stranger, the eye of a man, it's the old army game, the train's roaring again—she gave him the glad eye, the mad eye, the sad eye, he terrified gave it back. Why Jeffrey, why stranger, she said bitterly, brittley, why Dennis, why Ferris, don't you like me, don't you love me, I'm so gay, I'm so light, I bounce here and there like a light rubber ball—yet you tremble, you shrink . . . can I help it if I've lost the track? The eye of a man, the eye of a man—then off with you Jeffrey, I'll have me the next one—Terrill, Terrill? eyes like Brownlow, voice like Ferris, will I never see a whole new man again? They danced and they danced and they swayed and they bent, faster and faster his arms went around her, the arms of the stranger, the lone wolf Terrill, the weak-willed Terrill, haven't I met you before Mister Terrill, maybe in an art colony maybe on a boat? (Norah, Norah, I saw you with Mr. Middleton, dancing and dancing, Norah you wouldn't ever, would you Norah, oh I'd kill you, Norah, I'm so glad to be back, to be with you again, darling Norah, I love you Norah, I feel as though I'd been on such a journey.) Why yes, Mr. Draper, delighted I'm sure, you look like somebody I vaguely know, like everyone I somehow know—amusing? the younger generation? oh yes, oh yes, we're all of that, ah no we don't give a damn for anything, only aspirin the morning after —but you, don't you feel the shaking of the boat, the roaring of the train? (No, I don't like her Norah, I'm afraid of her, I don't like my women clever, darling, I like them to be like you, listen Norah, promise me something, I'm drunk but I want you to promise me something) hurry, Mr. Middleton, whirl me, whirl me, before I change trains and jingle-jangle along again on my fast-express, the twentieth century unlimited, twentieth century unspirited, hell-bent for nowhere our fast-express, the only non-stop through express. (No, I guess I want to promise *you,* Norah, listen darling, listen, I promise you never to leave you again, never to be unfaithful, I want to promise you that Norah, can I, can I—she kissed him warmly; he knew she was not asking him to promise, he knew that he would never keep it; but the promise *felt* good, lent him in the midst of chaos a certain queer stability—his cycle was done for a time, he had come home again to Norah) . . . Faster and faster their arms went around her, the fast train hurtling, no love just lust no joy no pain, Elizabeth saw the wreckage ahead, piled up ahead on the glittering twittering railroad track, she saw the train headed downward, the downhill special, she saw Bruno in his sailor-suit, Bruno on his bicycle, Bruno downhill headed . . . Faster and faster they spun and careened, Ferris-Terrill-Brownlow-Denny, no stopping them now they were headed for hell. . . . The wreck loomed larger, larger, she saw the disaster with her inside eye, Bruno pedalling on his bicycle, her mother calling from the nursery window, the ship was shaking, the whole train quaking like an avalanche . . . she saw the train, she was the train. . . .

Let me go, I dance faster alone, she screamed and danced from her partner's arms and danced down the vanished track to rescue Bruno, herself, the twentieth century—before it was too late.

O very good, ve-ry good, said old Miss Ballister, seeing one of those young things, sixty years her junior, gyrate and spin in a lettuce-colored dress, so gay, so young, so mad.

FOUR

Missis Flinders

"HOME you go!" Miss Kane, nodding, in her white nurse's dress, stood for a moment—she would catch a breath of air—in the hospital door; "and thank you again for the stockings, you needn't have bothered"—drew a sharp breath and turning, dismissed Missis Flinders from the hospital, smiling, dismissed her forever from her mind.

So Margaret Flinders stood next to her basket of fruit on the hospital steps; both of them waiting, a little shame-faced in the sudden sunshine, and in no hurry to leave the hospital—no hurry at all. It would be nicer to be alone, Margaret thought, glancing at the basket of fruit which stood respectable and a little silly on the stone step (the candy-bright apples were blushing caricatures of Miles: Miles' comfort, not hers). Flowers she could have left behind (for the nurses, in the room across the hall where they made tea at night); books she could have slipped into her suit-case; but fruit—Miles' gift, Miles' guilt, man's tribute to the Missis in the hospital—must be eaten; a half-eaten basket of fruit (she had tried to leave it: Missis Butter won't you . . . Missis Wiggam wouldn't you like . . . But Missis Butter had aplenty of her own thank you, and Missis Wiggam said she couldn't hold acids after a baby)—a half-eaten basket of fruit, in times like these, cannot be left to rot.

Down the street Miles was running, running, after a taxi. He was going after the taxi for her; it was for her sake he ran; yet this minute that his back was turned he stole for his relief and spent in running away, his shoulders crying guilt. And don't hurry, don't hurry, she said to them; I too am better off alone.

The street stretched in a long white line very finally away from the hospital, the hospital where Margaret Flinders (called there so solemnly Missis) had been lucky enough to spend only three nights. It would be four days before Missis Wiggam would be going home to Mister Wiggam with a baby; and ten possibly—the doctors were uncertain, Miss Kane prevaricated—before Missis Butter would be going home to Mister Butter without one. Zig-zagging the street went the children; their cries and the sudden grinding of their skates she had listened to upstairs beside Missis Butter for three days. Some such child had she been—for the styles in children had not changed—a lean child gliding solemnly on skates and grinding them viciously at the nervous feet of grown-ups. Smile at these children she would not or could not; yet she felt on her face that smile fixed, painful and frozen that she had put there, on waking from ether three days back, to greet Miles. The smile spoke to the retreating shoulders of Miles: I don't need you; the smile spoke formally to life: thanks, I'm not having any. Not so the child putting the heels of his skates together Charlie Chaplin-wise and describing a scornful circle on the widest part of the sidewalk. Not so a certain little girl (twenty years back) skating past the wheels of autos, pursuing life in the form of a ball so red! so gay!

better death than to turn one's back and smile over one's shoulder at life!

Upstairs Missis Butter must still be writhing with her poor caked breasts. The bed that had been hers beside Missis Butter's was empty now; Miss Kane would be stripping it and Joe would come in bringing fresh sheets. Whom would they put in beside Missis Butter, to whom would she moan and boast all night about the milk in her breasts that was turning, she said, into cheese?

Now Milcs was coming back, jogging sheepishly on the running-board of a taxi, he had run away to the end of his rope and now was returning penitent, his eyes dog-like searching her out where she stood on the hospital steps (did they rest with complacence on the basket of fruit, his gift?), pleading with her, Didn't I get the taxi fast? like an anxious little boy. She stood with that smile on her face that hurt like too much ice-cream. Smile and smile; for she felt like a fool, she had walked open-eyed smiling into the trap (*Don't wriggle, Missis, I might injure you for life, Miss Kane had said cheerfully*) and felt the spring only when it was too late, when she waked from ether and knew like the thrust of a knife what she had ignored before. *Whatever did you do it for, Missis Flinders Missis Butter was always saying; if there's nothing the matter with your insides—doesn't your husband . . . and Won't you have some fruit, Missis Butter, her calm reply: meaning, My husband gave me this fruit so what right have you to doubt that my husband . . .* Her husband who now stumbled up the steps to meet her; his eyes he had sent ahead, but something in him wanted not to come, tripped his foot as he hurried up the steps.

"Take my arm, Margaret," he said. "Walk slowly,"

he said. The bitter pill of taking help, of feeling weakly grateful stuck in her throat. Miles' face behind his glasses was tense like the face of an amateur actor in the rôle of a strike-leader. That he was inadequate for the part he seemed to know. And if he felt shame, shame in his own eyes, she could forgive him; but if it was only guilt felt man-like in her presence, a guilt which he could drop off like a damp shirt, if he was putting it all off on her for being a woman! "The fruit, Miles!" she said; "you've forgotten the fruit." "The fruit can wait," he said bitterly.

He handed her into the taxi as though she were a package marked glass—something, she thought, not merely troublesomely womanly, but ladylike. "Put your legs up on the seat," he said. "I don't want to, Miles." *Goodbye Missis Butter* Put your legs up on the seat. I don't want to—*better luck next time Missis Butter* Put your legs *I can't make out our window, Missis Butter* Put your "All right, it will be nice and uncomfortable." (She put her legs up on the seat.) *Goodbye Missis But . . .* "Nothing I say is right," he said. "It's good with the legs up," she said brightly.

Then he was up the steps agile and sure after the fruit. And down again, the basket swinging with affected carelessness, arming him, till he relinquished it modestly to her outstretched hands. Then he seated himself on the little seat, the better to watch his woman and his woman's fruit; and screwing his head round on his neck said irritably to the man who had been all his life on the wrong side of the glass pane: "Charles street!"

"Hadn't you better ask him to please drive slowly?" Margaret said.

"I was just going to," he said bitterly.

"And drive slowly," he shouted over his shoulder.

The driver's name was Carl C. Strite. She could see Carl Strite glance cannily back at the hospital; Greenway Maternity Home; pull his lever with extreme delicacy as though he were stroking the neck of a horse. There was a small roar—and the hospital glided backward: its windows ran together like the windows of a moving train; a spurt—watch out for those children on skates!—and the car was fairly started down the street.

Goodbye Missis Butter I hope you get a nice roommate in my place, I hope you won't find that Mister B let the ice-pan flow over again—and give my love to the babies when Miss Kane stops them in the door for you to wave at—goodbye Missis Butter, really goodbye.

Carl Strite (was he thinking maybe of his mother, an immigrant German woman she would have been, come over with a shawl on her head and worked herself to skin and bone so the kids could go to school and turn out good Americans—and what had it come to, here he was a taxi-driver, and what taxi-drivers didn't know! what in the course of their lackeys' lives they didn't put up with, fall in with! well, there was one decent thing left in Carl Strite, he knew how to carry a woman home from a maternity hospital) drove softly along the curb . . . and the eyes of his honest puzzled gangster's snout photographed as "Your Driver" looked dimmed as though the glory of woman were too much for them, in a moment the weak cruel baby's mouth might blubber. Awful to lean forward and tell Mr. Strite he was laboring under a mistake. *Missis Wiggam's freckled face when she heard that Missis Butter's roommate . . . maybe Missis Butter's baby had been born dead but anyway she had had a baby . . . whatever did you do it for Missis Flind . . .*

"Well, patient," Miles began, tentative, nervous (bored? perturbed? behind his glasses?).

"How does it feel, Maggie?" he said in a new, small voice.

Hurt and hurt this man, a feeling told her. He is a man, he could have made you a woman. "What's a D and C between friends?" she said. "Nobody at the hospital gave a damn about my little illegality."

"Well, but I do," he protested like a short man trying to be tall.

She turned on her smile; the bright silly smile that was eating up her face.

Missis Butter would be alone now with no one to boast to about her pains except Joe who cleaned the corridors and emptied bed-pans—and thought Missis Butter was better than an angel because although she had incredible golden hair she could wise-crack like any brunette. Later in the day the eight-day mothers wobbling down the corridors for their pre-nursing constitutional would look in and talk to her; for wasn't Missis Butter their symbol and their pride, the one who had given up her baby that they might have theirs (for a little superstition is inevitable in new mothers, and it was generally felt that there must be one dead baby in a week's batch at any decent hospital) for whom they demanded homage from their visiting husbands? for whose health they asked the nurses each morning second only to asking for their own babies? That roommate of yours was a funny one, Missis Wiggam would say. Missis Wiggam was the woman who said big breasts weren't any good: here she was with a seven-pound baby and not a drop for it (here she would open the negligée Mister Wiggam had given her not to shame them before the nurses, and poke contemptuously at the floppy parts of herself within) while there was Missis Butter with no baby but a dead baby and her small breasts caking because there was so much milk in them for nothing but a . . . Yes, that Missis Flinders was sure a funny one, Missis Butter would agree.

"Funny ones," she and Miles, riding home with numb faces and a basket of fruit between them—past a park; past a museum, past elevated pillars—intellectuals they were, bastards, changelings . . . giving up a baby for economic freedom which meant that two of them would work in offices instead of one of them only, giving up a baby for intellectual freedom which meant that they smoked their cigarettes bitterly and looked out of the windows of a taxi onto streets and people and stores and hated them all. "We'd go soft," Miles had finally said, slamming the door of the Middleton party; "we'd go bourgeois." Yes, with diapers drying on the radiators, bottles wrapped in flannel, Mr. Papenmeyer getting to know one too well—yes, they would go soft, they might slump and start liking people, they might weaken and forgive stupidity, they might yawn and forget to hate. "Funny ones," class-straddlers, intellectuals, tightrope-walking somewhere in the middle (how long could they hang on without falling to one side or the other? one more war? one more depression?); intellectuals, as Bruno said, with habits generated from the right and tastes inclined to the left. Afraid to perpetuate themselves, were they? Afraid of anything that might loom so large in their personal lives as to outweigh other considerations? Afraid, maybe, of a personal life?

"Oh give me another cigarette," she said.

And still the taxi, with its burden of intellectuals and their inarticulate fruit-basket, its motherly, gangsterly, inarticulate driver, its license plates and its photographs all so very official, jogged on; past Harlem now; past fire-escapes loaded with flower-pots and flapping clothes; dingy windows opening to the soot-laden air blown in by the elevated roaring down its tracks. Past Harlem and through 125th street: stores and wise-cracks, Painless Dentists, cheap florists; Eighth Avenue, boarded and plastered, concealing the subway that was reaching its laborious birth beneath. But Eighth Avenue was too jouncy for Mr. Strite's precious burden of womanhood (who was reaching passionately for a cigarette); he cut through the park, and they drove past quiet walks on which the sun had brought out babies as the fall rains give birth to worms.

"But ought you to smoke so much, so soon after—so soon?" Miles said, not liking to say so soon after what. His hand held the cigarettes out to her, back from her.

"They do say smoking's bad for child-birth," she said calmly, and with her finger-tips drew a cigarette from his reluctant hand.

And tapping down the tobacco on the handle of the fruit-basket she said, "But we've got the joke on them there, we have." (Hurt and hurt this man, her feeling told her; he is a man and could have made you a woman.)

"It was your own decision too," he said harshly, striking and striking at the box with his match.

"This damn taxi's shaking you too much," he said suddenly, bitter and contrite.

But Mr. Strite was driving like an angel. He handled his car as though it were a baby-carriage. Did he think maybe it had turned out with her the way it had with Missis Butter? I could have stood it better, Missis Butter said, if they hadn't told me it was a boy. And me with my fourth little girl, Missis Wiggam had groaned (but proudly, proudly); why I didn't even want to see it when they told me. But Missis Butter stood it very well, and so did Missis Wiggam. They were a couple of good bitches; and what if Missis Butter had produced nothing but a dead baby this year, and what if Missis Wiggam would bring nothing to Mister Wiggam but a fourth little girl this year—why there was next year and the year after, there was the certain little world from grocery-store to kitchen, there were still Mister Butter and Mister Wiggam who were both (Missis Wiggam and Missis Butter vied with each other) just *crazy* about babies. Well, Mister Flinders is different, she had lain there thinking (he cares as much for his unborn gods as I for my unborn babies); and wished she could have the firm assurance they had in "husbands," coming as they did year after year away from them for a couple of weeks, just long enough to bear them babies either dead-ones or girl-ones . . . good bitches they were: there was something lustful besides smug in their pride in being "Missis." Let Missis Flinders so much as let out a groan because a sudden pain grew too big for her groins, let her so much as murmur because the sheets were hot beneath her—and Missis Butter and Missis Wiggam in the security of their maternity-fraternity exchanged glances of amusement: SHE don't know what pain is, look at what's talking about PAIN. . . .

"Mr. Strite flatters us," she whispered, her eyes smiling straight and hard at Miles. (Hurt and hurt . . .)

"And why does that give you so much pleasure?" He dragged the words as though he were pounding them out with two fingers on the typewriter.

The name without the pain—she thought to say; and did not say. All at once she lost her desire to punish him; she no more wanted to "hurt this man" for he was no more man than she was woman. She would not do him the honor of hurting him. She must reduce him as she felt herself reduced. She must cut out from him what made him a man, as she had let be cut out from her what would have made her a woman. He was no man: he was a dried-up intellectual husk; he was sterile; empty and hollow as she was.

Missis Butter lying up on her pillow would count over to Missis Wiggam the fine points of her tragedy: how she had waited two days to be delivered of a dead baby; how it wouldn't have been so bad if the doctor hadn't said it was a beautiful baby with platinum-blond hair exactly like hers (and hers bleached unbelievably, but never mind, Missis Wiggam had come to believe in it like Joe and Mister Butter, another day and Missis Flinders herself, intellectual sceptic though she was, might have been convinced); and how they would pay the last instalment on—what a baby-carriage, Missis Wiggam, you'd never believe me!—and sell it second-hand for half its worth. I know when I was caught with my first, Missis Wiggam would take up the story her mouth had been open for. And that Missis Flinders was sure a funny one. . . .

But I am not such a funny one, Margaret wanted, beneath her bright and silly smile, behind her cloud of cigarette smoke (for Miles had given in; the whole package sat gloomily on Margaret's lap) to say to them; even though in my "crowd" the girls keep the names they were born with, even though some of us sleep for a little variety with one another's husbands, even though I forget as often as Miles—Mister Flinders to you—to empty the pan under the ice-box. Still I too have known my breasts to swell and harden, I too have been unable to sleep on them for their tenderness to weight and touch, I too have known what it is to undress slowly and imagine myself growing night to night. . . . I knew this for two months, my dear Missis Wiggam; I had this strange joy for two months, my dear Missis Butter. But there was a night last week, my good ladies, on coming home from a party, which Mister Flinders and I spent in talk—and damn fine talk, if you want to know, talk of which I am proud, and talk not one word of which you, with your grocery-and-baby minds, could have understood; in a régime like this, Miles said, it is a terrible thing to have a baby—it means the end of independent thought and the turning of everything into a scheme for making money; and there must be institutions such as there are in Russia, I said, for taking care of the babies and their mothers; why in a time like this, we both said, to have a baby would be suicide—goodbye to our plans, goodbye to our working out schemes for each other and the world—our courage would die, our hopes concentrate on the sordid business of keeping three people alive, one of whom would be a burden and an expense for twenty years. . . . And then we grew drunk for a minute making up the silliest names that we could call it if we had it, we would call it Daniel if it were a boy, call it for my mother if it were a girl—and what a tough little thing it is, I said, look, look, how it hangs on in spite of its loving mother jumping off tables and broiling herself in hot water . . . until Miles, frightened at himself, washed his hands of it: we mustn't waste any more time, the sooner these things are done the better. And I as though the ether cap had already been clapped to my nose, agreed offhandedly. That night I did not pass my hands contentedly over my hard breasts; that night I gave no thought to the nipples grown suddenly brown and competent; I packed, instead, my suit-case: I filled it with all the white clothes I own. Why are you taking white clothes to the hospital, Miles said to me. I laughed. Why did I? White, for a bride; white, for a corpse; white, for a woman who refuses to be a woman. . . .

"Are you all right, Margaret?" (They were out now, safely out on Fifth Avenue, driving placidly past the Plaza where ancient coachmen dozed on the high seats of the last hansoms left in New York.)

"Yes, dear," she said mechanically, and forgot to turn on her smile. Pity for him sitting there in stolid New England inadequacy filled her. He was a man, and he could have made her a woman. She was a woman, and could have made him a man. He was not a man; she was not a woman. In each of them the life-stream flowed to a dead-end.

And all this time that the blood, which Missis Wiggam and Missis Butter stored up preciously in themselves every year to make a baby for their husbands, was flowing freely and wastefully out of Missis Flinders—toward what? would it pile up some day and bear a Magazine? would it congeal within her and make a crazy woman?—all this time Mr. Strite, remembering, with his pudgy face, his mother, drove his taxi softly along the curb; no weaving in and out of traffic for Mr. Strite, no spurting at the corners and cheating the side-street traffic, no fine heedless rounding of rival cars for Mr. Strite; he kept his car going at a slow and steady roll, its nose poked blunt ahead, following the straight and narrow—Mr. Strite knew what it was to carry a woman home from the hospital.

But what in their past had warranted this? She could remember a small girl going from dolls to books, from books with colored pictures to books with frequent conversations; from such books to the books at last that one borrowed from libraries, books built up of solemn text from which you took notes; books which were gray to begin with, but which opened out to your eyes subtle layers of gently shaded colors. (And where in these texts did it say that one should turn one's back on life? Had the coolness of the stone library at college made one afraid? Had the ivy nodding in at the open dormitory windows taught one too much to curl and squat looking out?) And Miles? What book, what professor, what strange idea, had taught him to hunch his shoulders and stay indoors, had taught him to hide behind his glasses? Whence the fear that made him put, in cold block letters, implacably above his desk the sign announcing him "Not at Home" to life?

Missis Flinders, my husband scaled the hospital wall at four o'clock in the morning, frantic I tell you . . . But I just don't understand you, Missis Flinders (if there's really nothing the matter with your insides), do you understand her, Missis Wiggam, would your husband . . . ? Why goodness, no, Mister Wiggam would sooner . . . ! And there he was, and they asked him, Shall we try an operation, Mister Butter? scaled the wall . . . shall we try an operation? (Well, you see, we are making some sort of a protest, my husband and I; sometimes, she thought, recalling Norah, I forget just what.) If there's any risk to Shirley, he said, there mustn't be any risk to Shirley . . . Missis Wiggam's petulant, childish face, with its sly contentment veiled by what she must have thought a grown-up expression: Mister Wiggam bought me this negligée new, surprised me with it, you know—and generally a saving man, Mister Wiggam, not tight, but with three children—four now! Hetty, he says, I'm not going to have you disgracing us at the hospital this year, he says. Why the nurses will all remember that flannel thing you had Mabel and Suzy and Antoinette in, they'll talk about us behind our backs. (It wasn't that I couldn't make the flannel do again, Missis Butter, it wasn't that at all.) But he says, Hetty, you'll just have a new one this year, he says, and maybe it'll bring us luck, he says—you know, he was thinking maybe this time we'd have a boy. . . . Well, I just have to laugh at you, Missis Flinders, not *wanting* one, why my sister went to doctors for five years and spent her good money just *trying* to have one. . . . Well, poor Mister Wiggam, so the negligée didn't work, I brought him another little girl—but he didn't say boo to me, though I could see he was disappointed. Hetty, he says, we'll just have another try! oh I thought I'd die, with Miss Kane standing right there you know (though they do say these nurses . . .);

but that's Mister Wiggam all over, he wouldn't stop a joke for a policeman. . . . No, I just can't get over you, Missis Flinders, if Gawd was willing to let you have a baby—and there really isn't anything wrong with your insides?

Miles' basket of fruit standing on the bed-table, trying its level inadequate best, poor pathetic inarticulate intellectual basket of fruit, to comfort, to bloom, to take the place of Miles himself who would come in later with Sam Butter for visiting hour. Miles' too-big basket of fruit standing there, embarrassed. Won't you have a peach, Missis Wiggam (I'm sure they have less acid)? Just try an apple, Missis Butter? Weigh Miles' basket of fruit against Mister Wiggam's negligée for luck, against Mister Butter scaling the wall at four in the morning for the mother of his dead baby. *Please* have a pear, Miss Kane; a banana, Joe? How they spat the seeds from Miles' fruit! How it hurt her when, unknowing, Missis Butter cut away the brown bruised cheek of Miles' bright-eyed, weeping apple! Miles! they scorn me, these ladies. They laugh at me, dear, almost as though I had no "husband," as though I were a "fallen woman." Miles, would you buy me a new negligée if I bore you three daughters? Miles, would you scale the wall if I bore you a dead baby? . . . Miles, I have an inferiority complex because I am an intellectual. . . . But a peach, Missis Wiggam! can't I possibly tempt you?

To be driving like this at mid-day through New York; with Miles bobbing like an empty ghost (for she could see he was unhappy, as miserable as she, he too had had an abortion) on the side-seat; with a taxi-driver, solicitous, respectful to an ideal, in front; was this the logical end of that little girl she remembered, of that girl swinging hatless across a campus as though that campus were the top of the earth? And was this all they could give birth to, she and Miles, who had closed up their books one day and kissed each other on the lips and decided to marry?

And now Mr. Strite, with his hand out, was making a gentle righthand turn. Back to Fifth Avenue they would go, gently rolling, in Mr. Strite's considerate charge. Down Fourteenth Street they would go, past the stores unlike any stores in the world: packed to the windows with imitation gold and imitation embroidery, with imitation men and women coming to stand in the doorways and beckon with imitation smiles; while on the sidewalks streamed the people unlike any other people in the world, drawn from every country, from every stratum, carrying babies (the real thing, with pinched anaemic faces) and parcels (imitation finery priced low in the glittering stores). There goes a woman, with a flat fat face, will produce five others just like herself, to dine off one-fifth the inadequate quantity her Mister earns today. These are the people not afraid to perpetuate themselves(forbidden to stop, indeed) and they will go on and on until the bottom of the world is filled with them; and suddenly there will be enough of them to combine their wild-eyed notions and take over the world to suit themselves. While I, while I and my Miles, with our good clear heads will one day go spinning out of the world and leave nothing behind . . . only diplomas crumbling in the museums. . . .

The mad street ended with Fifth Avenue; was left behind.

They were nearing home. Mr. Strite, who had never

seen them before (who would never again, in all likelihood, for his territory was far uptown) was seeing them politely to the door. As they came near home all of Margaret's fear and pain gathered in a knot in her stomach. There would be nothing new in their house; there was nothing to expect; yet she wanted to find something there that she knew she could not find, and surely the house (once so gay, with copies of old paintings, with books which lined the walls from floor to ceiling, with papers and cushions and typewriters) would be suddenly empty and dead, suddenly, for the first time, a group of rooms unalive as rooms with "For Rent" still pasted on the windows. And Miles? did he know he was coming home to a place which had suffered no change, but which would be different forever afterward? Miles had taken off his glasses; passed his hand tiredly across his eyes; was sucking now as though he expected relief, some answer, on the tortoise-shell curve which wound around his ear.

Mr. Strite would not allow his cab to cease motion with a jerk. Mr. Strite allowed his cab to slow down even at the corner (where was the delicatessen that sold the only loose ripe olives in the Village), so they rolled softly past No. 14; on past the tenement which would eventually be razed to give place to modern three-room apartments with In-a-Dor beds; and then slowly, so slowly that Mr. Strite must surely be an artist as well as a man who had had a mother, drew up and slid to a full stop before No. 60, where two people named Mister and Missis Flinders rented themselves a place to hide from life (both life of the Fifth Avenue variety, and life of the common, or Fourteenth Street, variety: in short, life).

So Miles, with his glasses on his nose once more, descended; held out his hand; Mr. Strite held the door open and his face most modestly averted; and Margaret Flinders painfully and carefully swung her legs down again from the seat and alighted, step by step, with care and confusion. The house was before them; it must be entered. Into the house they must go, say farewell to the streets, to Mr. Strite who had guided them through a tour of the city, to life itself; into the house they must go and hide. It was a fact that Mister Flinders (was he reluctant to come home?) had forgotten his key; that Missis Flinders must delve under the white clothes in her suit-case and find hers; that Mr. Strite, not yet satisfied that his charges were safe, sat watchful and waiting in the front seat of his cab. Then the door gave. Then Miles, bracing it with his foot, held out his hand to Margaret. Then Mr. Strite came rushing up the steps (something had told him his help would be needed again!), rushing up the steps with the basket of fruit hanging on his arm, held out from his body as though what was the likes of him doing holding a woman's basket just home from the hospital. "You've forgot your fruit, Missis!"

Weakly they glared at the fruit come to pursue them; come to follow them up the stairs to their empty rooms; but that was not fair: come, after all, to comfort them. "You must have a peach," Margaret said.

No, Mr. Strite had never cared for peaches; the skin got in his teeth.

"You must have an apple," Margaret said.

Well, no, he must be getting on uptown. A cigarette (he waved it, deprecated the smoke it blew in the lady's face) was good enough for him.

"But a pear, just a pear," said Margaret passionately.

Mr. Strite wavered, standing on one foot. "Maybe he doesn't want any fruit," said Miles harshly.

"Not want any *fruit!*" cried Margaret gayly, indignantly. Not want any fruit?—ridiculous! Not want the fruit my poor Miles bought for his wife in the hospital? Three days I spent in the hospital, in a Maternity Home, and I produced, with the help of my husband, one basket of fruit (tied with ribbon, pink—for boys). Not want any of our fruit? I couldn't bear it, I couldn't bear it. . . .

Mr. Strite leaned over; put out a hand and gingerly selected a pear—"For luck," he said, managing an excellent American smile. They watched him trot down the steps to his cab, all the time holding his pear as though it were something he would put in a memory book. And still they stayed, because Margaret said foolishly, "Let's see him off"; because she was ashamed, suddenly, before Miles; as though she had cut her hair unbecomingly, as though she had wounded herself in some unsightly way—as though (summing up her thoughts as precisely, as decisively as though it had been done on an adding-machine) she had stripped and revealed herself not as a woman at all, but as a creature who would not be a woman and could not be a man. And then they turned (for there was nothing else to stay for, and on the street and in the sun before Missis Salvemini's fluttering window-curtains they were ashamed as though they had been naked or dead)—and went in the door and heard it swing to, pause on its rubbery hinge, and finally click behind them.

THE END

AFTERWORD

Janet Sharistanian

i

When her career was cut short by cancer at the age of thirty-nine, Tess Slesinger had published one novel, *The Unpossessed* (1934), a collection of short fiction titled *Time: The Present* (1935), and numerous uncollected short stories, in addition to screenplays and works in progress, including a Hollywood novel.[1] Born in 1905, Slesinger was reared in an assimilated, middle-class, third-generation Jewish family in New York in which she was the only daughter, indulged by her parents and three older brothers.[2] The family's attitudes included indifference to Judaism, marked openness about sexuality, a strong concern for literacy, self-expression, and vocation, and an interest in the systematic analysis of personality. Though the children felt loved by both parents, the relationship between mother and father was marked by a steady underlying current of hostility. This, along with Mrs. Slesinger's extremely strong personality, had an impact upon all the children. Tess's reaction to her parents' relationship helped form her personal values, including her strong desires for both autonomy and intimacy, and her thematic interests, especially her need to understand the inextricable relationships between individual, family, and social structure.

Slesinger's mother, Augusta Singer Slesinger, had left school after the eighth grade to work as a bookkeeper for her father, who disliked entrusting that sensitive work to persons outside the family. Mr. Singer, a Russian Jewish immigrant, had made a great deal of money manufacturing men's and women's clothing and investing his profits in tenement housing on the Lower East Side. At nineteen Augusta married Anthony Slesinger, who came to the United States from Hungary as a child, graduated from City College of New York in 1889, and then studied law at Columbia

University, but did not complete the degree. Instead, marriage interrupted and altered all his plans. Soon after the wedding he and his brother-in-law, an erstwhile newspaper cartoonist, were persuaded to join Mr. Slesinger in his garment business. His daughter Augusta, with her appropriately imperial name, would likely have made a better recipient of the property and responsibility, had cultural patterns encouraged such an arrangement. Tony, though a charming person, was easily dominated, rather ineffectual, and an unhappy choice for running a business. Nor was his brother-in-law any better at the task. For years Tony toiled on in the garment business, his fortunes sometimes respectable but rarely reliable, his skills not of a kind to offset the waxing and waning of the economy.

In the meantime Augusta, who in the late 1880s attended classes at City College which aroused her interest in the developing social sciences, began working early in her marriage at various social-welfare agencies. This was work that she enjoyed and did energetically and well, though its justification among relatives and friends was the need for two incomes in a growing family in which the husband's capacity as a provider was proving insufficient. Eventually, Augusta became the director of a child guidance clinic and thereafter executive secretary of the Jewish Big Sisters. By Tess's teens, her mother was helping to establish the New School for Social Research, one of whose administrators, Dr. Alvin Johnson, credited her with bringing the psychologist Alfred Adler there to teach,[3] and where she took courses almost continually. After her children were grown, Augusta Slesinger's professional and intellectual horizons broadened further. In 1931, when her daughter's fiction was being widely published, Mrs. Slesinger began practicing as a lay analyst. In the mid-1930s she became a patient and student of Erich Fromm and Karen Horney. During the last six years of her life (Augusta Slesinger died in 1952), she researched and wrote a book describing her contribution to psychoanalytic technique, called "looking in and self-sensing," which substituted the analysis of daydreams for that of dreams in the treatment of children. She completed the manuscript, which unfortunately seems to have disappeared, a week before she died. At her death, she was noted as a member of the group of practitioners responsible for the development of psychiatric case work.[4]

Because of the sharp differences in their personalities, because Augusta Slesinger enjoyed steady professional success while Anthony Slesinger's status in the public world was insecure, and because Anthony was doing unpalatable work in what had been his father-in-law's business, there was considerable tension in their relationship. Moreover, these difficulties were exacerbated by cultural constructions of gender, which defined both parents as somewhat deviant from prescribed norms of femininity and masculinity. Nevertheless the marriage limped along until the day after the Slesingers' fiftieth wedding anniversary, when they separated permanently, never to see one another again.

Slesinger's current readers often find her fiction startlingly reflective of their own worries about sexuality, reproduction, heterosexual relationships, family conflicts, work, and social change. In particular, her filtering such issues through the voices, thoughts, and emotions of diverse, yet well-defined, female characters strikes a responsive chord. That her writing can be so contemporary despite its reliance upon stereotypes of male and female "nature" typical of the early decades of the century is undoubtedly due, in part, to her background. Unusually progressive in its childrearing practices and work patterns, Slesinger's family provided her with complex experience made generally familiar only recently as the movement of large numbers of middle-class mothers into wage labor, and contemporary feminism's insistence on generalizing about private experience, have exposed the complicated connections between domestic and public life.

Certainly it was from her mother, unusual among women of her period and class in working continuously along a developing career path, that Slesinger gained a strong sense of vocation. Yet precisely because of Mrs. Slesinger's competence, energy, and power, there was conflict between mother and daughter as well. From both her own struggles with her mother and from observing the conflicts between her parents, one can assume that Slesinger learned a good deal about the difficulties of achieving equality in personal relationships and the complicated ways in which women and men think about and live with each other. In both her writing and her life, one can see Slesinger meditating upon and striving to envision a better relationship between the sexes and a more satisfactory adjustment between public and domestic existence than she observed in her own family or the wider society around her.

Slesinger went to Ethical Culture Society schools, which were vaguely socialist in orientation and primarily attended by children of acculturated Jewish families. She spent summers at camp in the mountains or at the shore. At Swarthmore College she impressed friends with her knowledge of Freud and professors with her writing. She graduated in 1927 from the Columbia University School of Journalism, where she studied fiction writing with novelist, critic, and folklorist Dorothy Scarborough, best known for a desolate and controversial novel of Texas life called *The Wind.*[5]

In 1928, after stints on several New York newspapers and other short-term jobs in journalism and retailing, Slesinger married Herbert Solow, a brooding, scholarly political journalist who was assistant editor of the *Menorah Journal.* The *Journal* had been started in 1915 as an attempt to create a Jewish humanism in America, but by the early years of the Depression it turned to the Left and was grappling with the complexities of Marxist thought.[6] Through Solow, Slesinger (who retained her name) became part of the intense, young, left-wing group surrounding the brilliant Elliot Cohen, then editor of the *Journal* and later founder of *Commentary.* The *Journal* coterie has since been identified as the earliest source of the enormously influential New York literary Left.[7] Cohen's circle included Lionel (and slightly later Diana) Trilling, Clifton Fadiman, Henry Rosenthal, Anita Brenner, Felix Morrow, and Albert Halper, among others. At its fringes were such figures as Sidney Hook and Max Eastman. All considered themselves intellectuals, had ambitions as writers, and, as the 1920s drew to a close, became increasingly involved in left-wing politics. In these political activities and debates Slesinger sometimes participated, though if one were to judge from her later writing, she as often sat quietly, observing and absorbing.

Determined from childhood to be a writer and nothing else, Slesinger had gradually transformed youthful tall tales into rudimentary sketches and then into short stories. Her closest childhood friendship, which lasted until her death, was with another artistically ambitious girl, later the New York artist Dorothy McDonald. The friendship was crucial for both, since in their experience girls went to college but no women were creators in the arts. At college, Slesinger had impressed classmates and instructors as having genuine talent. Now her marriage and political associations provided her with ample and fertile material for fiction. The group's constantly percolating discussions broadened her range of knowledge and sharpened her analytical abilities. Encouragement and criticism were provided by such friends as Fadiman (subsequently her editor at Simon & Schuster) and Cohen, who gave her work a good dcal of attention, whom she strongly admired, and whom Trilling later characterized as the best teacher of writers he had ever known.[8]

Beginning early in 1930 Slesinger's short stories and nonfiction began appearing in swift succession in such magazines and quarterlies as *American Mercury, Forum, Menorah Journal, Modern Quarterly, The New Yorker, Pagany, Scribner's, Story Magazine, This Quarter,* and *Vanity Fair.* Some of these pieces concentrate on the psychological dimensions of personal relationships, and draw upon Slesinger's experiences as daughter, wife, lover, writer, and (briefly) teacher. Others, more capacious in vision, show the interaction between character and milieu, the ways in which class, race, work, or politics impinge upon personality. In *The Unpossessed* Slesinger would combine her ability to dramatize the impact of large-scale events on individual lives with her understanding of the psychological and social complexities of interpersonal relations, particularly between women and men. But even in her earliest stories, Slesinger exhibits her characteristic style, which combines wit and energy with emotional nuance, and with an ability to present in prose a variety of personalities and social types.

"Mother to Dinner," published in March 1930 in the *Menorah Journal,* is a useful example of Slesinger's psychological fiction because it explores the conflict between "feminine" and "masculine" characteristics which would be an important component of *The Unpossessed.* Additionally, by inscribing this conflict in the protagonist's hidden thoughts and emotions, rather than revealing it through her speech and actions, the story points toward the difficulties of self-expression experienced by the more sympathetic characters of both sexes in *The Unpossessed* and the special difficulties the female characters have in making any claims for themselves upon the world.

The story begins as Katherine Jastrow, who still thinks of herself as Katherine Benjamin, prepares in an increasingly agitated manner for the meal her parents will share with her and her husband Gerald this evening. Outside the "sodden" air builds up to a storm. Inwardly, Katherine struggles between conflicting feelings of identification with mother and husband and divided feelings about each of them individually. Her domestic and social habits are those of her mother, patterns of female culture passed down from one generation to the next, "little rituals" that bring with them "a horde of vague recollections." Yet young, slim Katherine knows that it is silly to walk through her domestic routines "with her mother's tired, elastic step, the step of a stout woman who has shopped all day," and indeed she suffers from matrophobia, or the fear of becoming one's mother. She is tempted to agree with Gerald that her mother's habit of "attaching significances to every . . . moment, . . . [is] 'imbecilic' " and accuses herself of sharing only the small details of life with her mother "because you knew she wouldn't understand the important ones." But she is also repelled by Gerald's logic and intelligence, his ability to "shed" sentiment "like a wet bathing suit," emerging from it "cool and casual, forgetful and untouched." These are the mental habits of a person who values only action in the public world and is contemptuous of the small anecdotes of private life. Besides, Gerald is a "stranger" whom she "could never visualize" at his office and who knows nothing of her twenty years of life but the last two.

Thus Katherine muses and frets as she prepares for the meal that she dreads, hoping "nervously that Gerald would not be insolent and argumentative, that her mother would not be stupid. . . . She must protect them both," she thinks in the first section of the story. But by the final section panic has overtaken protectiveness. As the doorbell rings Katherine wishes that "one of them, Gerald or her mother," were dead.[9] Mrs. Slesinger never forgave her daughter for this parable of conflict between the maternal and the masculine.

"Jobs in the Sky," published in *Scribner's Magazine* in March 1935, represents Slesinger's broader perspective. It explores work, economic status, and the connections between individual identity and social role that she developed at greater length and in a more intellectualized context in her novel. Written—like most of Slesinger's fiction—from an interior perspective, and shifting in point of view as it moves from character to character, "Jobs in the Sky" captures the intensifying rhythms of work in a large department store during the Christmas rush. The identity of each clerk and department head is submerged in his or her function and hierarchical position: "the hat girls in their drab black dresses and exquisitely sheer-hosed legs," the "floorwalkers [who] adjust their button-holes and their smiles, mov[ing] here and there with dignity." At the same time there is a strange pleasure for these functionaries in acting out their roles effectively in the flow of motion and excitement and the richly detailed, almost theatrical setting.

Yet behind the general issue raised by the story—is there such a thing as meaningful work?— is the specific issue raised by its Depression-era context—is there work to be had at all, and if so, by whom? Like Miles Flinders's boss in *The Unpossessed,* Mr. Marvell (the "M" in "M & J Department Store") knows how to play on the fear of unemployment as he delivers this year's version of his annual Christmas message:

> In conclusion it is good-will that counts good cheer is the baist policy the spirit of Christmas all year round is our slogan we are one big femilay and we spread our good cheer our customers expect it demand it PAY for it and now my friends I wish each and every a merry and profitable Christmas KEEP ON YOUR TOES ALL DAY OUR PROFIT IS YOUR PROFIT IT MAY BE THAT YOU CAN WIN YOURSELF A PERMANENT POSITION my friends I thank you each and every one.

Interestingly, as in *The Unpossessed,* it is women and working-class young people who are most expendable, farthest from centers of power. At the close of the story middle-aged Miss Paley, a teacher for years before she lost that job, makes "her exit from the Commercial World. . . with a last bewildered look," floating out with "her handkerchiefs, her pencils, and her varicose veins." The other salespeople are "all. . . kind to her," yet "really hurrying her a little, too, hurrying her out of their lives—Miss Paley was bad luck." Their attitude is shared by young Joey Andrews, the kid from the slums, who "In all his life. . . had never been so happy" as when he got this job. He turns "back with relief to his salesbook" until, finally, he understands the point of the words being addressed to him: " 'different with you, you are young, . . . You are young and life holds many opportunities,' Mrs. Summers says, smiling and smiling."[10] Though Slesinger herself was young and her life full of promise, she understood the difficulties that could be involved in surviving, even without dignity.

ii

After publishing her novel in 1934 and her collection of short fiction in 1935, both well reviewed, Slesinger set out for the West Coast to begin anew. She was brought to Hollywood by Irving Thalberg to work on the screenplay of Metro-Goldwyn-Mayer's *The Good Earth,* which set the original standard for multi-million-dollar film productions. She quickly became fascinated by the young craft of screenwriting, particularly the working out of relationships among dialogue, image, and camera angle, and by the scope, complexities, and contradictions of the film industry. In the decade from 1935 until her death, Slesinger wrote the scripts for seven films that were produced and for many others whose final lodging was the shelf rather than the screen. Often she worked in collaboration with her second husband, Frank Davis, an M-G-M producer who deliberately transferred his loyalties from management to labor when he joined his knowledge of films with Slesinger's skills as a writer to form a well paid screenwriting team continually in demand. In addition to *The Good Earth* (finally released in 1937), Slesinger's credits include *Girl's School* (Columbia, 1938), based on her novella "The Answer on the Magnolia Tree" (which is in turn based on her year's experience as a private-school teacher); a proto-feminist film directed by Dorothy Arzner, Hollywood's only female studio director, entitled *Dance, Girls, Dance* (RKO, 1940); and *A Tree Grows in Brooklyn* (Twentieth-Century Fox, 1945), the first film directed by Elia Kazan.[11]

Despite the frustrations of being hired to adapt rather than to create, and of adjusting to the constantly evolving collaborative process of filmmaking, Slesinger enjoyed her new work. She had many other reasons for remaining in southern California, including steady employment and financial independence, circumstances rare enough for any writer or woman, and especially so during the 1930s. There were also professional collaborations and friendships with some of the hundreds of writers then working in the film industry or living on the coast, including Sidney Buchman, George Kaufman, Tillie Olsen (then Tillie Lerner), Clifford Odets, Dorothy Parker, Maurice Rapf, Preston Sturges, and Donald Ogden Stewart. Escape from the past and enjoyment of a new life in a different and hospitable environment, a successful second marriage and a thriving family, and the bonus, in a gratifying mingling of the public and the private, of collaboration with her husband were certainly major factors in Slesinger's decision to remain permanently on the West Coast. Finally, Hollywood provided Slesinger with political activity of a kind suited to her temperament and with rich material for what was to have been her second novel.

In Hollywood, Slesinger continued the intermittent political activism that went back to her New York years. There, for instance, she had participated in the 1934 strike against Macauley Company publishers. When they had picketed to support the clerical workers' demands for better working conditions and the right to bargain collectively, eighteen writers were thrown in jail. After vigorously defending themselves, they were released, and saw the Office Workers' Union demands met. Radical writer John Howard Lawson wrote in the *Daily Worker* that this was an important political action, both because it represented "one of the first concrete victories achieved by white collar workers" and because in it writers acted "in a professional capacity dealing with conditions in their own field."[12] While living on the West Coast, Slesinger, though neither a theoretician nor a partisan, continued to support such left-wing causes as the freeing of Tom Mooney, the release of the Scottsboro Boys, the fighting of the Abraham Lincoln Brigade in the Spanish Civil War, and the activities of the Hollywood Anti-Nazi League. She served on the executive board of the Motion Picture Guild, organized for "the production of liberal and progressive films";[13] and she participated in a Marxist study group. But her most active and influential political period came during the formation and attempted dissolution of the Screen Writers Guild, a context in which she personally had a great deal to offer, to gain, and to lose.

Years later Frank Davis called the intense and complicated maneuvers that attended the establishment of the Guild possibly the most dramatic and climactic episode in Slesinger's life. The Guild was originally organized in 1933 under the leadership of John Howard Lawson, a committed Communist and later a member of the Hollywood Ten. In a day when producers frequently called in a dozen or more writers to work on a single script, and then awarded precious credit for the work to whichever writer they arbitrarily chose (often the last one they remembered seeing), writers wanted more control over their labor in particular and a more orderly and democratic division of power in the industry in general. Moreover, when Roosevelt temporarily closed the banks and halted all money transactions in March of 1933, the studios responded by cutting the salaries of their writers by fifty percent, though most of them earned very little and industry profits were high.

Slesinger joined the Guild immediately upon arriving in Hollywood, at a time when the studios, frightened by its increasing power, maneuvered the creation of a paternalistic counter-organization and then forced the union underground in 1936. Meeting secretly to keep the organization alive despite company edicts against fraternization among writers and the fears of some of their colleagues that the union was merely a Communist front, Lawson, Slesinger, and others also had to fight against studio attempts at blacklisting that foreshadowed the 1950s. Warned by Thalberg that she owed her living and therefore her loyalty to the studio, that the Guild was an attempt at domination by East Coast organizations and the enemy of the motion picture industry, that its leaders were " 'a bunch of bastards, sons of bitches, and God damn Reds,' "[14] and that in any case unions were good only for laborers, Slesinger nevertheless refused to resign. Instead, Slesinger testified at the 1937 hearings held in Los Angeles by Roosevelt's newly established National Labor Relations Board, which concluded in 1938 that the producers has illegally conspired to block the writers' attempts at collective bargaining. By 1941 the Guild had negotiated its first certified contract for writers working in the industry.[15]

This trade-union activity undoubtedly served, for Slesinger, as a political endeavor with specific practical consequences, a context in which talk could be turned to action. She valued politics as an integral part of daily life, not as an abstract mode of thought. Even this pragmatism is tempered, I believe, by the influence of her mother's Freudianism, which sees individuals as at the mercy of psyche and history rather than in charge of personal change. Certainly Slesinger had broadly Left values and concerns. But during her marriage to and divorce from Herbert Solow, whose own political odyssey during the thirties was extremely complicated,[16] her response to the internecine warfare among left-wing writers and politicos in New York was skepticism toward the attempts of intellectuals to be, as Irving Howe later put it, *of* the workers, "even if they were *for* and *with* them."[17] She regarded intellectuals as "a class by themselves" because their interests are "not essentially remunerative."[18]

Though Slesinger believed in socialism both as the only way out of the impasse of the moment, and as a means of creating a more equitable future society, she had an individualist's horror of group ethics and Party discipline and a writer's unwillingness to have her subjects dictated to her. In part for these reasons, she never joined the Communist Party. Yet during the late 1930s her waning faith in the Soviet Union as an heroic social experiment was sufficiently buttressed by a growing perception that Hitler, not Stalin, was the greater enemy. Consequently a profound disorientation in her political outlook, though it began with the Moscow Trials of 1935–38, came only with the Nazi-Soviet pact of 1939. In short, aside from her feminism, the values of Tess Slesinger during the Depression are typical of those of many left-wing writers: a broadly socialist orientation kept in check by doubts about political solutions in general and the role of the intellectual in particular.

However, in her unfinished novel Slesinger continued to explore the complex relationships among history, politics, personality, and behavior. She had intended to complete the book after scripting *A Tree Grows in Brooklyn,* when she planned to return to the full-time writing of fiction. Instead, she died before the film was released, in early 1945. The manuscript, which I reassembled several years ago, is about 150 pages in length, and divided into sections labeled Notes, Characters, and Beginning (of which there are several versions). The material and Slesinger's discussions with Davis suggest that her aim was to write about Hollywood not from the viewpoint of its elite, as F. Scott Fitzgerald did in *The Last Tycoon,* nor from that of its thrill-seeking aspirants and fans, as Nathanael West did in *The Day of the Locust.* Instead, she wanted to create a more comprehensive novel about Hollywood written from the perspective of the ordinary talented workers of the film industry. As she had lived and worked in Hollywood, she had also systematically studied the various departments in the studio. Thus, the typical 1930s emphasis on earning a living would have been set in the context of conflicts between the facts of life in the film industry, the fictions that it creates, and the causes that it espouses.

In the manuscript one catches glimpses of Slesinger's respect for the competent, dedicated professionals upon whom the industry depended. In a sketch of the cutter or film editor, for instance, "The feel of the film was good to his fingers, cutting them, clinging, then sliding through, and every infinitesimal motion of his trained hand muscles a delight of skill and familiarity. . . ."[19] One also sees Slesinger's sensitivity to the ironic discrepancy between noble political intentions and the imperfect and self-deceived individuals who attempt to carry them out. She notes, for example, the "actor who came to meetings [regarding the Scottsboro case] with his sideburns and his beard belonging to his part, and [who] always managed to inject a Napoleonic [*sic*], or a peasant, or a kingdom prince, into the meetings." A longer sketch describes "Brick," the political organizer, as "a brilliant imitation of a complex human being." The portrait turns upon the question of who, literally and psychically, this man is, who has so thoroughly adapted himself to the contradictory demands of Party-line politics and Hollywood luxury that all signs of a purely private self have been obliterated.[20] Other bits of plot and sketches of characters include female clerical workers, stars, and producers' wives. These portraits of women suggest that Slesinger intended to incorporate her feminist perspective into this larger canvas. A sketch entitled "The Old Man's Wife" (based loosely on Irving Thalberg and his wife Norma Shearer), for example, explores the discrepancies between the Mary the Old Man has invented and the actual woman, hidden in their "chivalrous," "charming" marriage, "Every step . . . molded on picture ideals." Yet the idealized relationship has such a "semblance of reality" that though Mary "was intuitive enough to sense everything that was going on," she was "not strong enough to oppose it."

Had Slesinger been able to complete her projected novel, she might have left a serious Hollywood story with a broad social perspective. Unfortunately, as Mary Anne Ferguson has put it, Slesinger had "everything but time."[21] And yet, of course, her one published novel offers its own form of literary timelessness. Lively, even controversial in Slesinger's own day, *The Unpossessed* has survived to become a feminist classic in ours.

iii

The Unpossessed was published in 1934, two years after Slesinger's divorce from Solow. The novel's general subject is the place and purpose of the intellectual, its source is the *Menorah Journal* and Slesinger's marriage, and its specific focus is the relationship between politics and sexual politics. The book met with considerable acclaim, controversy, and commercial success, going through four printings and a British edition.

The characteristic tone of the reviews was one of excited praise. Reviewers for major newspapers spoke of Slesinger's "keen mind" and "cutting wit,"[22] calling the book "a brilliant. . .first novel"[23] and its author "a very real. . .talent."[24] Where their enthusiasm was qualified, frequently the qualifications themselves constituted a form of appreciation. For instance, the *New York Times* book critic termed *The Unpossessed* "imperfect" for being "both clever and wise," which in a writer as young as Slesinger was "a rare combination,"[25] while another reviewer felt the book fluctuated "between being good and being brilliant" and pronounced *The Unpossessed* "one of the very best of recent American novels."[26] E.H. Walton's summary is representative: "There is something curiously final, definitive, about this extraordinary first novel. Slashing, witty, vehement, both comic and heart-breaking, it makes the ordinary novel of contemporary New York seem pallid and synthetic. . . . *The Unpossessed* has so much bite and drive that one can forgive minor faults."[27]

The problems that reviewers saw in the novel can be divided into two categories: flaws that one might logically expect in the first novel of a young writer whose experience of life and control over her material are still developing; and problems of evaluation that arise when the reader tries to set the book into its historical context. Most obvious in the first category of flaws is occasional overwriting. Because both the narrative voice and the characters rework all thought, emotion, and action in language, the style has a certain nervous verbosity befitting its intellectual characters but sometimes annoying to the reader. Another problem is the structural looseness of the episodic plot, which can, however, be defended as appropriate to the irresolution of the characters' dilemmas as individuals and participants in a social movement.[28] Finally, there is the uneven density of the novel, which, though it dramatizes the intersection between private and political spheres of commitment and action, has more depth in presentations of the former sphere than of the latter.

Reviewers also raised issues of broader importance that would reappear in later, more fully developed criticism of Slesinger. One was the question of who the characters were based upon. For instance, one journalist reported that arguments were raging about the accuracy of Slesinger's character studies, and defended her characterizations on the grounds that he knew some of the individuals upon whom they had been based.[29] Whether the novel was a *roman à clef* is significant for biographical and critical as well as journalistic reasons, for it raises the question of the relationship between fact and fiction in a novel that consciously responds to a particular moment in history. That is, what are the novelist's documentary responsibilities to her material, and how much fictional license does she possess? In fact, all of the characters are either composites or clearly distinguished in some salient fashion from their sources, indicating that Slesinger considered herself to be writing fiction, not untransmuted autobiography or factual documentation. Her associates were the occasion for the novel rather than its justification. Like the writer in her short story "A Day in the Life of a Writer," she might have admitted that "I am a natural liar, I prefer a jumbled order to chronology, and poetry to logic; I don't like facts, I like to imagine their implications."[30]

The second issue was the question of Slesinger's ideological stance: that is, whether she had one, and if so, whether it was the "correct" one. The issue arose because *The Unpossessed* satirized the Left from within in a period during which writers were pressured not only to join ranks with the proletariat, but to close ranks against those whose writing was ambivalent or hostile toward socialism. Literature was seen literally as a tool in the class struggle. That Slesinger's ambivalence included a feminist perspective exacerbated the reactions against her. Thus Philip Rahv, reviewing *The Unpossessed* in *New Masses,* welcomed Slesinger's satirical portrayal of Comrade Ruthie Fisher, the false Communist, but complained that the novel failed to provide "a disciplined orientation for radicalized intellectuals."[31] Joseph Freeman, writing in *The Daily Worker,* condemned praise for the book as "bourgeois"and "reactionary," and used its publication as an occasion to argue that intellectuals have no separate or independent status or problems, but are wholly "auxiliary troops of the various contending social groups." Because Slesinger did not ascribe the political and sexual problems of her women and men solely to class or material conditions, Freeman considered *The Unpossessed* to be "a study in social impotence without any real explanation of that impotence."[32]

Whatever the contextual problems raised by *The Unpossessed,* it was clear that Slesinger had produced, in her first novel, a book that dealt with significant concerns and exhibited unusual ability. Technically, *The Unpossessed* is noteworthy for its adaptation of new stylistic and structural devices to subject matter ordinarily treated, especially during the 1930s, in realistic or naturalistic modes.[33] Her form and style were inspired not by Joyce, Proust, or the early Hemingway (as has been claimed) but by Virginia Woolf and Katherine Mansfield, whose work Slesinger eagerly awaited and read. From a biographical perspective, the book is revealing in its separation of the author into the two main female characters, one representative of 1930s intellectual radicalism, the other shaped by the Bohemian permissiveness of the 1920s. In terms of subject, it is remarkable as one of the rare novels of the period to deal with radical urban intellectuals.[34] Written out of an unprogrammatic feminism, *The Unpossessed* expresses repugnance at the way ideological absolutes repress and distort private life, and questions the relationship between individuals' political views and ideals and their personal behavior. Slesinger treated her characters with irony and, occasionally, with wicked humor. But she also took them seriously, conscious at once of their difficult relationship to their times, their genuine superiority of mind, and their egotistical frailty as ideologues and human beings.

" 'When intellectuals can do nothing else they start a magazine,' " Irving Howe wrote in 1954 about the founding of *Dissent.* Three decades later, reflecting on that sentence, he noted that it rapidly became "a text for ironic commentary" but counters, "might not the irony be a little misplaced? For starting a magazine, as even right-wing intellectuals would later discover, can also be a way of doing something, a way of thinking in common, and from thinking in common who knows what else may follow?"[35]

Similarly *The Unpossessed,* whose alternating scenes of public and private activity are organized around the long-planned founding of a Magazine of social thought by a small group of left-wing intellectuals and student followers, moves between ironic satire of and empathy toward its characters. On the one hand, the Magazine's founders (all male) seem motivated by an unacknowledged search for personal salvation—intellectual in the case of college professor Bruno Leonard, moral in the case of New Englander Miles Flinders, sexual in the case of Jeffrey Blake, the Don Juan of the typewriter, who shakes up women just as he does bootleg cocktails—as much as they are by the desire to help change the world. On the other hand, as intellectuals they know that they have only the tools of mind and word with which to understand and respond to reality. The Magazine will be their way of reestablishing communication between the intellectual and the mass of society, and in the process possibly of affecting the latter.

Yet when the abstraction "society" is broken down into its component parts, this intention is not so easy to sustain. For instance, Bruno Leonard recognizes the intellectual vulgarity of his working-class student followers, who want to drive the search for political positions into the erecting of absolutes on even trivial matters. At the same time he feels awkwardly in their power because they are poor and hungry, while he is only disoriented. *Petit bourgeois* Mr. Harrison, the office-furniture salesman, who provides the Magazine with its filing cabinets, beams with pride at his sales record and his product. His understanding of social class extends only to filing cabinets—they come in infinitely subtle gradations, though as a sociologist of office furniture he can distinguish among them all—and he is not interested in listening to a lecture on social stratification or revolutionary change. He is an individualist, who can achieve success because he knows how to sell filing cabinets. As for the upper class, occupied by the Middleton family consisting of Merle, a vague "plaster-cast Venus"[36] always accompanied by her psychiatrist, Al, a wisecracking but shrewdly honest businessman, and son Emmett, the lost sheep among Bruno's Black Sheep, they have nothing to offer to the cause of social change but (paradoxically) money. This they spend lavishly in the penultimate chapter of the novel, when they give a wildly satirized yet horribly painful "radical chic" party.

Where, then, *is* society? Though the male intellectuals raise this question in their voluminous discussions, and expect to address it in their Magazine, they fail to realize that part of the answer lies with the people who share their daily lives. Thus "society" resides to some extent in minor characters like Mr. Papenmeyer the grocer and Mrs. Papenmeyer the Flinders' landlady, or in Arturo Teresca the would-be great composer, now leader of Art Terry's Society Band; but more importantly, it is embodied in the major female characters of the novel.

Margaret Flinders, wife and working woman, is drawn from Slesinger's experience: she is the socially conscious, yet confused, educated, middle-class young woman of the 1930s. She is married to Miles Flinders, an intelligent, highly principled, but congenitally dour young man whose life is divided between underemployment in a petty, undignified, and increasingly unremunerative office job and ambitions for the new magazine and the social revolution of which it aims to be a part. Margaret questions her recently acquired radical intellectualism, which rejects the validity of private experience and the traditions of her middle-class family. At the same time she recognizes the economic and political upheavals of the times. Because of these conflicting feelings and their attendant behavior, she fails to live up to the expectations of her judgmental husband, who is dedicated to radical change for the betterment of the masses. Yet he cannot act, has no faith in the future, and only resentfully interacts with the ordinary persons who shape his daily routine. A limited truce between Margaret and Miles is effected when they fall in love for a second time, but this can only be temporary, since Miles believes that it is futile to search for happiness in human life. Happiness is for pigs, he tells his wife. They wallow in it, but humans cannot expect to retreat from disappointment, failure, and suffering into some domestic haven in a heartless world.[37] At the same time Margaret suspects that his philosophical detachment is in part an unseen cloak for resentment at being tied down to the complicated give-and-take of marriage with its necessary compromises, including a wife who brings in more and more of the household income. Margaret's worst suspicions are confirmed when Miles forces her to have an abortion, ostensibly for political and economic reasons. He can commit himself in theory to humanity, but not in practice to the love or needs of his wife.

The final chapter of this novel was originally published as a short story entitled "Missis Flinders." Rejected many times before Whit Burnett and Martha Foley published it in *Story,* it was the first fiction dealing with abortion to appear in a magazine of general circulation.[38] Margaret comes home from the hospital with the basket of fruit Miles has given her instead of with a baby. By placing "Missis Flinders" at the end of the novel, immediately following the chaotic party for the Magazine, Slesinger suggests that irresolution is inevitable in both political and domestic life unless principles and politics are translated into daily behavior.

The novel is not a polemic; Slesinger pays close attention to both Flinders' lonely thoughts, churning emotions, and genuine suffering. Yet there are also some special similarities among the female characters: they are lost souls in a male ideological universe that refuses to see women.

The other central female character in *The Unpossessed,* Elizabeth Leonard, is an expatriate art student with cropped hair and boyish ways, a product of the sexual permissiveness of the 1920s. She strongly resembles the autobiographical figure in Slesinger's "Memoirs of an Ex-Flapper," who, writing in retrospect, depicts herself and her friends emerging as "hard-boiled veterans" of a war they never went to with uniforms, codes, and traditions of their own, the burden of which was "to keep moving and . . . stay away from home."[39] Moreover, this flapper is a logical extension of young Tess, who had not a *bas mitzvah* but a much more unusual *rite de passage,* when her brothers sang and danced around the table to celebrate their sister's first menstruation, an event which an astonished neighbor still remembered decades later. One can easily imagine a younger Elizabeth Leonard as the author of the little black notebook entitled "Adolescent Youths—Their Methods *and* Mistakes" which Tess kept in 1921 and 1922. In it she rated her numerous boyfriends according to their looks, brains, sense of humor ("Good, except where he's concerned"), charm, and masculine charm (evidently she saw a difference between these). She passed judgment freely ("Will be a stout, prosperous golfer at forty, 'playing around' with his friends' wives"). And she expressed a coolly ironic attitude toward sex ("Met him at a susceptible time—first boy after camp. Liked him because he was a boy"). Both Elizabeth and her creator are members of the sexually free generation of women coming to maturity in the late teens and early twenties of this century. According to Lewis Terman's 1938 survey of middle-class females, "Women born after the turn of the century were twice as likely to have experienced premarital sex as those born before 1900, . . ."[40] The flapper, broadly described by historian Mary Ryan as "a solipsistic, hedonistic, and privatized femininity, a gay abandonment of social housekeeping, women's organizations, and dogged professionalism,"[41] resembles Elizabeth Leonard, at least until the novel's close.

But the novel also questions the meaning and results of this early-twentieth-century sexual and personal liberation. Having absorbed the masculine gospel of freedom, independence, and emotional uninvolvement from her alter ego (and distant cousin) Bruno Leonard, Elizabeth has lived for a decade on "the Bohemian train of fast living."[42] At the novel's end, emotionally desolate after years of artistic and sexual dilettantism, Elizabeth returns from Paris to New York ready to make a personal commitment to Bruno, who loves her as genuinely as he can love someone who so closely resembles himself. But Bruno, already distraught with his friends' and followers' impossible demands that he lead them out of their wilderness, is unable to respond. Moreover, his inability to reach out to Elizabeth helps render him psychologically unprepared to deliver the obligatory speech at the benefit party, which ends as he collapses in a frenzy of public self-denunciation.

Slesinger's point here is that politics must begin with and circle back to home. Without some integration of public and private life (which Slesinger saw in heterosexual terms), without some integration of theoretical absolutes and relativities of daily existence, of expectations for revolutionary change and acceptance of the past and present, ideology is self-defeating because it is incomplete. In her short fiction, Slesinger developed the theme of the relationship between politics and sexual politics, using it to encompass the experience of working-class people. Two stories from *Time: The Present* can serve as representative examples. In

"The Friedmans' Annie," based to some extent on domestic arrangements in the Slesinger household, a German maid follows both the example of her immigrant boyfriend and the advice of her prosperous Jewish mistress in adapting to American patterns of behavior and internalizing middle-class values. As a result, she is constantly taken advantage of by what she now considers her family. Yet when her once ambitious boyfriend Joe, finding upward mobility impossible in such hard economic times, expresses disillusionment in the language of both anti-Semitism and increased class-consciousness, Annie, offended by his bigotry, proud of her economic self-reliance, and unwilling to exchange one form of domestic servitude for another in more squalid circumstances, is unable to break away from her surrogate family to marry him. At the end of the story, which ironically echoes the ending of *The Unpossessed,* she is left with a hand-me-down black hat, stripped of its decorative rose, instead of with a husband. Annie is trapped between two countries, two cultures, and two classes, partially because she cannot deny her experiences as a woman.[43] Like Margaret and Elizabeth in *The Unpossessed,* Annie's problems come in part out of historical circumstances shared with men, and separately out of gender.

In "The Times So Unsettled Are," two high-spirited newlywed Americans (apparently based on Slesinger and Solow, who spent part of their honeymoon in Austria) live briefly in post-war Vienna, where they become unlikely friends with Heinrich and Mariedel, a working-class couple who cling to one another out of desperate loneliness caused by the losses of the First World War. When Heinrich, who has been dedicated to revolution, is killed in the shelling of the Socialist workers' tenements, an event that signified the end of democratic rights in Austria, Mariedel is then left so rudderless in both personal and public life that she is unable to grieve. Since she has been supporter rather than armed revolutionary, her task is to endure the special pain of being left behind, of being acted upon rather than acting. Mariedel escapes to America to begin a new life in the aura of her friends' happiness, only to discover, when they temporarily rejoin to meet her, that they have been divorced.[44]

One of Slesinger's central concerns, the intersection between gender and history, is of interest to other women writers of the thirties as well. As Elaine Hedges has pointed out in her work on Meridel Le Sueur, in both her life and art Le Sueur is conscious of the position of women. Though Le Sueur found the thirties a time of "intensely satisfying work," and though she was nourished by her participation in organizations of the Left, she was also chastized by individual men and women for some of her writing. Le Sueur was criticized, for example, by editors of *New Masses* who found that her reportage in "Women on the Breadlines" was full of a " 'defeatist attitude' " and " 'nonrevolutionary spirit.' "[45] In *The Girl,* a novel drafted in 1939 but not published until 1977, Le Sueur depicted both the suffering and the pleasure of heterosexual working-class women who momentarily transcend the oppressions of class and gender as they "renew their commitment to life and to the future" when "the Girl's" child is born.[46] Similarly, Tillie Olsen's novel *Yonnondio: From the Thirties,* also written then but published in 1974, records her consciousness of both class and gender. According to Deborah Rosenfelt, Olsen also experienced hostility from male cultural leaders on the Left about the articulation of female experience.[47]

All three of these women writers of the thirties, and others as well, share the experiences of female activists, despite the differences among them of class, race, marital status, even ethnic origins. As women, they understood the sexual division of labor first hand, as well as the male chauvinism within the intellectual and the working-class Left. As early as 1920, Crystal Eastman anticipated the special conflicts of women on the Left:

> Woman's freedom, in the feminist sense, can be fought for and conceivably won before the gates open into industrial democracy. On the other hand, woman's freedom, in the feminist sense, is not inherent in the communist ideal. All feminists are familiar with the revolutionary leader who "can't see" the women's movement. "What's the matter with women? My wife's all right," he says. And his wife, one usually finds, is raising his children in a Bronx flat or a dreary suburb, to which he returns occasionally for food and sleep when all possible excitement and stimulus have been wrung from the fight. If we should graduate into communism tomorrow this man's attitude to his wife would not be changed. . . .[48]

Like Eastman, Slesinger understood that ideologies, whether bourgeois or socialist, which presuppose the invisibility and subordination of women and trivialize their experience, limit the fulfillment of women, of men in their relationships with women, and of ideals of social equality.

The feminist values that infuse Slesinger's work—and the work of other women writers of the thirties—suggest to those charting the period between the granting of suffrage and the late sixties that these "forty years in the American wilderness"[49] need to be re-visioned. Instead of a waste land, these years may reveal a continuing tradition of feminist values if not of action. The feminist consciousness in the work of Slesinger and other women writers of the thirties will help to explain the origins of contemporary feminism's insistence that "the personal is political."

Clearly, Slesinger is part of this tradition. Yet it would be a mistake to argue that in *The Unpossessed* she located the center of supreme value in the women characters. Miles and Margaret Flinders perceive the world in radically different ways, he—the absolutist male—in terms of logic and abstract principle, she—the accommodating female—in terms of emotion and the claims of biology. Yet at many points the narrative voice sympathizes with Miles instead of with Margaret, and satirizes the latter for her balmy sentimentality. On the other hand Elizabeth and Bruno Leonard, both caught in endless complexities and ambiguities, neither absolutists, are both quite androgynous and very like each other—and their mating never even takes place. In short, each couple (as well as the other important couples in the novel) fails both itself and the larger society. Indeed, it may be that the novel's most unusual aspect is not that it satirized the Left from the perspective of an insider and a feminist, or that it attended to craftsmanship, relied on autobiographical subjects, or exhibited hostility to political abstractions, all of which, as Richard Pells points out, were presumed to be synonymous with indifference to mass suffering according to the literary theory of the Depression.[50] Instead its most striking characteristic may simply be that in a period that asked artists to embody the solutions to large-scale social problems in their work, it raised difficult questions about whether any solutions were possible.

iv

Reconstructing the biography and rereading the fiction of Tess Slesinger thus offers contemporaries fresh insights of value. First, rescuing this "stranded ghost,"[51] to use Virginia Woolf's phrase, provides us with writing that is fresh, vibrant, and distinctive—sympathetic to the lives of both women and men, serious in its concerns, yet at the same time full of wit and energy. Second, as Jean Strouse, biographer of Alice James, has observed, studying "semiprivate lives" halfway between the obscure and the extraordinary offers us "new ways of looking at the intersection of public and private experience without the obfuscation of myth."[52] Since Slesinger was a writer as well as a woman, a wife, and a mother, we may discover why her life was semi-private by asking the question raised in Tillie Olsen's *Silences:* Was Slesinger silenced?[53] In her own life, Slesinger eventually found it possible to reconcile the demands of public and private existence. Moreover, she was on the way to producing an important second novel when she died.

A revival of Slesinger's fiction contributes to the reassessment of the 1930s which has been gathering momentum for several decades in a stream of history, biography, memoir, anthology, correspondence, and reprint.[54] Politically, a reinterpretation of the Depression has moved beyond inflexible, sometimes anachronistic, labels. Aesthetically, fresh evaluation has rejected former stereotypes of thirties literature as narrow, dull, "proletarian," and hence devoid of interest. Instead, critics rediscovering the diversity of style, form, and subject matter of thirties fiction are finding works of considerable aesthetic merit. Not surprisingly, many of these were written by women especially sensitive to their own complex status in the patriarchal thirties, and yet invisible in the social and literary histories of the period until recently. All of them—Tillie Olsen and Meridel Le Sueur who can speak for themselves, Olive Tilford Dargan, Josephine Herbst, and others who cannot—deserve reassessment as writers and activists. Like the others, Slesinger brings something special to revaluations of both feminism and radical politics. In her case, it includes a sophisticated and urbane wit and a clarity of perception which allowed her to see through the intellectuals who thought that all understanding was theirs.

Janet Sharistanian
University of Kansas, Lawrence

Notes

Research for this essay was supported in part by the University of Kansas General Research Fund and the National Endowment for the Humanities.

1. *The Unpossessed* was first published in New York in 1934 by Simon & Schuster and reprinted by Avon Books in 1966 with an Afterword by Lionel Trilling. *Time: The Present,* originally published by Simon & Schuster in 1935, was reprinted by Quadrangle Books in Chicago, with the addition of the story "A Life in the Day of a Writer," under the title *On Being Told That Her Second Husband Has Taken His First Lover and Other Stories* in cloth in 1971 and in paper in 1974. The novel was, appropriately, dedicated "To My Contemporaries"; the collection, "To My Mother and Father."

2. My primary sources for information on Slesinger's life are interviews and correspondence with her relatives, friends, and professional associates, including Michael Blankfort, Frank Davis, Peter Davis, Dorothy McDonald, John McDonald, Tillie Olsen, Maurice Rapf, Carol Krusen Scholz, and Donald Slesinger, to whom I am deeply indebted; manuscript material including short fiction, articles, filmscripts, the Hollywood novel manuscript, letters, notebooks, etc.; archival materials at Metro-Goldwyn-Mayer, RKO Radio Pictures, Twentieth-Century Fox, and the Library of the Academy of Motion Picture Arts and Sciences; and other materials. Biographical information is also contained in Shirley Biagi, "Forgive Me For Dying," *Antioch Review* 35, no. 2-3 (Spring-Summer 1977), pp. 224-36.

3. In the eulogy Johnson delivered at the New School for Social Research the day after her death, January 7, 1952.

4. Obituary, "Mrs. A. Slesinger, Psychoanalyst, 79," *New York Times,* January 7, 1952, p. 4.

5. For a reprint edition see Dorothy Scarborough, *The Wind,* Foreword by Sylvia Ann Grider (Austin: Univ. of Texas Press, 1979). The novel, published in 1925, was later made into an M-G-M movie starring Lillian Gish.

6. See Alan M. Wald, "The Menorah Group Moves Left," *Jewish Social Studies*

38, no. 3-4 (Summer-Fall 1976), pp. 289-320. The article includes an extensive discussion of *The Unpossessed* (pp. 311-19) that differs from my interpretation.

7. Alan M. Wald, "Herbert Solow: Portrait of a New York Intellectual," in *Prospects: An Annual of American Cultural Studies,* Vol. 3, ed. Jack Salzman (New York: Burt Franklin & Co., 1977), p. 419.

8. Lionel Trilling, "On the Death of a Friend," *Commentary,* February 1960, pp. 93-94.

9. Slesinger, "Mother to Dinner," in *On Being Told...,* pp. 89-116.

10. Slesinger, "Jobs in the Sky," in *On Being Told...,* pp. 143-69.

11. One of Slesinger's more interesting unproduced scripts, which she and Davis constructed on their own, was based on the life of Elizabeth Blackwell, the first woman doctor in the United States.

12. John Howard Lawson, "Change the World!," *The Daily Worker* [New York edition], June 28, 1934, p. 5. Lawson also wrote about the strike ("Writers Arrested Picketing Macaulay Publishing Offices") in the June 7, 1934 edition of the same paper (p. 5). Slesinger is mentioned in both accounts.

13. Jay Martin, *Nathanael West: The Art of His Life* (New York: Farrar, Straus & Giroux, 1970), p. 351.

14. From the transcript of Slesinger's testimony before the National Labor Relations Board hearing, Los Angeles, October 1937. The side of Thalberg revealed in her testimony, and the character based upon him in her Hollywood manuscript, are sharply at variance with the portrait of Thalberg as a noble and beleaguered leader and artist, a kind of Diaghilev of film, which F. Scott Fitzgerald presented in Monroe Stahr, the protagonist of *The Last Tycoon* (New York: Scribner's, 1941).

15. In addition to Martin's biography of West, three important sources of information on the formation of the Screen Writers Guild are Larry Ceplair and Steven Englund, *The Inquisition in Hollywood: Politics in the Film Community, 1930-1960* (Berkeley: Univ. of California Press, 1983); Dave Davis and Neal Goldberg; "Organizing the Screen Writers Guild—An Interview with John Howard Lawson," *Cineaste* 8 (Fall 1977), pp. 4-12, 58; and Nancy Lynn Schwartz, *The Hollywood Writers' War* (New York: Knopf, 1982).

16. Wald, "Herbert Solow," provides an extensive discussion of Solow's political history.

17. Irving Howe, *A Margin of Hope: An Intellectual Autobiography* (New York: Harcourt Brace Jovanovich, 1982), p. 83.

18. From a letter of Slesinger's to Simon & Schuster, which the company excerpted on the book jacket.

19. I am grateful to Slesinger's son, Peter Davis, for permission to quote from the manuscript of this novel. Additional material about and from the manuscript may be found in Janet Sharistanian, "Tess Slesinger's Hollywood Sketches," and in "Tess Slesinger's Hollywood Gallery," *The Michigan Quarterly Review* 18, no. 3 (Summer 1979), pp. 429-38 and 439-54.

20. Brick was based upon Stanley Lawrence, who came from New York to California as a Communist Party organizer although he was out of favor with the Party hierarchy. His activities there and later in Spain were attempts to reinstate himself politically. Eerily, in her notes Slesinger imagined his death in the Spanish Civil War several months before it actually occurred.

21. Mary Anne Ferguson, "Tess Slesinger," *American Women Writers: A Critical Reference Guide from Colonial Times to the Present,* ed. Langdon Lynn Faust, abridged ed., Vol. 2 (New York: Frederick Ungar, 1983), p. 238.

22. Lewis Gannett, *New York Herald Tribune,* May 10, 1934, p. 10.

23. Ferner Nunn, *The Nation,* May 23, 1934, p. 598.

24. Herschel Brickell, *New York Post,* May 12, 1934, p. 11.

25. J.D. Adams, *New York Times,* May 20, 1934, p. 6.

26. Robert Cantwell, *New Outlook,* June 1934, p. 53.

27. E.H. Walton, *Forum,* July 1934, p. 4.

28. Robert M. Adams, in a review of the 1964 reprint, argues this point and also notes that since the experimental structural devices of modernist literature have become assimilated into mainstream writing, the novel's later readers are less likely to be uncomfortable with its structural looseness than some early readers were. Robert Adams, "Restorations," *The New York Review of Books,* October 20, 1966, p. 28.

29. Brickell, p. 11.

30. Slesinger, "A Life in the Day of a Writer," in *On Being Told. . .,* p. 384.

31. Philip Rahv, *New Masses* 11, no. 9 (1934), pp. 26–27.

32. Joseph Freeman, *The Daily Worker* [New York edition], June 2, 1934, p. 7.

33. Wald, "Menorah Journal," p. 313, sees the novel's structural and stylistic forebears as male, its thematic analogues as female. I would argue that Slesinger is responding to female models in both respects.

34. Richard H. Pells, in *Radical Visions and American Dreams: Culture and Social Thought in the Depression Years* (New York: Harper & Row, 1973), makes this point (p. 404), but sees the book's subject matter and its feminist perspective as at odds with one another: *"The Unpossessed*. . . [is] one of the few depression novels that tries to understand urban radicals, though *even here* [emphasis added] the issues ultimately become more sexual than political;. . . ."

35. Howe, *Margin,* p. 235.

36. *The Unpossessed,* p. 305.

37. The phrase is from the book by Christopher Lasch, *Haven in a Heartless World: The Family Besieged* (New York: Basic Books, 1977).

38. "Missis Flinders" first appeared in *Story Magazine* in December 1932. In the tenth anniversary issue, in which Burnett and Foley reprinted it as one of the ten best stories they had printed in the first decade of the magazine (during which *Story* had published nearly a thousand short stories), Burnett commented: "to Palma de Majorca [where the magazine was being published in 1931–32] came 'Missis Flinders,' by Tess Slesinger, which cross-sectioned the mind of a woman foregoing motherhood. It had been rejected all over America, and when it appeared in *Story,* it was the first story with its subject matter ever to appear in a magazine of general circulation" (*Story Magazine,* May-June 1941, p. 28).

39. Slesinger, "Memoirs of An Ex-Flapper," *Vanity Fair* 43 (December 1934), p. 27.

40. William H. Chafe, *The American Woman: Her Changing Social, Economic, and Political Roles, 1920–1970* (New York: Oxford Univ. Press, 1972), p. 95.

41. Mary Ryan, *Womanhood in America from Colonial Times to the Present,* 1st ed. (New York: New Viewpoints, 1975), p. 256.

42. Chap. 3, Part II of the novel is entitled "The Fast Express" and versions of this phrase, including the one quoted, form a *leit motif* running (like a train) through the chapter.

43. Slesinger, "The Friedmans' Annie," in *On Being Told. . .*, pp. 255–90.

44. Slesinger, "The Times So Unsettled Are," in *On Being Told. . .*, pp. 65–86.

45. Elaine Hedges, "Introduction" to Meridel Le Sueur, *Ripening: Selected Work, 1927–1980* (Old Westbury, N.Y.: The Feminist Press, 1982), pp. 8–11.

46. Hedges, "Introduction," p. 12.

47. Deborah Rosenfelt, "From the Thirties: Tillie Olsen and the Radical Tradition," *Feminist Studies* 7, no. 3 (Fall 1981), pp. 389-94.

48. Crystal Eastman, "Now We Can Begin," reprinted in *Crystal Eastman on Women and Revolution,* ed. Blanche Wiesen Cook (New York: Oxford Univ. Press, 1978), p. 53.

49. The phrase comes from Barbara Sinclair Deckard, Chap. 11, "Forty Years in the Desert: American Women, 1920–1960," *The Women's Movement: Political, Socioeconomic, and Psychological Issues,* 3rd ed. (New York: Harper & Row, 1983).

50. Pells, *Radical Visions,* p. 154.

51. Virginia Woolf, "The Lives of the Obscure," *The Common Reader: First Series* (New York: Harcourt, Brace, 1925), p. 110.

52. Jean Strouse, "Semi-Private Lives," in *Studies in Biography,* ed. Daniel Aaron (Cambridge, Mass.: Harvard Univ. Press, 1978), pp. 114, 129.

53. Tillie Olsen, *Silences* (New York: Dell, 1979), especially "One Out of Twelve: Writers Who Are Women in Our Century," pp. 22–46, and "The Writer-Woman: One Out of Twelve—II," pp. 177–255.

54. Some representative titles include the following: Margaret Breneman-Gibson, *Clifford Odets, American Playwright: The Years from 1906 to 1940* (New York: Atheneum, 1981); Jack Conroy and Curt Johnson, eds., *The Anvil Anthology, 1933–1940* (New York: Lawrence Hill, 1973); Malcolm Cowley, *The Dream of the Golden Mountains: Remembering the 1930s* (New York: Viking, 1981); John P. Diggins, *The American Left in the Twentieth Century* (New York: Harcourt Brace Jovanovich, 1973); Irving Howe, *A Margin of Hope;* Alfred Kazin, *New York Jew* (New York: Knopf, 1978); Meridel Le Sueur, *Ripening;* William L. O'Neill, *The Last Romantic: A Life of Max Eastman* (New York: Oxford Univ. Press, 1978); Richard H. Pells, *Radical Visions;* Deborah Rosenfelt, "From the Thirties"; Lois Scharf, *To Work and to Wed: Female Employment, Feminism, and the Great Depression* (Westport, Conn.: Greenwood Press, 1980); Robert Shaffer, "Women and the Communist Party, USA, 1930–1940," *Socialist Review* 45 (1979) pp. 77–118; Edmund Wilson, *The Thirties: From Notebooks and Diaries of the Period,* ed. Leon Edel (New York: Farrar, Straus & Giroux, 1980).

The Feminist Press offers alternatives in education and in literature. Founded in 1970, this non-profit, tax-exempt educational and publishing organization works to eliminate sexual stereotypes in books and schools and to provide literature with a broad vision of human potential. The publishing program includes reprints of important works by women, feminist biographies of women, and nonsexist children's books. Curricular materials, bibliographies, directories, and a quarterly journal provide information and support for students and teachers of women's studies. In-service projects help to transform teaching methods and curricula. Through publications and projects, The Feminist Press contributes to the rediscovery of the history of women and the emergence of a more humane society.

FEMINIST CLASSICS FROM THE FEMINIST PRESS

Antoinette Brown Blackwell: A Biography, by Elizabeth Cazden. $16.95 cloth, $9.95 paper.

Between Mothers and Daughters: Stories Across a Generation. Edited by Susan Koppelman. $8.95 paper.

Brown Girl, Brownstones, a novel by Paule Marshall. Afterword by Mary Helen Washington, $7.95 paper.

Call Home the Heart, a novel of the thirties, by Fielding Burke. Introduction by Alice Kessler-Harris and Paul Lauter and afterwords by Sylvia J. Cook and Anna W. Shannon. $8.95 paper.

Cassandra, by Florence Nightingale. Introduction by Myra Stark. Epilogue by Cynthia Macdonald. $3.50 paper.

The Convert, a novel by Elizabeth Robins. Introduction by Jane Marcus. $6.95 paper.

Daughter of Earth, a novel by Agnes Smedley. Afterword by Paul Lauter. $6.95 paper.

The Female Spectator, edited by Mary R. Mahl and Helen Koon. $8.95 paper.

Guardian Angel and Other Stories, by Margery Latimer. Afterwords by Louis Kampf, Meridel Le Sueur, and Nancy Loughridge. $8.95 paper.

I Love Myself When I Am Laughing...And then Again When I Am Looking Mean and Impressive, by Zora Neal Hurston. Edited by Alice Walker with an introduction by Mary Helen Washington, $9.95 paper.

Käthe Kollwitz: Woman and Artist, by Martha Kearns. $7.95 paper.

Life in the Iron Mills, by Rebecca Harding Davis. Biographical interpretation by Tillie Olsen. $4.95 paper.

The Living Is Easy, a novel by Dorothy West. Afterword by Adelaide M. Cromwell. $7.95 paper.

The Maimie Papers. Edited by Ruth Rosen and Sue Davidson. Introduction by Ruth Rosen. $11.95 paper.

The Other Woman: Stories of Two Women and a Man. Edited by Susan Koppelman. $8.95 paper.

Portraits of Chinese Women in Revolution, by Agnes Smedley. Edited with an introduction by Jan MacKinnon and Steve MacKinnon and an afterword by Florence Howe. $5.95 paper.

Reena and Other Stories, selected short stories by Paule Marshall. $8.95 paper.

Ripening: Selected Work, 1927–1980, by Meridel Le Sueur. Edited with an introduction by Elaine Hedges. $8.95 paper.

The Silent Partner, a novel by Elizabeth Stuart Phelps. Afterword by Mari Jo Buhle and Florence Howe. $6.95 paper.

These Modern Women: Autobiographical Essays from the Twenties. Edited with an introduction by Elaine Showalter. $4.95 paper.

The Unpossessed, a novel of the thirties, by Tess Slesinger. Introduction by Alice Kessler-Harris and Paul Lauter and afterword by Janet Sharistanian. $8.95 paper.

Weeds, a novel by Edith Summers Kelley. Afterword by Charlotte Goodman, $7.95 paper.

The Woman and the Myth: Margaret Fuller's Life and Writings, by Bell Gale Chevigny. $8.95 paper.

The Yellow Wallpaper, by Charlotte Perkins Gilman. Afterword by Elaine Hedges. $2.95 paper.

Women's Studies in Italy, by Laura Balbo and Yasmine Ergas. A Women's Studies International Monograph. $5.95 paper.